A sliver of fire seared W... he heard the deep roar of a shotgun. Acting out of sheer reflex, he jerked the Navy and placed five shots in the precise spot he had seen the muzzle flash. There was a momentary lull while everyone stood rooted in their tracks, then the stablehand lurched out of a dark passageway between two buildings. The shotgun fell from his hand, and he teetered there like a tree rocking in the wind. His legs gave way all of a sudden, as if chopped from beneath him, and he pitched facedown in the street.

Hardin felt something warm and sticky soaking his shirt front, and without realizing it, his knees buckled and he found himself sitting in the road. From a great distance he heard the raspy croak of his own voice.

"Can you beat that? The sonovabitch hit me."

NOBLE
OUTLAW

MATT
BRAUN

St. Martin's Paperbacks

NOBLE OUTLAW

Copyright © 1975 by Matthew Braun.

ISBN: 0-312-95941-9

Printed in the United States of America

Popular Library edition published 1975
St. Martin's Paperbacks edition/September 1996

10 9 8 7 6 5 4 3 2 1

For the Adair Clan,
family, friends, and plain good folks

BOOK ONE
1868–1871

CHAPTER 1

1

The boy sat beneath a tall pecan tree beside the creek bank. Overhead the leaves rustled in a gentle summer breeze and somewhere in the distance a lone crow cawed in warning. Splintered shafts of sunlight, fading slowly into dusk, filtered through the pecan grove and sent sparkles of gold dancing along the stream. Across the water, beyond another stand of trees, lay a lush meadow, brilliant with bluebonnets and scarlet buckeyes. But the boy saw none of this. Nor had he heard the sentinel crow raise its strident call. He was concentrating on the gun.

Working with meticulous care, he measured powder from a flask into the pistol chambers. It was a weapon that had seen much abuse, worn and scarred, a veteran of untold battles in the late war. Yet it was serviceable and fired true, and the boy counted it his most prized possession. The man who sold it to him, a gimp-legged survivor of Shiloh and Vicksburg and other bloodbaths, had instructed him briefly in its use. According to the former Confederate, once a sergeant in Nathan Forrest's cavalry, it was the finest sidearm to emerge from the war. A Navy Colt with an octagonal barrel bored for .36 caliber. Light and well-balanced, quick to draw, yet powerful enough to down any man struck squarely in the vitals.

Sometimes, when he came to the pecan grove to practice, the boy stargazed a bit, conjuring up gory battlegrounds and bluebelly Yankees. In his mind's eye he saw them fall before the leaden jolt of his little gun like hay under a scythe. The Navy bucked and spat, belching orangey streaks of flame, and the whimpering Northerners toppled over in neat, winnowed rows. It was a pleasurable pastime, this killing of Yankees, and if he thought on it hard enough he could even visualize himself as having been there. Behind the gun, pulling the trigger, cutting them down with precision and unerring aim. He liked to imagine the cavalry engagements, the thunderous charge of horsemen, and the deadly Navy sweeping the field with a sharp, barking sting. At times, if he really put his mind to it, he was one of them. Astride a fiery stallion. Out in front, where the fighting was the thickest. And always the little Navy was in his hand drilling holes that spurted bright crimsoned fountains and left the earth puddled with blood.

Seating a ball in the last cylinder, he tamped it down hard with the loading lever. Then he hauled out caps and pressed them snugly in place on the nipples at the back. The Navy was ready to fire.

The boy stood and walked to the edge of the creek bank. Each evening, when the work was done, he came here to practice. Over the past month, since buying the pistol, he had taught himself to use it with considerable skill. Sometimes it was difficult to sneak away from the farm and his father's watchful eye, but seldom a day passed that he didn't manage to fire at least twenty or thirty rounds. At first he had used the trees for targets, notching out an X with his knife for a mark. As he grew accustomed to the Navy, and gained a feel for its balance, he steadily became more accurate. Under twenty paces he found that he no longer needed sights. The gun became an extension of his arm, much as a pointed finger, and in three out of five shots he could place the slug within a handspan of the mark. Along the creek some half-dozen tree trunks were now pitted and scarred where he had fired on them from varying angles. Within the past week he had added a new twist to the game, stretching himself for a more finely attuned sense of aim, and every evening his last full load was reserved for this sterner test.

Grasping a stoppered bottle, he lofted it in a shallow arc upstream. The bottle sank in a small silvery splash, then popped to the surface and came bobbing downstream as the current caught hold. He held the gun at his side, waiting, eyes fixed on the tossing bubble of glass. As it passed an overhanging limb his arm swept upward and locked shoulder-high. The Navy jumped with a sharp crack and a geyser of water erupted inches behind the bottle. Thumbing the hammer, he triggered two quick shots, missing by an even wider margin. Then he steadied himself, swinging the barrel in a smooth, unhurried arc, and fired again as the bottle passed directly to his front. Glass shards leaped skyward in a watery explosion and the back half of the bottle disappeared. The front half settled deeper, tilting upright, and for a moment part of the neck and the cork stopper bobbed nearly motionless in the stream. Deliberately, sighting along the barrel with both eyes, he feathered off the last round. One edge of the cork shredded as the slug skimmed past and thunked into the water. An instant later the bottle upended and sank from sight.

Standing there, the boy grunted to himself with a mixture of disgust and pride. He had rushed the first three shots, ignoring everything he had learned about the deliberation needed for accuracy. Hurry had caused him to waste lead, and had the bottle been a Yankee he might never have got the fourth shot off. It was a lesson he would tuck away and remember. There was a fine borderline between fast and sudden, and the man who rushed merely hurried his departure to hell.

Still, he had hit the cork. Something he'd never before pulled off. That last shot was the most near perfect he had yet made. Unhurried, with just the right blend of target and barrel centered in his eyes, and the silky touch of a butterfly on the trigger. It was a hell of a shot, and he had every right to gloat a little bit.

Except for one thing.

Instead of his last shot it should have been his first. When he could wing the necks off bottles first crack out of the box then he'd have something to crow about. Until that day rolled around, though, he still had a lot of powder to burn.

Dusk was fast approaching and he set such thoughts aside for another time. It would never do to be late for supper, and he had a good half-mile run back to the farm. Quickly, he disassembled the pistol and scrubbed it thoroughly with lye soap and a thin wire brush he'd bought in town. Then he dried it, wiped the parts with a greasy rag, and put it back together. Satisfied that it was free of grit and burnt powder, he wrapped the Navy in an oilskin cloth, and along with his loading gear, stuck it in a tanned cowhide bag. After drawing the thongs tight, he crammed it beneath the stump of a dead tree that had been struck by lightning three summers back. The summer the war ended.

Brushing twigs and leaves into the stump hole, he removed all sign from the hiding spot, then took off in a dogtrot toward home.

Less than ten minutes later he skidded to a halt behind the barn and started drawing deep breaths as he crossed the yard. When he entered the kitchen he had his wind back and a look of youthful innocence plastered across his face. It was a look he had cultivated since childhood, and around the Hardin household it came in uncommonly handy.

His mother turned from the stove and inspected him critically for a moment. Then she blew a wisp of damp hair from her forehead and nodded toward the front of the house.

"Your father wants to see you in the parlor."

"Aw cripes, Ma, I haven't done nothin'. What's he want now?"

"Don't try and wheedle me, John Wesley. You just march in there and find out for yourself." She brushed at the stray lock of hair and went back to the stove, muttering to herself. "Lord save us, I mortally never saw a boy so set on getting himself into meanness. Never in all my born days."

The youngster watched her slam lids and bang pots for a

minute, then abruptly decided he would get no help in that direction. The only thing left was to face the music, and he headed for the parlor wondering what hymn his old man would dust off this time.

James Hardin was exactly where the boy expected to find him. Seated in his rocker with a Bible laid out across his knees. Though a farmer by necessity, he was a preacher in his spare time and all day on Sundays, a man who had heard the calling and ministered to a flock of Bible-thumping Texans in the little town of Mount Calm. Most of the time his face was set in an astringent expression, as if his jaws had been broken and wired shut. Yet in his off moments, when he wasn't thinking so hard on the Lord's business, he could display a rare gift for understanding and forgiveness. This clearly wasn't one of those moments, though. Nor did he look in any mood to forgive his second-born, the one he'd named after the founder of the Church. The rocker squeaked to a halt and he stabbed with a bony finger at a chair on the opposite side of the fireplace.

"Sit down, Wes. I have something to ask you."

He waited while the boy crossed the room and took a seat. At times like this he wondered where he'd gone wrong. How a man could raise two sons as different as day and night. Joe, his eldest, was a fine upstanding Christian. Already had his own farm and a family that brought pride to the Hardin name. But Wes seemed cast from a different mold entirely. At fifteen he was the unchallenged hellion of Mount Calm. Big for his age, so large that his father hadn't tried to whip him in over a year, he was forever starting fistfights at school. And there were reports that he had recently shown a remarkable interest in a certain girl. All of which embarrassed the old man as a preacher and disturbed him as a father. Yet not nearly so much as he was at this very moment. Particularly if what he suspected was actually true.

Fixing the boy with a stern look, he demanded, "You have a gun, don't you?"

"A gun! Where'd you get an idea like that, Pa?"

"None of your tomfoolery, now. I followed you today and

lost your tracks in the woods. But on the way back I heard gunfire from the direction of the creek. It was you, wasn't it?''

The boy's ears reddened and his tone was hotly defensive. ''Well, cripes a'mighty, Pa, what if it was? Everybody else has got a gun. Why shouldn't I have one?''

''It's the Devil's handiwork. An instrument of death and damnation.'' There was a harried sharpness in the old man's words. ''Do you want your soul to burn in eternal perdition?''

''C'mon, Pa. God's not gonna send me to hell for shootin' up a few trees.''

'' 'He that diggeth a pit shall fall into it.' Ecclesiastes. Chapter Ten, verse eight.''

The youngster deliberated an instant and then brightened.

'' 'The words of the wise are as goads.' Ecclesiastes. Chapter Twelve, verse eleven.''

''That's blasphemy, Wes. Blasphemy!'' James Hardin's voice shook with indignation. ''You will go fetch that gun and bring it back to me. Before supper. Is that understood?''

''Pa, I'll sure give 'er a try. You bet'cha I will. But if I'm not back by the time you get done eatin', don't start to worryin' over it. Tell you the truth, I'm not real hungry anyhow.''

The boy came to his feet and headed toward the kitchen, then changed his mind and went out the front door. When the latch clicked shut the old man wearily knuckled his brow and uttered a long sigh. After a while his eyes drifted to the Bible and his lips began to move in silent invocation.

2

Wes Hardin rode into his uncle's farm outside Livingston three days later. After a night of bickering over the gun, interspersed with threats of hellfire and damnation, he at last finagled his way around the old man. While his father never suspected that he had been flimflammed, it was actually the boy who planted the thought and nurtured it along. Perhaps Mount Calm, with all its temptations, was a bad influence. If he spent the summer working on Uncle Barnett's farm it might just get him started on the straight and narrow. The elder Hardin had swallowed it hook, line, and sinker, and appeared relieved to have the headstrong youngster off his hands.

But if the old man breathed easier, Wes was positively glowing. For one of the few times in his life, he was out from under his father's thumb. Not unlike a spirited pony with its fetters removed, he felt wild and free as the wind. Upon leaving the house he had to restrain himself from jumping up in the air and clicking his heels, and it was all he could manage to hide the grin that threatened to spill over. Bursting with energy, the boy quickly put his newfound freedom to practical use.

He circled back to the creek and collected his gun.

Afterward, with the Navy stuck in his belt, he turned his horse east toward Livingston. With the gun loaded and resting comfortably against his belly, he felt a yard wide and ten feet tall. Riding along the public road, his own man at last, he could only marvel at the hullabaloo raised by his father. The way he had it figured, anybody who worked like a man ought to be treated like a man. Yet his father still thought of him as a child, and all too often acted as if he didn't have sense enough to come in out of the rain. Which was a damn poor way—leastways from where Wes stood—to treat somebody who was full-grown and able to think for himself.

That he had sprouted tall and lithely muscled, bigger than most men, wasn't something people had to be told. Already he was just a shade under six feet, with lean flanks and broad shoulders, and farm work had turned his body hard as nails. He moved with the effortless, catlike grace of an athlete, and those who went against him in a slugfest came away looking as if they had tangled with a buzzsaw. After whipping everyone in school, there wasn't a boy left in Mount Calm who cared to try him on for size.

The next step, logically enough, would have been to test

himself against grown men. Trading blows, feeling his fist crunch against meat and bone, was something he enjoyed, a rough-and-tumble sport in which he took considerable zest and went out of his way to promote. Yet the men of Mount Calm, pool hall loafers and regulars at the town's one saloon, evidenced no great rush to butt heads with this young bull. Something about the square jaw and the wild look to his pale gray eyes gave them pause. They merely watched as he swaggered about town, waiting expectantly for somebody to knock the chip off his shoulder. But none of them felt the urge personally to test his grit. Though unspoken, there was common agreement on the subject.

It wouldn't do for a man to get tromped by an overgrown boy.

None of this fazed Wes one way or the other. He liked to fight and would gladly accommodate anyone looking for trouble. But he rarely started it. Contrary to what the townspeople thought, he wasn't spoiling to hand out lumps and bruises. Nor did he throw his weight around or act the part of a bully. He was simply a cocky kid, with a hair-trigger temper and a sledgehammer in each fist. Trouble sought him out like iron filings drawn to a magnet. Other boys took offense at his devil-may-care manner, and seemed gripped by some curious compulsion to taunt him over the line. In all the years he had attended the Mount Calm school, he'd never started a fight. Yet it was only after he had thrashed every boy in school, and some of them twice, that they had really had enough.

This was another of those things his father had never understood, or accepted as truth. Fighting was wrong, a sin according to the Gospel. He laid the blame on Wes, branding him a hotheaded troublemaker, and had taken him to the woodshed more than once to quell his pugnacious spirit. Within the last year, though, the boy had shown signs of rebelling. No longer would he meekly submit to the beatings, and considering his size, the trips to the woodshed had ceased. Instead, Reverend Hardin counseled him to turn the

other cheek and reflect on the teachings of the Lord God
Jehovah.

Wes found the advice impractical, if not downright foolish. The way he saw it, turning the other cheek merely got
a fellow two black eyes instead of one.

The three-day ride to Livingston gave him time to ponder,
among other things, the wisdom of his father's religious zeal.
It was a difficult life, being a preacher's son, particularly with
the added burden of having been named after the founder of
the Methodist sect. People expected too much of him, like
goodness and mercy and turning the other cheek. While he
was his father's son, he just wasn't built that way. Only a
simpering pisswillie let another fellow walk over him, and
he'd roast in hell before he showed the white feather. Anybody who pushed him would get pushed back, and the
rougher they shoved the better he liked it.

Now, there was this big rhubarb about the gun. Thou shalt
not kill! Vengeance is mine, saith the Lord! His father had
trotted out Scripture like a pitchman selling snake oil off the
tailgate of a wagon. But so far as the boy could see, the
whole windy sermon had been little more than a contradic-
tion in terms. The meek might inherit the earth, but if they
did, it was strictly an accident of nature. Like a tent show
freak or a two-headed calf. However humble and righteous
they were, God sure as hell didn't give them much help along
the way.

The truth of that was plain to see in the way the war ended.
If the Confederates had had more guns and less God it would
have been a different story. That God hadn't waved his
magic wand and made the South victorious ought to have
been clear to everybody. But it appeared to be a message
that was lost on the meek and humble servants of the Lord.

Since the summer of '65 the Union Army of Occupation
had ruled Texas with an iron hand, conquerors in the harshest
sense of the word. Carpetbaggers had swarmed in from the
North, hovering over the land like vultures drawn to ripe
meat. Next came the scalawags, southern-born turncoats,

swearing allegiance to the Union in return for a license to
rob their neighbors and kin. Between them they held every
public office of importance across the state, and their dictates
were enforced by the bayonets of federal troops.

Worse yet, Union commanders held the power of life and
death over the people. Their word was law, without appeal
or mitigation. The verdict of a military tribunal could send
a man to prison for defaming the flag. Or hang him for some
trifling offense that became heinous only when committed
by a Southerner. It was a land where all men were held equal
before the law—guilty whatever the charge—just so long as
they were white and native-born.

Not unlike the seven tribes in the Old Testament, the Confederate states had been shunted aside by their God, left to
the questionable mercy of a conqueror who believed that an
eye for an eye was but the first step along the road to retribution. Yet there were still men, Reverend James Hardin
among them, who abhorred the use of guns and counseled
the virtue of meek submission.

It confused Wes not so much as it annoyed him. A man
should fight whatever the odds, especially if he was in the
right. To back off and hide behind the good book was just
plain foolish. The Lord worked in mysterious ways, well
enough, but that didn't include wet-nursing dimdots and
fainthearts. Leastways if He was to be judged on past per-
formances, it appeared the Lord always threw the game to
the side that carried the stoutest club.

Shortly before sundown of his third day on the road Wes
neared the farm of his uncle. Suddenly he felt a surge of
excitement come over him and his irksome ruminations were
quickly forgotten. Barnett Hardin was a great bear of a man,
ham-fisted and loud and uncommonly profane. Not at all like
his preacher brother. The boy had always admired him, finding it easy to overlook any minor flaws of character, and the
summer ahead promised grand things. As he rode into the
yard and piled off his horse there was a booming shout from
the barn. A moment later his uncle appeared and lumbered
toward him like a boar grizzly walking upright.

"Gawdamn my soul, is that you, Wes?" Barnett Hardin smote him across the back and almost wrenched his shoulder out of the socket shaking hands. "Jesus Pesus Christ! You're growed up, boy. Damn me if you're not."

Wes grinned and turned the color of ox blood. "Well, I still got a ways to go."

"Horseapples! I'll bet you could give me a good tussle right now. How much you weigh? Two hunnert? Little more, mebbe?"

"Aw, quit your joshin'. I'm nowhere near that. Hundred and seventy at the outside. And I don't want to wrestle you, neither."

"The hell you say. Them that eats has got to fight for their supper around here." The older man cocked one eyebrow, inspecting the pistol, and rapped him in the belly. "See you got yourself a peashooter. Figger you was gonna meet up with some robbers, did you?"

"That's sorta why I'm here." Wes touched the Navy and suddenly wished he'd hidden it in his saddlebags. "Pa and me had it out 'cause I got myself a gun and he sent me over to spend the summer with you. Guess he had some idea you'd get me straightened out. Likely he's already got a letter posted with all the particulars."

"Why, Christ A'mighty,'course he does, boy. When it gets here we'll have ourselves a high old time readin' all that hellfire and brimstone talk he writes. Oughta be a barrel of laughs."

"You mean it's awright? I can keep the gun."

"Shore you can. Just so you don't shoot your toes off." The boy's look of relief brought a rumbling chuckle. "Listen, Wes, a gun ain't no worse than the fella behind it. That's a lesson I learned in the war. A man that can't be trusted is just as dangerous without a gun as he is with one. You tuck that away and keep it in mind."

"I will for a fact. You bet'cha I will. Makes sense too."

"Let's get ourselves some supper and then I'm gonna let you try puttin' a knot in my tail. Hunnert-seventy, you say? Damn, we gotta get you fattened up, boy."

Barnett Hardin clapped a paw over his shoulder and steered him toward the house. As they went through the door Wes smiled to himself and wondered how it would come out.

He'd never wrestled a real live gorilla before.

3

Along about sundown Wes unhitched the team from the traces and led them toward the barn. It had been a brutally hot day and he was glad to see it done with. Barnett Hardin played no favorites when it came to work and he demanded as much of the boy as any field hand. Not that Wes minded. He had worked hard ever since he was old enough to spit, and a little sweat was good for the joints. Kept them well oiled. However much was asked of him by his uncle, he gave it willingly. He was being treated like a man for the first time in his life and he meant to earn his keep. But there was one part of the bargain he hadn't counted on, and it was fast wearing him down to the nubbin.

After supper every night his uncle insisted they lock horns in a free-for-all wrestling match. Wes hadn't minded the first night, or even the second, but a solid week of such nonsense had left him half crippled. He was so sore he could scarcely walk, black and blue from stem to gudgeon, and once or twice he felt as if his spine had come unsnapped. The worst part of it was, he hadn't once thrown the old devil. Taking hold of Barnett Hardin wasn't much different from trying to stuff hot butter in a wildcat's ear. Whichever way a man twisted that mountain of flesh was all over him, grappling and heaving until he was dumped. Slammed to earth with close to three hundred pounds pulverizing him like sandstone in a rockcrusher.

Still, sore as he was, he didn't exactly begrudge his uncle the somewhat one-sided brawls. It took a little longer each evening to pin him, and along the way he got in some pretty good licks of his own. In a way it was sort of educational,

despite the fact that he was giving away better than five stone
in weight. The tricks he picked up might come in real handy
someday, and when it got right down to cases, he had nothing whatever to be ashamed of. Anybody who could last ten
minutes with that old woolly-booger had earned the right to
strut his stuff.

That was the problem in a nutshell. Barnett Hardin was
starved for rough-and-tumble, the no-holds-barred fracas that
country folk thrived on as entertainment. Over the years he
had cracked his neighbors' skulls and wrenched their backs
with childlike gusto, and there wasn't a man in Polk County
who dared risk his limbs by stepping into the circle. They
had simply admitted to themselves and each other that he
couldn't be beaten, and afterward avoided his offers to wrestle as if he had an advanced case of leprosy.

This left Barnett Hardin high and dry, not unlike a beached
whale. None of his neighbors would sacrifice themselves to
his lust for head-thumping, and most even went out of their
way to sidestep his bone-crushing handshake. A few years
back he looked around one day and suddenly discovered that
he was fresh out of playmates. The only alternative, and it
was really little more than a passing thought, was to wrestle
his field hands. Lots of them were strong enough to give him
a good tussle, and since their emancipation, not a few would
have relished the idea of putting a couple of knots on his
head. Trouble was, a white man, particularly a landholder,
couldn't lower himself to butt heads with a common black.
Maybe they were free, liberated from bondage by the Union
juggernaut, but they were still niggers. Nothing changed that
in Texas. Not Abe Lincoln or U.S. Grant or Jesus Christ
resurrected and riding a broomstick.

Things being what they were, Barnett Hardin looked on
Wes as something heaven-sent, a prayer answered. Like a
captive participant, a gladiator-in-residence of sorts, the boy
had no choice but to join in the fun and games. For all his
rough ways, though, the older man was hardly an ogre. He
handled Wes with brute gentleness, much the same as a sow
bear cuffing her cubs, and took care never to inflict any last-

ing injuries. Right at the moment the strapping youngster was the only opponent he had, and he wasn't about to spoil the game with an excess display of strength. Yet he took certain pride in his roughhouse skills, and it never occurred to him to fake a fall. If the boy whipped him it would be done fair and square. Otherwise sport would become farce, and the arena a stage upon which he alone played the fool.

Wes had only a mild awareness of most of this, and even if he'd understood it fully, it would have done little for his lumps and bruises. He was stiff and sore and felt as though he'd come off second best in a skirmish with a meat grinder. As he led the team of horses into the barn it came to him that he was dreading suppertime. Somewhat ruefully, he was forced to admit that his uncle hadn't been joshing after all. Visitors to the Hardin farm really did have to fight for their supper.

After the horses were stalled, he grained and hayed them, then lugged in water from the well. All the time he was working he kept his eye on the milking stalls. Barnett Hardin's pride and joy was five butterball milk cows, and the small herd was the sole responsibility of a Negro freedman who went by the name of Mage. For the past week Wes had tried to make friends with the black man, only to find himself rebuffed with short answers and unintelligible grunts. Slowly he caught on that his uncle purposely kept Mage working around the barn, off away from the other field hands. The man was a troublemaker, what white folks called uppity, and was best left to his own company. Unlike most former slaves, Mage took little solace from his newly won freedom. He worked grudgingly, and seemed to resent every drop of sweat shed on behalf of a white landowner.

Wes simply quit talking to him after the first couple of days. It was like trying to make friends with a mean dog. But he kept an eye on the man all the same. Anybody who was that stiff-necked and surly wasn't to be trusted, and some sixth sense warned him to watch his step. Mage was broad as a singletree, with a girth to match Barnett Hardin himself, and he considered the barn his own personal bailiwick. Under the circumstances, it was best to ignore him and leave him to his cows. From the little the boy had observed, they were the only friends he had anyway.

With the horses stalled for the night, Wes suddenly became aware of the rumble in his own belly. Supper and then a brief flurry with his uncle. Afterward, like the livestock, he could call it a night and get some rest himself. That's how he'd come to think of it, and as he passed the milking stalls, his mind turned to the evening's chief sporting event. Somehow he had to figure a way to outsmart his uncle. It was a surefire cinch he couldn't outwrestle a mountain of blubber, and the situation seemed to call for new tactics all the way round. Something shrewd and crafty.

Pondering on it, he awoke with a start as the stall door slammed open in his face. Mage backed out carrying a bucket of milk in each hand and, too late, the boy tried to swerve aside. They collided head-on and the black man lurched backward, sloshing milk over the barn floor.

"You blind or sumthin'?" he demanded churlishly. "Watch wheah you goin'!"

The words brought a rush of anger flooding over Wes, and with it the realization that this was no accident. It was intentional.

"Boy, you are some kind of stupid, and you don't fool me for a minute. Anybody put your brains in a jaybird he'd fly backward."

Mage squinted hard, his muddy eyes flecked and smoky. "Who you callin' *boy*, white trash?"

"You"—the youngster's temper exploded—"you sorry sonovabitch!"

The black man backhanded him without warning and the whole left side of his head went numb. The blow brought a brassy taste to his mouth and flashing lights swirled before his eyes. Then he pulled himself together, set his jaw at a determined angle, and waded in. Mage uncorked a looping haymaker that would have demolished a stone privy, but it whistled harmlessly through the air. Crouching low, Wes ducked and let go two splintering punches on his chin.

Nothing happened. The black man just stood there, unfazed, blinking his eyes. For a moment Wes couldn't believe
it. Never before had anybody stayed on his feet when he
gave him the double whammy. There was something spooky
about it, and all too suddenly, he realized he was in way over
his head. This black glob of bone and gristle was about to
tear his wings off. Squash him like a fly.

Barnett Hardin materialized out of nowhere and slammed
Mage up against the wall with a crash that shook the entire
barn. He rammed his forearm up under the black man's chin
and bore down hard on the windpipe. Mage thrashed and
sputtered, gasping for air, and his eyes bulged out of their
sockets. Hardin held him pinned, nostrils flared with rage,
and his words crackled like spitting grease.

"Lemme tell you somethin', coon! Touch that boy again
and I'll peel your hide down to the bone. You hear me
talkin'?"

Mage bobbed his head, unable to speak, hanging limp
against the wall. After a moment Hardin released his hold
and stepped back, jerking his thumb toward the door.

"Get your ass on over to the cabins. And don't lemme
hear of you bellyachin' to anybody about this. Not unless
you want another dose of the same."

The black man clutched at his throat, sucking wind, and
shot Wes a look of raw hatred. Then he seemed to wilt before
Hardin's glare and scuttled through the door without a word.
Still rubbing gingerly at his windpipe, he crossed the yard
and headed toward a row of cabins in the distance. He didn't
look back and his pace slackened only after he had passed
the main house.

Barnett Hardin watched after him for a long while in silence. At last, he turned to face the boy and his gaze was
somber, troubled.

"Son, I hate to say it, but I think it'd be best if you went
on back to your daddy's place."

"You mean I gotta leave?" Wes gawked at him in disbelief. "Just because I swapped punches with a burrhead?"

"I don't like it any better'n you, but that's how she shapes up."

"But I didn't do nothin'. It was him that started it. I just give him back what he dished out."

"Mebbe so, but there's more to it than that." The older man kneaded the back of his neck with a thorny paw, then went on lamely. "Ever' so often the Freedman's Bureau holds a meetin' in town and Mage is always up there shoutin' louder'n anybody else. Just as sure as God squats he's gonna raise a holy stink about this. Bright and early the next mornin' I'll have a bunch of pettifoggin' Yankees out here askin' damnfool questions that ain't got no answers."

He faltered and gave the boy a sheepish look. "Times bein' what they are, it'd be better for me if you wasn't here. That way them carpetbaggers won't have nothin' to get their hooks into and I can waltz 'em around till they run out of wind. See what I'm gettin' at?"

Wes shrugged and glanced away. "Yeah, I guess so. It's just that I don't like runnin'. Specially when I haven't done nothin'."

"None of us do. But sometimes a man ain't got no choice."

Barnett Hardin threw an arm over his shoulder and led him toward the door. As they came outside he stopped and watched Mage disappear into a rickety cabin in the colored quarters. After a moment he hawked and spat, eyes rimmed with disgust.

"We're livin' in sorry times, boy. And gettin' sorrier ever' day."

4

Bright golden streamers arched skyward as sunrise broke across the land. Somewhere in the distance a meadowlark greeted the day, and perched on top a fence, a speckled rooster with a great comb flapped his wings and crowed de-

fiantly. It was the time when life awakened and stirred, and
all about the farm there was a calliope of grunts and snorts
and bawling moans.

Wes led his horse from the barn, saddlebags strapped behind the cantle and a sack of oats tied to the saddle horn. He
had been up since false dawn, somehow anxious to be gone
from this place, and he was ready to travel. Though he had
hoped to avoid last-minute goodbyes, he was a moment late
in taking the stirrup. The front door opened and his uncle
stepped out of the house, walking toward him in that peculiar, shambling gait.

"Gawd A'mighty, boy, what's your rush?" Barnett Hardin halted a couple of paces off and gave him a quizzical
frown. "There ain't no need to go tearin' out of here like
your pants was on fire."

"Nothin' holding me now, I guess." The youngster's tone
was flat and short, and he found it difficult to meet the older
man's gaze. "Thought I'd put some distance behind me before it turns off hot."

"Yeah, I s'pose it is better ridin' early like this." Hardin
glanced eastward, studying the ball of fire slowly cresting
the earth's rim. "Looks like it's gonna be another scorcher."

Wes just stood there, groping for words, feeling awkward
and uncomfortable. This wasn't the way he wanted it between them. Stiff and formal, like strangers making small
talk. But the thoughts rattling around in his head could hardly
be spoken aloud. Not to his own kin.

The silence deepened and presently his uncle shot him a
sidewise look, clearly unsettled by the boy's attitude.
"Y'know, Wes, part of growin' up is knowin' when to pull
in your horns. There's days the odds don't favor a man.
Them that's got any sense learns to swallow their pride and
wait for a better time to do the fightin'."

"I never run from nothin' in my life."

"You will, son. Sooner or later we all do. Life's got a
way of breakin' a man to halter, and them that can't accept
it are in for some hard licks."

Again the boy fell silent, staring at the ground. They stood that way for a while and finally Barnett stuck out his hand. "Tell your pa I sent my best. And try not to be too hard on us old folks, boy. Mortals are mighty puny creatures when it comes down to cases. I reckon that's something you'll have to learn the hard way, just like the rest of us."

Wes gave his hand a couple of shakes and let go. Then he swung aboard his horse and reined it out of the yard at a brisk lope. Despite himself he looked back, and quickly wished he hadn't. Hardin was still standing there, like a tree taken root, and his wife had come to the door. They both waved but the boy couldn't bring himself to wave back. He jerked his head around and gigged the horse with his heels.

After rounding a curve, where the road meandered through a grove of trees, he slowed the horse to a walk. He was glad his aunt hadn't showed up till the very last. Bessie Hardin was wholly unlike her husband, without his thick skin and hard ways. Last night had been bad enough, sitting there in growing silence while she tried to smooth over the strained feelings. They had no children of their own and she had taken it hard, his being forced to leave. Thinking back on it, he was sorry he couldn't have made it easier for her. But there were times when a fellow simply couldn't get his jaws unlocked, and the way things were, maybe it was best for all concerned that he'd kept his mouth shut.

As far back as he could remember, he had looked up to Barnett Hardin. Idolized him for his bearish strength and booming laugh and blasphemous disregard for all that was holy. The very things his own father wasn't, and never would be. Had anyone told him Barnett Hardin could be made to haul water, back off from a fight, he would have laughed himself hoarse. Such a thing wasn't possible with a man who had stood off Indians and built a farm for himself from raw wilderness, the Hardin who had come through the war decked out with honors and a chest full of ribbons. Yet, possible or not, it was true. The toughest man he'd ever known had shown the white feather. Just because a burrhead might sic a bunch of carpetbaggers on him.

It was enough to make a buzzard puke. A grown man, and

a Hardin at that, who'd learned to squat every time a Yankee
yelled frog. Just the idea of it set his stomach to churning as
though he'd swallowed a jar of butterflies.

Suddenly the boy's horse spooked, plunging sideways, and
for an instant it was all he could do to stay in the saddle. He
hauled up short on the reins, sawing cruelly at the bit, and
managed to work his mount back onto the road. Then, hardly
able to credit his eyes, he saw what had turned the horse
skittery.

Mage was standing in the tree line on the opposite side of
the road.

The black man had a gnarled oak limb in his right hand,
and there was a peculiar glint in his eye. Without a word he
moved out of the trees and onto the road. His purpose was
clear and the club alone was explanation enough. He meant
to brain himself a white boy, even the score for yesterday's
humiliation. As the gap closed, he darted forward in a sudden, bounding leap, waving his arms and howling like a ban-
shee.

Arrghhh!

The horse reared and Wes clutched at the saddle horn to
hold his seat. For the merest fraction of a second he considered riding off, leaving the black man to eat dust and choke
on his own curses. Then it was too late. Mage jumped clear
of the flailing hooves and swung the club in a whistling arc.
The blow caught Wes in the left side and his ribs buckled
in a shower of fiery sparks that numbed him clean to the
shoulder. Hardly before he realized what was happening, he
felt himself falling, sledged out of his saddle by the impact
of the stout limb. The ground came up to meet him in a rush,
and air exploded from his lungs as his battered ribs absorbed
the shock.

Mage swatted the horse on the rump, and as it broke away,
he stepped forward. Just for a moment he stood there, towering over the youngster, slowly thumping the club against
the palm of his free hand. Then his mouth split in a wide,
pearly grin.

"Well now, what you say, *boy?* Ready to meet yo' Maker?"

Wes pulled the Navy in a single motion and shot him three times. It was done without thought, a reflex action, and the black man appeared as surprised as the boy. Bright red dots, side by side, blossomed at his beltline, and the third slug caught him just below the brisket. He reeled backward in a limp, nerveless dance, and then, as if his legs had been chopped from beneath him, he collapsed and sat down heavily in the road.

They stared at each other for what seemed a long time. Neither of them said anything, almost as though it had gone beyond mere words and must now be resolved in an older way. At last, gathering himself with a supreme effort, Mage came to his knees and commenced pushing himself erect with the club as a support. Wes raised the pistol, thumbing the hammer back to full cock, and very carefully shot him between the eyes. The black man's skull blew apart in a misty spray of bone and gelled brains, and he toppled over backward into the dust. His hand twitched spastically, grasping the club in a death grip, then he lay still.

The boy just sat there, staring at the body. He felt nothing. Neither remorse nor anger. Instead, he was gripped by a queer fascination at how easy it was to kill. His hand was steady, his mind clear, and he remembered every detail from the moment he pulled the gun to the last shot. It was hardly any different from drilling lead into a tree, or bursting bottles. Except the slug made an unusual sound when it struck bone and meat. Sort of a mushy splat. Like thunking rocks into a muddy creek bank.

But there was something else, now that he thought on it. Perhaps it was easy to kill but men damn sure didn't let go of life without a struggle. Not if this burrhead was any example, they didn't. Two slugs in the gut and a third in the chest and he'd still had plenty of starch left over. Apparently some men took a powerful lot of killing before they were dead. More than he had suspected, or would have believed

if he hadn't seen it for himself. Only after the sorry bastard
had been drilled through the head did he finally give up the
ghost.

It was a point worth remembering, and he filed it away
for future reference. A gut shot, or centering a man in the
chest, was easiest. But there was a strong chance it wouldn't
put them down for good. Next time he'd have to shoot a lot
straighter. The heart or the head. First crack out of the box.
The thought gave him a bad moment, and his nerves jangled
a little as he glanced over at the body. If the black scutter
had been using a gun instead of a club it might have been a
different story. Four shots to ring the gong was three too
many.

Uncoiling, he climbed painfully to his feet and walked off
toward his horse. By the time the flies settled over that hunk
of meat in the road, he had a hunch he'd better be long gone
from Polk County.

Not long after sundown, two days later, Wes reined to a
halt in the yard of his brother's farm outside Prairie Hill. He
felt surprisingly good considering he'd ridden better than a
hundred miles with a bucket of coals simmering in his rib
cage. All the same, he wasn't sure he could have stood another hour of jouncing around in the saddle. Just then, having
solid earth under his feet sounded real inviting.

He dismounted, took three steps toward the house, and fell
flat on his face.

5

Joe Hardin wasn't a paragon of virtue, for he'd sowed
some wild oats in his time, but that was before he settled
down. Since then he had taken to religion as though every
day was a brand-new revival meeting, and in a remarkably
short period of time, he'd become a Christian with his boots
firmly planted on the road to salvation. Upstanding, honest,
forthright, and straitlaced as a whalebone corset. He had seen

the light, and his conversion, in no small part, was brought about by the inducements of his wife, Ruby May. She was a buxom, good-natured, apple-cheeked girl who knew how to ying Joe's yang in all the right ways. Together, though they were still in their early twenties, they had built themselves a farm, whelped three kids, and maneuvered Joe into the post of deacon at the Prairie Hill Methodist Church.

They were prosperous, in a hardscrabble sort of way, reliable as a horse wearing blinders, and possessed of a faith that could have withstood an acid bath. Reverend James Hardin thought they were about the slickest thing ever to come down the pike, and every now and then, they had to admit that he was pretty close to right. The Good Lord had provided them with a bountiful life, and with a little judicious tugging in the right spots, they had become one of the leading families in their community. Like his father, Joe's neighbors thought he was something on a stick, and he meant to cultivate their support for all it was worth. Someday, the Lord willing, of course, he might just wind up one of the big augurs in Prairie Hill. With God on his side, Joe had more visions than a Comanche witch doctor. And none of them small pickings, either.

As Ruby May was quick to point out, Joe Hardin aimed high.

It was understandable, then, that Joe greeted his younger brother with something less than open arms. While Mount Calm was ten miles up the road, the people of Prairie Hill had heard an earful about Wes Hardin. Bad news travels best, and what with Methodists being a close-knit bunch, Reverend Hardin's flock had spread the word about his wild and unruly son. Local gossips were hard put to explain how the eldest son had come out so righteous and the youngest a practicing heathen, and for his part, Joe tried to ignore the whole affair. Like a cat scratching dirt over its mess, he figured to bury the stink beneath a layer of good works and flawless conduct.

Yet, when he let himself think about it, generally after

Ruby May was asleep, he couldn't help but envy Wes just
the least little bit. In a manner of speaking, the kid had life
by the balls.

Joe had discovered sometime back that the straight and
narrow was a tedious path. Fun and games—especially wine,
women, and song—were strictly forbidden. That Wes had
charted a different course for himself struck Joe as sinful and
wicked, but not without certain redeeming qualities. In his
secret moments, he found himself wishing he had sown a
few more wild oats before shouldering the old rugged cross.

Still, his backsliding was but a thing of the moment, fleeting and soon smothered in righteous thoughts. When he entered the house after a hard day in the fields, he decided to
have it out with Wes. The boy had been here four days now,
and despite Joe's incessant badgering, he had explained nothing of his condition or his reason for leaving Uncle Barnett's
place. His one slip, stated with considerable gloom, was the
request that their father be kept in the dark about his return,
which in itself was highly suspect.

It was time for some talk. Straight from the shoulder.

Wes was seated in a rocker, watching Ruby May prepare
supper. His ribs were bound tightly, and any sudden movement brought a wince of pain, but he was on the mend. Two
days in bed, at Ruby May's insistence, had done wonders
for a couple of cracked ribs. As the door opened, he glanced
around and smiled warmly at Joe.

"Evenin', Brother. How goes the battle?"

"Well enough, I reckon."

Joe hung his hat on a peg, crossed the room to where Ruby
May fluttered around a scorching stove, and gave her a quick
peck on the cheek. Not to be distracted, she went right on
with her cooking. After a moment he turned, came back, and
took a chair across from the boy. Outside, the children were
whooping and hollering, but he seemed unaware of the
racket. Settling back, he gave Wes a dour look.

"I think it's time you spilled the beans."

"Cripes, you gonna start harpin' on that again?"

"Now I'm just gonna say this once, and you'd better listen

good.'' Ruby May paused at the harsh tone and darted a glance at her husband. His face was flushed and his knuckles turned white where he gripped the chair. ''You come to my house all stove up and we took you in. But everything's a big dark secret and you won't say nothin'. I got a family to think about and that entitles me to some answers. If you're in trouble I'll do my best to help you, but you stay clammed up and you're not welcome here no more. That's all I've got to say.''

Wes shifted uncomfortably in his chair, stung by the anger in his brother's words. He'd always resented Joe, thinking of him as a mama's boy, forever buttering up their folks to make himself look good. Like it or not, though, he was forced to admit that Joe had a point. This was his house and it was only fair that he called the shots under his own roof. That didn't mean Wes had to like it. But circumstances being what they were, he was obliged to supply some answers. Pony up or get out, which was a mighty slim choice.

Still, Joe had asked for it, and it might be fun to watch him squirm. Wes set the rocker in motion and smiled as though he had a mouthful of feathers.

''I killed a man.''

''Oh, my God.'' Ruby May dropped her stirring spoon and clapped her hands over her mouth.

Joe sort of recoiled, as though he'd been slapped in the face, and his eyes bugged out. ''Killed a man? What man? Where?''

''One of Uncle Barnett's hired help. A burrhead. He come at me with a club and I shot him.''

''Well, where was Uncle Barnett? What'd he say?''

''I dunno. It happened down the road from his place, and since I was leavin' anyway, I just kept on makin' tracks.''

''Whoa, back up a minute. How come you was leavin'? You was supposed to stay there the whole summer.''

Wes quickly sketched the story for them, starting with the fight in the barn. As he talked, it became apparent that he had no remorse whatever about killing the black man. But his remarks about Barnett Hardin were sharp and biting. The

disillusionment had festered, gnawing on his insides, and he
made no bones as to how he felt. When he finished, Joe
scowled and shook his head with mild disgust.

"You've got a lot to learn, bubber. In case you don't know
it, Uncle Barnett has never swore an oath of allegiance to
the Union. He's what the Yankees call an un-reconstructed
Rebel. He can't vote or hold public office, and if them carpetbaggers took a notion, they could steal that farm out from
under him quicker'n you can say scat. Now that don't mean
nothin' to you, naturally. But if you'd broke your back for
twenty years scratchin' and grubbin' you might be whistlin'
the same tune."

The boy blanched, eyes round as saucers. "Judas Priest.
He never said nothin'. Not a word."

"He wouldn't. That's his way. But that's water under the
bridge. We've got something more important to talk about."
Joe scooted up on the edge of his chair, talking intensely, as
Ruby May came to stand at his shoulder. "Wes, you've
killed a colored man. That doesn't seem to faze you even a
little bit, but you'd better get the cobwebs out and start
thinkin'. We're livin' under military law, and next to shootin'
a Yankee, the worst crime you can commit is to kill a tar-
baby. You get yourself caught and that's all she wrote.
They'll hang you deader'n a doornail."

"It was self-defense!" Wes blurted hotly. "How do you
think I got these busted ribs?"

"That don't mean a hill of beans. They'll stretch your
neck anyway. I'm tellin' you, the Army plays for keeps."

"He's right, Wes." Ruby May's face was pale and she
couldn't seem to keep her hands still. "They hang men every
day down at Austin for lots less."

The youngster blinked and suddenly lost his cocky look.
"Maybe they won't know it was me. I mean, there was nobody around and I got out of there plenty quick."

"They'll find out," Joe countered. "Once they start
talkin' to Uncle Barnett's hands they'll put two and two together."

"That sort of puts me between a rock and a hard place, don't it?"

"Well, you was right in stayin' away from Pa's place. That's the first spot they'll look. Now we've got to figure out someplace where you can get lost for a year or so. Give it time to blow over."

"How about China?" Wes grinned weakly. "That's pretty far off."

"You think you're jokin', but that's about what I had in mind. I was figurin' maybe Mexico would turn the trick."

"Mexico! Holy cow, there's nothin' down there but a bunch of greasers. Besides, I don't like their food. Tried it once and it like to melted my teeth."

"Better tortillas and peppers," Ruby May observed, "than a noose around your neck."

Wes started to answer but they suddenly heard a commotion out front. A wagon rattled into the yard and the children began jabbering at someone. Joe hurried to the door, waving the boy back, and stepped outside. Peering through the window, Ruby May and Wes saw Joe talking to Jack Oliphant, who owned a farm down the road. The conversation was short and clearly of a serious nature. Moments later Oliphant climbed into his wagon and Joe rushed back toward the house. When he came through the door his jaw was set in a grim line.

"Oliphant says there's four soldiers in town askin' questions about me. He overheard 'em in the store and beat it out here to warn me."

"They're on to me, just like you said." Wes puzzled over it a minute, then nodded. "Yup, that's it. Probably checked Pa's place first and figured they'd look here next."

"C'mon, bubber, we gotta get you out of here." Joe headed for the door but suddenly turned into the bedroom. A moment later he emerged with a double-barreled shotgun. Frowning, he thrust the greener and a bag of shells into the youngster's hands. "I don't hold with killin', but there weren't no Yankees when the good book was written. Just

promise me you won't use it unless they get you backed into
a corner."

"You got my word on it, Brother. Cross my heart."

Joe hustled him out of the house with Ruby May wringing
her hands and screeching for the children to get inside.
Within minutes they had a saddle slapped on his horse and
paused for a last handshake. Wes tried to thank him but Joe
would have none of it. He boosted the boy up, popped the
horse across the rump, and let go an earsplitting Rebel yell.
The horse took off as though he had been shot out of a
cannon, and as they rounded the corner of the barn headed
south, Wes glanced back over his shoulder. But instead of
waving he swallowed hard and urged his mount into a headlong gallop.

Four bluecoats had just ridden into Joe Hardin's yard.

Shortly before sunset, Wes booted his horse across a shallow stream and dismounted in a thick stand of cottonwoods
on the far side. There was no way he could outrun the soldiers, that was obvious now. They had been gaining on him
steadily, with a good two hours of daylight left, they would
overtake him long before dark. It was stand and fight or be
run to earth. Which seemed more likely with each passing
minute. His side hurt so bad he could scarcely breathe, and
he would never have held on till dark anyhow. Better to have
it done with here, on ground of his own choosing, where he
had the advantage of surprise.

Walking to the forward edge of the tree line, he stopped
behind a huge cottonwood and cocked both hammers on the
shotgun. The wait was shorter than he had expected. When
he heard hooves splashing in water he stepped clear of the
tree, raising the shotgun to his shoulder. The soldiers were
in single file, sweaty and cursing, suspecting nothing. He
pulled the first trigger and the lead trooper was snatched from
his horse as if struck by a thunderbolt. Then the second barrel
roared and the man next in line somersaulted backward into
the stream. The youngster flung the shotgun aside, jerked the
Navy Colt, and hammered two slugs into the third trooper
as he clawed frantically at his holstered pistol. The soldier

at the rear was gone, pounding back across the prairie, before the boy could get off another shot.

Wes stood there for a long while, staring down at his handiwork. It was queer, unreal somehow, like a bad dream. In the space of a week he had killed four men. With hardly any effort at all. But he sensed that it wouldn't end here. After gunning down a black and three Union troopers, every bluebelly in Texas would be dogging his trail. The race had only started, and second best was a one-way trip to the gallows. Stuffing the pistol in his belt, he retrieved the shotgun and headed back through the trees. Barnett Hardin had been right.

Things were getting sorrier all the time.

CHAPTER 2

1

A long, dreary winter passed uneventfully and spring came once again to the land. After his brief spate of killing the summer before, Wes had somehow managed to stay out of trouble. This in itself was a remarkable feat for a boy who attracted misfortune the way horse dung draws flies. But the more striking accomplishment, by far, was that he had also managed to elude Yankee justice. Perhaps the only thing that saved him was a masquerade of sorts, cloaking himself in a highly unlikely disguise.

Wes Hardin had become a schoolteacher.

The irony of it was inescapable, and in guarded moments, Wes felt like the leading character in an outlandish farce. That he had pulled it off seemed a bizarre joke on everyone involved. All the more so since he had become something of a celebrity in the little town of Pisga.

The summer before he had stayed on the run for close to a month after ambushing the Union troopers. Seldom did he spend more than one night in the same spot, gradually working his way west, toward the remote backcountry of the great Texas plains. The thought of fleeing to Mexico, as Joe had suggested, was discarded out of hand. Texas was his home, a land peopled with his own kind, and he couldn't bring himself to leave it. Of equal significance, it was a big country, stretching from sunrise to sunset for close to a thousand miles. He figured that a lone boy, especially one who kept his wits about him, wouldn't have any trouble getting lost in the far-flung wilderness to the west.

Somewhere on the Brazos his mother had kin, and that became his immediate goal. If the Yankees came after him then he would simply pull another disappearing act. Yet, curiously enough, he found the western reaches of the Brazos a perfect sanctuary. Comanches and Kiowas were a constant threat, but Yankee patrols seldom ventured that far from outlying army posts.

In time, it became apparent that the Union forces were not hounding his trail. While he expected pursuit of some kind, absolutely nothing happened, almost as if his name had been mislaid by the authorities in Austin. As days turned into weeks, it slowly came clear that he hadn't reckoned with the truculent nature of his fellow Texans. Under Reconstruction politics hundreds of men had been declared outlaws, and certain parts of Texas were in what amounted to a state of armed insurrection. The Army of Occupation faced a monumental task policing its rebellious wards, and was kept busy merely trying to stop the flames of discontent from spreading. Shootouts between Federal troops and wanted men were so commonplace that they hardly warranted newspaper coverage. Unlike other Confederate states, Texas had not accepted the yoke of oppression with either manners or grace. Fiercely independent, nearly impossible to intimidate, the Texans fought back with every means at hand. And in the general turmoil, a hot-tempered kid who had seemingly vanished from the face of the earth was soon forgotten. The Army had its hands full merely catching the dumb ones.

Through his kinfolks on the Brazos, Wes began an exchange of letters with his parents in early July. Reverend James Hardin was mortified that his youngest son had fallen prey to Satan's wiles, but expressed hope that the boy's soul might yet be salvaged. Then, toward the latter part of the summer, Wes received an astounding piece of news. With the help of a fellow minister in Pisga, his father had secured for him the position of schoolteacher. Pisga was a small town, hardly more than a backcountry crossroads, without

the funds to attract a highly educated man. Despite the
youngster's age and his lack of experience, the townspeople
were delighted when he arrived a week before the fall term
began.

Wes discovered the reason for their high spirits only after
school officially opened. The children, most of them from
surrounding farms, were a diabolic lot. They had scared their
last teacher into an early retirement, and considered it a personal affront that the town fathers had hired a replacement
with such ease. But if adults and children alike took Wes for
an easy mark, they were in for a rude awakening. He knew
every trick in the hellraiser's handbook, having invented
many of them himself, and the problems of higher education
in Pisga were solved in a most elemental fashion.

The school bully, a lard-faced lout who at seventeen was
still struggling to escape the fifth grade, unwittingly volunteered himself as an object lesson. On the second morning
of the new term Wes thrashed him within an inch of his life,
and offered to give his father a dose of the same if there
were any objections. There were none. Peace reigned at the
Pisga country school, and by whatever means, the parents
were elated that discipline had been asserted.

Throughout the winter Wes taught his converts everything
he knew, which was considerably more than they had learned
in the past. In the process he became something of a hero to
the kids and a much-sought-after guest in the homes around
town, especially those with grown daughters. People found
it difficult to believe that he was scarcely older than many
of his students. The last year had matured him greatly—after
killing four men he tended to act and think beyond his
years—and he now found himself more comfortable in the
company of men several years his senior. The townspeople
of Pisga were both bemused and intrigued by the enigma
they saw before them. A schoolteacher who carried a gun.
A boy who handled himself like a man. A rough-and-tumble
scrapper of considerable skill who went out of his way to
avoid trouble.

It was a puzzle.

Perhaps the most baffled of the lot was Neal Bowen, owner of Pisga's most imposing structure, the general store. Wes had taken a shine to his daughter, Jane, and since Christmas had been courting her on a steady basis. Bowen tended to worry a lot anyway, always looking on the dark side of things, and the young schoolmaster left him vaguely uneasy. Not that he had any reason for his suspicions. The boy didn't drink or smoke. Nor did he gamble or frequent the pool hall. He attended church every Sunday, sang hymns in a loud, husky baritone, and could quote Scripture like a preacher. But Bowen's wariness persisted all the same. A man without visible vices was generally a man with things to hide. Even if the man was a boy.

Wes had two things working for him, though. He had charmed Elizabeth Bowen, the old man's wife, into thinking he was a gentleman and a scholar. A fine catch for their daughter. Someone to be gaffed fast and led to the altar before his eyes strayed to greener pastures.

The other thing in his favor was Jane Bowen. Though she was young Hardin's age, hardly anybody would call her a girl. She had blossomed early and ripened fast. Anything in Pisga that wore pants had his eye on her, and under normal circumstances she would have been married off inside a year. But things ceased being normal a couple of months after Wes came to town. Every time they were within sight of one another it was as if her eyes were fastened on something sweet and sticky.

Between mother and daughter, Neal Bowen didn't have a prayer. He was outflanked at every turn, and generally put to rout with a barrage of female chatter.

That was the way it stood the night Wes came to supper. It wasn't the first time he'd been invited to share their table, but it was a very special night. School had let out for the summer that day, and feminine intuition was working overtime. The prize catch hadn't yet proposed, and both the Bowen women were nervous wrecks for fear he would ride out of Pisga and never look back. Jane was especially skittish, and with good reason. Her young gentleman caller had

taught her much in the past few months, and having lost her
virtue, she was not about to lose her man. Not without a last-
ditch fight.

Jane looked so ravishing that Wes couldn't do justice to
the spread laid out in his honor. Her dark hair was piled up
in a fancy twist on top of her head, glinting with auburn
flecks of rust from the lamplight, and her eyes sparkled with
an animation that seemed to devour him bit by bit. She had
chosen a fluffy blue dress, his favorite color, and by sheer
coincidence, it displayed the firm roundness of her breasts
with stunning effect. Wes needed little imagination about the
rest of her. What he couldn't see was vivid in his mind's
eye, and he had a hunch that dessert might turn out to be
extra special.

Toward the end of the meal Elizabeth Bowen finally
popped the question that had preoccupied her thoughts for
the past week. "Wes, now that school is out, what are your
plans for the summer?" Before he could reply, she hurried
on. "I'm sure Mr. Bowen could arrange something for you
at the store."

Neal Bowen gave her a dour look, but he shouldn't have
bothered. Wes wasn't about to get himself snookered into
becoming a ribbon clerk. "Well, ma'am, I've given that a
lot of thought, and understand, I'm not sayin' anything
against storekeepin'. It's just that I had my mind set in another direction. I've got a cousin that's been workin' steady
for a big rancher and I figured he might be able to get me
on for the summer."

"A drover?" Elizabeth Bowen was appalled by the idea.

Jane looked crushed and the old man could scarcely hide
his grin. There was an awkward silence and then Wes went
on to explain that he needed some fresh air and sunshine. A
tonic of sorts, to get him in shape for another winter in the
one-room schoolhouse. The women perked up at that, and
later, when he asked Jane to go for a walk, she gave him a
bright little nod.

Outside, they walked toward a cottonwood grove north of
town. They had a special place there, secluded and private,

where they often met beside a small creek. Neither of them said much as they strolled along, arm in arm, but Jane snuggled close as they approached the trees. After he spread his coat on the ground, and they were seated near the stream, he tried to kiss her. She pulled back, elusive but not out of reach, and gave him an inquisitive, sideways glance.

"Wes, did you really mean it? What you said about coming back in the fall."

" 'Course I did. Only I'll be back lots of times before school starts. Cripes, Richland's not more'n a good ride from here."

"Richland?"

"Sure. Didn't I tell you? That's where I'll be workin'. The Richland Bottoms."

Her smile went smoky and warm, like an autumn sunset, and she cuddled back in his arms. "Oh, sugar, you make me the happiest girl alive. I just feel like dancing on air."

He brushed her lips with a soft kiss and his voice went husky. "Sure you wouldn't feel like somethin' a little more vigorous?"

"Why, Wes Hardin! You're a wicked, sinful man." Her mouth crinkled in a teasing smile and she lay back on the ground. "The way you read a girl's mind is a caution. Honestly, it's just not fair."

They fell back on the coat, a tangle of arms and legs, smothering one another with kisses. Along the creek the crickets quit chirruping, as if waiting, and after a while a soft, hungry moan joined with the sound of rushing water. The moon filtered down through the trees, bathing them in streamered light, and the moan became more urgent, demanding.

The crickets listened quietly, and then, satisfied, went back to their nightly serenade.

2

Working cattle wasn't the picnic Wes had envisioned. The days were long, hot, and dusty. Sleep was a sometimes thing, and the grub, while filling, was strong on heartburn and short on savory. The pay was considerably more than he had earned as a schoolteacher, but astride a cow pony, thirty a month and found came the hard way. He was battered and bruised, and generally collapsed on his bunk at night as if he'd been wrestling a pack of bears since sunrise.

All the same, Wes took to the life like a speckled pup with a bowl of cream. Simp Dixon, a distant cousin on his father's side, hadn't told him it would be easy. Quite the contrary, Dixon had been at some pains to convince him that it was a tough and sometimes hazardous job. But never dull, and in its own thorny way, a barrel of laughs. Wes found that true enough. After sixteen hours in the saddle, sporting an assortment of aches and pains, a man went out of his way to laugh. Invented things to raise a chuckle around the bunkhouse. Otherwise he could never have faced another gray dawn and the chance to do it all over again.

The first month had been the hardest. Though Wes could sit a horse well enough, he had never been aboard the hurricane deck of a cow pony. Mostly they were of mustang stock, small and quick-footed and fiery-tempered. Like all cowhands, he was given his own string of ponies the day he signed on with the Slash O spread. Much to the delight of the other hands, he discovered that no amount of breaking ever fully tamed a wild horse. Shortly after dawn the wrangler would drive the remuda in and the next hour was something on the order of a three-ring circus. Saddling a snorting, flailing bundle of dynamite was only the first step. Some of the horses had to be blindfolded or tied down just to get the bridle on and the cinch snugged tight. Then the real fun commenced. Early in the morning ponies were frisky and full of devilment, and the kinks had to be ironed out before they could be used to work cows. The older hands took immense pleasure in watching a greenhorn test out his string, not unlike curious onlookers drawn to the scene of a natural disaster. They generally ganged around, grinning and expectant, offering Wes free advice on the quirky ways of mustang stock. More often than not they were rewarded with a humdinger performance.

By rough count, Wes was bucked off forty-three times the first week. Apparently that was the barrel of laughs Simp Dixon had told him about, and the second week was only slightly less hilarious. He ate dust twenty-six times in topping off a string of twelve ponies. But he kept climbing back on, goaded by a bulldog determination to stick, and toward the end of the month the others quit joshing him so much. Among themselves, they agreed he had the grit to make a good hand. Time and hard knocks would turn the trick.

Wes found out quickly enough that hard knocks were easy to come by in a cow camp. Longhorns were wilder than the mustang ponies, and if anything, more dangerous. Where a pony would stomp a man all in good fun, a longhorn meant business. Pushed too hard, or cornered in the brush, a mossyhorn would turn and fight like a Bengal tiger fresh off a patch of locoweed. The first time the youngster roped an outlaw steer he discovered that the hardest part of catching a longhorn was in letting go. As a breed they were cantankerous, short-fused, and born man-haters, which was what kept the job from getting dull. Every day was sort of the first day of a man's life, and if he got careless it could easily become his last.

But Wes stuck, observing and learning as he went along. While he had joined the spring roundup late, there were still enough cows to go around. Tom Hardesty, owner of the Slash O, planned on sending four herds up the trail to Abilene that summer. Some eight thousand longhorns had to be caught and trail-branded in the course of a few short months. Between this and branding calves, every man on the place had all the work he could handle. By the time the spring gather was finished Wes was carrying his own weight, making up with spirit and persistence what he lacked in skill. While Hardesty passed him over for a spot on one of the trail crews, he didn't feel slighted. He was making good money, enjoying himself, and had put on better than ten pounds of whipcord muscle. It was a good life, carefree and unfettered, and with each passing day it exerted a stronger hold on him. So much so that it caused him no end of trouble back in Pisga.

Three times since signing on with the Slash O he had made a lightning trip to see Jane Bowen. Much to her father's undisguised glee, and Jane's dismay, he looked more like a cowhand and less like a schoolteacher with each visit. Their last night together, some two weeks back, had been nothing short of catastrophic. Jane had burst into tears, convinced he was dallying with her affections, and wound up calling him a fiddle-footed saddle tramp. Wes eased her fears before riding out the next morning, but secretly he was rather pleased with himself. He had the best of both worlds. A ripsnorter of a job and a pretty girl clutching at his shirttail. It was a dandy life, and for the moment, suited him just right.

Late one afternoon, riding back to the Slash O compound with Simp Dixon, he found himself lecturing on precisely that subject. That was the way people talked to his cousin anyhow, as if enlightening a backward child. Simp's real name was Jack, but nobody had used it since he was a kid. In the family they joked about it, dusting off an old saw and revamping it to fit the boy. Simple's not the same as stupid, except where Simp is concerned.

Yet, for all his slowness, Simp wasn't a man to cross. He was dangerous as a bee-stung bear, and had proved it by killing a couple of men in saloon-room shoot-outs. One of the deceased happened to be a soldier, and like Wes, Simp was wanted by the Union Army. With ferretlike cunning, some sort of instinctual urge for survival, he had lost himself on the vastness of the Slash O spread. The only time he went to town was when he needed a woman so bad his teeth hurt, and that was about once every six months. In the way of a simple man, he had simple needs, but people were still careful that he never caught them laughing at him.

Being kin, Wes was allowed liberties denied others. It was apparent in the worldly tone he took with Simp on the topic of women.

"Y'see, the way to handle a female is to keep her guessin'. Never let her get set so she can start workin' them female tricks on you. They're slick that way, and if you don't stay a step ahead of 'em, they'll punch your ticket real fast."

Simp thought it over for a while and finally screwed up his face in a quizzical frown. "I don't get it. Why d'ya have to stay a step ahead of 'em?"

" 'Cause they're all the time chasin' you. Tryin' to get a wedding ring through your nose."

"I ain't sayin' you're wrong, but that don't exactly hold water. Now you take me, fer instance. I don't never recollect no female chasin' me. Fact is, it's always been the other way around. I can't hardly name you a time I didn't wind up payin' fer it. 'Cept fer ol' Mollie Pritchard back home, and she just give it away to anybody."

Wes took a closer look at his cousin and had to admit that he had a point. Simp was a wiry feist of a man, with a crooked nose and scraggly yellow teeth. Nothing much to look at and even less to smell. The only time he took a bath was when it rained, and even then, he'd never been known to shed his long johns. Wes thought about it a moment longer and then had to hold back a chuckle. He had forgotten the cardinal rule. For Simp, things had to be kept simple.

"Well, Simp, it's like this. Y'know how a cow'll let three or four bulls come up and sniff her before she finally gives in? That's the way women are. Scatterbrained and fickle as all get-out. I guess you just haven't nosed the right woman yet."

"Balls o' fire!" Simp's eyes lit up like soapy agates. "You mean when I find me the right one and give 'er a good sniff she'll start chasin' me like this gal is doin' you?"

"Damn bet'cha, that's what I mean. She'll run right up your back and throw a half-hitch on you. Quicker'n scat."

"Keeerist! I sure wish I knowed where she was. I'd go

coldnose 'er so fast it'd make your head swim.''

Wes started to laugh, but the sound died in his throat as they came over a low rise. The Slash O compound was less than a quarter mile off and what he saw froze his blood. Five Union soldiers sat their horses near the bunkhouse and a sixth was talking with Tom Hardesty in front of the main house. The youngster reined his pony in sharply and Simp followed suit. They just sat there gawking, too startled to speak, and at last Simp whistled under his breath.

"Guess I went tomcattin' in town once too often."

The youngster stiffened as the soldiers swung their mounts out of the yard and headed up the rise. "Hardesty's sicced 'em on us."

"That bastard'd sell his mother if it was a Yankee talkin'."

"What about it? Think we can outrun 'em?"

"After we worked the ass off these horses all day? They'd catch us 'fore we hit the river." Simp wheeled his pony around and spurred hard. "C'mon! Let 'em think we're makin' a run fer it."

The boys disappeared over the rise at a gallop as the soldiers pounded toward them. On the back slope Simp suddenly yanked his pony to a halt and spun about, facing the crest of the hill. He jerked his pistol and motioned back the way they had come.

"When them bluebellies top that rise, open up on 'em. Only chance we got is to get 'em before they get us."

Simp wasn't overly bright, but Wes had to give him credit for a wolflike cunning. It was the best chance open to them, and under the circumstances, likely to be the only one they would get. Then, quite suddenly, the time for thinking was past. They heard the thud of hooves and the Yankees came boiling over the hill.

Within a heartbeat both boys cut loose and it was as if the soldiers had been enveloped in a swarm of hornets. Three troopers were flung from the saddle in the opening blast and another man's horse bolted straight out across the prairie. Before the remaining troopers could get untracked slugs were frying the air around their ears. One man doubled over and tumbled to the ground, and the second crested the rise raking his horse in headlong flight. For a moment the boys just sat there, hardly able to believe they had pulled it off. Less than ten seconds had elapsed from first shot to last, and between them they had killed four men.

Wes came out of the trance an instant before Simp, but they were both of the same mind. The fighting was done with, at least for now. It was time to run. To put miles between themselves and the Slash O, and find a new hole. Someplace where Yankees were scarce and men on the dodge were made welcome. A far place. Long gone.

Hunched low over their ponies, they rode west toward the Richland Bottoms.

3

Fort Griffin was a star-spangled oasis in the middle of nowhere. The last stop between the rolling prairies of west Texas and the vast, uncharted wilderness of the Staked Plains. Some politicians considered it the forerunner of settlements that would one day dot the great buffalo ranges west of the fort. But for those who had seen it, there was nothing civilized about this remote way station. It was raw and crude, a small slice of hell fashioned in man's own image.

The fort was situated on a hill overlooking the Clear Fork of the Brazos, and below, along the riverbank, was what had once been a grungy frontier outpost. Just that spring, though, the village had suddenly come of age, transformed in an explosive burst of energy into a regular little metropolis. It was called The Flats, and as a commercial enterprise, it was devoted almost exclusively to man's gamier pursuits in life.

Over the past winter word had gone out that Griffin was to be the scene of the next buffalo slaughter. Within months, from every corner of the plains, the race was on. Scenting fast money on the freshening winds, the flotsam of humanity descended on the Clear Fork of the Brazos. They all came—

hide hunters, gamblers, cutthroats, and harlots alike—
spurred on by greed and the chance for a quick kill. The lure
was as old as man himself, and in keeping with the nature
of the beast, the entertainment was lusty and uncomplicated.

Sprawled out across the flats at the foot of the hill, the
town had shot up at a dizzying pace as the horde swarmed
into this new mecca of fast women and easy money. Mer-
chants and tradesmen and slick-talking speculators vied with
the sporting crowd for choice locations, and whole caravans
of lumber were freighted west as row upon row of buildings
sprang up overnight. Where before there had been only a
store and a saloon, there were now three grand emporiums
and a half-dozen new watering holes. The tent hotel of earlier
times had given way to a two-story frame structure, and
along the river stood a clutch of bawdy houses to rival anything west of Kansas City.

The town's single street was a regular beehive of activity.
Mule skinners cursed and shouted, cracking their whips from
atop huge Studebaker freighters, as they jockeyed for position before the stores with an unending stream of hide wagons. Hitch racks in front of every building were jammed with
horses and every corner was crowded with knots of men out
to see the elephant. Hunters, cowhands, and soldiers turned
the boardwalks into a rowdy jostling match as they made
their way from one dive to the next. Dance halls and saloons
shook with the strident chords of rinky-dink pianos and the
sprightly wail of an occasional fiddle. Louder still, drowning
out all else, came the raucous babble of men busily engaged
in sampling the local firewater. Women stood in the doorway
of every dive, decked out in gaudy dresses and paint-smeared
faces, and their laughter racketed along the street in shrill
invitation to anything that wore pants.

It was a carnival come to life. Squalling, blustery, a vol-
atile mix of popskull whiskey, loose women, and a small
army of men flinging their money to the winds. A place
where a man could lose himself in the riotous crowd, simply
vanish in a sea of faces that all looked the same.

Which was precisely what Wes Hardin had done.

After the one-sided shoot-out at the Slash O, he and Simp Dixon spent a couple of weeks dodging army patrols and finally decided to split up. Together, with their descriptions plastered over half of Texas, they drew too much attention. Separately, they stood a better chance of moving about unnoticed, or so it had seemed at the time. Less than a week later Wes heard that Dixon had been cornered and killed while attempting a midnight visit with his family. Though the boy hadn't seen his own parents in more than a year, any thought of sneaking into Mount Calm quickly went by the boards. He headed west, toward the Brazos, where there were fewer towns and a scarcity of Yankees.

While news traveled slowly on the outer fringes of civilization, he learned a short time later that Union troops had ceased to pose a threat. Instead, he had a new enemy, and from all reports, one even more relentless and vengeful than the occupation forces.

Earlier in the year a Republican carpetbagger, E. J. Davis, had taken office as governor. Within six months, through manipulation and outright intimidation, he had gained control of the legislature. Having won his office through fraud and voting laws which disenfranchised all former Confederates, Davis immediately took steps to quell the unruly Texans. In late June he engineered a bill authorizing a State Police force, and on July 1 it became law. With his own personal janissaries, Davis was now the law in Texas, responsible for maintaining order among a conquered people who refused to knuckle under. As an object lesson to the masses, he published a wanted list which outlawed nearly two thousand men. One of the names on the list, charged with the murder of seven men, was John Wesley Hardin.

The State Police swarmed across central and eastern Texas. Though commanded by white officers, their ranks were comprised mainly of freed blacks and northern rogues, men owned body and soul by the carpetbagger machine. They ransacked houses, arrested scores of men without warrant, and quickly became known for their brutal methods. Within a fortnight close to a dozen prisoners had been killed while attempting to escape. Those newspaper editors who hadn't yet lost their backbone found it curious that in each case the prisoner had been shot in the back. While unarmed. It made for interesting speculation.

Wes Hardin speculated only briefly. The handwriting was on the wall, and he saw his own name there in bold, black letters. Drifting steadily westward, where the State Police had not yet ventured, he rode into Griffin in late July. The Flats was a haven for wanted men, a remote frontier way station where law officers simply didn't exist. The Army was concerned more with Comanches and Kiowas than with white fugitives, and what little law the town got was strictly hit-and-miss. It was every man for himself, and in a very real sense, Judge Colt proved to be the Court of Last Resort.

Soon after he hit Griffin the youngster joined forces with John Collins. They met in a saloon-room-brawl, standing back to back for mutual protection, and afterward, over drinks, discovered that each had something the other wanted. Collins was a gambler by profession, but what he won at the tables had lately been lost in racing horses. Though he owned a blooded stallion, he lacked a skilled rider, and the boy seemed to fit the ticket perfectly. For his part, Wes aspired to bigger and better things. The little he'd seen of the sporting crowd left him goggle-eyed. Men won and lost more in a single night than he could earn in an entire year as a cowhand. He saw it as an act of Providence that he and John Collins had been thrown together. The gambler would teach him all there was to know about the vagaries of poker and faro and chuck-a-luck, and in time he visualized himself as a full-fledged member of the fraternity. A true high roller.

Oddly enough, the partnership worked from the very outset. Collins was a loner by nature, quiet and reserved, a man who stayed alive through cold calculation of those he met across a gaming table. He dressed immaculately, went clean-shaven, and despite his chunky appearance, had the deft touch of a magician in his hands. This, along with a derringer that could materialize out of thin air, had won him the respect of the sporting crowd. But never before had he teamed up with another man, honest or otherwise. Wes was the first, and only after the boy had won a race astride the stallion did Collins fully accept him as a confederate.

That night Wes got his opening lesson in the ancient art of legerdemain. After supper they retired to Collins' hotel room and the gambler began a step-by-step demonstration of why the hand is quicker than the eye. He shuffled, allowed the boy to cut the deck, and then dealt a hand of five-card stud. Wes had learned the rudiments of poker in the Slash O bunkhouse, but he was mildly puzzled by Collins' performance. Obviously something was being taught here, and though he watched attentively, he saw nothing out of the ordinary.

Collins' face was impassive, a blank. "How would you bet your hand?"

Wes had a pair of queens and the gambler had an ace high showing. Still in a bit of a quandary, the youngster shrugged. "I'd bet the limit. Odds are you haven't got nothin' to go with that ace."

A slight smile ticced the corner of Collins' mouth. He flipped his hole card and exposed a second ace. "Kid, there's about a hundred different ways to cheat a man with a deck of cards. I just used three of them on you."

The boy gave him a level gaze. "Don't call me kid."

Collins regarded him thoughtfully for a moment, then nodded. "Fair enough. But that doesn't change anything. You were still suckered and you didn't catch it."

"I'm used to playin' with honest people."

"Then you'd better steer clear of saloons and gaming dives."

"Meanin' nobody plays straight."

"Let me put it to you this way. Whether you're straight or crooked is up to you. But if you try gamblin' without being able to tell the difference, you'll lose your ass in a hurry. That's what separates the men from the boys. Knowing how to spot the tricks."

"Which one are you"—Wes eyed him closely—"straight or crooked?"

"You'll figure that out for yourself when you get good

enough.'' Collins riffled the deck, never bothering to look at
the cards. ''Time for school. I'll show you what I did a
minute ago, and when you get to where you can catch me
most of the time, we'll go on to the slicker stuff.''

In slow motion, his hands moving with the languid grace
of a sleek cat, Collins began the lesson. First he shuffled and
asked Wes to cut. Then, with sleight of hand so simple it
was audacious, he collected the deck and switched it back
into the original order. Next he demonstrated dealing seconds, deftly slipping the top card aside just enough to
squeeze out the card below. Lastly, employing various fingers in distinct and separate movements, he showed the
youngster how to deal from the bottom of the deck. Finished,
he set the cards aside and the enigmatic smile returned.

''That's what I did. Think you could spot it at regular
speed?''

''Christ A'mighty.'' The words were awed, almost rev-
erent. ''I barely saw you do it just now.''

''Then you'd better watch close and practice like hell.''
Collins' stony mask cracked long enough for a small grin to
peek through. ''That is, if you're still of a mind to be a
gamblin' man.''

''You damn bet'cha I am. Just keep dealin' till I get the
hang of it. Way you work them pasteboards, I'm likin' this
game better all the time.''

Collins let the mask fall back in place and began shuffling.
His hands caressed the cards with the soft, fluttering touch
of a butterfly, and after the cut, he dealt another hand of
stud. Only this time he made the sucker bet all the more
enticing.

Kings for the boy and aces for himself.

4

They rode into Towash like a couple of errant knights
returned with the Holy Grail. Collins wore the customary
garb of a gambler, undertaker black with a downy white shirt

and a diamond stickpin, which was only a cut above the attire
he generally affected when Lady Luck set him astraddle a
winning streak. But his partner bore only scant resemblance
to the young bumpkin he had taken under wing some six
months past. Wes was decked out in a candy-striped shirt
and knee-high *vaquero* boots, with jangly roweled spurs that
sparkled in the wintry sunlight. Around his waist was a silvery concho belt and cinched over his hips was a gun belt
that would have done justice to the most fearsome Mexican
bandido. The sombrero he sported was merely frosting on
the cake.

With a monkey and a bass drum, they could have drawn
a crowd.

All of this was not without some little forethought on Collins' part. Whenever they hit a new town the contrast was
certain to start talk. A professional gambler and a spiffy kid.
It was a combination that aroused considerable curiosity, and
had much the same effect as a candle on a flock of moths.
Most folks figured them for a pair of sharpers, and rightly
so. But human nature being what it is, the rubes couldn't
resist trying them on for size. Win, lose, or draw, it was sure
to be worth the price of admission.

The partnership of Collins & Hardin had prospered exceedingly since they joined forces at Fort Griffin. The youngster proved to be an apt pupil, practicing diligently and
soaking up the tricks of the trade like a fresh sponge. Gifted
with strong, supple hands, he soon acquired the knack of
manipulating a deck of cards, and if so disposed, could make
the pasteboards all but sit up and bark. Collins was at first
amazed by the boy's dexterity and nimble wits, and in no
small degree, gratified by his protégé's thirst to learn. Before
long he felt like a master imparting the wisdom of the ages,
and in the youngster's deft performance he saw something
of himself made to live again.

Oddly enough, Wes discovered that the older man was a
rarity among his breed, an honest gambler. Except in a
crooked game. When Collins found himself head to head
with a tinhorn he had no compunctions whatever about turn-

ing the tables. And the startling part was that he could out-
slick the slipperiest sharper around. But given his choice, he
preferred an honest game. Strategy, a working knowledge of
the odds, and a good bluff, he explained to Wes, made gambling a higher form of science. Cheating was a crutch, a
device employed by dullards who lacked either the wits or
the savvy to hold their own with a true high roller. Yet there
was a time for all things. If some penny-ante cardsharp tried
to improve the odds, a man had a moral obligation to trim
his wick. The money was not to be sneezed at, naturally, but
that was purely secondary. The important thing was to beat
a tinhorn at his own game. Leave him busted and bruised, if
not wiser. A believer, of sorts, in the follies of a sparrow
trying to fly high in the company of chicken hawks.

Wes listened and learned, absorbing in months the cagey
gambits accumulated by Collins in a lifetime of courting the
fickle lady. But it was a fair exchange, for in the process he
pulled his own weight where it counted most. Astride the
back of the blood bay stallion, Steeldust.

Collins had won the horse in a poker game, and quickly
taken a fancy to the sport of kings. West of the Mississippi,
though, the sport had been altered somewhat. Cow ponies
weren't much on the long stretch, but they were chain lightning over the short haul. Over a period of time the distance
had been reduced to accommodate the quick-starting, tough-
bottomed little fire-eaters commonly used on cattle spreads.
Instead of a grueling mile, the race had become more of a
sprint, something on the order of a quarter mile. While the
run was over and done with hardly before it began, this in
no way diminished the ardor of those addicted to fleet ponies
and fast money. A race was a major event, and in the far-
flung towns of west Texas, men leaped at the chance to bet
their favorite.

From Fort Griffin, Collins had taken the youngster on a
six months' odyssey of the gambler's circuit. West along the
Pecos, then south to the Rio Grande, and at last, a wide swing
north toward the more settled areas. In that time Wes had
been exposed to every gaming dodge in the book, and aside

from the real artists, he could hold his own in pretty fast company. Though they seldom played at the same table, except to team up in a crooked game, the boy could even give Collins a stiff way to go. Still, his greatest contribution to the partnership had been aboard Steeldust. Which was what brought them to Towash. The stallion had gained a certain fame throughout west Texas, losing only once ·in the last several months, and there were towns standing in line to match their local champion against this explosive bay.

Christmas Day in Towash had become something of a tradition. A day to make a man's sporting blood run hot, and even more than the Fourth of July, a day when everybody cut the wolf loose. The lure was the Boles Racetrack, a hard-packed quarter mile that had felt the drumming hooves of many great horses. People came from as far as Dallas and San Antonio, and they brought with them some of the finest horseflesh in the Lone Star State. If not the most important race in Texas, it was one of the wildest. In a mad rush of betting, men wagered every dollar they possessed, and when the lust took hold extra hard, some went so far as to mortgage their farms and next year's crops. Short of a wife's virtue, anything was negotiable in Towash on Christmas Day.

Collins timed their arrival perfectly. Soon enough to enter Steeldust in the race, but with only a couple of hours to spare. The sporting crowd scarcely had time to look the stallion over, which was precisely as the gambler had planned it. The favorite was a roan stud, called Big Red, from over around Nacogdoches, and despite Steeldust's growing reputation, the odds held firm to the very last. With Wes doing the betting—to all appearances a slick-eared kid decked out to look like Sudden Death from Bitter Creek—they were able to get down better than two thousand dollars before starting time. Collins sort of hung around in the background, observing, immensely pleased with himself and his young partner. Unless he had miscalculated, Santy Claus was about to make it a Merry Christmas they would long remember.

The first groans went up when Wes shucked out of his spurs and fancy gun belt and climbed aboard Steeldust.

Everybody was struck by a sudden notion that things weren't as they appeared. Like maybe the kid had sunk the gaff and was about to land himself a barrelful of suckers. Though the weather was brisk and windy, several men found themselves sweating freely, and their qualms were lessened not at all when the starter fired his pistol.

Big Red broke to the front, taking a lead of a length and a half. But he held it for less than a furlong. Steeldust suddenly exploded from the pack, churning at the hard-packed earth, and yard by yard the gap began to close. Then they were nose to nose, the blood bay and the great roan, and an agonized roar went up from the crowd as Steeldust edged ahead. Big Red came on valiantly, narrowing the lead to inches, and for a moment it appeared that the favorite might yet pull it off. Seemingly without effort they had made it a two-horse race, and they thundered along side by side, some thirty yards separating them from their nearest rival. With the finish line in sight, locked in a dead heat, Wes played his joker at last. Bending low, he slammed his heels into the stallion's ribs.

Steeldust rocketed forward as if he'd been shot out of a cannon. The bay hated nothing worse than to be spurred, but it was a fury the boy had learned to harness. Now, enraged by the insult, Steeldust simply ran off and left Big Red. Driving hard, with Wes scrunched down tight against his neck, the stallion crossed the finish line six lengths in front of the Nacogdoches roan.

The crowd was curiously silent as the youngster slowed Steeldust and turned him, trotting back down the track. While there was some sullen muttering to be heard, most of the onlookers were rankled not so much with the boy and the horse as with their own gullibility. They hadn't been hornswoggled, for Steeldust was a name known to all. But they had swallowed the bait, in the form of a big roan stud, and they were finding it damnedly hard to digest.

Two hardcases, men Collins had never seen before, couldn't get it down at all. When he and Wes finally worked their way through the crowd to the stakeholder, the strangers were standing nearby. As Collins collected their winnings, one of the men spoke up in a disgruntled voice, loud enough to make sure that everyone within earshot heard clearly.

"Mister, that was real slick. Lettin' that kid suck ever'body in. You two must've had plenty of practice."

Collins turned his head just far enough to rivet the loud-mouth with a quizzical frown. "You accusing me of something, friend?"

The stranger held his gaze for a moment, then snorted. "Well, Jesus Christ! Don't get your nose out of joint. I was just sayin' you work good together."

"Much obliged." Collins pocketed the money and turned away with Wes at his side. "Bet on Steeldust next time. He's surefire."

"Hey, looky here, you don't seem like a man to take a feller's poke and run. How about givin' me and my sidekick a chance to get some of it back?"

Collins stopped and again fixed him with a curious look. "What'd you have in mind?"

"Nothin' much." The stranger shrugged, almost too casually. "Maybe a little poker. Leastways if you're partial to the game."

The gambler studied both men for a moment, then nodded. "Matter of fact, I am. You know Dire's Store?"

"Sure. That's the one right in the middle of town."

"There's a back room with a card table. We'll meet you there after supper."

Collins walked off and Wes fell in beside him. The strangers exchanged sly looks and suddenly broke out grinning. Heads together they turned and marched off in the opposite direction.

The game was less than an hour old when Collins' hunch proved correct. The men were tinhorns, and inept tinhorns at that. Jim Bradly, the loudmouth, had a thick brushy beard and smiled a lot, like an amiable cockleburr. His partner, Hamp Davis, was sad-faced and skinny as a hound dog, and spoke only when a grunt wouldn't suffice. Somewhere he'd lost one ear, and the empty spot made him seem even more forlorn. But for all the contrasts in look and manner, they shared the same affliction. Neither man could cheat worth a damn.

Wes and the gambler were slowly trimming them, feeding one another good hands and bumping the pot with sucker raises. But the youngster's temper was steadily getting the better of him. The two sharpers were so clumsy he felt humiliated merely to be in the same game with them. Finally, when Davis awkwardly palmed an ace, Wes slammed his fist down on the table.

"The next sonovabitch that sneaks a card, I'm gonna shoot his other ear off. Savvy?"

Davis put on his best hangdog look, but Bradly demanded churlishly, "You sayin' we're cheatin'?"

Wes raked him with a cold glare. "What I'm sayin' is that the both of you don't know beans from buckshot about what you're tryin' to do. Why don't you just give it up and we'll call it quits?"

Bradly hawked, clearing his throat, vaguely unsettled by the boy's cocksure tone. After a moment he glanced over at Collins. "Mister, you better put that rooster to crowin' on some other roof."

"He's old enough to wipe his own nose," Collins said evenly. "Unless you figured to do it for him."

There was a long silence, and at last, Bradly slumped back in his chair. "Shit. We're wastin' time. Play cards."

Wes grinned. "Funny, how it's always the loser shoutin' for somebody to deal."

"Sonny, you keep askin' for it," Bradly rasped, "and you're gonna get it."

The youngster smirked and ran his fingers through the stack of coins in front of him. "Looks to me like I've already got it."

Bradly muttered something under his breath and snatched his cards from the table. Without a flicker, Davis fumbled the ace back into the deck and grunted to himself. He still

couldn't believe the kid had caught on. Not so quickly anyhow.

Shortly before midnight it was done. Collins and the boy
walked from Dire's Store with every nickel the tinhorns had
between them. Crossing the street, headed toward a saloon,
the gambler chuckled and slewed a sidewise glance at Wes.

"You shouldn't let a pair like that get your goat. Spoils
the fun of watchin' them fry in their own fat."

Before the youngster could answer a slug whistled past
him and the sharp crack of a pistol echoed up the street.
Behind them, Bradly jumped off the boardwalk and rushed
forward, cursing as he triggered another shot. But his aim
was as bad as his poker. The ball sailed harmlessly by and
shattered the saloon window.

Wes spun, crouching low, and drilled him square in the
chest. Bradly stumbled to a halt, planting a slug in the earth
at his feet, then toppled forward like a felled tree. The boy
calmly shot him in the head and looked up just as Davis
scampered back into the store. Holstering the Navy, Wes
turned and strolled away as if he hadn't a care in the world.

Dumbfounded, Collins just stood there a moment, staring
at the body. Then his lips moved, mouthing words heard only
by himself and the dead man.

"Mother of God. Ain't he a sudden little bastard?"

5

Pisga appeared unchanged. Seated astride a grullo gelding,
Wes studied the town as a soldier might reconnoiter an enemy stronghold. From a distance, atop a small knoll west of
the business district, he saw nothing out of the ordinary. The
night wind was chill and the dim twinkle of lamplight below
gave him a warm feeling down in the pit of his belly. But it
was a fleeting sensation, put to rout by a gritty wariness that
chided such foolish notions. There was no safe place. There
were only places less dangerous than others.

Still, he couldn't ignore the gut feeling about Pisga. A
good feeling. Unless the State Police were better bloodhounds than the Yankee Army, this was one place they
wouldn't have nosed out. Aside from his family, he'd never
told a living soul about Jane Bowen and his winter as a
schoolteacher. Not even John Collins knew about it, though
in the end, he'd felt obligated to tell the gambler most everything else.

It saddened him in a queer sort of way. Not having a
partner any longer. But Collins had been right, and wholly
justified in the stand he took. A gambling man, one who rode
the circuit regular as clockwork, couldn't afford trouble with
the State Police. Sheriffs and town marshals could be bought
off, or wheedled into looking the other way. But a man who
valued his hide didn't monkey with the governor's hired mercenaries. After Wes spilled the beans, admitting that his
name was on the now infamous wanted list, Collins had
wasted little time in dissolving the partnership. The gambler
did so reluctantly, swilling himself blind drunk in the process, for he had grown fond of the boy. What with him being
a confirmed loner, that was no small honor in itself. Yet,
drunk or sober, he hadn't wavered.

The killing in Towash would eventually find its way to
the wrong ears. The youngster's name would be linked with
his own, and before long the State Police would show up
looking for both of them. It was a risk he couldn't afford to
take. Much as he liked the boy, and needed him aboard Steeldust, the odds dictated only one choice. They had to go their
separate ways.

They parted outside Towash the morning after Christmas.

Wes felt no bitterness toward the gambler. Nor could he
fault the man. Collins had taught him a trade. Educated him
in tricks that remained a mystery to all but the most skilled
high rollers. And perhaps the last lesson had been the most
profound of all. Only a fool buys chips in another man's
fight. In that there was a kernel of wisdom, one he wouldn't
soon forget.

But never had he felt so alone, or at a loss for what came

next. He had the clothes on his back, close to a thousand dollars in gold, and a grullo gelding. That and a pair of hands trained to earn him an easy living.

Yet, of all he possessed, it was the gelding he prized most just at that moment. He had bought the grullo from a *vaquero* down on the border, after busting the man in a monte game. Dusky blue in color, with a sound bottom and strong lungs, the horse was built to last. Times before, when he'd been on the dodge, Wes had learned that endurance was what counted. A wanted man, with the law on his tail, was a goner unless he had something underneath him that wouldn't quit. The grullo was no quitter, and in that he found comfort. So long as the State Police didn't take him by surprise, he had a fair chance of pulling through.

With no real destination in mind, he had ridden aimlessly for a couple of days and awoke one morning with a sudden yearning to see Jane Bowen. Nearly seven months had passed since his last visit, and by now, like as not, she was married off to some ribbon clerk with a bright future. But he still wanted to see her, and like a bear overcome with a taste for honey, he headed east into the hornet's nest. Where the State Police swarmed in droves, and carpetbagger law still ruled the land.

Now, two days after New Year's, he brought the grullo down off the knoll and rode into Pisga. Skirting the business district, he swung north around town and approached the Bowen house from the back. After tying the gelding in a stand of live oaks, he stuck to the shadows and worked his way around to the front porch. When he yanked the pull bell it suddenly came to him that he reeked with sweat and a week's accumulation of grime. It was too late to back off, though. If she was still here, not yet married off, she'd have to take him as he was. Or not at all.

The door opened and Jane gave a small, stifled cry. Her hand flew to her mouth and she gaped at him in bemused wonderment. Several moments passed before she found her voice, and even then it came in a near whisper.

"Wes?"

"It's me, in the flesh." His stomach churned, and flipped

over in a full somersault, but he flashed a cocky grin. "Big as life and twice as ornery."

"You've changed." Her eyes took in the fancy duds and the gun belt, and she seemed to shrink back. "Or maybe it's the clothes."

He doffed the sombrero and shuffled his feet. The jingle-bobs on the big, roweled spurs chimed softly, and all of a sudden he felt very out of place. Like a kid playing the tough hombre and botching it all to hell.

"I was just passing through. Thought I'd stop by and say hello." Edging away, he smiled weakly and started to turn. "Nice seein' you again. Didn't mean to bust in on you so sudden like."

"Wes Hardin!" Her crisp tone stopped him cold. "You come into this house. Right this instant!"

Grabbing his hand, the girl tugged him through the door and into the parlor. Neal Bowen froze halfway out of his chair, and his wife sat immobile, her face drained of color. Then the old man sank back in his rocker and pinned the youngster with a glacial stare. Jane wasn't exactly radiant, but she managed a brave smile and dragged Wes a couple of steps closer.

"Mama! Daddy! Look who's here. It's Wes."

That much they could see for themselves, and the sight clearly wasn't to their liking. They gave his *charro* getup a hard once-over and frowned as if somebody had just broken wind. After a long, turgid silence, Bowen finally grumped out a few words.

"Well, Hardin, how are things in Mexico?"

Wes turned the color of beet juice, acutely aware of his peculiar garb. "Tolerable, I guess. Met some nice people down that way."

"You should have stayed. Or isn't the law after you anymore?"

"Law?" the boy echoed hollowly.

"I'll be frank with you, Hardin." The merchant's tone was clipped and stiff. "We accepted you into our home and you deceived us. You were wanted by the law then, and doubtless you're wanted by the law now. I have no use for a man who wantonly takes the lives of other men, and even less use for a liar.''

"Daddy!" Jane cried. "That's not fair. Give Wes a chance to explain.''

"Explain what? That he's a liar and a killer, and from the looks of him, half greaser.'' Bowen stabbed out with a bony finger. "You're not welcome in this house, Hardin. And I'll thank you to leave my daughter alone. She'll have no truck with the likes of you. Do I make myself clear?''

The youngster's hackles pricked up as though he'd heard a new verse in an old sermon, and for an instant, he glared back in baffled fury. Then his temper came unhinged.

"Lemme tell you somethin', old man. I've been listenin' to that sanctimonious hogwash all my life. You high-and-mighty hypocrites sit back on your perch and play God judgin' people like me. And it don't even matter that maybe I had to shoot to save my own skin. All you can do is get puffed up with righteousness and start shoutin' *burn the sinner!* Well, Mr. High and Mighty, I'm here to tell you—just lookin' at you makes me sick to my stomach.''

Bowen flushed and sputtered something unintelligible, but Wes cut him off. "Don't say nothin', you hear me! Don't even open your mouth. I'm gonna walk out of here and I'm not comin' back. But you say one more word and you'll wind up eatin' with store-bought choppers.''

The boy spun on his heel and stormed out of the house. Jane hesitated a moment, almost mesmerized by the raw terror on her father's face, then turned and darted through the door. She caught Wes as he barreled around the corner of the house and clutched desperately at his sleeve.

"Wes! Please, Wes. Don't leave like this.''

"Like what?'' He jerked his arm loose and stalked off into the darkness. "You want me to go back in there and apologize? Tell him what a swell feller he is for showin' me the gate?''

"You know that isn't what I mean. I defended you, didn't I? Answer me, Wes, didn't I?''

Something in her voice stopped him, a tiny cry of helplessness, and his anger simmered down as fast as it had boiled over. Sheepishly, he turned back and gave her a crooked grin. "Yeah, I guess you did, at that. I was so mad I plumb forgot."

She came into his arms and their lips met in a hungry yearning too long denied. When they parted, at last, she peppered his face with wet, sticky kisses. "Oh, Wes, I love you so much. Honestly, I do. Late at night I lie awake thinking about you and I break out in goose bumps all over. It's shameless, but I can't help it. I won't ever love anybody but you."

"Then let's get married. Tonight." He lifted her chin, searching her face intently. "We'll get some preacher out of bed and just put all this behind us. Ride off and never look back."

Her eyes went misty, the color of damp violets, and she shook her head. "I can't."

"What do you mean, can't?"

"I want to. It's all I've ever wanted. Since the first day we met. But I just can't till you clear yourself with the law. Don't you understand? I couldn't live that way. Always on the run. Never knowing from one minute to the next if you'll get killed—or have to kill somebody else."

"No, I don't understand. You're startin' to sound like your pa."

"That's not true"—she stamped her foot with tart annoyance—"and you know it very well."

"Well, by Jesus Christ, it's all I keep hearin'. And it's enough to gag a dog off a gut wagon." He crammed the sombrero on his head. "Tell you what. You and your goose bumps think it over, and if I get the chance, I might just stop by next time I'm in town."

Wheeling around, grinding his teeth in a burst of temper, he strode off toward the live oaks. Jane stood rooted, speechless, unable to move or call out. After what seemed a lifetime, she heard the faint thud of hoofbeats and a moment later the night went still. Then her knees went shaky and she began to cry. Very slowly she lowered herself to the ground and buried her face in her hands. But it helped not at all.

The flinty soil consumed her tears and nothing changed.

CHAPTER 3

1

Like a young hawk gaining its wings, a remarkable change had come over Wes Hardin. Those who knew him best merely nodded wisely and observed that strange things often happened to a boy when he turned seventeen. Others, especially those meeting him for the first time, found it difficult, if not impossible, to believe that he wasn't older. But there was no mistaking the steady look in his eye and his assured manner in dealing with the vagaries of life. Whatever the reason, the boy had set aside boyish ways. Tall and resolute, square-jawed with a brushy mustache covering his upper lip, he spoke and acted with the bearing of what he had become. A man.

Yet, if Wes Hardin had been a defiant boy, he had matured into a dangerous man. Within the crucible of death and gunsmoke and Yankee injustice had been fired a confirmed fatalist. Time and eight dead men had numbed him to the sight of death, hardened him to the act of killing. However unnatural, the outgrowth was an utter contempt for those who opposed him and a blind disregard for the consequences to himself. What others took to be rashness, or an excess of courage, was neither of those things. It was simply a complete and immutable absence of fear.

Though still headstrong and short-fused, Wes had learned to control his temper. Where before he had exploded with the suddenness of a firecracker, he now harnessed his anger to better effect. Cool and detached, calculated in a deadly sort of way, he appeared devoid of nerves in a tight situation. Here again, it was not a matter of icy bravery. Instead, it hinged on a single imponderable. He feared nothing that walked, talked, or crawled, and the offspring was a steely audacity that left other men vaguely uneasy in his presence.

Carpetbagger justice was in no small part the moving force behind his stoic outlook on life. The State Police had hounded him relentlessly, dogging his tracks from town to town across the state. Early in the spring, while visiting his parents for the first time in more than a year, he had narrowly escaped capture. Perhaps more than anything else, it was the thought of his family in jeopardy, badgered and ruthlessly questioned by black officers, which brought about the transformation. Where in the past he had run from the dreaded State Police, avoiding confrontation, he now took no steps whatever to elude them. He went where he wanted, when he wanted, supremely untroubled by the possibility that he might be caught.

This process of growth and maturity had revealed itself in other ways as well. Looking back, he was able to understand Jane's reluctance to take him on his own terms. In time, he even came to accept her deep-seated apprehension, and saw himself as something of a lout for the way he had acted. Certainly there was no place for a wife and family in the life he led, and in truth, that was what Jane had tried to tell him. While some six months had passed, he hadn't worked up the nerve to visit Pisga again, but he had written her several letters as he drifted from town to town. Whether she still waited for him, or had, after all, married some ribbon clerk, was an uncertainty that rode with him constantly. But it was something he accepted as inevitable, at least for the moment. Until Texas changed, and Yankee rule ended, he would remain what a topsy-turvy world had made him. A man outside the law.

Still, with all its assorted miseries, life hadn't been unkind to him. Cards and horse racing kept him well supplied with funds. Women found him easy on the eyes, yet he was free to come and go as he chose. Within the sporting crowd he was respected more than most, both as a gambler and a man ever willing to toe the mark. All in all, whenever he paused to reflect on it, he had no room for complaint. Things weren't exactly perfect, but they could have been a hell of a lot worse.

Along the way, he had even acquired a new partner. Upon skipping out of Mount Calm a step ahead of the State Police, he had taken refuge with the Barrickman clan, distant relatives on his mother's side of the family. There he had renewed a boyhood friendship with his cousin, Alec Barrickman. After a week of swapping tall tales, Alec decided the fast life sounded better than farming, and when Wes rode out, he tagged along. Here, too, the change in the young outlaw was evident. Though Alec was a couple of years older, there was never any question as to who called the shots. Wes figured he'd served his apprenticeship, and anyone who sided with him now would have to settle for second fiddle. That or nothing. Unless somebody put a shotgun on him, he had taken orders for the last time in his life.

Barrickman was a gangling, rawboned sort of fellow, with more spunk than savvy. Towheaded, with a wide gap between his front teeth and a quid of tobacco stuffed in his cheek, there was something of the hayseed about him. But he was bright enough, and early on it became apparent that they made a good team. With his country-boy smile and china-blue eyes, people right away took Barrickman for a natural born sucker. Wes taught him a few tricks, mostly how to boost a pot when dealt a loaded hand, and a steady stream of tinhorns were left scratching their heads over the young sodbuster's astounding luck. All the same, the senior partner saw to it that his cousin stayed out of straight games. Barrickman had an unnerving habit of drawing to inside straights and trying to bluff on a busted flush, which tended to whittle down the profits at an alarming rate.

Toward the middle of June, Hardin & Company drifted into the town of Horn Hill. There was a circus running full blast, drawing crowds from several counties, and the place swarmed with pigeons ripe for the plucking. Wes hadn't killed anybody since the Towash shoot-out, and as near as he could tell, the State Police had lost his scent. This, combined with the carnival mood of the town, made him a little less wary than usual. Barrickman was horny as a goat anyway, so he promised the junior member of the firm that part of their time would be devoted to the ladies of Horn Hill.

All the same, business came first.

That afternoon Barrickman went into what, by now, had become their standard routine. Wandering into a saloon, he flashed a fistful of double eagles and quick as a wink found himself engaged in conversation with a couple of sharpers. As it always did, the discussion ultimately worked around to the game of poker, and the young bumpkin allowed himself to be steered to the table. Magically, a deck of cards appeared, and by the third drink, things were off and running. Standing at the bar, Wes waited until another farmer had taken a seat in the game and then ambled over. The tinhorns sized him up as yet a third mark and invited him to take a chair. Their smug looks made it all the easier. Moments ago they were matching one another for drinks and suddenly— magi-presto—they had stumbled into a field of clover.

It took Wes only one turn as dealer to figure out the play. They were using strippers, and rather crudely shaved at that. In his hands the cards began performing wonders, and queer as it seemed, the young hayseed across from him started raking in some dandy pots. Wes worked on the premise that a man with larceny in his heart was the biggest sucker of all. But the kill had to be made fast, before the sharper suspected that someone had outslicked him at his own game.

The end came less than a half hour after Wes joined the game. He dealt one tinhorn a full house and the other four deuces. Alec Barrickman, after drawing three cards, wound up with his old standby, four nines. The farmer dropped out when the raising began, and by showdown time, the two sharpers had bumped the pot with all they had, pinky rings included. Gleefully, all wide-eyed innocence and boyish smiles, Barrickman dragged in the pot with his thorny paws.

The tinhorns just sat there, clicking their teeth like a couple of rabid skunks. In the parlance of the sporting world, they had been gaffed on their own play.

After leaving the card sharps to lick their wounds, Wes deposited Barrickman in a pool hall, where he couldn't get himself into any mischief. Then the young outlaw went looking for a straight game. He found it in the Bella Union Saloon, and about three hours later came out wishing he hadn't bothered. Lady Luck had dumped all over his head, handing him a steady run of second-best, and he had dropped better than a hundred dollars. Still, not once had he violated the cardinal rule as laid down by John Collins. Unless the other fellow cheated first a man played whatever he was dealt. There was always another day, and more often than not, the fickle lady smiled on those who kept the faith.

Barrickman wasn't even remotely interested in the details. He was tired of cards and sick to death of pool. What he wanted most was a greased pole, and after the debacle at the Bella Union, Wes had to admit he could use a little diversion himself. In high spirits, certain they would hit pay dirt of a different sort, the youngsters set out in the direction of the circus.

More quickly than they expected, good things began to happen. A brace of apple-cheeked farm girls had eluded their parents, and with only the mildest coaxing, the party shortly became a foursome. Arm in arm, the girls squealing and the boys licking their chops, they struck off down the midway to see the sights. As in most small-time carnivals, the tent barkers were the best part of the show. The bearded lady turned out to be a scraggly old crone with a face full of fuzz and the world's strongest man almost had a stroke lifting a midget pony. But it was fun, and the girls' squeals were growing louder, which the young gamblers took as a good sign, so nobody was overly disappointed that the freaks didn't live up to the barker's spiel.

After watching a fire-eater singe his tonsils, the foursome sailed back onto the midway laughing and snuggling closer with every step. Wes figured a few more shows ought to turn the trick and he steered them toward a tent proclaiming the eighth wonder of the world.

Whatever the colossus was, they never got to see it. A fight broke out behind them and a circus roustabout burst out of nowhere on the dead run. He scattered the foursome with a rough shove and lumbered on toward the fight. Wes's re-action was sheer reflex. Rushing back, he grabbed the man's shoulder and spun him around.

"Mister, somebody ought to learn you some manners. There's a couple of ladies back there that's got an apology comin' to 'em."

"Out of the way, rube. Less you want your face smashed."

"Smash and be damned! I'm kind of a smasher myself."

Somehow it wasn't the youngster's day. Sparkling lights danced before his eyes and the next thing he knew, he was flat on his back. Instinct alone saved him. As the roustabout tugged at a gun in his waistband, Wes cleared leather and stitched three slugs straight up his front. The last one caught the circus tough just below the hairline and his skull blew apart in a frothy pink gore. Wes was on his feet and running before the man hit the ground. Somewhere in the background he heard the girls shrieking at the top of their lungs and a murderous outcry from the crowd. Then he was around a tent and going strong. Barrickman loped up beside him, pant-ing hard, and threw him a wild-eyed look.

"Gawd A'mighty! You play for keeps, don't you?"

"Alec, lemme tell you somethin'. And don't you never forget it. Any man worth shootin' is worth killin'."

Wes cast a peek over his shoulder and saw a mob hard on their heels. Digging harder, he sprinted off, roaring in Bar-rickman's ear as he went past."

"Now, run, you horny sonovabitch! Run!"

2

After Horn Hill young Hardin became even bolder. Somehow tucking tail like a whipped dog didn't sit well on his stomach. Granted, to stand his ground and face the mob would have bordered on suicide. A stranger in a small town would have had less chance than a snowball in hell. Especially if the sheriff had taken a notion to consult his wanted circulars. They would have strung him up before he had time to take a deep breath. And Barrickman alongside him. Sort of a grand finale to their circus holiday.

People were like that. Nothing tickled their fancy quite so much as a good hanging. The longer a man danced on air, slowly choking with bulged eyeballs and swollen tongue, the better they liked it. It was a sight to be savored down to the tiniest detail, something that added spice to dull conversation on a cold winter night.

Yet, for all the ghoulish mood of the people, Wes was still irked at being forced to run. Discretion was the better part of valor—that was one of his father's favorite little gems—but in the last two years he had damned sure had his share of running. A double helping, and then some. Upon fleeing Horn Hill, quirting his horse into the pitch-black night, he decided it was the last time. He would run no more.

With Barrickman in tow, he turned east, straight into the jaws of the governor's meat grinder. It was a nervy act of defiance, an engraved invitation to the State Police. They would come after him, of that he was sure, for his name was known and word of his presence in east Texas wouldn't be long in reaching Austin. But it hardly seemed to matter. In fact, he welcomed it. Killing saloon toughs and circus roustabouts had somehow lost its zest. It was time to get down to serious business. Put the nutcracker to work on those who had hounded him and shamed his family—the carpet-baggers and their pack of hired cutthroats.

Late in July, Wes and Alec Barrickman rode into Evergreen. The young outlaw now had a price of one thousand dollars on his head, but he entered the town openly, with no attempt to conceal his identity. Reward dodgers bannering his name, with a charcoal sketch bearing a fair likeness, were tacked on the notice board outside the sheriff's office. As he rode by, it gave him a moment of perverse amusement. The circulars showed a youthful, clean-shaven face, without a sign of his cookie-duster mustache.

On impulse, he reined in and dismounted. Scrounging around in his saddlebags, he found a stub pencil and walked to the notice board. Wetting the pencil on the tip of his tongue, he carefully blacked in a brushy mustache on the sketch. Stepping back, he studied his handiwork for a moment and then grunted, better satisfied with the likeness. Chuckling to himself, he swung aboard the grullo and reined back into the street.

Barrickman had sat spellbound through the entire performance, and now he gave the youngster a look of popeyed disbelief. "Wes, I'll swear to Christ, you got more balls 'n a bulldog. That or you ain't playin' with all your marbles."

"Well now, Alec, suppose you gimme the straight goods"—Wes smiled, thoroughly delighted with himself—"which one you figure it is?"

Barrickman wasn't that thick. However casual, the question called for a bit of diplomacy. "My pap used to tell about a feller that hunted bears with a switch. Folks always allowed as how he was strong on guts, and smart too,'cause he never once tangled with anything he couldn't handle."

Wes burst out laughing and heeled the grullo. "Quit your fibbin' and c'mon. Let's go see what's happenin' at the races."

Saturday was race day in Evergreen and the sporting crowd generally flocked in for the occasion. Wes figured to get down a few wagers on the ponies, and afterward, scare up a poker game in one of the dives along Main Street. Since Horn Hill he'd gone through a long dry spell, playing hide-and-seek with the fickle lady. Luckily, the youngsters had stumbled across enough card slicks to keep them in funds,

and he still had close to five hundred dollars in his saddlebags. Today he felt good, though, and he had a hunch the
tide had changed. Any gambler worth his salt knew the feeling, and being a superstitious lot, they followed the oldest
adage in the profession.

Get a hunch, bet a hunch.

Which was precisely what Wes did. But the ponies he
liked apparently weren't listening. One faltered on the get-
away, four in a row came in a strong second, and the sixth
went berserk, pitching his rider ten yards short of the finish
line. All in all, it was a bleak afternoon. The young gambler
had dropped better than three hundred dollars and unless
something changed fast, he was seriously considering another line of work. That or scouting up a voodoo witch doctor and buying himself a whole string of juju charms. Headed
uptown from the racetrack, he had the distinct premonition
that if he plucked a rose it would vanish in a puff of smoke
and leave him holding a fresh horse turd.

Barrickman said little or nothing as they prowled the dives
along Main Street. He had learned some time back that with
Wes in a foul mood a man did well just to keep his mouth
shut. Shortly before sundown, though, they wandered into
the Acme Saloon and Gaming Parlor and Wes seemed to
perk up the least bit. This was clearly the local hangout for
the sporting crowd. There were faro layouts and chuck-a-
luck along one wall and a whole row of poker tables on the
opposite side. With the races over, the place had drawn a
full crowd and the action was running heavy. Aside from
that, the atmosphere alone told Wes they had found Evergreen's leading spot. Unlike saloons which catered to rowdy
cowhands, a real gaming den was quiet as a church. Gamblers didn't like distractions or noise, complaining it broke
their concentration, and a loudmouth ran the risk of getting
his skull peeled with a bungstarter. Other than a murmured
drone of conversation, the only sound here was the clink of
gold coins and a random curse whenever a man's cards fell
the wrong way.

The youngsters bellied up to the bar and ordered whiskey.

Wes was a sipper, generally nursing the same drink for a couple of hours. Rotgut impaired a man's reactions, not to mention clouding his judgment, and he had observed that hard drinkers usually finished last. At cards or in a fight. A sober man had the edge, and Wes sort of liked it that way. Besides, the stuff most joints served tasted like sheep dip anyhow. So there wasn't much sense in floating his gizzard just to be sociable. Better to keep the edge.

Wes turned, hooking his elbows over the counter, and made a slow survey of the action. There were chairs open at a couple of tables, and from the looks of things, the betting was light. Which, at the moment was just about his speed. Less than two hundred dollars damn sure wouldn't go far in a table stakes game. He was on the verge of giving it a whirl when a man seated at the nearest table climbed to his feet and strolled forward. The stranger halted a few steps off and leaned into the bar.

"Funny thing. I been watchin' you and I got a feelin' you're somebody I oughta know. Curious, ain't it?"

Wes uncoiled, freeing his gun hand. "You writin' a book or was you just born nosy?"

"Don't get your dander up, neighbor." The man extended his hand. "S'pose I go first. Name's Bill Longley."

Wes pumped the hand a couple of times and let go. He'd heard of Longley, and none of it good. Wanted for several murders, and according to reports, most of the victims bushwhacked. On top of that, he was a queer-looking bird. Tall, almost gaunt, with a lantern jaw and eyes deep-set under a ridged brow. His bony wrists dangled from the sleeves of a frayed hickory shirt and his feet were about the size of nail kegs. Taken at a glance, he made an unlikely-looking gambler and seemed built all wrong for gunfighting. Which might account for his reputation as a backshooter.

"Most folks call me Wes Hardin."

Longley nodded. "Yep, thought so. Seen the posters out on you. Guess it was the soup-strainer that throwed me." He paused, twisting his jaw in a crooked smile. "Workin' sorta close to home, ain't you? What with Austin bein' so handy,

I mean. Last I heard you was out west somewheres.''

The youngster shrugged, revealing nothing. "Some folks might say you're kind of handy yourself.''

"Yeh, but I'm used to them nigger lawdogs. Eat 'em for breakfast.''

"That a fact? I'm sort of partial to dark meat myself.''

"Hey now, neighbor, you're talkin' my kinda talk.'' Longley jerked his thumb back toward the poker table. "How'd you like to join a little game we got goin'? Be proud to have you sit in.''

Wes held back hard on a grin. It was like a wolf being asked to come play with sheep. Whatever else he was, Longley had the look of a born loser.

"Sure, why not? I got some time to kill. Might even get lucky and win a couple.''

The statement proved prophetic, in a way Longley and his friends could hardly believe. The young gambler hit a streak that was nothing short of stupefying. He caught straights and flushes and full houses, and three of a kind so often it was downright embarrassing. Once, defying the laws of poker and ordinary horse sense, he dragged down a pot on a jack high. Barrickman stayed at the bar, chuckling to himself as he swigged whiskey, certain beyond doubt that his cousin was goosing the odds with some slick tricks.

Similar thoughts occurred to the players themselves, but somehow the idea wouldn't hold water. Hardin didn't win just when he was dealing. He won damn near all the time, no matter who dealt. If they were being fleeced, the bastard was either a swami or a gypsy in disguise. Otherwise, it was pure outhouse luck.

And in that, they were right. Wes felt the lady riding his coattails, and he laid on strong. His luck had returned with a vengeance, and as a practical matter, it was like taking candy from babes. Everything he did was not so much right as faultless. Within an hour he had busted the four men flatter than flat. Dead broke.

Longley took it hardest, fancying himself the he-wolf of Evergreen and Jacinto County. But for all his fearsome reputation, he was a poor judge of character. More than money, he had lost face, and in a moment of rash bravado, he decided to sprinkle a little salt on the kid's tail. As Hardin pulled in the last pot, Longley shifted in his chair and dropped his hand below the table.

"Y'know, it's a funny thing. We heard them nigger police had sweet-talked some wanted men into playin' Judas goat. Spyin' on white folks and turnin' them in for the reward. What with you showin' up so sudden and all, I just been sittin' here wonderin' if maybe you got yourself a deal with them nigger-lovers in Austin."

Wes met his look with an icy smile. "Longley, you got about three seconds to back off. Then I'm gonna put a leak in your ticker."

A tomblike silence settled over the table and Longley swallowed nervously. Something in the kid's eyes told him he'd made a big mistake. If he so much as flicked an eyelash he was dead as a doornail. Evergreen's premier badman pasted a waxen smile on his face and made a game try at laughing.

"Why, hell, Hardin, I was just funnin'. Way you hauled our ashes I figured you owed us a little sport. No harm done."

"Much obliged, gents." The young gambler stood, stuffing the last of the coins in his vest pocket. "See you in church."

Hitching back his chair, he walked straight to the door and pushed through the batwings. Barrickman was only a step behind, and as they climbed aboard their horses, Wes grunted sardonically.

"That's rich. First man I ever really wanted to kill and the sorry shitheel lost his nerve. Alec, I tell you, there just ain't no justice."

Reining back, he spurred the grullo down Main Street past the sheriff's office. The reward dodger was exactly as he had left it, penciled mustache inky black in the gathering twilight.

3

Less than a week later Hardin & Company was dissolved. Unforeseen events conspired to end the partnership, and Wes reluctantly sent Barrickman back to the family farm. They parted outside the town of Kosse, in the dead of night, horses lathered from a long run. As he watched his cousin ride off, Wes was struck by the eerie feeling that life or fate, or perhaps some flaw in his own character, destined him to go it alone. Reflecting on it further, it came to him that maybe John Collins had been right after all. Some men simply weren't suited to lasting alliances with other men.

A lone wolf had only himself to worry about.

That was it in a nutshell. Responsibility. A sense of obligation to the man who rode beside him. The constant worry of being concerned about the other fellow's welfare. An infernal irritant that preyed on the mind like worms gnawing on rancid meat.

There were those seemingly born to such things. Men like his father, who saw themselves as the shepherd of the flock, their brother's keeper. They gloried in it, lived for nothing else, found their mission on earth in an everlasting vigil over their fellow man. Perhaps, at root, this was what separated Christian from heathen, sinner from saint. If so, then as his father had so often prophesied, he was doomed to the fires of eternal damnation. But if it was already ordained, if he was slated for hell with a one-way ticket, then he sure as Christ wouldn't make the trip oozing despair for the clods around him.

Better to ride alone, cover his own tracks, and to hell with the fainthearts.

The trouble had started earlier that night, shortly after they rode into Kosse. Barrickman got himself involved with a saloon girl, and in the heat of the moment, went a little too far. The girl's lover, a gambling man Wes knew from his Brazos days, took exception to Barrickman's pawing and rough talk. Within moments Barrickman was backed into a corner, clearly outclassed and only a step away from the grave. Had it been someone else, Wes would have washed his hands of the whole mess. But this was his cousin, blood kin. After soothing words and a couple of warnings failed, there was only one way out. He killed the gambler.

Though he had been recognized, and the State Police were sure to pick up his trail, that bothered him scarcely at all. The thing that had him boiling was the senselessness of the whole affair. Never before had he killed a man in cold blood, a man who had done him no wrong, knowing even as he forced the fight that the gambler was a walking dead man.

Somehow it grated on him that the gambler hadn't yet cleared leather when the first slug knocked him head over heels. All the more so since it was Barrickman's fight. A killing that served no purpose, could have been avoided except for the goatlike lust of a green plowboy.

Afterward, Wes made no bones about it. Barrickman was to return to the farm, and that was final. More than a liability, he had become a luxury Wes couldn't afford. Killing men who deserved it was one thing. The dead littered along his trail, each and every one, had asked to be buried. But pulling someone else's fat out of the fire, killing when there was no need, was a whole different ball of wax. It made him want to puke.

Barrickman had taken it hard, pleading to be given another chance. The words fell on deaf ears, though. Wes bowed his neck and that was the way it ended. Under a cloud of gloom, tail between his legs, Barrickman headed back to the family farm. The fast life he longed for had, after all, been a little faster than he could handle.

Wes watched him ride away and felt a moment of regret. But in the same instant a flood of relief swept over him. Somehow, by whatever force of nature, he was meant to be a loner, obligated only to himself and the dictates of what was best for Wes Hardin. It was a lesson he wouldn't soon forget.

With that, he pulled the grullo around and struck out for

Mount Calm. A dead gambler, needlessly killed, would soon put the law on his tail. Before it was too late, he had a need to see his folks again. Why or to what purpose was a question that had no answer. But it had to be now. Some inner voice told him that the next time would be a long haul down the trail.

Dusk had fallen as Wes crossed the creek. Avoiding Mount Calm, he'd spent last night and most of the day making a wide swing to the north. It seemed unlikely that the law would have a watch on the farm, but it was a risk to be considered all the same. Better to approach from the blind side, through the fields, just in case. Caution wasn't his strong suit, yet there were times when it paid to step light. Like tonight. Shooting his way out of the Hardin household would be about the last straw.

The one that broke James Hardin's back.

The old man already had a mighty cross to bear, what with his son an outlaw and the congregation clicking their tongues with shock. If the law ever cornered him at the farm, and he had to fight his way out, that would finish it. Preacher Hardin would pass on to his reward out of sheer mortification.

After unsaddling, Wes hobbled the gelding and left him to graze near the creek. A short walk through the woods brought him to a field, and from there he was within a stone's throw of the house. Gaining the barn, he hunkered down in the shadows and spent a quarter hour watching and listening. Satisfied that everything was as it should be, he finally climbed to his feet and made a dash for the back door.

When he entered the parlor, Sarah Hardin uttered a sharp gasp and jumped from her chair as if galvanized. Tears welled up in her eyes and she crossed the room like a distracted ghost, locking him in a fierce hug. Never given to display of emotion, she had changed markedly since his trouble with the law, almost as if the dam had burst and the love hoarded in his childhood must be lavished on him while there was yet time.

Somehow it made him uncomfortable and he pulled back

after giving her a peck on the cheek. "How are you, Ma?"

"Fine, Son. Just fine." She dabbed at the tears and took hold of herself. "Just seeing you does wonders for me."

"Then I'm glad I came."

James Hardin hadn't moved from his rocker, and the youngster sensed that this time was to be no different from his other visits. They were of the same flesh and blood, but in spirit nothing kindred bound them together.

"Hello, Pa."

"Wes, this is your home and you're welcome here night or day. But I don't hold with firearms." He shook a finger at the holstered Colt. "I'd take it kindly if you'll leave that on the back porch."

"Sorry, but I guess I can't do that, Pa. Things the way they are, I rest easier with a gun in reach."

"Tools of Satan! Haven't you learned that yet?"

"Please, James. Please don't spoil it." Sarah Hardin stepped between them, beseeching the old man with her eyes. "We see him so little. Couldn't it be nice for a change? Just once?"

Something passed between them, and after a moment, he nodded. "Sit down, Wes. The way your mother worries about you, I suppose some things just have to be overlooked."

"I don't mean to worry you." Wes lowered himself onto the settee and his mother came to sit beside him. "I'd change it if I could. But that bunch down in Austin don't seem to see it the same way."

"You're trying to reform, then?" His father fixed him with a baleful look. "Is that what you're telling me?"

"Well, in a manner of speakin', I guess you could say that."

"How? What path has this reformation taken?"

Wes shifted uncomfortably. "I'm not sure I follow you, Pa."

"Very well, let's take an example. Have you stopped gambling?"

"No. Not just exactly. But it's an honest livin'. I don't cheat nobody."

"Have you stopped consorting with Jezebels?"

The youngster darted a glance at his mother and saw her redden. "Well, Pa, that's sort of a loaded question. Any way I answer, I'm gonna come up on the short end."

"Have you stopped killing your fellow man?"

"Pa, you're makin' it awful hard for me to hold my tongue. You know well and good I've never killed anyone that wasn't tryin' to kill me."

"According to the State Police, who were here this afternoon, you killed a man not twenty miles from this very room just last night. They say you bulled your way into a private argument and forced him to fight you. I suppose that was self-defense, also?"

"Now, hold on a minute. I can explain—"

"They say that John Wesley Hardin has now killed nine men. Nine human beings."

Wes wasn't about to correct him. The count was ten, but apparently the law hadn't connected him with the circus roustabout. "You want to hear my explanation or are you just gonna sit there and rake me over the coals?"

"What I want to hear," James Hardin countered, "is how my son has set about reforming himself."

"I guess I haven't. Not the way you look at things. I'm just tryin' to mind my own business and stay a step ahead of the Yankees. Maybe someday they'll figure out I'm the wrong fellow to monkey with and then they'll leave me alone."

" 'Whosoever shall exalt himself shall be abased. And he that shall humble himself shall be exalted.' St. Matthew. Chapter Twenty-three. Verse twelve."

"Yeah? Well try this one on. 'Where there is no law, there is no transgression.' Romans. Chapter Four. Verse fifteen."

"Meaning?"

"Meanin', as long as the carpetbaggers are runnin' Texas there's no way somebody like me can come clear. They got my name down on the wanted list and nothin' is gonna change that. Not you or your Scripture or all the hallelujahs this side of kingdom come.''

The old man set his rocker in motion and gazed off into space. ''For once, I believe we are in agreement.''

Wes blinked with surprise. ''We are?''

''Since this afternoon I have given it a great deal of thought. Until Texas is readmitted to the Union there is no salvation for you here. Afterward, when Texas is again governed by Texans, perhaps some form of amnesty can be worked out. Despite our prayers, that is still a long way off, however.''

James Hardin brought his rocker to a halt and riveted the youngster with an owlish stare. ''I believe you should go to Mexico. And stay there until the ashes of war have been scattered. It will be better for you and for all concerned.''

''All concerned, meanin' you and Ma.''

''And your brother. The entire family suffers from the shame you've brought to the Hardin name.''

Curiously, Wes felt nothing. Only a stinging numbness, as if he'd passed his fingers over an open flame. ''Maybe you've got somethin', at that, Pa. Mexico might just fit the ticket.''

''I'm glad you agree. It's wisest all around.''

Sarah Hardin stood and looked down at her son. ''Could you eat if I put something on the table?''

''Ma, it's the funniest thing.'' Wes jumped to his feet and briskly rubbed his hands together. ''All of a sudden, I'm so hungry I could eat a bear.''

As they walked toward the kitchen, the old man's chair creaked and he began rocking slowly back and forth. It was a sad thing he had done. But necessary. However much it sorrowed him personally, it was for the good of the family. Then he heard the youngster laugh out in the kitchen and he nodded, grunting to himself.

That was good. The boy had taken it well.

4

There was no doubt whatever in Jane's mind. When the doorbell rang she knew it was Wes. All along she had held to an unshakable conviction that he would return. It had never been a matter of if he would come back, but only when.

She flew across the parlor, heedless of her father's scathing look. Dutiful, raised to respect her elders and obey unquestioningly, she had at last rebelled on the subject of Wes Hardin. So long as he was an outlaw, she wouldn't marry him. That much she had promised. But she meant to see him whenever and wherever possible. After several stormy sessions, her father resigned himself to this stalemate of sorts. Wisely, he hadn't pressed the issue further. To do so would have driven her into the young hellion's arms all the faster, and perhaps out of the Bowen household forever.

Jane threw open the door and slammed it behind her. Startled, Wes backed up a step as she flung herself on him, peppering his face with warm, sticky kisses. She had saved his letters, knew practically all of them by heart. Stiff and formal and clumsy as they were, she had every certainty that he loved her. Alone in her room at night, she lay wakeful, her mind flooded with wicked thoughts of their moments together. Face flushed, loins and breasts aching, she could close her eyes and feel their bodies engaged. Know again the touch of his corded muscles and his weight upon her, thrusting, filling her emptiness. She needed him and her need knew no shame. However silly or sinful or unwise, she was consumed with want for this boy who wrote clumsy, unforgettable letters. .

Wes was no slouch himself when it came to kissing, and he planted one on her that made up for all the months of being apart. At last, when they broke for air, he grinned and gave her a sly look.

"Seems like somethin's changed since the last time I was here."

"Nothing of the kind." Her lips curved in a teasing smile. "I've just decided I love you, that's all."

"That's all!" he blinked, somewhat taken aback. "Holy Moses."

"And I've also decided you love me."

"Well, I'll be double-dipped. You're just a sackful of surprises, aren't you?"

"But that doesn't mean I'll marry you. Not just yet, anyway."

"Here we go again. Same song, second verse."

"Wes Hardin, you're impossible." She kicked him in the shin and stalked off indignantly. "A girl tells you she loves you and is willing to wait for you and give you time to get yourself straightened out, and all you can do is poke fun at her. You're just a big, overgrown ingrate!" She stamped her foot in exasperation.

"Now hold off a minute." The girl's sudden flare of temper left him a little nonplussed and he hobbled across the porch, surprised she could kick so hard. "Hell's fire, you didn't say nothin' about all them things. Waitin' for me, I mean. And givin' me a chance to get clear with the law."

"Land's sakes, I said I loved you, didn't I?" She put on her best pout, casting him a hurt look. "And don't curse. It's not gentlemanly."

Still somewhat baffled, he moved up behind her and gently took hold of her shoulders. "You really meant it? You'll wait?"

"Of course I meant it, you big ninny. Why do you think I waited all this time for you to come back?"

"Danged if I know. I sort of halfway figured you'd be hitched up to some stiff-necked church deacon by now."

"Oh, men! You're all blind as bats." She spun around and thrust herself into his arms. "Mercy sakes alive, leave a girl a little pride. Don't make me spell it out for you."

Wes just stood there, tongue-tied, struck by a sudden fit of speechlessness. There was something different about her.

Older and wiser. More woman than girl. In the face of her unabashed candor, it took him a moment to collect his wits. Presently, he cleared his throat, sensing that she meant to wait him out. Then he smiled.

"Come to think of it, I got a couple of surprises myself. That's why I'm here. To tell you I'm headed for Mexico."

"Mexico!" Jane blurted the word in an incredulous whisper. "You mean across—over the border?"

"Yep, I'm gonna lay low down there till the Yankees call it quits and go home. Way I got it figured, that's about the only way I'll ever come clean with the law."

"But that could take years. Forever."

"Mebbe not. Most all the Confederate states are back in the Union already. My pa says it won't be long before Texas sees the light and gets itself readmitted. Then we'll have Texans runnin' things again and I can work out some kind of amnesty deal."

Jane cocked her head, scrutinizing him closely. "Wes, be honest with me. Whose idea was this—about you going to Mexico?"

Her steady gaze bored into him, insistent, demanding frankness. "It was my pa's idea. He sprung it on me last night. Said it'd be best if I just vamoosed for a while and let the dust settle."

Something in his tone, and the hangdog look on his face, told the tale. Jane scarcely needed an explanation. The elder Hardin had banished his son, and much as Wes tried to hide it, he was grievously hurt. Outlaw and outcast weren't the same. A man could live with one but he could only sorrow with the other. Still, there was something else at work here. A thought that occurred to her only on the moment. In Mexico, Wes at least had a chance. There was nothing for him in Texas but Yankee justice. And the gallows.

She brightened and playfully tugged at his mustache. "Lordy mercy, you got me talking so much I near forgot about this sticker patch. When did you grow that?"

"Few months back." He swiveled around to give her a look from another angle. "Like it?"

Lifting an eyebrow, she studied him with mock serious-ness. "Well, it does make you look older." Then she gig-gled. "They say everybody in Mexico wears mustaches. Maybe if you get one of those sombreros like you used to wear you'll fit right in."

"You might have somethin' at that." Her mood was con-tagious and his glum look disappeared with mercurial swift-ness. "Them señoritas are real pepperpots." Knuckling the ends of his mustache, he grinned. "Wouldn't surprise me none if they swooned dead away when they get a gander at this."

"Now, if that isn't just like a man." She stuck out her lip in a little-girl sulk. "Scarcely betrothed and he's already thinking about other women."

"Betrothed!"

"Well, of course, silly. What did you think I was talking about a minute ago?"

"I dunno." Things were happening a little too fast and he just stared at her, thoroughly dumbfounded. "All I heard you say was that you were gonna wait for me."

"Gracious sakes alive, Wes Hardin! You don't think I would wait on a man I wasn't betrothed to. What kind of a girl do you take me for?"

"Why, sure. I mean, yeah, I understand why—" Flustered now, he stopped and drew a deep breath. "What I'm tryin' to say is that I wouldn't have it any other way. But what changed your mind so sudden?"

"Nothing changed it. I always meant to marry you." She batted her eyelashes and smiled. "I just decided to tell you about it, that's all."

"I'll be damned." His bafflement was profound but it abruptly gave way to concern. "Say, what about your old man?"

"Oh, don't worry about Daddy. When the time comes I'll just twist him around my little finger. I've done it before."

Wes had no doubt of that. He was struck by the thought that inside this innocent-looking creature lurked a real spit-fire. Tonight he'd seen a wholly unsuspected side of her character, and like as not, there was more where that came from. He had a sneaking hunch he'd taken on more than he'd bargained for.

Ducking his head back at the house, he grinned suggestively. "If you've got your daddy's number then I don't reckon he'd mind if we took a walk."

Jane laughed. A low, throaty laugh that sounded wicked as sin itself. "You're a naughty man, Wes Hardin. I declare, you just make a girl break out in goose bumps all over."

"What d'you wanna bet I can't cure 'em?"

She giggled and he broke out in a chortled belly laugh. Arm in arm, stifling the temptation to share their high spirits with the world, they stepped off the porch and walked toward the corner of the house.

Within moments, the darkness swallowed them from sight.

An hour later Wes kissed the girl one last time and left her at the front door. As he headed in the direction of the live oak grove, his mind was a grab bag of conflicting emotions. Never in his life had he been so happy. Or so sad. She was his woman. By her own word. Willing to wait however long it took. Yet ahead of him loomed Mexico, and before he saw her again, he had an idea things would get mighty bleak. South of the Rio Grande began to sound worse all the time. A small slice of hell.

Moving through the trees, he was absorbed with the thought, aware of nothing around him. As he halted beside the grullo, hand stretched out to untie the reins, somebody jammed a gun in his back.

"Stand real easy." The man behind the voice nudged him with the pistol. "Just flinch and you're cold meat."

Wes froze stock-still. Whoever the voice belonged to, he was all business. A hand snaked around and relieved the youngster of his Navy, and Mexico suddenly seemed a long way off. An eternity instead of mere miles.

They stopped the next evening beside a small creek. By now Wes saw himself as the greatest jackass of all time. He'd walked into the trap like a dimdot with a head full of sawdust. Suspecting nothing. His captors were divided on the subject. Captain Dan Stokes of the Texas State Police was interested only in the reward and the fame of dragging John Wesley Hardin alive and kicking into the Austin jail. The other one, a black private named Jim Smolly, thought it was funny as hell. The big tough hombre collared with no more fuss than a freshly weaned pup. It was a fine joke.

After ordering the manacled young outlaw to lend a hand with camp chores, Stokes cautioned the black man to remain alert and take no chances. Then he rode off toward a nearby farm to obtain grain for the horses. Smolly flashed a broad, pearly grin, chuckling to himself. The thought of this half-witted kid giving him any trouble was so farfetched he couldn't help but laugh.

"Off yo' hoss, killer." Dismounting, thoroughly amused with himself, he walked to a stump and took a seat. "Start collectin' us some wood fo' the fire. Gonna be a long night."

Watching Stokes disappear in the distance, Wes had an idea it would be the longest night of the black man's life. Stepping down from the saddle, he kept the grullo between himself and Smolly. His wrist flicked, just the way John Collins had taught him, and a derringer appeared in his hand. Unhurried, calm as an undertaker, he moved clear of the horse and shot the black man twice at point-blank range.

Smolly hurtled backward over the stump and fell spread-eagled on the grass. Working faster now, the youngster searched him, found the keys, and unlocked the manacles. Then he retrieved his Navy from the black man's saddlebags, climbed aboard the gelding, and spurred south at a fast lope. The look on Smolly's face at that last instant stuck in his mind and he burst out laughing.

Yassuh, burrhead. It's gonna be a long night.

5

The sun hung suspended in a cloudless sky as Wes rode out of Belton. Nightfall was some three hours off and he meant to be far down the road before darkness. Outside the town he put the gelding into a fast trot and the edgy feeling slowly began to fade. It made him uneasy to travel during daylight, and the risk of entering a town bothered him even more. Still, a man had to eat and vittles didn't grow on trees. The general store in Belton had seemed the safest bet, and despite his misgivings, things had gone pretty smoothly. Near as he could tell, nobody had given him a second glance. All the same, he was glad to be on the road again. Out in the open, with room to maneuver, where he couldn't be taken by surprise.

Here lately, he'd had a gut full of surprises. And then some.

Though he had escaped handily enough, he wasn't interested in another scrape like the one last night. Sticking to back roads and wagon trails, he had skirted Waco and Temple, bearing generally south and west. Early that morning, after riding through the night, he had holed up to let the grullo graze awhile. But a couple of hours was all he allowed himself, then it was back in the saddle. He had in mind to make dust, and lots of it, before word reached Austin. If he didn't make it around the capital sometime tonight, or sunrise at the latest, there was a damn strong likelihood he'd never make it.

Yet, even as he dodged around through the backcountry, skirting the larger towns, Wes was gripped by a sense of self-loathing. He was on the run again. Something he'd sworn wouldn't happen. It was as if he'd taken an oath and broken it. Not to someone else but to himself. Which made it all the harder to swallow.

Thinking back on it, he felt like a willow in a strong wind. Whichever way the breeze blew, that was the way he leaned. One day he would make up his mind to something, determined that it would be just that way, and quicker than scat it got changed. Events or circumstances or some damned thing seemed to be rolling dice with his life. Not to mention people. A whole batch of them, with nothing better to do than nose around in his affairs.

The hell of it was, he let them get away with it. Like this
little sashay down to Mexico. He'd let his father browbeat
him like some harelipped pisswillie without a mind of his
own. Shame him into running. Instead of standing up to the
old man, telling him to jam all that sanctimonious crap about
God and family, he'd caved in without a fight. Just laughed
it off—as if it didn't mean a hill of beans. That was it in a
nutshell. A willow bending with the wind. Taking the easiest
way out.

Sometimes, looking back, it seemed he had no more spine
than a toad. Otherwise, he wouldn't let himself get waltzed
around that way. Like a puppet on a string, dancing to whatever tune somebody thought best. Even this thing with the
State Police wasn't all that different. Lots of men would have
stood their ground and fought it out come hell or high water.
The way Simp Dixon had done. Instead of skittering off after
every killing like a mouse in a nest full of snakes.

Of course, Simp Dixon was dead. And so was everybody
else who had stood and fought. That was no small thing. A
dead man, for all the grit he showed, was still dead. Done.
Finished. Nothing more than a hunk of meat for the worms
to commence pulverizing.

It was damned confusing. This thing of being pushed and
pulled in opposite directions. Somewhere along the line, it
seemed as though a man ought to make up his mind and
stick with it. Quit swapping ends every time the wind shifted.
But where to draw the line was a question that defied answer.
The more he grappled with it, the less certain he became.
Which was goddamned perplexing for a fellow who thought
he had life by the short hairs.

Then again, maybe it was like what he'd read in books.
Wisdom came not with age but with doubt. A man who knew
all the answers actually knew nothing. Only a skeptic discovered the truth. That being the case, though, growing up
was a damn sight more trouble than he'd suspected.

Separating the men from the boys was a first-class pain in
the ass.

Along about sundown, still pondering the riddle, Wes

forded the Lampasas at the Belton Road Crossing. As he kneed his horse up the far bank, where the road cut through a stand of pecan trees, he decided that maybe there wasn't any answer. That a fellow did the best he could, juggling circumstances whichever way seemed right, and when he got all through, he was a man. What kind of man he turned out to be was perhaps not so much a matter of shifting winds and the tides of fate, but rather how good a juggler he'd become along the way. If he couldn't keep the balls gyrating in the air, sort of harness the vagaries of life to suit himself, then he deserved whatever he got. Boiled down that way, it came out pretty simple. Whatever got shoved up a man's ass was done not just with his consent, but with him lending a helping hand.

The youngster grunted, beaming inwardly, satisfied that at least part of the riddle had come clear. Maybe with time, and poking around in his head a little more, he would solve the whole damn mess. If not, he stood about as much chance as a one-armed juggler in a high wind. The kind that life gobbled up in its own special meat grinder. Only most times the man was spit out, looking much as he always had, and it was his balls that got pulverized.

Which made him no man a'tall.

Jarred loose from his reverie, Wes suddenly hauled back on the reins. He couldn't move, as if somebody had sewed his puckerhole shut and nailed him to the saddle. None of it seemed real, yet queerly enough, it was big as life and a yard wide.

Standing before him in the road was Captain Dan Stokes.

Wes just sat there in a witless stupor for perhaps a half-dozen heartbeats. Before he could collect himself, somebody off to his left thumbed back the hammer on a shotgun. Then, from the other side, came the metallic snick of a Colt being eared back to full cock. They had him stoppered and corked like a jug of molasses.

Stokes shifted to the right a couple of steps, pistol held at his side, and again, the voice was all business. "Hardin, you make any sudden moves and you're a goner. Now step down

out of that saddle real easy like, and don't make me guess
what you're doin' with your hands.''

The young outlaw sighed, weighing the alternative, and
decided it was no choice at all. They had him snookered,
and this time they'd plugged all the holes. Very carefully, he
placed both hands over the saddle horn and stepped down
off the gelding. Footsteps broke out all over the place—front,
and sideways—but he didn't bother looking around. It was
such a pitiful goddamn mess he couldn't bring himself to
look them in the eye. All of a sudden, he felt green as a
gourd and not a hell of a lot smarter.

Ten minutes later they had him trussed up like a Christmas
pig. Hands manacled, feet bound together, and propped back
against a tree with a rope around his throat. Captain Stokes
overlooked none of the salient details this time out. He relieved Wes of the Navy, slipped the derringer out of its
spring-loaded wrist rig, and even collected his jackknife. The
three of them, Stokes and a couple of underlings, stood
around watching him a minute and one of the men made a
crack about a snake with his fangs pulled. Stokes lambasted
him hotly, recalling Jim Smolly's abrupt demise the night
before, and warned both men to be on their toes at all times.

"What we got here ain't a snot-nosed kid," he observed
dryly. "It's a natural disaster. Like a tornado or a prairie fire.
Them that didn't believe it found out the hard way."

Afterward, with dusk settling over the wooded stream
bank, they made camp for the night. While one of the men
hobbled their horses, the other built a fire for coffee and
broke out jerky and hardtack. When the coffee boiled, Stokes
dug a bottle from his saddlebags and laced everybody's cup
with a short dose. Squatted around the fire, swigging their
brew and munching a cold supper, they congratulated themselves on a good day's work. A short ride come first light
would put them in Austin, and the jingle of gold was so real
it was already burning a hole in their pockets.

Hardly to his surprise, nobody offered to feed Wes. They
had him pegged for the gallows, and as one of the men com-

mented, there was no sense pouring oats down a dead mule. Watching them, a couple of things became apparent to the youngster. They had ridden hard and fast to cut him off, and they weren't about to be done out of the reward money. Over and above that, this bunch was far more dangerous than the mushhead he'd killed last night.

Stokes was a seasoned man hunter. That was plain from his manner and the slick way he had of outguessing those he hunted. Though it went against the grain, Wes couldn't help admiring him the least bit. The man was good at what he did, and that commanded a certain amount of respect. But the other two were a different story entirely. Shiftless and grungy, willing to cut a man's throat for a hot meal or a shot of red-eye. Northern white trash who had been given a badge and a license to kill. If anything, they were more dangerous than Stokes. Given a choice, they would have just shot him in the back and to hell with the manacles.

The thought sparked another, whetting the young outlaw's curiosity. Glancing across the fire, he studied Stokes awhile and finally decided there was no harm in asking.

"Cap'n, you've got me puzzled about somethin'. Mind answerin' a question?"

Stokes's flinty gaze came level and he shrugged. "Seein' as you're the guest of honor, I guess it'd be awright."

"You've had two chances to gun me down. I was just wonderin' why you didn't."

"Best reason on earth. We been huntin' you two years and folks has got to thinkin' you're some kind of cross between the Holy Ghost and a wild tiger. When they stretch your neck down at Austin lots of people is gonna get educated real quick."

"So you held off drillin' me for the good of Texas?"

The lawman allowed himself a tight smile. "Nope. It'd give me considerable satisfaction shootin' you, but I got an idea it's gonna be lots more fun watchin' you swing."

Wes accepted the statement for what it was, a blunt truth. He felt no rancor but he was still curious. "Just one more and I'll shut up. How'd you figure I'd be comin' through at this crossin'? I didn't know myself till I woke up this mornin'."

"Weren't hard. You was headed south and I knew you'd stay clear of big towns. I killed a horse gettin' to Waco and picked up these boys." He ducked his chin at the policemen and they grinned in unison. "Then we rode like hell to beat you here. Less you turned off west somewheres, it figured you'd come through Belton. 'Pears I was right."

The two grinners busted out laughing and Wes lapsed into silence. Stokes just smiled and let it drop there. He wasn't much of a talker anyway and made it a rule never to waste the few words he spoke on the likes of outlaws. The threesome went back to their celebration, passing the bottle back and forth around the fire. The policemen, Anderson and Roberts, did most of the gabbing and Stokes just kept his thoughts to himself. But they all did their share of drinking, and by full dark, the bottle was empty. When Stokes declared it was time for sleep none of them were feeling any pain. Anderson was ordered to stand for the first watch and warned again to stay alert. Just before he rolled into his blanket, Stokes glanced across at the youngster.

"Don't try nothin' funny. Be a shame to havta kill you now."

Wes took him at his word. For the better part of an hour. Then Anderson started nodding, warmed by the fire and the whiskey, and within moments he was fast asleep. Working quietly, Wes slipped the rope off his throat and into his mouth. Gnawing furiously, he cut through the hemp in a matter of minutes. Without a sound, he untied his feet and stood. Briefly he debated making a run for it and just as quickly discarded the idea. It was too risky. Besides, Stokes wasn't a quitter, and the next time out he might just finish the job.

It had to end here.

An inch at a time, silent as a night hunting owl, he moved around the fire. Anderson didn't awaken as he eased the shotgun from the man's slackened grip. But when he earred both hammers back the whole camp came alive. Roberts raised up, directly beside Anderson, and the first blast shredded both men with buckshot. Farther off, back away from the fire, Stokes made a grab for his pistol. Then he stopped, staring into the big black hole centered on his belly. After a moment his gaze came level and their eyes locked.

"Sorry, Cap'n. I'd sort of got to like you."

Stokes shrugged, wooden-faced. "Luck of the draw."

Wes pulled the trigger, gutting him just above the belt buckle. But Stokes's last words hung in his ears over the roar of the shotgun. Slick as he was, the man hunter had lived a lifetime without learning the most important lesson of all.

The luck of the draw depended entirely on who was dealing.

CHAPTER 4

1

Abilene was situated on the edge of a vast prairie which sloped imperceptibly toward the timbered bottomland of the Smoky Hill River. As a town it wasn't much to look at. Just a crude collection of rough-sawn, false-fronted buildings clutched together across from the limestone bluffs on the south side of the shallow stream. Yet, in that sweltering summer of '71, it was one of a kind. A diamond in the rough. The premier cow town on the great western plains.

In Abilene, men who had met under less favorable circumstances, at Shiloh and the Wilderness and Gettysburg, once more came together. They gathered not out of friendship or with the uneasy camaraderie that sometimes exists between former enemies. Nor was there any spirit of reconciliation among them. They met again for a more practical purpose—mutual profit—to exchange Yankee gold for Texas cattle. It was a motive reasonable men understood, and while neither side thought of the other as reasonable, they bartered each summer on the banks of the Smoky Hill in a state of armed truce.

The town itself was a gaudy, ramshackle affair devoted exclusively to avarice and lust. There were some thirty buildings along the main street, dedicated for the most part to separating the Texans from their money. Saloons, dance halls, gambling dives, and whorehouses predominated. With the exception of two hotels, a mercantile emporium, one bank, and a couple of greasy spoon cafes, the entire business community of Abilene was crooked as a dog's hind leg.

When Wes rode into town in early June, he was short on illusions but chock full of great expectations. Bright-eyed and bushy-tailed, if somewhat cynical. Among Texicano trailhands legends had already sprung up about the lusty antics of this Babylon of the plains. While there was every certainty that they would be cheated, flimflammed, and hornswoggled—milked dry of three months' pay in a single week—they came eagerly, with boundless spirits, to this mecca of shady ladies and slick-fingered gamblers. They begrudged the Yankee bloodsuckers every hard-earned nickel, departed town with swollen heads and empty pockets, but they returned each summer with the youthful vigor of bulls in rut. There was nothing like it on the face of the earth, and crooked or not, it was worth the price of admission.

Unlike most cowhands, Wes came to Abilene less out of design than sheer chance. Last summer, after killing four State Police in twenty-four hours, he had struck out for Mexico in a blaze of dust. Newspapers bannered the story in all its gory details, and the name of John Wesley Hardin crackled across Texas like chain lightning. His name became a household word, and the exploits of a lone youth, boldly defying the rascals in Austin, acted as an elixir on the soured spirits of his fellow Texans. The backcountry people, oppressed by Yankee invaders for five long years, took him into their hearts. Among them spread tales of his fearlessness and ferocity, and before long they spoke of him as the daring lad who championed the cause of all men against injustice and tyranny. He was a hero, homegrown and bigger than life. A will-o'-the wisp, with godlike luck and a smoking six-gun, who had made Governor Davis and his ruthless hooligans the laughingstock of Texas.

Still, fame had its price, and the carpetbagger regime quickly upped the ante. Hardly before he crossed the Rio Blanco south of Austin, the young outlaw had a reward of three thousand dollars on his head. Dead or alive. Governor Davis and Attorney General Horace Davidson made no secret of their heartfelt wish that he be brought in stiff as a board. They wanted the man not so much as they wanted his cadaver.

But the youngster was, after all, no less mortal than other men, and scarcely immune to his growing fame. The tales he heard, concocted in equal parts of wishful fancy and pure horsedung, bore only scant resemblance to Preacher Hardin's wayward son. Unfazed, he took a closer look at himself and decided the people had hit the nail on the head. Instead of a desperado and murderer, he was a defender of the faith. Marching in the vanguard of those sworn to oust the Yankee conqueror. Somehow, it had a better ring to it, and with only the slightest effort, he found it wholly believable.

Struck by a random impulse, along with this new vision of himself, he chucked all thoughts of Mexico. Texas was where he belonged, among his own kind, and with spirits restored, he rode east into Gonzales County. There he received a lordly welcome from the Clements tribe, twice-removed cousins of uncertain lineage. Although the family brewed moonshine with a deadly kick, and kept half the country in a suspended state of ossification, its chief claim to fame was four strapping brothers. Hellraisers of the first order—Manning, Gip, Jim, and Joe—they lionized Wes in the manner of the one who had brought glory to the family name. In turn, Wes found himself among kindred souls, and their pride in his quickness with a gun made him cockier than ever.

They were well matched, these four brothers and the young outlaw. The Clements boys were tough as mules, raw-boned and coarse, with skin weathered the color of whang leather. There was a noisy vitality about them, and whatever job they tackled, they worked harder than a gang of coons climbing a greased pole. Every spring, ranchers in the county competed to sign them on as trailhands, and after wintering with the tribe, Wes was just naturally considered part of the bargain.

Early in February they hired out as a group to Columbus Carol, a vinegary old cattleman with the disposition of a constipated Gila monster. The spring gather was finished just short of a month later and they headed a herd of fifteen hundred longhorns north toward the Red River, where Texas ended and the Chisholm Trail began. The three-month drive proved uneventful; discounting a couple of stampedes and Wes's killing a *vaquero* in a brief, but memorable, gunfight. The greaser was given an unceremonious burial, and the young outlaw's reputation went up another notch as the Clementses brayed about his speed with childlike gusto. Columbus Carol left the entire crew slack-jawed with astonishment when he went so far as publicly to congratulate the boy and offer him a job as *segundo*. While Carol's demonstrated passion for busthead whiskey and saloon brawls made the job something more akin to bodyguard, Wes found the notion to his liking and readily accepted.

Upon fording the Smoky Hill in early June, Carol's herd was driven to a holding ground at Cottonwood Springs north of town. There the hoary old cattleman intended to wait for a rise in the market and force some Yankee swindler to pay him top dollar. Most of the crew was let go, but Wes and the Clements brothers were kept on the payroll to nursemaid the longhorns through their wait. It promised to be an ordeal, for Kansas summers sizzled one day and scorched the next. All the same, the inducements to stay on were strong. The pay was steady and down the road a piece was that tabernacle dedicated to man's raunchier instincts. The place called Abilene.

Carol selected Manning and Wes to accompany him into town for the first night's winging. Gip, Jim, and Joe grumped around camp a lot, kicking at stones and bellyaching in general, but it was a waste of breath. The old man listened for all of sixty seconds and then blistered them good. Somebody had to watch over the herd, and what with it being a democratic outfit, he'd taken a one-man vote and elected them to office. Their chance to turn the wolf loose would come the next night, and that was that. An hour later, hair slicked back and reeking of bay rum, Carol and the two youngsters rode out of camp.

Along the way, the cattleman mellowed and grew expansive, reminiscing over similar excursions in the past. He'd been up the trail every summer since '69, when Joe McCoy and the Kansas Pacific slapped Abilene together. To hear him tell it, they were headed toward the world's foremost den of iniquity. Wicked, depraved, and dangerous as a teased rattler. All of which seemed to please him mightily. They were off to see the elephant, he declared, and it was a sight to make a sporting man's blood run hot.

Just last summer he'd seen Bear River Tom Smith tame an entire town with nothing but his fists. Whipped the living bejesus out of a half-dozen hardcases, pausing only long enough to dust off his tin star, and spent the rest of the season trading smiles with the politest bunch of trailhands ever hatched. But that didn't last long. Some sodbuster perforated Bear River Tom while he wasn't looking and put an end to his bare-knuckle style of law enforcement. Of course, sodbusters were sneaky, and known backshooters, so it was hardly more than could be expected.

Now, according to word along the trail, Abilene had hired itself a real pisscutter. Fellow name of Hickok, better known as Wild Bill. If the newspapers could be believed, he had killed close to fifty men. But then, newspaper editors were the biggest liars on earth, so most of it was likely horsefeathers and hogwash. Just the same, this Hickok had killed three or four toughnuts over in Hays City, and there was a story around that he'd stood up to a tinhorn in Springfield and drilled him dead center at seventy-five yards. What with one thing and another, it seemed like Hickok might be the real article after all, even if he hadn't killed the full fifty. Folks that had seen him said he was a fish-eyed bastard, cold as a witch's tit and mighty intolerant. Took a dim view of Texans trying to hurrah his town.

Columbus Carol was a man quick to give advice, but he seldom took it. His own or anyone else's. After lecturing the boys all the way into town, cautioning them to steer clear of the law in general and Wild Bill Hickok most particularly, he proceeded to cut the wolf loose with a vengeance. They hit four saloons and a whorehouse in rapid succession, leaving in their wake two crippled bouncers and an apoplectic madam. When they slammed through the doors of the Alamo Saloon Carol was pickled to the eyeballs and had himself primed for a real knock-down-drag-out.

Bulling his way through the crowd, Carol elbowed room for the three of them at the bar and stood there staring at a huge ornate mirror flanked on either side by fake Renaissance nudes. After a couple of minutes he swelled up like a dead toad in a hot sun and commenced pounding the counter with a meaty fist.

"I can lick any lily-livered sonovabitch in this joint!" Listing to port, he slowly came around and faced the crowd. "First come, first served. Who wants to get knocked on his ass?"

Dimly, he became aware that somebody had already taken him up on the offer. Only it was all out of kilter, wrong somehow. The man standing before him was wearing a star and he had a gun rammed into Carol's belly.

"Mister, you're headed for the lockup. 'Bout the only choice you got is how you go. Which way's it gonna be?"

Manning Clements was blind drunk and could hardly keep his feet. But Wes had been sipping all night and was stone cold sober. Shifting away from the bar, he assessed the lawman with a quick once-over.

"You Wild Bill Hickok?"

"Not that it makes a whole hell of a lot of difference, but I'm Carson, chief deputy. Any objections?"

The youngster's arm moved and the Navy appeared in his hand, cocked and centered on the deputy's shiny badge. "Only objection I've got is that you're standin' in my friend's road. Suppose you put that popgun back in the scabbard and haul ass out of here."

Carson regarded him with a quizzical scowl. "Sonny, you're gonna meet Mr. Hickok sooner'n you expected. And you won't like what he's got to say."

"Last man that called me sonny ended up worm meat. Now, you gonna pull freight or do I have to shoot your ears off?"

The lawman spun on his heel, holstering his pistol, and stalked off through the crowd. As he slammed the batwing doors open, Wes gave him a parting volley.

"Tell Mr. Hickok the name's Hardin. Wes Hardin."

2

The name John Wesley Hardin was not unknown in Abilene. Reward dodgers had been circulated from Texas to neighboring states, and the young outlaw was the subject of idle speculation among peace officers throughout the Southwest. A kid of eighteen who had killed ten men was a curiosity in itself, and hardly to be taken lightly. While Texans were known to exaggerate on occasion, the circulars were taken at face value. Anybody who had walked away from that many gunfights, whatever his age, was no joke. Quite clearly he played for keeps, and wasn't overly concerned with the rules.

The marshal of Abilene had given the matter weighty consideration. Though his name implied differently, Wild Bill Hickok was a man of craft and cunning, wily in a deceptive sort of a way. It was this unobtrusive canniness, rather than his speed with a gun, which had kept him alive through a long and checkered career as a lawman. Last evening, when Tom Carson returned to the office in a rage, Hickok had done nothing. Sifting his options, he chose to ignore the brash young gunman. The alternative was to take his four deputies and invade the Alamo, which was bursting at the seams with drunk Texans. Likely that would have resulted in a pitched battle and left the saloon littered with dead men. Among them, perhaps, Mr. James Butler Hickok. It was an idea he found both repugnant and rash. Better simply to wait and let it fizzle out in its own time.

By morning, Hickok was convinced he had acted wisely.

the owner of Abilene's most profitable gam
and pugnacious in appearance, with piercin
bristly mustache, he was a Texan by bi
trade. Strictly as a sideline, sort of
was also a deadly gunfighter. But
who played the odds, weighing
care of one versed in the ar

Seated across from him
young man who only
Carson's tail. While
made clear, he h
mutual interes
more than t
son had
and de
son

being jackassed around by a hard-nosed kid. He meant to keep the peace, as well as his job, and despite the city council's professed support, that was easier said than done. Reflecting on it over his morning coffee, Hickok silently patted himself on the back for his clever handling of last night's fracas.

John Wesley Hardin was but a single gnat in a swarm of insects. One he couldn't afford to swat. Not just yet, at any rate. Time was on his side, and if a man studied on it hard enough, there was generally a way to exterminate a trouble-maker without upsetting his own applecart. Several ways, in fact. Most of which, somewhere along the line, he had employed with considerable guile.

Down the street at that very moment, another man was considering the same problem, although from a slightly different vantage point. In the back room of the Bull's Head Saloon, Ben Thompson had embarked on a scheme that for cold and ruthless calculation was the equal of Hickok's spidery patience. Thompson, in partnership with Phil Coe, was

ng dive. Squat
g eyes and a dark
th and a gambler by
a sporting diversion, he
like Hickok, he was a man
g each move with the precise
of survival.

was Abilene's latest celebrity. The
last night had tied a can to Deputy
the gambler's purpose had not yet been
d invited Wes over to discuss the matter of
. The fact that it served Thompson's interest
e boy's was only incidental. Long ago, Thomp-
ade what he considered a vital discovery about life
ath. Sometimes it was easier to kill a man, and per-
lly less dangerous, simply by planting a seed and watch-
g it grow.

Thompson had talked around in circles for the better part
of twenty minutes, playing on the youngster's cock-of-the-
walk manner. Everyone in Texas had heard of Ben Thompson and his skill with a gun, and the boy positively glowed
with each word of praise. Presently, the gambler decided it
was time to sink the gaff. Leaning back in his chair, hands
locked behind his head, he chuckled warmly.

"Yeah, they'll be tellin' that story for a long time to come.
Tom Carson euchred like some greenhorn fresh off the train.
You know, he claims he's kin to ol' Kit Carson. Always
braggin' about his famous relative. I got an idea there's
gonna be a lot of salt rubbed in that wound."

"I hadn't heard that." Wes shook his head in mild disbelief. "If it's a fact then the blood must've got thin as beet
juice by the time it sifted down to Tiger Tom."

"Tiger Tom!" Thompson erupted in a whooping belly
laugh. "Christ A'mighty, I'll have to remember that one. The
boys won't never let him live it down."

They sat there for several moments, Wes beaming and the
gambler chortling appreciatively. After a while, though,

Thompson seemed to sober, as if struck by a sudden thought, and his eyes took on a somber cast.

"There's another side to that coin, of course. Carson's strictly penny-ante. Nothin' you couldn't handle. But Hickok's a bad man to tangle with. You're gonna have to watch out he don't get the drop on you."

"Get the drop on me?" The youngster gave him a quizzical frown. "You mean he don't come at a fellow straight out?"

"That's exactly what I mean. Most of them he's killed got took from the blind side. Never had a chance. Case you haven't heard, he's got no love for Texans, neither. What with him havin' fought for the bluebellies, he figures Southerners are lower'n snake turds."

"Well you damn bet'cha I'll be on the lookout. Course, I'm not tootin' my own horn, you understand, but I'll tell you one thing. He starts any monkeyshines with me and I'll put some leaks in him they'll never get plugged up. That Wild Bill stuff don't faze me none. He bleeds just like everybody else."

Thompson rubbed his jaw, mulling something over, and finally looked up. "You know, it just come to me. You might be the one."

Wes blinked. "The one what?"

"Why, the one all the trailhands have been waitin' on. Hickok gives 'em a hard way to go, bustin' heads and throwin' people in the lockup if they look at him cross-eyed. So far, though, nobody's had the gumption to try punchin' his ticket. I got an idea you're the one that could cut him down to size."

"You're talkin' about killin' him."

The gambler's mouth creased in a tight smile. "You just got through sayin' a minute ago that he bleeds like everyone else."

Something in Thompson's eyes touched a nerve, and the youngster instantly came alert. "If he needs killin' so bad, why don't you do it yourself? What I heard, you're no slouch with a gun."

"Well, you know how it is. A man operatin' a business can't get involved in these things. In a manner of speakin', I'm kind of like the cowhands. Just have to wait till someone comes along that can give Hickok a dose of what he deserves. Way you talked, I thought it might be you."

Wes wasn't quite sure of the game, but one thing was plain to see. Whatever his reason, the gambler wanted Bill Hickok dead and buried. However slyly, a baited hook had just been dangled in front of his mouth.

"Ben, I'll tell you how it is with me. I don't do nobody's fightin' but my own." Uncoiling from the chair, he came to his feet. "Much obliged for the invite and the conversation."

They stared at one another a moment, understanding of sorts passing between them, then Hardin turned and walked through the door. Thompson muttered an oath, scowling, and slammed his chair to the floor. Somehow, he felt as though he had egg on his face.

Late that afternoon Wes wandered into the Alamo Saloon. Columbus Carol had given him the day off, a reward of sorts for saving the cattleman from a night in Abilene's jail. The youngster found it an excellent idea, but for reasons all his own. After making his brag last night, all but daring Hickok to come after him, it wouldn't do to hide out in a cow camp. That would mark him as gutless or scatterbrained, or both. Make him a laughingstock, and through him, put all Texans to shame. What with the Clements boys beating the drum about his bulldog grit, and everybody glad-handing him all over the place, he felt a certain obligation not to let them down. Things being the way they were, he had a reputation to maintain. Not so much for himself as for Texas and Texans.

Or so he told himself, at any rate.

Throughout the day he had leisurely prowled the town, inspecting the stores and the stockyards, taking dinner in one of the cafés and pausing for drinks in a couple of the saloons. Abilene in daylight was pretty tame, and sort of hard on the eyes. The buildings were constructed of bare, ripsawed lumber and looked as if they had been thrown together with spit and poster glue. But the town itself interested him little, if at all. He merely wanted to be seen, to let folks know that he was out and about and available. Just in case Abilene's fire-eating marshal had any notions about settling last night's score.

Apparently that wasn't the case. Hickok failed to put in an appearance and the only man Wes spoke with at any length was Ben Thompson. Nursing a drink, seated at a table in the back of the Alamo, the youngster was still hashing that one around. A word here and a word there, mainly from bartenders, had erased part of the mystery. Earlier in the season, Hickok and Thompson had evidently had a falling out. Something about a bawdy sign Thompson had hung outside the Bull's Head. Harsh words had been exchanged, and it was even money that the two men would butt heads before the trailing season ended. Plain to see, Thompson figured he'd save himself some trouble by egging a slick-eared squirt into starting a shoot-out with the marshal.

Only it hadn't worked. Wes had made himself available, but as he'd told Thompson, it was strictly his own fight. Other people, the gambler included, would have to do their own dirty work. Except that there hadn't been any fight. Nor the least sign of Hickok. That was a new riddle to ponder, but for the moment the young outlaw set it aside. The Clements boys were due in town any minute now and his mind turned to the night ahead. Swigging his drink, he commenced planning how he'd show them the elephant. A guided tour of Abilene's spiffy cathouses and the better watering holes.

Along about the third sip, though, he started thinking on a different kind of game altogether. Bill Hickok marched through the door, walked straight to the bar, and proceeded to knock back a couple of quick ones. Wes had heard about him, but in person the lawman was a real eye-duster. Black frock coat, hair that hung down over his shoulders, and a droopy mustache that cleared his jawbone. The face was sullen, like an old bull on the prod, and his eyes put the boy in mind of smoky agates, opaque and lusterless, lacking expression.

Still, appraising him closer, Wes decided he wasn't half as fearsome as folks made out. Likely he got into his pants one leg at a time, just like everybody else, and he damn sure wasn't immune to lead poisoning. Anybody that'd march around in a getup like that, odds were he'd assay out to about twelve ounces of bullshit to the pound. Slick and cagey, dangerous in an underhanded sort of way, the same as Thompson had warned him.

Hickok wheeled away from the bar and headed toward the back of the saloon. His manner was casual, unhurried, and as he stopped in front of the table, he nodded agreeably.

"I reckon you must be Wes Hardin."

The youngster smiled, looking him over. "And I could make a wad of money bettin' you're Wild Bill Hickok."

"Mind if I take a chair?"

"Help yourself."

The lawman seated himself and slouched back, folding his hands across his stomach. "Figured we might have ourselves a little talk."

"Folks always said I was a good listener. What you got on your mind?"

The cocky tone grated on Hickok's nerves, but he restrained himself, playing it loose and easy. "Well, for openers, let's just forget about last night. Carson made a horse's ass out of himself and we'll let it drop there."

"Sounds fair." Wes couldn't figure it, but he was curious to see how the next card fell. "Where's that leave us?"

Hickok's gaze clouded over, and it was a moment before he spoke. "I understand you had a powwow with Ben Thompson this mornin'."

"Word gets around, don't it?"

"Soon enough. Which brings up the question I come here to ask. Are you plannin' on takin' a hand in Thompson's fight?"

Wes smiled, glad to have it out in the open. "Marshal, I

make it a habit to stick to my own business. The only fight I've got is what the other fellow starts. Course, I also make it a habit never to back off if a man steps on my toes.''

Hickok bristled, unaccustomed to threats, veiled or otherwise. ''I guess you know I got a dodger on you. Pretty fat reward, too.''

The young outlaw regarded him evenly, still smiling. ''Lots of men have tried collectin' it. Turned out a little different'n they expected, though.''

They stared at each other in silence for a long while. Then, cocking one eye, Hickok smiled. It was an odd look, somehow out of character, as if his face might crack from the smile and shatter into small pieces.

''You're a game lad, Hardin. I like that. You stay away from Thompson, and behave yourself, and we'll get along just fine.''

''Why, sure we will, Marshal. Live and let live. That way nobody steps on the other fellow's toes. Pleases me a whole lot, you feelin' the same way about it.''

Hickok had the distinct feeling this smart-aleck kid was laughing at him. But he didn't press it further. Standing, he scraped back his chair and nodded, then headed for the door. As he walked off, Wes grinned, holding back hard on a chuckle.

The game was getting better all the time. Fast and foxy, and more fun than a barrel of monkeys. A real gutbuster.

3

The truce lasted four days.

On the evening of the fourth day, while taking supper in Abilene's leading greasy spoon, Wes became involved in a slight misunderstanding with a Yankee mule skinner. They exchanged a few heated words, and in the salty parlance of his trade, the teamster thoughtlessly remarked on the ancestry of Texans. Something about bitches in heat whelping flannel-mouthed kids. At that point, things got serious. They quit trading insults and started swapping lead, and the mule skinner wound up on the cafe floor. Stone cold and stiffening fast.

Wes had a fair idea as to what came next. The marshal and his four deputies would swarm over the place like a herd of bee-stung bears. What with the reward on his head, and his sassy attitude toward Hickok & Company, it would be shoot first and ask questions later. The odds told him to fold his cards and await a new deal. Which was precisely what he did.

Hardly before the gunsmoke settled, he charged out of the cafe and scampered aboard the grullo. Then, as if the gelding's tail was on fire, he beat a hasty retreat to Cottonwood Springs. It wasn't exactly the proudest moment of his life. Nor was it an act designed to boost his stock among Texans. But under the circumstances, it was judicious as hell. While nobody liked a quitter, especially if they were merely spectators to the blood and gore, he had lived to fight another day.

Overnight, tossing and turning in his blankets, he wrestled with that stickery bit of wisdom. It was but a minor skirmish, he told himself. Insignificant and without lasting effect. Certainly one battle didn't make a war. And a single step backward didn't offset what had gone before.

All the same, his pride had taken quite a drubbing. Everybody in Abilene, particularly the Texans, thought he was the Curly Wolf from Bitter Creek. The way he'd strutted his stuff around town, and lipped off to Hickok face to face, was by now a tale of stupendous proportions. A whopper that gathered momentum, and considerable embellishment, with each telling around cow camp fires. Yet, despite the wisdom and foresight and common ordinary horse sense of last night's decision, one fact stood out like a diamond in a goat's ass.

He had tucked tail in a cloud of dust.

The thought left his mouth bitter with the taste of ashes. When he crawled out of his blankets with first light, he could scarcely face himself, much less the Clements brothers and old man Carol. That they thought none the less of him, voicing agreement that he had played it cagey, did little to salve his gloomy spirits. In other camps, around other cook fires, men wouldn't be so charitable. Instead of Curly Wolf, he'd likely get dubbed with a new nickname. Something like Lickety-Split. Ol' Cut' 'n Run. Or Balls o' Fire.

Worse yet, Columbus Carol wanted him to keep right on running. After a pot of coffee, and a couple of thunderous farts, the old vinegarroon lit into him with spurs flying.

"Use your gawddamn brain. The same as you done last night. That was smart thinkin', scootin' out of town the way you did. And you'd better go right on thinkin' the same way. Hickok and his pack of lawdogs are gonna come lookin' for you sure as shit stinks. Hang around and they'll nail your hide to the wall."

"I'll be go to hell if that's so!" Manning Clements glanced around at his brothers and they nodded vigorously. "Long as we're backin' his play, they'll get more'n they bargained for."

"Close that flytrap and keep it shut," Carol growled. "Between the four of you there ain't enough sense to fill a thimble. You try backin' his play and the whole lot of you will get yourselves killed."

"Boys, I hate to admit it, but he's right." Wes gave his cousins a glum look. "This is my fight, and you'd just be buyin' yourselves a peck of trouble."

Carol squinted hard. "Mebbe you ain't any brighter'n they are. This ain't Texas, y'know. You kill any lawmen up here and ever' sonovabitch and his dog'll be out takin' potshots at you."

"Guess I can't argue with you there." The youngster studied on it a moment, torn between an acute case of pride and the old man's unassailable logic. "Tell you how it is, though. That teamster pulled first, and I killed him fair and square. If Hickok wants to make somethin' of that, then I reckon I'll just stick around and oblige him."

There was a long silence as they waited for Carol to explode. But he was curiously quiet, staring off into the distance with a tight scowl. At last, he grunted and jerked his chin in the direction of town.

"Well it appears like you're gonna get your chance. Unless I'm wide of the mark, that's the law, and they ain't out huntin' jackrabbits."

Everybody swiveled around with a start and caught sight of a tiny dust cloud far across the prairie. As they watched, it steadily grew larger, moving ever closer. Whoever it was, they were on a beeline leading straight to the camp.

"Whole bunch of 'em," Gip Clements muttered grimly.

"I make out three." Carol shaded his eyes against the early morning sun. "Four at the outside."

Wes popped to his feet, suddenly galvanized into action. "Manning, you and the boys saddle up and get on out with the herd. Whatever happens, just stay clear of it. I'm not funnin', neither. Stick to your business and let me handle this my own way."

Unhurried, moving with icy calm, he walked to the wagon and pulled a double-barreled shotgun from beneath the seat. Times before, when he had been outnumbered, he'd learned a fundamental truth. There was nothing like a double dose of buckshot to even out the odds. By the time he'd checked the loads and turned back, the Clementses were at the picket line, hastily slapping saddles on their ponies. Carol hadn't moved, still squatted before the fire, watching the dust cloud. Wes walked directly to a shallow gully, some half-dozen paces behind the old man. As the Clements brothers mounted and rode off, the youngster hunkered down in the draw and earred back both hammers on the shotgun.

Some minutes later, Tom Carson rode into camp, flanked by a couple of hard-eyed deputies. They reined to a halt, alert and tense, eyes flickering around the clearing. Carol held his spot before the fire, watching them, and at last Carson's gaze swung around.

"We're lookin' for Wes Hardin."

"You're a mite late, Deputy. He headed south last night." The cattleman gestured with his cup. "Welcome to coffee, though. Even got some beans left over if you're hungry.''

Carson dismounted and the other men stepped down beside him. Advancing on a line, still somewhat skittish, they stopped on the far side of the fire. Heaving a sigh of disgust, Carson screwed up his face in a baleful frown.

"Old man, you give us some straight talk or I'm gonna peel your head. Get the idea?''

"Boys, the only thing I can give you is some coffee.'' Carol stood and walked to the end of the fire, where a coffeepot hung suspended over a bed of coals. The lawmen watched suspiciously as he slung grounds out of a cup and filled it from the pot. "Ain't the best coffee you ever drunk, but it's hot and black.''

"Freeze!"

Startled, Carson and his deputies looked around and found themselves staring into the beady black eyes of a ten-gauge greener. Behind it, looming up out of the gully, stood the young outlaw. At that range, centered about chest-high, the scattergun looked like a double-barreled cannon.

They froze stiff as marble statues.

Wes had a finger curled around both triggers, and with Carol out of the line of fire, he held all the aces. If he touched off a double blast the lawmen were dead in their tracks. They knew it and he knew it. After a moment, fairly certain they wouldn't try their luck, he smiled.

"Shuck them guns. Slow and easy.''

The lawmen obeyed, carefully exaggerating each move. When their pistols hit the dirt, Wes relaxed a little and his mouth split in a wide grin.

"Now shuck your duds. And don't nobody get sudden.''

Carson stared at him dumbly for a second, then blanched with rage. "Goddamnit, Hardin, there's no call for that. It's enough you got the drop on us. Just call it quits and let us ride off.''

"C'mon, Tiger Tom.'' Wes waggled the end of the shotgun. "Skin down.''

The deputy glared and gritted his teeth, making knots in his jaws. But he skinned down. So did the other two, all the while eyeing the scattergun nervously. Within moments they stood barefooted and stripped, Carson in underdrawers and the pair of hardcases in filthy long johns.

Wes looked them over and then grunted, satisfied, "If I was you boys, I'd make it back to town before the sun gets too high. And give the marshal a message. Tell him the next time somebody steps on my toes they won't get off so light."

The lawmen hobbled back to their horses and gingerly mounted. Without a word they reined about and struck off toward Abilene. Wes scrambled out of the gully and walked forward to stand beside the old man. They watched in silence as the horses and their lily-skinned riders disappeared across the prairie. After a while Carol snorted and shook his head.

"Bub, I'll say one thing. You sure know how to rub a man's nose in it."

4

Wes hadn't left camp for nearly a week. Most of the time he sat beside the creek, beneath a towering cottonwood, brooding on his troubles. One day blended into the next, and with each passing sunrise he grew increasingly surly and cross-tempered. Try as they might, the Clementses and Columbus Carol couldn't get him to talk. It seemed he had shut them out, withdrawn into himself, and they were completely baffled. The John Wesley Hardin they knew was alive, full of piss and vinegar, scrappy as a bobcat. This man was a stranger, someone who might have wandered in off the trail. He ate and slept and worked. But mostly he just brooded, and kept to himself.

It all started the morning he'd jackassed the lawmen.

The Clements brothers hadn't quit laughing for hours afterward, doubling up convulsively every time somebody retold the story. Old man Carol, who tended to take the dim view, even cackled about it in a dour sort of way. Yet, for all their joshing and high spirits, the most they got out of

Wes was a bemused smile. That afternoon he turned moody and went off to sulk beneath the cottonwood.

What the others didn't understand was that the youngster himself was thoroughly bumfoozled. He'd turned the tables on Abilene's lawdogs, restoring his standing among Texicanos, but he still couldn't set foot in town. According to the grapevine, Hickok had threatened to kill him on sight, and to compound matters, the marshal kept himself surrounded by a gang of deputies at all times. It took Wes a couple of days to sift it all out in his head, and even then, the question was thorny as a briar patch. How to regain the limelight in Abilene without getting himself, and a whole bunch of well-meaning friends, shot to pieces in the process?

The only solution he saw was to kill Hickok.

But that was a damn sight easier said than done. Especially when the sorry devil never stepped outdoors without a couple of gunhands flanking him on either side. The real stickler, though, was why it even mattered. What difference would it make if John Wesley Hardin never again set foot in Abilene? Why didn't he just climb on his horse and get the hell on back to Texas? Puzzling on it, the young outlaw went round and round in circles, arriving every time at what seemed the dumbest answer of all. He was just too muleheaded—too infernal proud—to quit the fight. Which left him exactly where he'd started.

Stalemated. An impasse which seemingly defied answer.

Wes was still scratching his head when the big dogs rode into camp. Shanghai Pierce, Print Olive, and Bob McCulloch. Three of the largest cattlemen in the Lone Star State. Their outfits trailed close to fifty thousand steers to railhead every year, and when they talked, men stopped to listen. That they had come to the camp of Columbus Carol was no small event. The old man and his hands couldn't have been more surprised if the three wise men had galloped in aboard wild-eyed camels.

The queer part was that they had come to see Wes. After everyone squatted down around the fire, and coffee had been poured, the cattlemen wasted little time. Shanghai Pierce started it off.

"Hardin, we've come to ask a favor. You ever hear of a fella named Billy Coran?"

"Why, sure," Wes acknowledged. "He's foreman of the XL. Their camp's about five miles east of here."

"He was foreman of the XL," Pierce corrected him. "This mornin' one of his hands shot him in the back. A greaser that calls himself Juan Bideno."

Carol muttered a curse under his breath and the Clementses glanced at one another with shock. Billy Coran was widely respected among cattlemen and that he'd been murdered made his death doubly distressing. Wes hadn't known the man personally, but he could understand the anger of the three ranchers squatted across the fire.

"I'm sorry to hear that. From what I've heard about Coran, he deserved better."

"Goddamn right, he did!" Print Olive rasped. "Never even had a chance. Bideno gunned him down with no warnin' a'tall. Nothin'!"

"That's why we're here," Pierce added. "The greaser took off like a scalded goose. We sorta hoped you wouldn't have no objections to runnin' him down."

"Me?" Wes was genuinely surprised.

"There'd be a reward in it. A thousand, anyway. Mebbe more after we pass the hat."

"You're barkin' up the wrong tree. I never killed anybody yet for blood money."

"Well, it ain't the money, just exactly, that brought us here. We're askin' as one Texan to another."

"Yeah, but why me? Why don't you sic the law on him?"

Olive broke in, his voice husky and short. "Hardin, I'm gonna level with you. We don't want that greaseball brought in. We want him dead and buried. Everybody says you're chain lightnin' with a gun and we figure you're the man for the job. It's just that simple."

"Besides which," Bob McCulloch observed, "the nearest

U.S. marshal is in Topeka. By the time he got on the trail Bideno would be in the Nations. That happens, we might as well kiss him goodbye.''

''There's another thing, too.'' Pierce studied the ground a moment, then looked up. ''You been on the dodge longer'n most and you ain't never been caught. That gives you an edge nobody else has got.''

Wes smiled in spite of himself. ''Meanin' it takes one to catch one.''

''Naw, hell, that ain't what I meant a'tall.'' Pierce bit the words off, gruff and hard. ''I just meant there's less chance of him foolin' you than anybody we can think of.'' Then he stopped, struck by what he'd just said, and a slow grin spread across his face. ''Come to think of it, I guess that's the same thing, ain't it?''

The youngster couldn't help but like these men. They'd told him straight out, making no bones about it. What with him on the owlhoot so long, they figured he could outguess a common backshooter. It was a form of honesty, raw and simple, that he could appreciate. Besides, as they'd said, Coran was a Texan. So it was only right that a Texan be the one to down his killer.

''Lemme ask you a couple of questions. Has this Bideno ever been on the dodge before? For killin' or anything else?''

Olive took the lead on that. ''Nope. I asked the same question myself. Up till this mornin' he was straight as a string. Last night him and Billy had words, and evidently he got juiced up and went off his rocker. That don't excuse it none, though. He's still got to pay the price.''

''After he killed Coran which way did he head?''

''Due south,'' McCulloch said. ''Like as not he'll make a run for the Nations.''

Wes nodded, as if the answer merely confirmed his own suspicions. ''Gents, I'll run him down on two conditions.''

The cattlemen stared back at him, waiting.

''First, I want a warrant chargin' him with murder.''

''You'll have it,'' Pierce agreed.

"Second, I want a lawful commission as deputy sheriff."

"Holy jumpin' Christ!" Olive barked. "You don't want much, d'you?"

"I've already got my own troubles with the Kansas law. If I kill another man, I want it legal and aboveboard."

"You got yourself a deal." Pierce came to his feet. "I don't know how the hell we're gonna do it, but we'll get you a badge. Now, when can you be ready to ride?"

"The minute I see that tin star."

"Fair enough."

The three men walked briskly to their horses and mounted. But at the last minute Shanghai Pierce turned in the saddle and looked back.

"Say, we heard how you snookered Hickok's boys. Pretty slick. Everybody sorta figures you chalked one up for our side."

Then they were gone, pounding back toward Abilene. Carol and the boys stood there watching for a while and the old man finally glanced over at Wes.

"If I was a bettin' man, I'd say you had something up your sleeve."

The young outlaw grinned. "You'd be bettin' a surefire cinch. Them fellas don't know it, but they just put Mr. Wild Bill Hickok between a rock and a hard place."

Shortly before noon two days later, Wes Hardin and Jim Rodgers rode into the town of Bluff Creek. A mile or so outside the town limits was the state line, and across it, Indian Territory. The Nations. Here was where the chase ended. If their quarry had eluded them, taking refuge somewhere on tribal lands, then the hunt was finished. A washout. Yet, it was just possible the Mexican thought he was safe this far south. Whichever way the coin fell, there was only one way to find out.

The men separated and started checking opposite sides of the street.

Rodgers was an XL hand and could recognize Bideno on sight. Shanghai Pierce and the others had sent him along so identification would be certain if the *vaquero* was caught.

Hardin was to call the shots otherwise, and that's how it had worked out.

The young outlaw set a killing pace right from the start. They had been out of the saddle only three times in the last thirty-six hours, just long enough to swap horses with trail crews outside Newton, Wichita, and Cow House Creek. Along the way cowhands told them of a Mexican headed south at a fast clip, and what Wes suspected from the outset became more evident by the hour. Bideno was an amateur bad man, and like most beginners, he had reacted out of blind panic. Instead of twisting and doubling back, trying to hide his tracks, he had stuck to the Chisholm Trail as if glued on course. By the end of the first day it was no longer a matter of outguessing him. It came down to the knotty imponderable of whether or not they could overtake him.

And now they were about to find out.

Before Wes had gone halfway down the street a cow pony erased the question mark. It was standing hipshot, lathered with sweat, at a hitchrack in front of a saloon and hash house. And burned on its rump was the XL brand.

Taking it slow and easy, just another cowhand looking for a drink, he pushed through the doors. The place was empty, quiet as a tomb. A bartender was polishing glasses and looked up without interest as he approached.

"Saw your sign out front. Where d'you serve the eats?"

The barkeep jerked his thumb toward the rear. "Back room."

"Lookin' for a friend of mine. Mexican. He back there?"

"Could be. One came in about ten minutes ago."

"Guess I'm done lookin'. Much obliged."

Wes walked to the rear of the saloon, pulled his gun, and stepped through the door with the pistol at his side. Bideno was alone in the room, seated with his back to the wall. He looked up, fork caught in midair as the youngster entered.

"Bideno, you're under arrest for murder."

The Mexican just stared at him for a couple of heartbeats, completely befuddled. Then he dropped the fork, shoving away from the table, and made a grab for his gun. Wes shot him once, squarely in the forehead, splattering brains and bone matter across the far wall. Bideno pitched forward, up-ending the table, and crashed to the floor in a storm of broken glass and dinnerware.

Standing over him, it occurred to Wes that the man really was an amateur. The rankest kind. Fool enough to make his play when somebody had the drop on him. Then again, maybe he'd had the right idea after all. This was quick, over and done with, even painless. Brought back alive, the Texans would have strung him up slowly and let him swing a while. Most likely by the balls.

The young outlaw grunted, smiling to himself, and tipped his hat to the corpse.

Goodbye, Bideno. Hello, Mr. Hickok.

5

The celebration was long and noisy, punctuated time and again by a chorus of eerie, high-pitched Rebel yells. The gang of Texans floated from one dive to the next on a sea of busthead whiskey, and wherever they went, the drinks were on the house. Abilene welcomed John Wesley Hardin back with open arms. Already the story had circulated about his daring ride south and the gunfight that brought speedy justice to a godless assassin. Cowhands and townspeople stood in line to shake his hand, pat him on the back, and tell him what a grand fellow he was. While the Fourth of July was still a week off, the youngster's return seemed a tailor-made excuse to commence the festivities a little early. The town had itself a genuine, dyed-in-the-wool hero. And its citizens pulled out all the stops, toasting him in a raucous, earsplitting orgy of good cheer.

Just as Shanghai Pierce had promised, the hat was passed and the young outlaw came up with a purse of better than a thousand dollars. Pierce, along with Olive and McCulloch and Carol and the Clementses and the XL hands, appointed themselves his official escort. Wherever he went they formed a beefy wedge around him, clearing a path through the wild and unruly crowd. They toured cathouses, dance halls, gambling dens, and saloons in the whirlwind of shouted toasts and riotous laughter. Shanghai Pierce and the Clements brothers were especially vocal in their praise, bragging long and loud to each new audience. But they held the limelight only briefly.

It was the youngster that people had come to see. He was the star attraction of this impromptu road show and they demanded to hear him speak. The first couple of times, Wes was flustered, unaccustomed to addressing large throngs of gaping onlookers. Slowly, though, he warmed to the subject, aided in no small part by the liberal doses of popskull forced on him at each stop. With every retelling of the story his memory was jogged, and little details began drifting back to mind. The look on Bideno's face. The sheriff of Bluff Creek turning apoplectic at the thought of a corpse on his hands. The spontaneous roar of approval from spectators when Wes offered to stand the cost of burial. Adding a piece here and a piece there, he embroidered a story as he went along, lending it embellishments that made the telling more colorful, if not exactly accurate.

The crowds ate it up, stomping and shouting and straining to touch him. And at the very last, when he pulled Jim Rodgers forward to share the credit, they went jubilantly mad. It was a fine touch, the mark of a generous man, and he played it all with the aplomb of a medicine-show quack pitching the rubes.

Curiously enough, though, Abilene's leading citizen had failed to put in an appearance. Wild Bill Hickok was conspicuous by his absence, and the fact scarcely went unnoticed. The marshal had sworn to kill this young Texan on sight, and among the town's gamblers, there were many laying odds that he might yet give it a try.

If the thought had crossed Wes's mind, it apparently bothered him not at all. He was having the time of his life, the center of attention in a swirling maelstrom of rabid admirers, and living it to the hilt. Whatever happened would happen,

and when it did, he had every confidence he could handle it
slick as spit. This was his night to howl. The highwater mark
in a not uneventful month along the Smoky Hill. And he
meant to make the most of it.

Standing at the bar in the Alamo, surrounded by friends
and well-wishers, he found the life of a celebrity much to
his liking. It was the first time anyone had ever patted him
on the back for killing a man, much less lined his pockets
with gold. Aside from the firewater he'd downed, the experience itself was a heady sensation. Yet, back in some hidden
cranny of his mind, the irony was all but inescapable. Bideno
had made it an even dozen, and for this last killing he was
lionized and swamped with accolades. But of the twelve men
who had fallen before his gun, the Mexican deserved death
neither more nor less than the others. In every case, they had
gone up the flume with reason.

It was a special blend of irony. Bittersweet and somehow
confounding.

Shanghai Pierce was holding forth in the voice he generally reserved for special occasions, such as weddings, funer-
als and saloon-room oratory. It had been likened to the
trumpeting of a bull elephant in mating season. Only louder.

"Boys, I'm here to tell you, I've seen 'em all." He
paused, flashing a mouthful of teeth, and threw an arm over
the youngster's shoulders. "Saw Thompson down in Austin.
And King Fisher in Tascosa. Even saw Clay Allison in a
shoot-out once. But there ain't nobody—*nobody on God's
green earth*—that can hold a candle to this boy. He's greased
lightnin'. Half wolf and half alligator. A natural-born buzz
saw. So fast he leaves ordinary men blinded and suckin'
wind."

"Hey, Wes," somebody shouted, "show us yer draw!"

"Yeh, Wes, c'mon! Whip out that ol' thumb-buster."

The crowd took up the chant, demanding a demonstration.
Shanghai Pierce beamed proudly, and the Clements brothers
danced and shouted louder than anybody else. They weren't
to be denied, and presently, when the din became thunderous,
Wes shrugged modestly. He stepped away from the bar, flex-

ing his wrists, and a deadened silence swept back over the room. Every eye in the saloon was wide and unblinking, riveted on the nervy young gunfighter.

Wes dropped into a crouch, hand poised over his holster. He froze there for the merest fraction of an instant, then relaxed and stood erect. The room was quiet as a graveyard, and the men waited breathlessly, expecting him to make his move at any moment.

He grinned, glancing around at the rapt faces. "Wanna see it again?"

There was an interval of leaden silence as the crowd stared at him in oxlike amazement. Then someone caught on. It was a joke. He hadn't moved at all. The entire room exploded in paroxysms of laughter. Men doubled over, clutching their bellies, and others reeled drunkenly as tears sluiced down over their cheeks. Shanghai Pierce was right, they bellowed at one another, choking on fresh bursts of laughter.

The kid was so goddamned fast you couldn't even see it!

Smiling, pointing his finger at the thunderstruck Clementses, Wes joined in the merriment. After a while, when the laughter subsided a bit, Shanghai Pierce swelled up like a rooster and waved his arms for quiet.

"What d'ya think now? Ain't that the suddenest thing you *never* seen?"

This brought on a fresh burst of knee-slapping but back in the crowd someone shouted over the uproar, "That's quick awright, Shanghai. But there's one gunhand you ain't yet mentioned."

Pierce glared back at the doubter with an owlish frown. "Yeah, who's that?"

"Ol' sour-mouth himself. Wild Bill Hickok!"

"Jesus Pesus Christ," Pierce groaned. "You haven't got sense enough to come in out of the rain. Why, it wouldn't be no contest a'tall. This boy has got him shaded seven ways to Sunday. You stand them up against one another and it'd be like askin' Wes Hardin to commit murder." The cattleman grinned and looked around at the youngster. "Ain't that right, Wes?"

Abilene's star attraction didn't say a word. His eyes were fastened on the door and it was several moments before it registered on the crowd that he wasn't just stargazing. They turned as a man, and there was a sudden intake of breath, as if everybody in the room had been goosed with a hot poker.

Standing in the door was Bill Hickok.

The marshal strolled forward and a path opened before him through the crowd. He halted a couple of paces off and nodded to Wes. Then his head swiveled around and he nailed Shanghai Pierce with a sullen scowl.

"Mister, you got a big mouth."

Pierce swallowed hard. "If a man don't wanna hear then he shouldn't listen."

"In my town there's not much I don't hear. Scissorbills like you, I got a special place for 'em down at the jail. Maybe you'd like to see it?"

"Guess not."

"Then keep your lip buttoned." Hickok's gaze came back to the young outlaw. "Hardin, it appears you're keepin' bad company. Thing like that could get a fellow behind the eight ball real easy."

Wes smiled but a pale glint surfaced in his eyes. "I'm generally pretty picky about my friends. That way I don't have to think about it if it comes down to backin' their play."

The challenge was unmistakable and Hickok went stiff as a ramrod. Everyone in the saloon held their breath, waiting for him to make his move, but he just stood there knotting his jaws. At last, the tension seemed to drain out of him and he shook his head in mild wonderment.

"You got your share of grit. I'll give you that."

"Why, Marshal, down where we come from"—Wes gestured at the men lining the bar—"that's common as milkweed. Thought everybody knew that. Texans have just naturally got more sand in their craw than any creature there is."

Hickok grunted. "Well, I suppose that's another can of worms altogether, and I didn't come here to spoil your party.

Just wanted to congratulate you on catchin' your man. That was a right smart piece of work.''

"Thank you, Marshal. I'm obliged for the kind words.''

"Look me up when you've got some time. We'll have a drink on it.''

With that, Bill Hickok turned and walked from the Alamo. Not a man in the room could credit his own ears. Abilene's fire-eating lawman had refused the goad and pulled in his horns. It surpassed belief. But more than that, it boggled the mind. Left a man's throat scratchy and raw with thirst.

And dumbstruck. Unable to fathom what he'd just seen.

Late that night, Wes lay restless and wakeful in his room at the American Hotel. Sleep eluded him, but it had nothing to do with the carousing or the excitement of his jubilant welcome back to Abilene. His thoughts dwelt solely on one man, an enigma that made little sense and even less reason. Oddly, he was reminded of one of his father's favorite homilies. The dog that barks least bites the worst.

Suddenly there was a click as the door latch sprang loose and he came erect in bed. Snatching the Navy from under his pillow, he thumbed the hammer back and waited. Slowly, an inch at a time, the door swung open. Silhouetted in the entranceway was the shadowy form of a man. Tall and heavyset. Something glinted in his hand, reflecting light from the dimmed hall lamp. Then he moved. The spill of light became brighter. And the thing in his hand was a knife.

Wes shot him and he lurched back through the doorway, disappearing from view. The youngster bounded out of bed, and crouching low, ducked into the hall. Down the passageway, he saw the man staggering toward the stairs, supporting himself with one hand against the wall. Wes thumbed off three shots, dusting him squarely between the shoulder blades. Like a great tree uprooted from the earth, the man swayed, stumbled forward another step, and then pitched headlong down the stairs.

Baffled, Wes started after him and abruptly slammed to a halt. Through the open window in his room, he heard the sound of running footsteps on the boardwalk outside. Darting back through the door, he moved to the window and looked out onto the street. Pounding toward the hotel at a steady lope was the town's entire police force. Hickok and Carson and three deputies.

The coincidence of it confounded him. Hickok and his whole pack of lawdogs so close to the very hotel where John Wesley Hardin was involved in a shooting. Then, in a great flash of illumination, it came to him.

This was no coincidence. Not by a damn sight.

The young outlaw stopped thinking and simply reacted. Jamming his hat on his head, he grabbed his boots and gun belt in one hand, scooped up his shirt and pants in the other, and stepped through the window onto the roof of the porch. When the lawmen burst into the hotel lobby, he leaped to the street and took off running in a spurt of dust. Somehow, though, he couldn't help but chuckle as he ran. Things seemed to have come full circle. Irony heaped on irony.

The bastards had sent him packing in his underdrawers.

BOOK TWO
1872–1874

CHAPTER 5

1

"Bump it a hundred."

"Friend, I got an idea you're tryin' to run a sandy on this ol' country boy. There's your hundred and I'll just kick 'er another two hundred."

"That's a lot of simoleons."

Wes flicked a sulphurhead and took his time lighting a cheroot. He puffed on it abstractedly, regarding the man across from him through a bluish haze of smoke. His appraisal was swift and penetrating. Invariably, when this man bluffed he made some flippant remark. Otherwise, if he held a strong hand, he kept quiet and tried to sucker his opponent into raising. It was a dead giveaway, an unconscious mental tic that sprang to life defensively, without thought or awareness. Thinking back over the night, better than twelve straight hours of steady poker, Wes couldn't recall a single time the man had deviated from this pattern. Now, with just the two of them left in the game, it was time to end it. Sink the gaff and put the poor bastard out of his misery.

"Tell you what, sport. I think I'm gonna have to stick with you. You caught me with my dauber down a couple of times tonight, but I figure I got your number this trip."

The youngster fumbled a fistful of coins from the pile in front of him, letting the tremor in his hand belie the braggadocio in his voice. Licking his lips with a quick, nervous swipe, he scattered several coins over the table.

"Your two hundred and I'll raise it another fifty."

"Fifty?" The man snorted and his mouth twisted in a derisive smirk. "Bucko, you're tryin' to buy yourself a pot. Trouble is, you're a little too cheap for your own good. I reckon I'm just gonna have to send you back to the well." He flung a handful of coins onto the table, then shot the boy a mocking smile and dumped a second handful into the pot. "Call your fifty and goose it three hundred."

The clink of gold was melodic, sweeter than song itself, a tune that convinced Wes he'd pegged his man right. With an idle air of disinterest, he pulled the cheroot from his mouth and gestured at the dwindling stack of coins in front of his opponent.

"How much you got there?"

The man blinked and his Adam's apple bobbed in a jerky gulp. Hastily, he counted his pile and glanced up. "Two hundred twenty."

Wes clamped the cheroot between his teeth and smiled. "I tap you."

Dazed, the man stared at him blank-eyed for a couple of seconds. Then he barked a shaky, gargled laugh and flipped his cards face up on the table. "I'm callin' your bluff, cousin. Read 'em and weep."

Wes studied the pair of aces a moment, saddened somehow that it had been so easy. Sighing, he spread his hand. "Three ladies."

Across from him, the man flinched, batting his eyes furiously. Abruptly, he shoved back in his chair and stood. "Think you're pretty slick, don't you? Well, lemme tell you something, bud. There'll be a next time. You just wait and see."

"I won't be hard to find. Johnny-on-the-spot, that's me."

The man muttered something unintelligible and stalked off. When he went through the saloon door he slammed it so hard the front windows rattled. The bartender glanced over at the boy with a look of profound relief and went back to polishing glasses.

Wearily, Wes slumped back in his chair, the money un-

touched. His eyes felt pebbled and gritty, and his mouth
tasted like the inside of a bat cave. Sort of rancid and foul.
There was a steady, throbbing beat at his temples, and his
bones ached as if he'd just been poured through a rockcrusher. Daylight streamed through the front windows, searing his eyeballs, and it occurred to him that one more drag
on the cheroot would just about polish him off.

Yessir. It was a great life. A laugh a minute.

Bad as he felt, the thought sparked a sardonic chuckle.
The trouble with being a gamblin' man was the suckers. Like
this peckerhead he'd just skinned. They were dull and witless, and most of them shouldn't be allowed loose without a
keeper. Trimming them was childishly simple, downright
boring. So easy a man had no need for the tricks of the trade.
He had only to play the cards he was dealt, watch closely,
and the damn fools would pinpoint their own weaknesses
every time.

The real high rollers were few and far between. Mostly in
the mining camps farther west, out in the mountains. Once
in a blue moon would he run across a game that put him to
the test, challenged his skill. The rest of the time was like
tonight. Long and tedious and boring. Deadly boring. When
it was over, he had the money but damned little satisfaction.
And in the end, that's what it was all about. He was bored
stiff. Winning wasn't fun anymore. Wasn't enough.

And hadn't been for a long time now.

Last summer, after departing Abilene one jump ahead of
Hickok and his assassins, Wes had returned to Texas. The
Clements boys had tagged along and they'd ended up right
back where they started, in Gonzales. But things had changed
while they were in Kansas. The State Police had perfected
an enviable spy system, and within days, word of his
whereabouts spread to Austin. Reckless and headstrong as
ever, Wes hung around in town as if he owned the place,
seemingly oblivious to the gathering storm generated by his
return.

Texas' most wanted desperado had become a source of
acute embarrassment to Governor E. J. Davis. Over the past

three years the young outlaw had killed seven law-
enforcement officers, and to pile insult on injury, the State
Police had twice had him within their grasp. Unless he could
be run to earth, hung or killed outright, the system of intimidation employed by Davis and his mercenaries was apt to
collapse throughout the entire state.

In September two black officers surprised Wes in a Gonzales grocery store. He killed both of them in a gun battle
lasting all of ten seconds. Later that month five State Police
rode into Gonzales County. But Wes had a spy system of
his own, comprised of friends and a whole gaggle of relatives. He ambushed the man hunters on a backcountry road,
dosing them with a double load of buckshot, and two of the
five made it back to Austin.

About then, Wes got the idea that Gonzales wasn't exactly
a health resort. He bid the Clements brothers goodbye and
rode west, headed back to the gambling circuit. It was an
easy life, with poker games and horse races to occupy his
time, and he drifted from town to town as the mood struck
him. Understandably, he found fame, not to mention a certain
notoriety, to be an asset among the sporting crowd. Men
spoke softly in his presence, the shady ladies thought him an
adorable young scamp, and he thoroughly enjoyed the loose
camaraderie of professional gamblers. But only for a while.

Slowly, the life began to pale on him. He drank more and
slept less, and became bored to distraction with the unending
grind. Towns ceased to have names, and the suckers all
started to look alike. Beneath his cold eyes and slick manner,
he was bedeviled by the need for something more. What, just
exactly, he wasn't certain. But one thing was for sure. Fun
and games aside, he wasn't cut out for the life of a wastrel.
Somewhere along the line, the scales had tipped, and he
found himself growing envious of men who lived straight
and slept without a gun under their pillow.

At least once a month, when he couldn't stand it any
longer, the youngster would sneak into Pisga to see Jane.
This went on throughout the winter, and every time they
were together he tried to work out some sort of compromise.

All of which came to nothing. However much he wheedled and coaxed, Jane wouldn't budge. She still loved him—and proved it with the abandon of a female wildcat—but she refused to marry him. Unless he quit the sporting life altogether, and somehow got himself straightened out, she was determined to stand her ground.

As winter passed, and the rolling grasslands again turned green, his thoughts came to dwell more frequently on Jane and the kind of life they could have together. Yet the where and the how continued to elude him. His alternatives were what they had always been, bad and worse. Surrender to the State Police was out of the question, something he never even considered. The next choice, skipping off to California or Oregon or New Mexico Territory, left him equally cold. Perhaps he was muleheaded, too stubborn for his own good, but he refused to be driven from his homeland. That narrowed it down to a single option. Head west and lose himself in the vast stretch of wilderness along the Brazos.

The thought alone appalled him. No towns. No people. No more poker games or horse races or fast times. Just the wind and the empty sky and the limitless plains stretching endlessly to nowhere. All it had to offer was Jane, and at first, she wasn't counterweight enough to offset what seemed a monumental sacrifice. The sporting life.

But as he considered it now, staring bleary-eyed at the pile of double-eagles in front of him, the sporting life had somehow lost its zing. Today, tomorrow, and yesterday all seemed to run together. Another town, another poker game, another night in some dingy whorehouse. There was a sameness about it—a grinding, monotonous, never-changing void— that suddenly overwhelmed him. Kicking his chair aside, he began stuffing coins in his pockets, determined at last how it would be.

Then he walked from the saloon and turned uptown toward the livery stable.

Three nights later, his mother beside him on the settee, he sat facing James Hardin again. They hadn't seen each other

in close to a year, and at first, the old man had raised cain
about the aborted trip to Mexico. Then, gaining his second
wind, he had thundered hellfire and damnation about Gonzales County, and the killing of three more peace officers. A
year older, more experienced, Wes simply let him sputter and
fume and finally run down. At last, when the tirade ended,
Wes told them what he'd ridden a hundred miles to say.

"I'm leavin' this part of the country, headin' out west.
Don't know exactly where I'm going, or when I'll be back,
so I felt obliged to tell you all goodbye. You done your best
to raise me proper and I figure it's time I tried puttin' it to
use."

There was a stunned silence as the elder Hardin and his
wife exchanged glances. Several moments passed before the
old man could collect his thoughts, and when he spoke, there
was a slight quavering in his voice. "Son, that's all I ever
wanted. I know you scoff at my ways, but what you've just
said simply strengthens my faith. The Lord has answered my
every prayer."

Sarah Hardin touched the boy's arm, willing herself not
to cry. "Where out west, Son? It would set my heart at rest
if I knew where you were and what you're doing."

"Ma, I can't tell you 'cause I don't know myself. I'm just
gonna head west along the Brazos and keep ridin' till I come
across the right spot. I'll know it when I find it. That's one
thing I've got no doubts about a'tall."

James Hardin lowered his head. "This my son was dead,
and is alive again. He was lost, and is found."

2

The sun dipped lower, where river and earth linked as one,
splashing great ripples of orange and gold across the water.
Overhead a hawk floated past on smothered wings, veered
slowly into the wind, and settled high on a cottonwood beside the stream. The bird sat perfectly still, a feathered sculp-
ture, flecked through with burnt amber and bronzed ebony

in the deepening sunlight. Then, with the lordly hauteur of taloned killers, it cocked its head in a fierce glare and looked down upon the intruders.

There were five men. A black and four whites scorched the weathered mahogany of ancient saddle leather. Their faces glistened with sweat as they wrestled a stout log onto their shoulders, lifted it high, and jammed the butt end into a freshly dug hole. Small rocks and dirt were then tamped down solidly around the log until it stood anchored to the earth as if set in stone. This was the last in a rough circle of wooden pillars embedded in the flinty soil. The men stood back a moment, breathing hard, and inspected their handiwork with a critical eye.

The black pulled out a filthy bandanna and mopped his face. "Jes' might hold 'em. If we's lucky."

A man next to him, shorter and sandy-haired, squirted the nearest post with tobacco juice. "Shit! Who you funnin', Lon? A goddamn grizzle bear with dynamite up his ass couldn't move one of them logs."

The black man just smiled. "You evah seen a bunch of mustangs when they was spooked?"

"What the sam hill's that got to do with anything? They're just critters, ain't they? Only got four legs, same as a cow."

"Lawdy me. Ain't you in for a s'prise, though. A mustang ain't no critter, Chub. It's a freak o' nature. Cross betwixt a ball o' fire and one o' them steam locomotives."

"What a crock! A critter is a critter. Hoss or cow don't make no nevermind."

"Boys, we got about an hour of daylight left. Little less jabber and come dark we might just have ourselves a corral."

The men turned to look at the rawboned youngster who paid their wages. While they were older, and perhaps more experienced, everyone understood who was boss. There was a quiet undercurrent of authority to his words, and when his pale eyes settled on a man, they seemed to bore right through. It was uncanny, this feeling, spooky in a weird sort of way. As if he could read the other fellow's mind, leave him stripped and vulnerable, his secrets a secret no longer.

They knew little or nothing of this youngster with the brushy mustache and the cold eyes. He was called Earl Roebuck. So far as they could determine he had neither family nor past. He volunteered nothing, and having looked him over, the men felt no great urge to ask questions. From his speech and manner of dress, they pegged him as a Texan; anything else was pure speculation, and best left that way. Yet there were many things they did know about him, bits and pieces gleaned from observation. A thinly sketched mosaic which told them not all, but perhaps as much as they wanted to know.

Earl Roebuck had a seemingly inexhaustible supply of bright golden coins. After hiring them in Fort Worth, he had outfitted them with extra horses; bought a wagonload of tools and gear; and laid in enough grub to feed a pack of wolves through the winter. He had asked few questions, satisfying himself that they were unmarried, in good health, and acquainted with the quarrelsome nature of cow ponies. In return, he told them he was outfitting a crew to hunt mustangs. The pay was forty a month and found, which was generous, although not unusual, considering the hazards of the job.

But the oddest thing about Earl Roebuck, and perhaps the most revealing, was that he evidenced not the slightest fear of being robbed. Not by them—though he had hired them out of saloons and knew nothing of their character—or by anyone else. Privately, and among themselves when Roebuck wasn't around, the men estimated that his saddlebags contained upward of three thousand dollars. A handsome sum by any yardstick, more than most men earned in a decade of back-breaking toil. Yet his attitude was cool and collected, utterly devoid of concern, as if he couldn't imagine anyone foolish enough to try robbing him. That alone told them much about their boss. The cocksure manner, the pale gray eyes, and the care he lavished on his Navy Colt simply rounded out the tale.

Earl Roebuck was a man who played for keeps.

All of the men had seen their share of hardcases. In Texas there was no scarcity of the breed. The young man who led

them now was cast from a similar mold, and yet, there was
something different about him. If anything, more deadly. He
never raised his voice, nor did he attempt to bully or browbeat, tactics commonly employed by self-styled bad men.
Instead, there was an inner calm about him, the quiet, cocksure certainty more menacing than a bald-faced threat. It was
a warning sign, a simple statement of fact. He was one of
those oddities of God's handiwork, a man who had purged
himself of fear. Looking into his eyes, they knew that if his
bloodlust were aroused, he would kill with the icy detach-
ment of a slaughterhouse executioner.

Still, as Earl Roebuck led them west along the Brazos,
they came to like and respect him. Though he was a hard
taskmaster, he demanded less of the men than he did of himself. Moreover, he was damned fine company, standoffish at
first, but slowly warming as he got to know them. By the
time their little column skirted Fort Griffin, which Roebuck
insisted be done at the crack of dawn, they discovered that
he had a dry incisive wit and a natural flair for leadership.
His orders were generally in the form of a request, stated in
a tone that was at once pleasant and persistently firm. He
chose good campsites, was constantly on the scout for Indians, and rotated the men on night watch without a hint of
favoritism. Their respect increased manyfold when it became
apparent that he had permanently assigned himself to the
dawn watch. Hostiles were partial to the early morning hours
for surprise attack, and every man in the crew knew it to be
the most dangerous time. It was but another clue to Roebuck's character, and while the men's trust and regard steadily multiplied, they never lost sight of the fact that he was
different.

In a way, it was like keeping company with an amiable
bear. So long as he wasn't crossed, he was the salt of the
earth. Aroused, he might just bite your head off.

West of Fort Griffin, where the Brazos split, Roebuck led
them along the Double Mountain Fork. This was virgin country, unknown to white men except for the military and buffalo hunters. These rolling plains were the ancient hunting

grounds of the Comanche and Kiowa, abounding with wild-
life. A vast, limitless land that swept westward in an emerald
sea of grass. The party moved at a snail's pace, for the wagon
slowed them considerably, and in a fortnight of travel they
sighted not a single human being. In an eerie sort of way, it
was as if they had entered another world, where man was
the outsider, marching backward in time and space into a
land where an older law prevailed, an atavistic law founded
on that most simple and most ancient expedient of all, survival.

Toward the end of May, near the headwaters of the Double
Mountain Fork and some hundred miles west of Fort Griffin,
Earl Roebuck found what he was looking for. A wide expanse of woodland, with cottonwoods along the river and a
grove of live oaks stretching southward for a quarter mile.
Bordering the shoreline there was a natural clearing, with a
rocky ford and stunted hills to the north, which would protect
it from the chill winter blast of a plains blizzard. He called
a halt and announced to the crew that their journey had
ended.

Standing there, gazing around the clearing, he felt a warm
glow down in the pit of his belly. The spot was made to
order, and somehow he sensed the rightness of it. Perhaps
of greater significance, though he was scarcely the superstitious type, he felt that time and place had joined hands to
give him a sign. That morning Earl Roebuck had turned nine-
teen.

The ensuing month had passed quickly, a time of sweat,
excruciating labor, and immense progress. Roebuck drove
himself and the men at a furious pace, working from dawn
to dusk, seven days a week. At the head of the list was a
project that left the crew more puzzled than ever about this
strange young man who had led them into the wilderness.
He informed them that two buildings must be erected, a main
house and a bunkhouse. Again, the men asked no questions.
They felled trees, snaked logs to the clearing, and worked
like demons under his relentless urging. Both buildings were
completed, including roughhewn floors and stone fireplaces,

within three weeks, although there still remained the moot question of who, besides Roebuck, was to occupy the main house.

Afterward, erecting the corral was child's play. Roebuck inscribed a circle on the ground, large enough to hold a hundred horses, and the men set about digging post holes. Once more, he drove them like a man possessed, never sharp or ill-tempered, but merely determined to see his vision a reality at last. For every drop of sweat they shed he shed double, and somewhere along the line a strange thing happened. He was still boss, and what he wanted was what he got, but curiously enough, the men came to feel that they were working not so much for him as with him. They had become a team.

Now, as dusk settled over the clearing, they stood back, weary and exhausted, and marveled on the fruit of their labors. Set off away from the river, shaded by tall cottonwoods, was a sturdy, shake-roofed log cabin. It had three rooms with windows overlooking the stream and an oak door four inches thick. Thinking back to the day they had hung that massive slab in the entranceway, the men still weren't sure if Roebuck meant to keep somebody on the outside from getting in or somebody on the inside from getting out. With time, they had come to accept these little mysteries as part of Roebuck's character. Simply another riddle to be dusted off occasionally and inspected as a child would scrutinize an old and treasured toy.

Across the clearing from the cabin, set flush with the tree line, was the bunkhouse. It was large but compactly built, with bunks on one side and the fireplace and a dining area on the other. Behind it, off in the woods, sat the men's pride and joy. A spiffy two-holer. So far as they knew, it was the first outhouse ever erected on the Double Mountain Fork of the Brazos, their elegant, if somewhat breezy, contribution to the advancement of civilization.

The corral sat squarely in the middle of the clearing, a short distance from the river. The cross posts were springy young logs, designed to absorb punishment from milling horses without breaking. They had been lashed to the ground posts with wet rawhide, and as the leather dried and shrank, the corral was fused solid, as though girded with steel bands. Looking at it now, the men agreed that Chub Poole might have been right after all. Nothing short of a cyclone on wheels would bust out of there. Common ordinary horseflesh wouldn't stand a chance.

Bunched in a loose knot, the five men stood there for a long while, recalling a grueling month comprised of aches and sprains and sweat-drenched days. They didn't say much, just nodding and looking, for none of them especially felt the need for words. Their creation spoke eloquently for itself. It wasn't fancy, or just exactly what a man would call handsome, but it was built to last.

Lon Hill, the black man, finally grunted and flashed a mouthful of ivory. "I got a notion Gawd never worked no harder buildin' the world. My bones feels like somebody been beatin' me with a iron switch."

"Cripes a'mighty, that ain't nothin'." Hank Musgrave, eldest of the bunch, sighed heavily. "My frazzle's fizzled so bad I couldn't pull my pecker out of a bucket of lard."

That got a chuckle, and heads bobbed in agreement. Not a man among them had energy left to work up a good spit. There was a moment of silence, as if everybody was waiting, and at last Earl Roebuck cleared his throat.

"Gents, you done yourselves proud. I'm beholden."

Looking from one to another, he held each man's gaze for a second and smiled. Then he turned and walked toward the main house. They stared after him, thick lumps clogging their throats, sort of tingly all over, and when he went through the door they still didn't move. None of them quite understood why, but his words had touched a nerve.

It was the finest compliment they'd ever been paid.

3

They came to the escarpment that guarded *Llano Estacado* in early July. Lon Hill was in the lead, for of the five men, he alone had seen the barren land that lay above. It was for this reason Earl Roebuck had hired him back in Fort Worth. The black man was many things—wrangler, bronc buster, mustanger—yet it was something more which set him apart from the others. He had trapped wild horses on the Staked Plains twice before, and returned to tell the tale. Locked in his brain was a map of this uncharted wilderness, their key into and out of a deadly hostile land. Without Lon Hill, or someone like him, venturing onto the high plains was a hazard few men cared to risk.

Late that afternoon they emerged from the steep, winding trail onto the plateau above. They halted to give the horses a breather and the men had their first look at *Llano Estacado*. Lon Hill had talked of little else since departing the Brazos, but nothing he'd said could have prepared them for the real article itself.

The plains stretched endlessly to the horizon, flat and featureless, evoking a sense of something lost forever. A thick mat of mesquite grass covered the earth, but hardly a tree or a bush was to be seen in the vast emptiness sweeping westward. It was a land of sun and solitude, a lonesome land. As if nature had flung together earth and sky, mixed it with deafening silence, and then forgotten about the whole mess. Nothing moved as far as the eye could see, almost as though, in some ancient age, the plains had frozen motionless for all time. A gentle breeze rippled over the curly mesquite, disturbing nothing, as if the wispy breath of a ghost had quietly drifted past. Perhaps more than anything else, it was this silence, without movement or life, which left a man feeling puny and insignificant, a mere speck on the sands of the universe. The Staked Plains did that to men, for in an eerie sense, it was like the solitude of God.

Distant, somehow unreal, yet faintly ominous.

Farther west the high plateau was broken by a latticework of wooded canyons, and it was in this direction that Lon Hill led Roebuck and his crew. These rocky gorges were all but invisible from a distance, and a man sometimes found himself standing on the edge of a sheer precipice where moments before there had been nothing but solitary space. Within these canyons was the breath of life, water, the only known streams in *Llano Estacado*. The men rode west not for the water itself, but instead because it served as a lure. A bait of sorts. It was near these streams that the wild horses roamed.

As they moved deeper into the trackless plains, Earl Roebuck had reason to feel pleased with himself. Back in Fort Worth, rather than hiring men at random, he had taken his time and selected with care. Every man in the crew had been chosen for a purpose, and while his judgment was hardly flawless, there was no deadwood among them. The past six weeks had proved a stern test, one that would have scattered lesser men by the wayside. Yet each of them had stuck, pulling his own weight, and by the sheer dint of hardships endured, they had dispelled any lingering doubt. These were tough men, determined and able, seared by wind and sun and time. They would stick to the last.

Lon Hill was perhaps the choice find of the lot. Freed at the end of the war, he had drifted into ranch work and quite soon shown a remarkable gift for the ways of horses. Though lean, he appeared built of gristle and spring steel, and it was a rare bronc that could unseat him. Better still, he had a head on his shoulders and knew how to use it. He was smarter than he let on, and while he played the feckless darky in front of white men, Roebuck observed that he generally got things his own way. That he outfoxed the others without them knowing it made him a prize catch indeed. Horse sense and brains seldom came in the same package.

Dolph Briscoe and Hank Musgrave were two of a kind. Not too bright but long on savvy. They understood hooved creatures better than they did men, and most of their lives had been spent aboard a horse. Their legs looked warped;

they were so bowlegged they tended to wobble when they walked. But when they stepped into a saddle some change came over them. They sat tall and easy, taking on the grace of men who had found their niche astride a spirited cow pony. Moreover, they were magicians with a rope, and it was for this reason that Roebuck had hired them. They could flatten a steer with loops that confounded the eye, and in another flick of the wrist have him hog-tied and begging for mercy. Savvy like theirs wasn't a gift so much as an art. It came only with time and unending practice.

The fourth member of the crew, Chub Poole, was also a specialist of sorts. Short and chunky, built low to the ground, but he had catlike reflexes and the strength of a young bull. There were few men his equal at wrestling steers or earring down a spooky horse. Unlike Briscoe and Musgrave, he also had something between his ears besides wax. His mind was as agile as his feet, and in a tight situation he was a handy man to have around. Aside from these more apparent traits, Poole had been selected for yet another reason. Earl Roebuck had a sixth sense for spotting men who could handle a gun. He suspected Poole's quickness and sharp reflexes weren't limited to manhandling livestock, and off in the wilderness as they were, having another fast gun along was something akin to an ace in the hole.

All in all, Roebuck felt like a man who had drawn to an inside straight and caught the right card. Watching them, as the little party moved across the high plains, a surge of confidence came over him. He had four good men, each leading an extra mount loaded with supplies, and they were headed into a country where mustangs were thick as blueberries. Suddenly he wanted to laugh. Jump up in the air and click his heels. For a man with a price on his head, he had the world by the balls.

A fortnight later, the trap was ready. Roebuck and his crew waited in a broad canyon, hidden against the sheer walls along both sides. Lon Hill was closest to the mouth of the canyon, the crucial position. The others were split into pairs

and spaced at half-mile intervals across from one another
farther down. All of the men had taken great care in con-
cealing themselves behind rocks and in scrub-choked gullies,
and now they stood fretful and anxious beside their fastest
horses. This was the day, and if they had calculated right,
all hell was about to break loose.

Their first herd of mustangs was due any minute now.

This was the hardest part. The waiting. Finding the canyon
had been fairly simple, for the grassy floor and the tree-
studded creek were alive with hoofprints. After that it was a
matter of Lon Hill bird-dogging the herd and determining
from their movements the best place to construct a trap.

The black man had needed less than a week to sniff out
the mustangs' grazing habits. Tagging along behind them, he
found that this herd was much like all bands of wild horses.
They browsed over a wide expanse of the high plains, always
drifting into the wind, and covered about twenty miles in
four days. What made it interesting was that it was always
the same twenty miles. The herd moved in a set pattern,
roughly an elongated circle, which ultimately brought them
back to their starting point. They stopped once a day to water, mostly at remote, pan-shaped basins on the plateau. But
every fourth day, a couple of hours before sundown, they
watered in the canyon. Warily, they then returned to the
plains along about dusk and spent the night in the safety of
open spaces.

Hill trailed them for six nights and five days before he was
certain of the pattern. Then he rode back to camp with the
news. Their grazing habits were regular as clockwork. And
just as predictable. With any luck at all, they could be
trapped in the canyon like a herd of sheep.

Roebuck listened, asked an endless stream of questions,
and followed the black man's advice to the letter. The men
worked three days out of four, avoiding the canyon completely on the day the herd came there to water. This was
part of the plan laid out by Hill, and it was based in no small
part on the cunning of the dun stallion that ruled the herd.

Sleek and barrel-chested, the stallion was heavily scarred

from a lifetime of fighting wolves and doing battle with young studs who tried to steal his harem. It was a full-time job, for the herd contained close to thirty mares, half again as many colts, and several yearlings. But the stallion was equal to the task. His strength and ferocity in a fight were balanced by the wisdom of age and an ever constant vigilance. He suspicioned anything that moved, and at the first sign of danger sent the herd flying with iron-jawed nips and whistling squeals of outrage. If the herd was to be captured, it was the stallion who must be outwitted. Under Lon Hill's directions, Roebuck and his crew set about accomplishing that very thing.

The trap itself was a simple affair, constructed along the lines of a funnel, but it was hellishly difficult to disguise. Since this was not a box canyon—the stallion would never water in a place that lacked an alternate means of escape—it was necessary to build two corrals where the sheer walls squeezed down to a narrow gorge. Built back to back, with a gate in between, the first was a catch corral, and the second was a larger holding pen to contain those already caught. The next step was by far the hardest. After cutting posts, the men constructed a half-mile-long fence on either side of the canyon. The fence fanned out from the corral entrance in a V shape, with the broad mouth facing the upper end of the canyon floor. If it worked, the herd would be tricked into the open throat of the funnel, then hazed down the narrowing fence and driven into the corral. With everything completed, the men came to the canyon before dawn on the eighth day and worked like demons cutting green junipers. These were used to hide the fences and corral, giving the trap a natural appearance. Once it was done, the men brushed their tracks from the canyon floor, erasing all human signs, and concealed themselves in the positions designated earlier by Lon Hill.

And now they waited. Deep shadows had already fallen over the canyon's westerly wall and sundown was but an hour away. The men began to sweat, despite a cool breeze, and their apprehension mounted as the fleeting sun dropped lower in the sky. Never before had the mustangs been this late. Unless they came to water soon it meant they weren't coming at all. Not tonight. Perhaps never again.

Then, quite suddenly, the herd appeared. One moment the mouth of the canyon stood empty and in the next, like some ghostly apparition, the mustangs simply materialized. A barren old mare, the herd sentinel, was in the lead. She came on at a stiff-legged walk, ears cocked warily, eyeing the canyon for anything out of the ordinary. At last, satisfied, she broke into a trot and led the herd toward the creek.

These wild horses were a sturdy breed, high in the withers and long in the shoulders, with a wide forehead, small ears, and a tapered muzzle. They had the spirit of their noble ancestors, the Barbs, and from generations of battling both the elements and predators, possessed an almost supernatural endurance. Honed by adversity to a single purpose—survival—they were the freest of all the earth's creatures. In motion, swallowing the wind, they could gallop to the edge of eternity and back again.

Behind the herd, the dun stallion came on at a prancing walk. Larger than the others, heavily muscled, he moved with the pride of power and lordship. Yet he was skittish as ever, nervously testing the wind, scanning the canyon floor with a fierce eye that missed not a rock or a blade of grass. He would water only at the very last, when the herd had taken its fill. Until then, protector as much as ruler, he would remain watchful and on guard, alert to any sign of danger.

Halfway between the canyon entrance and the creek, the stallion suddenly stiffened and whirled back. A vagrant breeze had shifted and with it came the most dreaded scent of all. The man scent. Pawing at the earth, nostrils flared wide, he arched his neck to sound the whistling snort of alarm.

Lon Hill shot him at that exact instant.

As the stallion went down, fighting death as he had fought life, the black man charged the herd. Instinctively, they wheeled away from the creek, prepared for flight. But their leader was down, legs jerking in death, and this strange new creature barreled toward them. It uttered the bloodcurdling scream of a cougar, and in its hand was an object that flashed fire and roared like thunder. Without their leader to command them, crazed with fright, the herd broke before Hill's charge and bolted down the canyon in a clattering lope.

The mustangs had gone only a short distance when other strange creatures came at them from either flank, screaming and firing guns. Their pace quickened, and tails streaming in the wind, the herd took off in headlong flight. Then, out of nowhere, two more riders appeared, forcing the herd straight down the middle of the canyon. Terrified, racing blindly in a thunderous wedge, the mustangs entered the juniper-lined funnel without breaking stride. The men on horseback stuck tightly to their flanks, hazing them onward with shouts and gunshots. Suddenly the funnel squeezed down to nothing, the only escape a narrow opening dead ahead.

Never faltering, the herd blasted through the corral entrance at a full gallop. The barren old mare and a yearling hit the far wall with a shuddering impact and toppled over backward, their necks broken. The rest of the herd slid to a dust-smothered halt, confused, then turned and started to retreat the way they had come. But the men were there, sliding long poles across the opening, and suddenly there was no escape. The mustangs milled about, wild-eyed and squealing, slamming against the corral at several spots. They tested the fence cautiously, though, with respect. For they had seen what happened to the old mare and it was lesson enough. Slowly their panic faded and they huddled together in the center of the corral, trembling and frightened, staring watchfully at the creatures who had captured them.

The men were shouting and laughing and slapping one another across the back. Briscoe and Poole even linked arms and danced a mad jig. But like the mustangs, their excitement slowly drained away. Instead, the hoots and laughter became a stilled amazement. Gathered before the corral gate, they just stood there, staring back at the horses. Somehow it wasn't yet believable, but what they saw was no mirage. They had actually done it. Trapped themselves a herd of woolly-booger mustangs.

Lon Hill was flashing ivory all over the place, proud as a peacock, and he finally got around to shaking hands with the boss. "Lawdy me, Mistuh Earl, ain't they a prize? Nothin' Gawd evah made that's prettier'n a wild horse."

"I guess not." Roebuck grinned, but his eyes were thoughtful, somehow distant. "Sorry you had to kill that stallion. I was hopin' to get a good stud horse for breedin'."

"Weren't no other way, Mistuh Earl." The black man met his gaze and held it. "The devil caught my scent, and he was fixin' to take 'em outta here lickety-split."

"You did what you had to. I know that, Lon. Guess I was just wishin' out loud."

"Well, bossman, you done got your wish." Hill dazzled him with a mouthful of teeth and gestured toward the corral. "Case you ain't had a gander, there's a couple of studs in there pushin' two years. And if I'm any jedge, they got their daddy's blood in 'em."

Roebuck studied the milling herd for a long while, sorting them in his mind. The studs were there right enough, a matched pair. In another year a man would be hard put to tell them from their sire. Of more immediate consequence, there were better than twenty head that could be sold off this year. His inspection finished, Roebuck turned back to the black man, and the corners of his mustache lifted in a wry smile.

"Lon, how long you reckon it'll take us to catch the next herd?"

4

A tangle of arms and legs, breathing hard, they slowly came apart. Jane sat up, straightening her skirts, and patted a stray lock back in place. Then she came into his arms again, suddenly reluctant to have it end so quickly. They didn't say anything for a while, just sat there underneath the oak hugging and kissing, listening to the katydids serenade the night. But the stillness gradually fanned her curiosity, and when she could bear it no longer, she pushed him away.

"Now that's enough! You promised to tell me and so far you haven't done anything but muss me up something awful."

"I don't recollect you puttin' up much of a fight."

"Wes Hardin, you—you're incorrigible! That's what you are. A wicked, naughty boy. Now, are you going to tell me or not?"

He smiled. "Well, first off, you've got the right fella but the wrong name. Figured if I was gonna have a new life I might as well have a new handle. Picked one out of a hat and came up with Earl Roebuck."

"Earl Roebuck?" Jane blurted the name, astonished and not a little mystified. Then she paused, repeating it several times to herself. At last, her cheeks dimpled in a smile and she gave his hand a big squeeze. "Oh, I like it! It's so dignified and—well, I don't know, almost like a banker's name."

"That's where I got it!" He let go a burst of laughter. "Off a bank window in Fort Worth."

"You didn't rob the bank."

"Course not. I just borrowed the name."

"But I don't understand, Wes. Why did—"

"Just for openers, you better get used to callin' me Earl."

"Oh, fiddlesticks. Stop playing silly games and tell me where you've been for the last three months."

"I'm not playin' silly games. That's my name now. And where I've been is out catchin' a bunch of wild horses."

She stared at him, thunderstruck, and repeated it in a tiny voice. "Wild horses. You mean real honest-to-goodness wild horses?"

"Yep, hired myself a crew of men and went pretty near to the headwaters of the Brazos before I found the spot I was lookin' for." He hesitated and gave her an earnest look. "Built a humdinger of a cabin. Got a parlor with a fireplace, and a bedroom, and a kitchen. Real fancy." Then, before she had time to interrupt, he went on. "Anyway, me and the boys took a little sashay out to the Staked Plains and when we come back we had ourselves close to two hundred head of mustangs. You're lookin' at a man of means, case you didn't know it. All honest and aboveboard, too."

"But I still don't understand." Her face crinkled in an exasperated little frown. "What earthly good are wild horses?"

"Money, woman. Money!" He cupped her face between his hands. "We're gonna break them horses and teach 'em some manners, and come fall, I figure to make myself about four thousand dollars."

Jane was visibly startled. That was almost as much as her father made in a year. And his was the most successful store in Pisga.

"That's wonderful, Wes. But how long can you go on catching wild horses? I mean, it's dangerous work, and surely it couldn't be too steady."

"The name's Earl. And don't you worry your head about wild horses. I don't plan on being a mustanger much longer. Just till we can get a herd of brood mares built up and start ourselves a real ranch."

"You mean it? You're going to be a rancher?"

"God A'mighty, haven't you been listenin' to a word I said? Why do you think I went to the trouble of buildin' a cabin and a bunkhouse and a corral? And near busted my back catchin' all them horses?"

Suddenly Jane was listening, very intently, and she understood at last. She fluttered her eyelashes and prompted him with a coy smile. "Tell me—Mr. Roebuck—why did you do all those things?"

" 'Cause I figured it was time I made an honest woman of you." He cocked one eyebrow in a mock scowl. "Unless you couldn't abide folks callin' you Mrs. Roebuck."

She laughed and clapped her hands like an exuberant child. "Oh, I could! Honestly, I could. I just don't care anymore, Wes. Just so long as we're together."

"Earl, damnit. Honey, you gotta get used to that. The name's Earl."

"I'll remember, I promise." She threw her arms around his neck and embraced him fiercely. "I wouldn't care if your name was Judas Iscariot. Just so we can get married."

Neal Bowen hardly shared his daughter's sentiments. In fact, he was livid with rage. He had hoped, with time, that she would outgrow her infatuation. Failing that, he had every confidence Hardin would get himself killed before too long. Either way the Bowen family would be shed of their own personal albatross and his daughter would again return to her senses.

When the youngster swept into the parlor with the news that they were to be married that very night, he was at first speechless. Then he went red as ox blood and began shouting. They stood there smiling at one another, arm in arm, as if he were some spoiled brat throwing a temper tantrum. Only by imposing an iron will was he able to calm himself. If anger wouldn't work, perhaps reason would. Facing them now, he took a firm grip on his rage and reversed tactics.

"Think for a minute, both of you. What kind of a life could you have together? Always running and hiding, never knowing when the law will kick down your door in the dead of night. That's not what you want for Jane, now is it, Wes?"

Jane countered with a fetching smile. "Mercy sakes alive, Daddy! You're just working yourself up for nothing. It's already settled. We have a ranch and a herd of horses and there won't be any more trouble with the law."

"But you can't know that for sure." The storekeeper was sweating freely now. "Why couldn't you wait a while? A year, even six months. Give yourselves a little time. If you really love each other a few more months won't make any difference. Now will it?"

That was his best shot, the irrefutable logic used by fathers since biblical times. But when he saw the look on their faces Neal Bowen knew he was licked. His last-ditch effort had just shattered to smithereens against a stone wall.

"Daddy," Jane said sweetly, "will you call the preacher over, or do you want us to run off and live in sin?"

Reverend Ira Suggs opened the good book and blinked sleep from his eyes. This whole affair seemed a trifle unorthodox and he had a strong hunch the Bowen girl was in a family way. If not, then he was going to be strongly indignant with Neal Bowen for rousing him at this ungodly hour. Barring a shotgun wedding or sudden illness, there was very little that couldn't await the light of day. The Lord hadn't said it just exactly that way, but Ira Suggs felt sure He would agree.

Still, the youngsters did make a handsome couple. And from the looks of her folks, it was entirely possible the girl was in a family way. Neal Bowen looked mad enough to chew nails, and his wife had reduced her handkerchief to a sodden ball of snot. The preacher sighed wearily and in a resigned monotone began the service.

"Dearly beloved, we are gathered together to join this man and this woman in holy wedlock—"

There was a short pause while Ira Suggs stifled a yawn. Then he graced the youngsters with a benign smile and went ahead. The bride and groom scarcely seemed to notice. Holding hands, eyes fastened on one another, the only sound they heard was silent.

Warm and throbbing, it passed softly between them.

5

Briscoe and Musgrave roped the horses selected by Lon Hill and dragged them fighting and kicking out of the corral. These were the mustangs the black man had picked to work on that particular day. Half of them were raw and untried, yet to feel a saddle or the weight of a man on their backs. The others were about half-broke, having been ridden and accustomed to a bridle, but they were still in school. As Hill had commented, they had a ways to go before earning a diploma from his bronc-bustin' academy.

The day's pupils were hauled down near the river and tethered to trees. Then the rest of the herd was driven from the corral and hazed through the ford to a lush grassland on the north side of the stream. There they could graze and water throughout the day, and toward sundown they would be driven back to the corral. Hank Musgrave was left to keep an eye on them, just in case some hammerhead took a notion to quit the bunch and head back to the wide-open spaces.

There was only a slim chance of this happening, though. The mustangs had learned that a bunch quitter quickly came upon hard times. Shortly after being captured on the Staked Plains, each of the horses had been roped and thrown to the ground. When released, the horse discovered that one of its front feet had been tied to its tail with a piece of rope. It was a practical device that kept the mustangs from running, and after they had dumped themselves a couple of times, they simply gave up trying. The men drove them out of the canyon and trailed them for two days in this manner. Afterward, with the ropes removed, the mustangs behaved themselves. They could be herded any way the men wanted them to move, and few of them needed a second dose. Another day roped foot to tail convinced even the most stubborn of the lot that it was better to stick with the bunch.

With the herd grazing peacefully now, the workday began. Dolph Briscoe brought one of the tethered horses back from the river and released it in the corral. This was a raw bronc, a big rangy buckskin, and it looked to be a lively session. Briscoe hitched his own horse outside the corral and stepped down with a lariat in his hand. Roebuck, along with Hill and Poole, awaited him at the gate, and they all four entered the corral at once. This was a job they had been at steadily for the past three weeks and there was little lost motion in their actions. Like a freshly oiled machine, with all the parts functioning properly, they worked well together.

The buckskin started racing around the far side of the corral as they fanned out and walked forward. Suddenly Briscoe's arm moved and the lariat snaked out, catching the mustang's front legs in a loop just as its hooves left the ground. Briscoe hauled back, setting his weight into the rope, and the horse went down with a jarring thud. Working smoothly, every man to his own job, the other three swarmed over the buckskin in a cloud of dust and flailing arms.

Poole wrapped himself around the horse's neck, grabbing an ear in each hand, and jerked it back to earth just as it started to rise. Almost at the same instant, Roebuck darted in with a length of braided rawhide and lashed the animal's back legs tight. While Poole kept the horse earred down, Hill slipped a hackamore over its head and Roebuck clamped hobbles around its front legs. Pushing and tugging, sometimes rolling the horse up on its withers, Hill and Roebuck then managed to cinch a center-fire saddle in place. As Hill jerked the latigo taut, Roebuck eased forward and tied a blindfold around the mustang's eyes.

The entire operation had taken less than a minute.

Quickly, the ropes were removed from the buckskin's legs and it was allowed to regain its feet. Blinded and dazed, still winded from the fall, the horse stood absolutely motionless. The hobbles around its front legs kept it from rearing or jumping away, and the blindfold calmed it into a numbed stupor. However unwilling, the bronc was ready for its first lesson.

Briscoe and Roebuck backed off and scrambled over the fence just as Jane walked down from the house. She couldn't bear to watch as the mustangs were thrown and tied—although she readily admitted that it was the most practical means of strapping a saddle on a wild horse—but she loved to watch the bucking. Briscoe touched his hat, grinning like a possum, and Jane gave him a winsome smile.

The sight of her was a constant source of agony to the men, for until Roebuck showed up with his new bride, they hadn't seen a woman in close to four months. The dresses she wore were simple gingham affairs, not meant to be suggestive, but they fit snugly across her tightly rounded buttocks and her fruity breasts. There was considerable moaning in the bunkhouse late at night, but the men treated her like a fairy princess come to life. Though unspoken, there was general accord that it was better to look and not touch than to have nothing at all to look at. They suffered in quiet agony.

Standing between her husband and Briscoe, Jane felt her pulse quicken. Poole had just handed the reins to Lon Hill and retreated back to the fence. The black man tugged his hat down tight and scrambled aboard the mustang. Whenever he mounted, no matter how many times Jane watched, she was always reminded of a monkey leaping nimbly to the back of a circus pony. One moment Hill was just standing there, and in the blink of an eye, as if springs had uncoiled in his legs, he was seated firmly in the saddle.

Leaning forward, Hill jerked the blindfold loose and let it fall to the ground. For perhaps ten seconds the buckskin remained perfectly still. The black man sat loose and easy, just waiting, his lips skinned back in a faint smile. Then he moved his foot, and in the breathless quiet of the corral, the jingle-bobs on his spurs gave off the thunderous chime of cathedral bells.

The buckskin exploded at both ends, like a firecracker bursting within itself. All four feet left the ground as the horse bowed its back and in the next instant came unglued in a bone-jarring snap. Then it swapped ends in midair and sunfished across the corral in a series of bounding, catlike leaps. Hill was all over the horse, bouncing from one side to the other, never twice in the same spot. Veering away from the fence, the bronc whirled and kicked, slamming the black man front to rear in the saddle, and sent his hat spinning skyward in a lazy arc.

Hill gave a whooping shout, and in the middle of a jump, decided it was time they got down to serious business. Lifting his boots high, he raked hard across the shoulders with his spurs, and the spiked rowels whirred like a buzz saw. The buckskin roared a great squeal of outrage, and this time went off like a ton of dynamite with a short fuse.

Leaping straight up in the air, the bronc swallowed its head and humped its back, popping the black man's neck with the searing crack of a bullwhip. A moment later it hit on all four

feet with a jolt that shook the earth. Then the horse went
berserk. As if willing to commit suicide in order to kill the
man, it erupted in a pounding beeline toward the corral fence.
Hill saw it coming and effortlessly swung out of the saddle
at the exact instant the mustang collided with the springy
cross timbers. Staggered, the horse buckled at the knees and
fell back on its rump. Like a drunk man, it just sat there for
several moments, shaking its head and making pitiful little
grunts.

Hill casually stepped back into the saddle as the mustang
regained its feet, then he rammed his spurs clean up to the
haft. This time there was less rage and less fight, ending in
a series of stiff-legged crowhops that lacked punch. The
black man hauled back on the hackamore for the first time,
shutting off the horse's wind, and reined it around the corral
in a simple turning maneuver. At last, he eased to a halt and
climbed down out of the saddle. The buckskin stood where
he left it, head bowed and sides heaving as it gasped for air.

Hill retrieved his hat and dusted it off. Jamming it on his
head, he walked toward the grinning foursome gathered outside the corral.

"That's gonna be a good hoss." He smiled and jerked his
thumb back at the spent mustang. "Got plenty of starch."

"He don't look so starchy now," Chub Poole cackled.
"Looks like somebody twisted all the kinks out of his tail."

"Aw, he's jest restin'. Figgerin' what he's gonna do next
time. Course, I'd bet a heap he don't run into that fence no
more."

Earl Roebuck laughed and squeezed Jane around the waist.
She had never seen him in such good spirits. Nor had the
men. They talked of it often in the bunkhouse. Since the lady
had come to stay, and Lon Hill started busting broncs, the
grim-eyed youngster was a changed man. Like night and day.

That evening the young couple came to sit on the front step
of their cabin. The sweet coolness of night had fallen over
the land and they could hear the crickets warming up along
the riverbank. There was a serenity about this place, some-

thing they both felt, almost as if there had never been another life except the one they shared here on the Brazos. Thinking about it now, Jane felt warm and giddy inside. These were the happiest days she had ever known. And she need look no farther for the reason than the man seated beside her.

"Penny for your thoughts."

His words jarred her reverie. She snuggled closer, burrowing deep into the hollow of his arm, and smiled. "I'm not sure I should tell you."

"Keepin' secrets on me?"

"No, but your head might swell up and bust."

He chuckled and gave her a bearish squeeze. "Try me. Can't hardly be worse'n it already is."

"I was just thinking how proud you make me. That it was you who built all this. The cabin and the horse herd and everything. Sometimes I have to pinch myself to make sure it's all real."

"Well, I had some help, y'know. It wasn't like I walked in here with an ax and a mouthful of nails and slapped it together all by myself."

"You're a paragon of modesty, Mr. Roebuck." Her voice had a teasing lilt. "I wouldn't be surprised but what you're blushing."

"Nope, I clean forgot how. Been too busy buildin' empires."

"See, I told you. It went right straight to your head."

"Judas Priest, can't a fella speak the truth in his own house?"

"Oh, you really are vain, Wes Har—" She clamped a hand over her mouth and giggled softly. "I mean, Mr. Roebuck. But it's still true. You're the vainest man I ever met."

"Caught you, didn't I? Any man that did that has got reason to be proud."

She laughed a deep, throaty laugh. "Maybe you don't catch me enough."

He considered it a moment and she could tell he was smiling. Then he chuckled, "I think you got somethin' there. What d'you say we hit the hay early tonight?"

"Mr. Roebuck, I thought you'd never ask."

Since they were of a mind, there seemed no reason for further talk. They stood and he lifted her over the step and set her on the floor inside the cabin. As he swung the massive oak door closed and barred it, she crossed the parlor and blew out the lamp. Then she laughed that laugh again, and he heard the rustle of her skirts as she headed toward the bedroom.

Curiously, he had no trouble finding her in the dark.

CHAPTER 6

1

Roebuck left the crew camped along the river outside town. There were several hours of daylight remaining but nobody questioned his decision to halt in midafternoon. The men were still hungover pretty bad, and just then, their only interest was in ridding themselves of the miseries. Trinity was scarcely more than a wide spot in the road, but it had a couple of saloons, and that was what counted most. A man wasn't picky about watering holes when his throat was on fire and his head felt like a melon about to burst. So far as the crew was concerned, Trinity would do nicely.

When he rode off headed south along the river road, the men gave him little more than a second glance. Trinity was in the opposite direction, but in the past year they had learned a vital lesson about Earl Roebuck. Like God, he moved in mysterious ways, and he didn't take kindly to questions. If he wanted them to know something, he told them. Otherwise, it was best to lie back and wait. While he was a damn good man to work for, and never put on any highfalutin airs, he still held his own counsel. That was his way, and however close the men felt to him, they knew better than to step over the line.

After he was out of sight, where the river took a sharp bend, Roebuck swung east and put the grullo into a steady lope. It pleased him that they hadn't asked questions. The fact that he had kin nearby was none of their business, and

under the circumstances, hardly explainable. The three-day
spree in Galveston had dampened their curiosity at any rate.
Busthead whiskey and fancy cathouses had a way of sapping
the juices, and right now they were more interested in re-
gaining their wind than they were in his little jaunt downriver. Satisfied with the way everything had worked out, he
put it from his mind and rode toward Barnett Hardin's farm.

Somehow, as his thoughts drifted back, there was a sense
of the unreal about this visit. It had all started here—not
quite four years ago—the day he'd killed the black freedman.
Yet it seemed he had lived a couple of lifetimes since that
day. Instead of twenty, he felt forty going on a hundred. A
man with few illusions left intact. Someone who saw life and
people not as he would have wished them to be, but simply
as they were. And the dozen dead men littered along his back
trail made the feeling no less intense. Coming here again,
where it had started, was strangely out of focus. As if it had
happened to someone else, in another lifetime, and he was
merely an observer peering through a frosted windowpane.

Still, for all the close shaves he'd gone through, things had
worked out pretty well in the end. This past year had been
as good as any man could ask for, and he had no complaints
about the time before. That was water under the bridge, and
with what he had now, there was nothing to be gained in
dwelling on the bad times.

It had been an eventful year on the Brazos. Last fall they
had sold close to a hundred head of saddle stock. Not mustangs but mannered horses, instilled with a healthy respect
for all mankind at the sure hands of Lon Hill. Trapping on
the Staked Plains had also been good, providing the Roebuck
spread with a fine herd of brood mares and another batch of
stock to be broken and sold. After a long winter, and a hectic
six weeks in the breaking corral, this new bunch had been
trailed to Galveston and sold to a dealer. From there they
would be shipped to various markets in the South where men
prized fiery-spirited horses. All in all, it paid handsomely.
Roebuck had cleared almost four thousand dollars for the
year and his brood mares would begin foaling next spring.

His vision of a horse ranch was only one step removed from becoming a reality.

Yet, the highlight of the year had nothing to do with horses. In May, a few days before Roebuck's own birthday, Jane had given birth to a squalling, lusty-lunged baby. It was a girl, which disappointed Roebuck only slightly, and they had named her Molly. Like her mother, she had a way with men, and inside of a couple of days everybody on the place had been bewitched by the tiny newcomer. Where the crew had simply been awkward and shy around Jane, they were completely spellbound by the baby. Somehow, in a way that seemed very personal, each of the men thought of himself as Molly's uncle. They never discussed it, and would have been mortified had anyone suspected their inner thoughts, but they felt it nonetheless strongly.

Jane herself had bloomed like a wild flower. Though reared to expect certain luxuries, she had taken to the frontier life with astounding gusto. There was nothing that fazed her, from cooking over an open fireplace to having her own husband as midwife, and she positively thrived where most women would have swooned dead away. The men thought her a great lady, and among themselves agreed that the boss was the luckiest sonovabitch on the face of the earth.

Earl Roebuck felt the same way. He had a fine ranch, a well-seasoned crew, and some nifty prospects for the future. But more importantly, he had Jane. And Molly. And a life that left him answerable to no man. So far as he could see, he had it all.

That thought was uppermost in his mind as he crossed a creek and heeled the grullo onto a rutted wagon road. The boy who had once killed a burrhead on this same road no longer existed. In his place rode a man who had won all the marbles. And on his own terms.

Barnett Hardin and the youngster came outside after supper to sit on the porch. They were stuffed full and feeling a bit sluggish from the heavy meal. But this hardly put a damper on their high spirits. There was an affinity between them that hadn't been dispelled by time or circumstance. More than blood, it was the kinship of strong men who each saw something of himself mirrored in the other. Hardin took a seat in a creaky rocker, motioning his nephew to another chair, and began loading his pipe. Then he struck a sulphurhead on his thumbnail and noisily sucked the pipe to life. Glancing up, he exhaled a thick cloud of smoke and smiled.

"Y'know, I hate to admit it, but I'm just the least mite envious. This place you got on the Brazos makes me wish I was twenty years younger. In a queer sort of way, a man's first scrap with the wilderness is the best time of his life. I don't understand just exactly why it's that way, but it's a fact all the same."

The younger man nodded, digesting the thought, and a slow grin spread over his face. "I never thought of it like that but I've got an idea you're right. Least ways this last year's been real good to me. Lots better'n I ever expected, that's for damn sure."

"Well, Christ A'mighty, boy! You had rough sleddin' there for a while." Hardin's words came out in little spurts of smoke. "What with one thing and another, it's a wonder you didn't get yourself skinned and hung out to dry."

"Yeh, I s'pose it is. Course, things have calmed down some since then."

"Not just exactly, it ain't. Mebbe Texas is back in the Union, but we still got Davis for governor. Long as he's got them nigger police backin' his play you're gonna stay on the wanted list. No two ways about it."

"I guess you're right." A sardonic smile flickered and in the next instant was gone. "Likely they figure I owe 'em some on account."

"Ain't no likely about it. Many of 'em as you killed they won't never forget your name. That's why I was so tickled when you told me you got a new handle. Best thing you could've done."

"Things the way they were, I didn't have much choice. Still goes against the grain, though, havin' to hide behind somebody else's name."

"Sure it does. But you got a wife and baby and a ranch to think about now. Like I said, it's the smartest thing you ever done."

The youngster got a far-off look in his eye, saying nothing, and after a moment Barnett Hardin snorted. "Hell's bells and little fishes! It ain't like it'll last forever. Lemme tell you somethin', Wes. Elections are comin' up next year, and there's a damn good chance Davis is gonna get his nose rubbed in it. If we can get a Democrat as governor, I got a notion the law might just forgive and forget."

"I'm not bankin' on it, but it'd sure be nice to quit this play-actin'. Sort of chafes a fellow's nerves after a while."

"I s'pect it does. All the same, you ain't killed nobody in over a year and the State Police ain't campin' on your tail. It's that new name that turned the trick. 'Cept for that there wouldn't be no Jane and there wouldn't be no baby girl. You can chew on that and you'll see I'm right."

"Course you are. I didn't mean I was thinkin' of pullin' anything stupid. Hell, I'm happy as a pig in mud the way things are. My name's Earl Roebuck and it's gonna stay that way."

"That's the ticket. You're young and you got plenty of time. Just keep the hell out on the Brazos till we get these carpetbaggers run off."

"Don't worry none on that score. Only time I come east of Fort Griffin is to sell horses. Got everything I need right where I am."

"By God, I'm glad to hear you say it. Only next time I want you to bring Jane and the baby. Don't rightly seem fair that you got a young'un and I ain't never seen her."

"Well, I would've brought 'em, but what with Jane just gettin' back on her feet I figured it was best to leave 'em at her folks. Just comin' in from the Brazos sort of took the starch out of her. Not that she's sickly or anything, but the rest will do her good. Next spring I'll bring 'em by for sure, though. You can count on it."

"Good. Your aunt would purely love to see that baby." Hardin puffed on his pipe a minute and gave the youngster a speculative look. "What about your folks? You plannin' on seein' them this trip?"

"Matter of fact, I am. Thought I'd sneak in for a quick visit on the way back to get Jane and Molly."

The older man smiled. "I'm real proud you patched things up with your pa. Every time we get a letter he don't hardly talk about nothin' but you. And, o' course, your ma misses you something fierce. They'll be tickled pink to see you're makin' out so well."

Bessie Hardin came through the door, drying her hands on a dish towel. The youngster stood and she motioned him back to the chair. "Now keep your seat and go right on visiting. I just thought you might want coffee, or maybe some more cobbler."

"Couldn't if I wanted to. I'm full as a tick. Besides, I told the boys I'd meet 'em in Trinity along about dark. Guess I oughta pull out pretty quick now."

"Think that's wise?" Hardin's gaze narrowed. "You go hangin' around towns and there's always the chance somebody'll spot you."

"Well, we didn't have any trouble in Galveston. And Trinity's sort of off the beaten path. I'd be surprised if anybody got curious."

"Just watch yourself. It only takes one miscue, y'know."

"Yeah, I learned that the hard way. Course, the way it worked out, the joke was always on the other fellow."

Barnett Hardin and his wife exchanged a quick glance. Then the older man grinned and a deep belly laugh rumbled up from his gut. He stood and clapped a thorny paw over the youngster's shoulder.

"I reckon it never was you that needed advice. It was them other fellers."

"Yessir, I guess it was. And hallelujah to that."

2

The game was less than an hour old and already Roebuck was far and away the big winner. While the stakes were small potatoes to him, it was plain that the other men were playing desperation poker. The money on the table was either all they had or more than they could afford to lose; they were taking reckless chances, defying both the odds and common sense, in an effort to recoup their losses. Some stayed, blindly counting on the draw, when they should have got out; others sweated inside straights or stupidly called raises when it was clear they were beat on the board. Fickle as ever, the lady allowed some of them to drag down an occasional pot. Since they wanted to believe, this was enough to convince them all that the worm would shortly turn. That luck would again come sit beside them. Lead them to that elusive pot of gold.

Roebuck was tempted several times to fold a winning hand, simply to lessen the mounting tension. But this went against his every instinct as a gambler. These men were both thick-headed and stubborn, and whatever drubbing they took was not so much a result of his skill as it was their own foolishness. They had ignored the cardinal rule of gambling—a man who bets money he can't afford to lose is beat before he starts. Roebuck wasn't a Good Samaritan where poker was concerned. Nor did he believe in charity to fools. He played the cards dealt him and he played to win.

Given different circumstances, perhaps Roebuck wouldn't have joined the game at all. Upon leaving Jane he had half-way promised he wouldn't backslide and let himself be lured to the gambling tables. Until tonight, it was a promise he had kept. But when he rode into Trinity, and found the crew at Gate's Saloon, he was quickly persuaded to change his mind. The men were already pretty well ossified, having hit the saloon some hours earlier, and he suddenly found their antics a little boring. The spree in Galveston had been enough to hold him for the year, but the men apparently meant to make the most of their brief respite from the Brazos. Briscoe and Musgrave were the worst, loudly proclaiming themselves the greatest mustangers ever to come down the pike. Poole wasn't far behind, and gaining ground with every shot of red-eye. Of the group, only Lon Hill still had his wits about him. The black man was the watchful type, particularly in a white saloon, and where the others swilled, he merely sipped.

Their tomfoolery was about what Roebuck had expected, though, and he didn't begrudge them another fling. They had worked long and hard over the past year, and he figured they'd earned the right to celebrate. But that didn't mean he had to get down and wallow with them. All the more so since whiskey generally left the taste of sheep dip in his mouth. After a couple of sociable belts, he left them to their own devices and wandered back to join the poker game.

Now, with most of the money on the table piled in front of him, Roebuck took up the cards to deal. The other men were about what he would have expected to find in a back-country poker game. Two hardscrabble farmers, a store-keeper, and the town loudmouth, who worked at the local livery stable. All of them had lost heavily and they were showing the strain, but the loudmouth was the only one who had so far voiced any grievance. Roebuck knew the type. A dimdot who gulped his whiskey and considered himself the world's shrewdest card player. The kind who was all wind and no whistle. A born loser.

Still, Roebuck had no qualms about trimming them. Anybody old enough to play was old enough to know when to quit. That most men didn't, and just sat there flinging good money after bad, wasn't his lookout. Nor did he have any misgivings that they might believe he was cheating. The deal passed from player to player, and regardless of who dealt, he was winning consistently. That spoke for itself.

After shuffling, and allowing the farmer seated on his right to cut, he dealt a hand of five-card draw. The man on his left, the storekeeper, opened for five dollars. The other farmer called, and with a gleeful cackle, the loudmouth raised ten.

The last man, the farmer who had cut, hesitated a long time, as if trying to change the spots on his cards. Finally he called. Roebuck had all he could do to keep a wooden face as he spread his own hand. Staring back at him were two pairs. Aces and treys.

"See the fifteen and bump it ten."

The storekeeper and the farmer swore in unison and pitched their cards to the center of the table. The loudmouth grumbled to himself a little bit, sneaking dark looks at Roebuck, and at last snorted derisively. He grabbed up a bunch of coins and flung them into the pot.

"Gonna make you stretch, Laddy. Your ten and ten more."

The farmer cursed under his breath and folded.

Roebuck merely smiled and started counting from the stack in front of him. "Like the fella said, when you got 'em, bet 'em. Call the ten and raise it"—he glanced up, still smiling—"how's fifty sound?"

The stablehand grunted as if he'd been kicked in the belly. But the whiskey had taken hold and he was too stubborn to back off now. "Call, by God! You ain't the only man that knows tit from tether."

Ignoring the jibe, Roebuck picked up the deck. "Cards to the players."

"Gimme two. And make 'em good uns."

Apparently the loudmouth had three of a kind. Or maybe a pair with an ace kicker. Either way it didn't matter. Roebuck dealt him two cards and carefully laid the deck on the table. Then he placed a double-eagle on top of his own hand.

"Dealer stands pat." He gave the other man a sardonic smile. "Your bet."

The stablehand blinked a couple of times and sweated out his draw. Evidently the cards failed to improve his hand, for when he glanced up his face was ocherous. "Check."

"Bet two hundred."

"Goddamnit, you know I ain't got that much."

"I'll tap you then. Call for what's in front of you."

Roebuck knew he wouldn't call. The hangdog expression

on his face told the tale. The bluff had worked. A moment elapsed, then the loudmouth slammed his cards to the table and knocked back a glass of whiskey in a single gulp. Smiling, Roebuck threw his hand on the deadwood and started to drag in the pot.

Suddenly the man snatched at the deadwood, trying to grab Roebuck's discarded hand. Roebuck leaned across the table and backhanded him in the mouth. The man's lip split, spurting blood, and he lurched erect.

"You sonovabitch! Nobody does that to me."

"Friend, I'll do worse than that if you don't keep your mitts out of the deadwood."

The stablehand was unarmed, so that meant rough-and-tumble if it came to a showdown. But forty years of beans and sowbelly were beginning to show at his waistline, and Roebuck had little doubt of the outcome. The youngster kicked his chair back and stood just as the saloonkeeper materialized at his elbow.

"Mister, don't pay no attention to Sam. He didn't mean nothin', honest. It's just whiskey talk. Look for yourself. He's so drunk he couldn't ride a hobbyhorse."

Roebuck's flinty gaze bored into the stablehand for a moment, then he shrugged. His voice was low-keyed, restrained somehow, but there was an undercurrent of deadliness in the words. "Get the peckerhead out of here. He's got no business playin' poker with grown men."

The barkeep circled the table and grabbed Sam by the shirt collar and the seat of his pants. Then he waltzed him across the room at a lively clip. But as they went through the door the stablehand twisted around and hollered back over his shoulder.

"You ain't through with me yet, you sorry bastard. Just hide and watch. You'll see!"

Drunk as they were, Roebuck's crew had wheeled away from the bar at the first sign of trouble. Now he smiled and waved them back, his brief flare of temper once again under control. Righting his chair he took a seat and glanced around at the dumbstruck players.

"Pardon the intrusion, gents. Who's dealin'?"

The storekeeper fumbled the cards together and commenced shuffling. Like a couple of mesmerized sheep, the farmers just sat there, staring vacantly at his shaking hands.

Late that night Roebuck emerged from the saloon trailed by three drunks and someone who looked like a glassy-eyed owl that had been dipped in tar. The notable difference was that Lon Hill could still walk, whereas the others sort of listed and swayed, taking two steps backward for every one step forward. Roebuck was somewhat ahead of the others and had just stepped off the boardwalk when a brilliant orange flash erupted across the street.

A sliver of fire seared his side and in the same instant he heard the deep roar of a shotgun. He knew he'd been hit, but somehow that seemed incidental, a mere trifle. Without thought, acting out of sheer reflex, he jerked the Navy and placed five shots in the precise spot he had seen the muzzle flash. There was a momentary lull while everyone stood rooted in their tracks, then the stablehand lurched out of a dark passageway between two buildings. The shotgun fell from his hand, clattering on the boardwalk, and he teetered there like a tree rocking in the wind. His legs gave way all of a sudden, as if chopped from beneath him, and he pitched face down in the street.

Roebuck felt something warm and sticky soaking his shirt front, and bright swirling dots appeared before his eyes. Quite without realizing it, his knees buckled and he found himself sitting in the road. Lon Hill loomed over him, and from a great distance he heard the raspy croak of his own voice.

"Can you beat that? The sonovabitch killed me."

As it turned out, the youngster was only half right. According to Dr. Jonas Stroud he should have been dead, but by some inexplicable quirk of fate, he wasn't. Less than an hour after the shooting, the physician operated and removed two buckshot that had passed through the kidney and lodged between the backbone and ribs. In the process he recognized Barnett Hardin's nephew for who he was, and inadvertently let slip to the crew that they were riding in fast company. All of which seemed a moot point since Stroud gave the young outlaw a fifty-fifty chance at best of pulling through. Unless he was confined to bed and kept completely inactive there were no odds. He would simply die.

Fearful of using opiates, due to the youngster's weakened condition, Stroud had operated without a pain-killer. Wes had stoically endured the scapel, and gritted his teeth all the harder when he heard the physician expose his identity. Now, stitched back together and bandaged tightly, he asked Stroud to summon his crew. They trooped in and ganged around the operating table, stone-cold sober and looking just the least bit sheepish. The youngster was ashen, but in full control of himself, and he smiled weakly.

"Boys, I guess the jig's up. I'm sorry I had to fool you like that, but it was better you didn't know who I was. Now that you do, I want you to make tracks and forget you ever heard of me."

Poole puffed up like a banty rooster. "Now just hold on a goldarned minute, Earl."

The young outlaw stopped him with a slight motion of his hand. "Chub, it's a little late to start arguin' with me. The doc will pay you fellows off out of my money belt and then I want you to vamoose. The State Police are gonna get wind of this, and if they catch us together you boys will swing right alongside me. You think about it and you'll see I'm right." Drained of strength, he managed one last smile. "Now scat, the whole bunch of you."

The men stood there several moments, wavering between loyalty to the man they knew as Earl Roebuck and the uncertain fate of riding with Wes Hardin. Bitter as it was, they had to admit he was right. Hank Musgrave started it off, and then, one at a time, they filed by and gave his hand a soft squeeze. None of them said anything and somehow that didn't seem in the least strange. It had all been said back on the Brazos.

When the door closed Wes lay there for a long while, trying to collect his thoughts and plan what to do next. Then, quite suddenly, he sensed that he wasn't alone. Turning his head, he saw Lon Hill standing just inside the doorway. The black man flashed a mouthful of ivory and met his stare straight on.

"Boss, you'd jest be wastin' your breath. Like it or not, you done stuck with me."

Hill cocked his hat back, grinned, and took a chair beside the door.

3

The room was still dark when Wes awoke. Through the window he saw a grayish tinge in the sky and estimated dawn was yet an hour away. Some inner mechanism had awakened him, a warning of sorts, and he lay there trying to unravel what it meant. Nothing stirred, and so far as he could tell there was no reason to take alarm. The house was quiet and there were no unusual noises from the farmyard. All of which didn't mean a hill of beans. Not after the last two months. The quiet times, especially when a man was sleeping, were the most dangerous of all.

Slowly, he ran his hand under the pillow and took hold of the Navy. Then he rolled sideways and eased his feet onto the floor. The wound in his side had healed nicely, but he favored it nonetheless. Sudden movements still brought a sharp pain, and while it curried him the wrong way, he had conditioned himself to taking things easy. Standing, he hobbled around the room, barefooted and silent. There were two windows, one at the side of the house and the other at the back. Some minutes passed as he scanned the yard, which was off a ways to the rear. He detected nothing out of the ordinary, but that did little to ease his jumpy feeling.

It was no false alarm. Not when it tugged him awake like this.

The past couple of months had given him a strong conviction about these hunches. Whether it was sixth sense or a deeper instinct of some sort seemed unimportant. He knew that he possessed it, whatever it was, and more significantly, he knew that it was almost unerring. Not infallible, but close. Damned close. The feeling was triggered by something inside him, always unexpected, and never once concerning itself with trifles. When it came, it came with dazzling clarity. And there was no muck of uncertainty. It struck hard and fast, and most of the time, dead center. On center often enough that only a fool would have ignored it. The proof was not so much in his head as in the simple function of his lungs.

This thing, whatever its name, had kept him alive.

Alert and edgy, he returned to bed and again lay down, with the Navy resting across his chest. Despite the early morning calm—what his eyes and ears took to be a good sign—he couldn't relax. Too much had happened since that night in Trinity. And none of it good. Looking back, he felt a profound sense of wonder. Not that he had survived that night, or recovered from the shotgun blast. But instead, that by hunch and a long streak of luck he had lived to greet the gloomy dawn of a September day.

Lon Hill had been as good as his word. The black man stuck with him, and foxy as ever, had cleverly engineered his escape. That same night Hill had cut the telegraph lines out of Trinity, sealing it off and delaying word of the shootout from reaching Austin. Then, shortly before dawn, he spirited Wes out of town in the back of a buckboard. It was rough going at first, for they were forced to hide in the heavy thickets along the river. After a week, though, Hill managed to sneak a quick powwow with Barnett Hardin and they were able to quit living like animals.

But instead of getting better, things got worse. Though Barnett Hardin's place was under constant surveillance, making it unsafe for them to stay there, he arranged for them to hole up with friends in Walker County. Texans were a prideful and independent lot, but they were united in one thing, their hatred of the carpetbagger regime. The name Wes Hardin had a certain magic about it, a symbol of sorts. One man fighting a lone fight against the brutality and injustice of Yankee tyranny. The youngster and his dusky watchdog were welcomed like victorious soldiers home from the war.

The jubilation proved somewhat premature, though. The State Police sniffed out their trail early in July, and within a span of six weeks they were forced to run on seven separate occasions. Wes was weak as a kitten throughout the entire ordeal, unable to sit a horse, much less turn and give fight as he had in the past. Lon Hill carted him from farm to farm in the buckboard, and each time, they escaped capture by what seemed a sheer stroke of luck.

It was during this deadly game of hide-and-seek that Wes first became aware of his hunches. Something akin to an itchy feeling would come over him, and an inner voice warned him of impending danger. Lon Hill believed in many things—among them voodoo witchcraft and the Lord God Jehovah—but his strongest faith was in the wolflike instincts possessed by certain men. Men like Wes Hardin. Whenever the young outlaw showed signs of that itchy feeling, Hill hurriedly packed the buckboard and they took off in a blaze of dust. That the hunches were virtually foolproof was borne out by the fact that they had misfired only twice. Of the seven times they ran, State Police stormed five hideouts shortly after they departed.

As if his wound and the relentless hounding weren't enough, Wes was further made miserable by concern for his family. Jane and the baby were still in Pisga, and through friends, he was able to send an occasional letter. But there was no way Jane could reply, and it was this loss of contact which he found unbearable. So long as they remained with the Bowens, she and the baby were safe, and for that he was thankful. Still, it did little to salve his need for them. Though the admission came hard, he couldn't elude a stark sense of emptiness. He was lonely, and for the first time in his life, he needed someone besides himself. It was a troublesome feeling, one he had difficulty in handling, particularly at night without Jane's soft warmth snuggled close to him.

Beneath it all, compounding his more immediate worries, was a hurt of a different sort. He had lost the ranch, and while the thought was bitter as wormwood, he never once tried kidding himself on that score. A year on the Brazos, filled with sweat and hope and great accomplishment, had simply gone down the drain. Poole and Musgrave and Briscoe were good men, loyal in a way he wouldn't have expected from hired hands. But they were heavy drinkers as well, and liquor tended to loosen a man's tongue. Despite their best intentions, sooner or later one of them would get crocked and spill the beans. Nothing was more natural when a man kept steady company with John Barleycorn, and before long they would all be bragging. Telling the world how they'd trapped mustangs with a fellow whose real name happened to be John Wesley Hardin. Much as it galled him, the young outlaw couldn't avoid facts.

Earl Roebuck was dead. And his dream on the Brazos had vanished in a puff of smoke.

None of this concerned him now, though. Instead, he lay in bed, wide awake and fretful, wondering if he was jumping at shadows. His nerves had been on edge for close to two months, and he was strung so tight he had begun to suspect his own hunches. Perhaps of greater consequence, he was just plain fed up with running. A week ago, with a premonition this strong, he would have rousted Hill from bed and made tracks. Now, irked by the constant harassment and feeling more his old self, he simply waited. The State Police weren't about to call it quits, and all of a sudden he just didn't give a damn. It was time to shove back.

A light rap on the door brought him out of bed in a single motion. He thumbed the hammer back on the Navy and waited. Then the doorknob turned, and in the deadened silence of the room, the creaky hinges sounded like the clatterwheels of hell. Lon Hill stuck his head inside.

"It's jest me, boss."

"Hell, c'mon in, Lon." Wes glanced sheepishly at the cocked pistol and slowly lowered the hammer. "Guess I'm a little spooky these days."

The black man swung the door open but held his position in the hall. "I s'pect you got reason." He jerked his thumb toward the front of the house. "Couple of fellas left their horses in the trees over by the creek. They's pussyfootin' this way and they got rifles."

Wes smiled grimly. "Looks like my itch was real after all." Snatching up his pants, he pulled them on, hurriedly hooked the top button, and jammed the Navy in his waistband. "Where are Dave and his wife?"

"Still sleepin'."

The young outlaw heaved a sigh of relief. Dave Harrel was an old friend of Barnett Hardin's, and it would be easier if he had no part in whatever happened. With that off his mind, he grabbed a shotgun leaning against the wall by the bed and turned back to the black man.

"You say there's only two of 'em?"

"That's all I seen."

"Good. Two're just about right. Say, how come you to spot 'em, anyway?"

Hill grinned. "Reckon I done caught your itch."

"Well, that's all you've caught. Get on back to your room and stay"—the black man's jaw clicked open but Wes's harsh scowl stopped him cold—"I haven't got time to argue. Just do like I say. And if they get me, you play dumb and act like you're Dave's hired help."

He brushed past Hill and hobbled off down the hallway. Entering the parlor, he moved quietly to a front window and peeked through the curtains. Two men were crossing the yard, rifles thrust out in front of them, peering suspiciously at the house. They both wore badges and had the unmistakable stamp of Yankee written all over them. Quickly, he moved across the room, earing back the hammers on the shotgun, and halted beside the door. Grasping the greener in his right hand, he threw the door open and dropped to one knee in the entranceway.

"Hands up!"

The policemen froze at his barked command. They gawked at him for an instant, goggle-eyed with disbelief, then the one on the right moved his rifle barrel. Wes pulled both triggers and the scattergun vomited a double load of buckshot. The officers hurtled backward, lifted from their feet by the impact, and slammed to earth with a dusty thud. One man's head was half gone and the other one had a hole the size of a saucer where his badge had been. The ground around them puddled with blood and muddy gore; there was scarcely any question about the outcome. They were dead and ripening fast.

Wes climbed to his feet and turned back into the house. Lon Hill was standing just behind him, clutching a battered Spencer carbine. The black man grinned.

"Looks like the magpies is gonna have eyeballs for breakfast."

"I thought I told you to stay put."

"Boss, you gonna have to speak louder. This ol' niggah's hard of hearin'."

"Yeah, sure you are. Like a fox." Wes smiled and shook his head. "Well, long as you're here, see if you can round up a shovel and we'll get those bastards planted."

"Yassuh, Mistuh Wes. You want one hole or two?"

The young outlaw flicked a glance back at the sprawled bodies. "One'll do fine. They can keep each other company."

Then he walked off down the hall. He could hear Maude Harrel screeching at her husband in their bedroom, and it grated on him that he had brought trouble to their doorstep. Suddenly he felt very tired and his side ached something fierce. A year on the Brazos had changed things not at all. It was like a lost man wandering in circles.

He was right back where he'd started.

4

The air was damp and chill along the river. Wes huddled deeper inside his blanket and tried to draw some warmth to his body. Though it was pitch dark, and the heavy thickets screened the campsite, he dared not light a fire. Instead, he sat with his back against a wagon wheel and shivered, forcing himself to ignore the pain in his side. Despite the cold, he felt flushed, just the least bit woozy, and sensed that he was running a fever. But this he also put from his mind. Until Hill returned there was nothing to be done. He closed his eyes, resigned to the wait, and blocked out all thought of pain and cold and chattering teeth.

They had been on the run for almost a week. Harried like animals with hounds set loose on their trail. There seemed no sanctuary, not after the gunfight at Dave Harrel's place; no matter how hard they pushed themselves, or how often they changed hideouts, the State Police were only a step behind. Finally, out of desperation, they had once again taken to the thickets. Here, at least, they could lose themselves for a while, and gain time to think.

Burying the dead officers at Harrel's had been futile, wasted effort. State Police were fanned out across Walker County in a massive search, and other officers had appeared that very afternoon asking questions. That they would return, nosing out the trail of the dead men, Wes had no doubt whatever. Yet he was in worse shape than ever, and hardly fit to run. The recoil from the shotgun, where he'd held it jammed against his side, had ruptured his wound. Maude Harrel fixed him a poultice of spider webs and chimney soot, but it merely slowed the bleeding to a steady leak. Late that night, though, he and Lon Hill took off in the buckboard anyway. As long as they remained at the farm, the Harrels were in danger of being killed, for it was only a matter of time until the law trapped them there. With them gone, Dave Harrel could claim he had harbored them at gunpoint, and there was no way of proving otherwise. It was no choice at all.

They ran and kept on running, driven, at last, into the thickets.

Now Wes gritted his teeth, closing his mind to the pain and the sweaty chills that swept over him. He focused instead on what seemed a more unsettling problem. Lon Hill was long past overdue, and it was unlike the black man to be late. Hill had ridden out around sunset, expecting to reach Barnett Hardin's place shortly after dark. Wes disliked drawing the old man deeper into his troubles, but he desperately needed a safe hideout. Someplace he could lay up until his wound healed fully and he was again fit to ride a horse. However distasteful the idea, he had nowhere else to turn for help. Barnett Hardin was his last hope. Yet, even as he mulled this over, it merely increased his concern for Lon Hill.

The black man might easily have been trapped at Hardin's farm. Or perhaps he was just fed up with the whole sorry mess and had kept on riding for parts unknown. The thought no sooner entered Wes's head than he discarded it. Lon Hill wasn't a quitter. Once he started something, he finished it, and he wasn't the kind to turn his back on a friend. The more likely possibility was that he had fallen into the hands of the State Police. And if so, God have mercy on his soul. They would brand him a renegade black, traitor to the very cause that had freed him. Justice would be swift and harsh. A shot in the back or a rope strung over the nearest tree. Wes saw it happening, etched clearly in his mind's eye, and the sight of it made his stomach churn.

Lon Hill deserved better than that.

The young outlaw was suddenly jarred out of his funk by a sound. A horse moving through the thickets along his side of the river. But there was something out of kilter, not as it should be. He listened closer, straining to catch the rustling sounds. Then he stiffened and threw the blanket aside. There were two horses. And Lon Hill hadn't left with an extra mount.

Scrambling to his feet, he grabbed the shotgun and ducked around behind the buckboard. Quietly, one notch at a time, he earred back both hammers and rested the barrels across the rear wheel. The horses came nearer, and while he could see nothing in the inky darkness, the noise pinpointed his target. That was the edge a scattergun gave a man, and why he always had one close at hand these days. Even in the dark it was deadly accurate, chunking a murderous storm of buckshot some thirty yards or farther. Shifting slightly, he trained the small cannon directly on the approaching sounds.

"Hold your fire, boss! We're comin' in."

Wes felt such a surge of relief that his knees went weak. Then his temper flared and he jerked erect. "Goddamnit, Lon, why didn't you call out sooner? And what the hell business you got bringin' back a spare horse?"

"Quit your cussin', boy. Both these saddles is filled."

Dumbfounded, Wes stared into the darkness with his mouth open. The voice was unmistakable, but it took him a moment to collect his wits. "Uncle Barnett?"

"Who'd you expect—Abe Lincoln?"

He heard the creak of saddle leather, and saw shadowy forms dismounting from horses. Lowering the hammers on the shotgun, he laid it in the buckboard and walked forward. The shadows became indistinct blobs, and the sheer bulk of one made mistake all but impossible.

"Guess you kind of threw me." Wes fumbled for words, still a little taken aback. "I never figured Lon'd bring you back out here."

Barnett Hardin laughed and clapped a bristly paw over his shoulder. "Lon didn't bring nobody. I brung myself."

"That's sure 'nough right, boss." The black man's ivories flashed in the dark. "Mistuh Barnett wouldn't have it no other way. Jest pointed me toward the river and said—*GIT!*"

"Well, to tell you the truth, Uncle Barnett, I wish you hadn't come. Don't misunderstand. I'm glad to see you and all that. But if the Yankees catch you with me that'll be all she wrote."

"Don't fret yourself about me. Case you forgot, I was killin' bluebellies before you learned to quit pickin' your nose." The old man's head swiveled around and even in the dark he seemed to be frowning. "What the hell you mean sittin' around here without a fire? Gawd A'mighty, boy, don't you know you can catch your death that way?"

"Things like they are," Wes said, "fires have a way of drawin' crowds. Lately most of 'em been wearin' a badge, too."

"Horseapples! Them police got more sense than to be stumblin' around in the thickets on a night like this." Hardin turned to the black man. "Lon, how 'bout rustlin' up a fire? Let's get this boy toasted a little on both sides and then we'll pour some of his aunt's special potion down him."

"Yassuh! Have 'er ready in a jiffy." Hill went into his darky routine and shuffled off to gather wood. "Lawdy me, I's glad you is here, Mistuh Barnett. He's been needin' the double whammy longer'n I can remember."

Wes narrowed his eyes suspiciously. "Just exactly what'd Aunt Bess send out here?"

"Why, I told you. It's her special potion." Hardin chuckled. "Sort of a broth—yellowroot, fresh kidney, oak bark—cures whatever ails you. Builds up your blood and flushes you out all at the same time."

The young outlaw groaned and sank down beside the buckboard. "Meanin', if it don't kill you then you're pretty sure of survivin' whatever it was that ailed you to start with."

The broth wasn't half bad, though. Presently, Lon Hill had a fire blazing, and after downing his aunt's magic remedy, Wes perked up considerably. Whether it was the curious-tasting broth, or simply having his chilled bones warm again, Wes didn't know and didn't really care. He was toasted to a crisp, pleasantly light-headed, and feeling no pain whatever. His only regret was that Bessie Hardin hadn't sent along a barrelful of the stuff. Even if it killed a man, at least he'd die happy.

After he'd finished, Wes glanced around the fire and gave the other men a dopey smile. "Whatever it was, that was mighty fine. We ought to bottle it and make ourselves a fortune."

Barnett Hardin just nodded, sucking on his pipe. Lon Hill hauled out the makings and started building himself a smoke. They exchanged glances and something unspoken passed between them. Several moments elapsed before the old man knocked the dottle from his pipe and looked up.

"Wes, I was talkin' things over with Lon, and the way we got it figured, you're about at the end of your string."

"The hell you say!" Wes slapped his knee and let go a goofy laugh. "I got lots of string left."

"Mebbe so. But if you don't get that hole plugged up decent, and stop flittin' around like a June bug, you're gonna have to unravel it six feet under."

"What're you talkin' about? I'm healthy as a horse."

"Sure you are. Any luck a'tall, you might last out the week."

"Your uncle's tellin' you right, boss." Hill lit his cigarette with a flaming stick, then let his gaze come level. "You got a leak that's gonna bleed you dry. And if that don't get you, the lung fever will." He gestured at the damp ground fog and the thickets surrounding them. "Man in your shape can't take it in a place like this."

"So what am I s'posed to do? Get the law to look the other way while I find myself a warm bed?"

"That's sort of what we had in mind." Hardin's lips were set in a grim line. "Leastways if we can get you to act sensible."

"Why hell, all us Hardins is sensible people." He gave them a glazed smile. "I thought everybody knowed that."

Barnett Hardin studied something in the fire for a moment. "Y'know, I got a good friend that's sheriff of Cherokee County. Fella name of Dick Reagan. He's a square shooter, and honest as sin."

"That a fact?"

"Yep. I was tellin' Lon about him. Said if we was to work it just right, Reagan would probably let you rest up in his jail."

Wes blinked and cocked one eye in a bemused scowl. "How's that again?"

"Well, it come to me, don't y'see, that Reagan's jail is a couple of counties away from here. Now, if we was to get him to hold you on some trumped-up charge and—"

"Whoa back!" Wes recoiled so hard he almost fell over. "That idea don't exactly touch my funny bone."

"Goddamn, lemme finish before you get your nose out of joint. Now, unless I heard wrong, you're wanted for a bunch of killin's down in Gonzales."

"What's that got to do with anything?"

"Suppose we was to have Reagan arrest you on some charge or other, and tell folks he was holdin' you for the Gonzales authorities." Hardin threw up his hand as the youngster started to interrupt. "Just hold your horses. That'd make it a county matter, wouldn't it? And the State Police couldn't touch you—ain't that right?"

"Hell, I guess so. I'm not no lawyer."

"Take my word for it. Now the other part is that Gonzales is a long ways off. And it could take them Gonzales lawmen a long time to hear that Dick Reagan is holdin' you for 'em. Maybe even a couple of weeks. Long enough, anyhow, for you to get yourself mended back together."

Hardin paused, and shot him a crafty look. "You startin' to get my drift?"

Wes digested it slowly, letting the words seep through his pleasant stupor. At last, he shook his head and grinned. "Maybe I'm crazy as a loon, but that's about the best son-ovabitchin' idea I ever heard in my life."

The old man beamed and traded smiles with Lon Hill. "I thought you might like it."

"I only got one question."

"Ask me anything. Solomon couldn't hold a candle to me tonight."

"How much liquor did you put in that soup?"

"Hell, that weren't liquor, boy. It was white lightnin'. Double distilled and spiked with tarantula juice."

They all burst out laughing, and Barnett Hardin's belly shook like a great mound of jelly. While everyone was in a good mood he fed Wes some more broth, and before long the youngster's eyes took on the luster of polished stones. After a while he just sort of keeled over and commenced snoring loud enough to raise the dead. The old man and Lon

Hill swapped looks again, and a rare feeling of kinship settled over them.

It had been a good night's work.

5

The soft metallic whine of a hacksaw on iron was lost in
the mournful chorus of hounds baying at the sky. Obscured
by low-scudding clouds, the moon cast a dim glow over the
earth, and the town of Rusk slumbered peacefully in the brisk
autumn stillness. It was past midnight, time for all respectable people to be in bed, and the citizens of Rusk were nothing if not respectable. They slept on untroubled and
undisturbed, secure in the blissful serenity of those committed to the straight and narrow.

Like the town and its people, the jail lay becalmed beneath
a shadowed moon. The only sound was that of steel teeth
steadily devouring iron bars. Yet it was a small sound, not
unpleasant in its hungry drone. Through the thick oak door
of the cellblock the sound was muffled further still, and the
night deputy, dozing quietly in the front office, heard nothing.

The jail's single occupant, Cherokee County's most illustrious boarder, took care that the steely blade hummed
smoothly, without distraction or undue noise. There was
every reason that the jailbreak should appear convincing, the
work of a lone prisoner aided by unknown confederates.
While hardly respectable by local standards—the townspeople thought of him as a misguided rogue—Wes Hardin was
nonetheless an honorable man. He had been well fed and
fairly treated during his brief confinement, and he meant to
leave the lawmen of Cherokee County with their reputations
intact. In all fairness, he could do no less. They were genial
hosts, ever willing to accommodate an old friend, and embarrassing them would have made it awkward as well for
Barnett Hardin.

Through an arrangement between his uncle and Sheriff

Dick Reagan, the young outlaw had surrendered himself on the courthouse steps some two weeks back. Word of his capture spread rapidly throughout Rusk, and in that time he had been the object of considerable speculation among the townspeople. At first, curious citizens flocked to the jail in droves, hoping to catch a glimpse of Texas' most famous desperado. But as quickly as they crowded through the door they were turned away, left to gather on the street and stare expectantly at the cellblock window. Sheriff Reagan made it plain that his prisoner was not to be put on public display. Instead, he would be held quietly and safely until Gonzales authorities came to collect him on several outstanding murder warrants.

Still, despite Reagan's discreet and somewhat stingy announcements, news of the capture spread within the week to other counties. As expected, State Police descended on the jail like sharks scenting warm blood, demanding custody of the prisoner. Reagan politely, but firmly, refused. They were told of the Gonzales warrants and informed that only a higher court order could supersede outstanding murder charges. Promising to return, they stormed from the jail and rode off toward Austin. The sheriff merely smiled and went on about his business. Nor was his prisoner overly concerned. The wheels of justice ground finely, and with elections approaching, Austin would consider at length before interfering in county politics.

Thereafter, young Hardin virtually had the jail to himself. A local sawbones, the only outsider allowed to see him, came by every day, and while patching him back together pumped him for juicy tidbits to pass along to the townspeople. His cell was warm and clean, the grub he ate came from the best cafe in town, and the Ladies Temperance Society kept him supplied with plenty of interesting reading material. Sheriff Reagan allowed him to exercise in the cellblock corridor, and once, late at night, even sneaked Barnett Hardin in for a quick visit. All in all, Wes took to it like a starved dog trailing a gut wagon. In close to two months of running, it was the first time he'd really stopped to draw a deep breath.

Perhaps as much as a good rest, it also gave him time to

think. Stretched out in his bunk, hands locked behind his head, he stared at the ceiling and slowly dissected his life. Taken as a whole, it wasn't much to talk about. Except for Jane and the baby he had little or nothing to show for his efforts. The ranch was gone, and with it his dreams of leading a straight life. In less than two months he had killed three more men, bringing the total to something over twenty. The state and several counties were keenly interested in stretching his neck. There was no sanctuary in any of his old haunts. Not on the Brazos or with the Clementses, and certainly not with his folks. And unless things changed drastically, he might as well forget about any kind of life with his own wife and child.

What with one thing and another, it was about as sorry as sorry could get.

But he'd never been one to dwell on past miseries. After hashing it over, and mentally kicking himself in the rump a couple of times, he began casting around for a solution. Something safe, so he could have his family with him, and yet nothing sneaky or fainthearted, for he still had to live with himself. That was a tall order, a compromise of sorts, and for a while it put him in a royal quandary. Then, out of a clear blue, he happened to remember Dewitt County and the Taylors.

The moment he thought of it he cursed himself for having overlooked it before. The Taylors weren't Hardin stock, and they were none too civilized, but they were still kin. As near as he could recall, old Pitkin Taylor was his mother's first cousin, and in Texas that made for close blood ties. Somewhat like a tribe, the Taylors stuck close to one another, and after whelping several generations of offspring, their numbers comprised a small army. He recollected his father commenting on occasion that the Taylor clan pretty well ran things to suit themselves in Dewitt County. While that had meant nothing at the time, it might now mean the difference between living free or resuming his one-sided race with the State Police. A county where his own kin called the shots seemed made to order. Not unlike a blind hog stumbling over an acorn, he had found a nifty compromise to all his problems.

That very night he made arrangements for his escape.

And now, as the shrouded moon played hide-and-seek in the clouds, and the town dogs closed down their nightly serenade, he sawed through the last bar. Gently, he lifted it from the window and laid it on the bunk, alongside its three mates. The hacksaw was placed squarely on the pillow, where it would be found and later marveled over as the townspeople recounted assorted versions of the daring escape.

Dusting iron filings from his hands, he turned and gave the cell a last inspection. Then, satisfied that everything was in order, he scrambled up the wall and disappeared through the window.

Outside, he kept low, sticking to the shadows, and sprinted toward the back of the jail. When he rounded the corner it was just as he had expected. A reunion of sorts. Lon Hill sat astride a flashy roan and beside him was the grullo gelding. Without a word, Wes swung into the saddle and they calmly walked their horses to the edge of town. There, no longer concerned with attracting attention, they spurred hard and took off in a pounding lope. Behind, they left a rooster tail of dust and the blissful, if somewhat unsuspecting, citizens of Cherokee County.

An hour later they reined to a halt along the banks of the Neches River. Wes unstrapped the holstered Navy from the saddle horn and buckled it around his waist. Then he laughed, suddenly galvanized by the sweet smell of freedom, and slapped the black man across the shoulder.

"Lon, you're a ring-tailed stemwinder. Damned if you're not! I don't know but a couple of men I would've trusted to pull that off tonight, and by Jesus, your name heads the list."

In all the months they'd been together it was the first time this mercurial youngster had spoken to him with such openness. Confused, his heart hammering with pride, Hill retreated behind his darky patter. "Weren't nothin', boss. Jest done what you tol' me, that's all. Hardest part was waitin'.

Not knowin' how you and that saw was gettin' along.''

"Hell, that's what I'm talkin' about. Any peckerhead can let fling when things bust loose. It takes guts to wait and play your cards right. Most men haven't got the sand for it. Just eats 'em up alive.''

The black man ducked his head, faltering for words. A moment passed and then Wes again started to speak. But something in his voice had changed. It was sober, the lightness gone, somehow reluctant.

"Lon, I sort of stretched it a minute ago. There's not another man on earth I'd sooner have side me than you. For my money, you're the pick of the litter. But I guess we don't always get things the way we'd like 'em. What I'm buildin' up steam to get said is that this here's where we part trails.''

Hill's chin snapped up and his muddy eyes glinted in the moonlight. "That a fancy way of tellin' me to haul ass?''

"Nope, it's a fancy way of sayin' I like you better'n any man I ever rode with. White or black. You stick with me and you'll get yourself killed. I know you'd do it anyway, regardless, so it's me that has to cut the knot. I hate it worse'n anything I ever done, but that's the way she's got to be.''

The black man studied him a long while, then quickly looked away. "Funny thing. What you said about likin' me. Guess I always felt the same way and jest didn't know how to say it.''

"Wasn't any need to say it, Lon. You showed it. Hadn't been for you I'd be worm meat right now.''

"Lawdy me, lissen to that man carry on. Feel like I been dipped in goosebutter.''

"Yeah, but it's a fact, all the same. I owe you, and the way I got it figured, there's only one thing that'll square accounts.'' Wes paused and gestured on an angle away from the river. "You head due west till you hit the Brazos and then you just keep right on ridin'. When you come to the ranch, step down and hang your hat. It's yours. I don't know anyone this side of hell I'd rather see have it than you.''

Hill swallowed hard and had to clear his throat. "Mistuh Wes, I know how much that place means to you. If you ever gets a notion—"

"Don't sit around lookin' for me. I'm headed in another direction. You just go on back to catchin' horses. And somethin' else. Anybody gives you trouble about ownin' that place, you tell 'em to button their lip or Wes Hardin'll come out there and shoot their balls off."

"I'll tell 'em that very thing. Be like showin' a spook the holy cross."

The young outlaw stuck out his hand. "Walk soft."

Lon Hill gave him one last flash of ivory. "You sleep light."

Their parting was as simple as that. With a final squeeze their hands came unstuck and they wheeled their horses in opposite directions. The pale moonlight filtered down over the plains, and they were in sight for a long while. But neither man looked back. There was no need.

CHAPTER 7

1

Spring came early to Dewitt County that year. It brought new life to the prairie and death to the Taylor clan. Along the Guadalupe, as the earth sprouted tall grasses and wild flowers bloomed, time was measured not by date or calendar, but by the day certain men were killed.

Pitkin Taylor, patriarch of the clan, had been murdered in his own front yard. His sons-in-law, Bill and Henry Kelly, were callously gunned down after being captured and disarmed. In retaliation, Bill Taylor, the old man's son, blasted William Sutton in the poolroom shoot-out, but unaccountably failed to kill him. There the matter stood on April Fools' Day.

A grim joke inscribed in blood.

Yet there was no laughter in Dewitt County, and few men took solace in graveside humor. Least of all John Wesley Hardin. In a very real sense, he had bought chips in a game where everyone lost. The stakes were ashes to ashes and dust to dust; aside from a glowing eulogy and plenty of company, the players could expect little on their journey to the Promised Land.

The young outlaw and his family had arrived on the Guadalupe in early January. Their Christmas had been sparse, spent dodging around backcountry roads, and they entered Dewitt County only one step ahead of the law. But all pursuit stopped there, and for a brief time they rejoiced quietly. The

Taylors gave them haven, and not even the dread State Police
dared challenge their kinsmen. It seemed, at last, that they
were safe, in a world apart, where carpetbagger justice was
a thing of the past, and men could again get on with the
business of living.

Quite soon, though, the bubble burst. Their refuge proved
an illusion, and in the light of day, reality was stark and cold
and never more blunt. They had merely traded one enemy
for another. And while at first it had seemed the lesser of
two evils, in some ways the State Police were a catwalk
compared to the dangers they now faced.

Not unlike many sections of Texas, where cattle was king,
Dewitt County was in the midst of a power struggle. Since
before the Civil War the Taylor clan had controlled the
county, and run it much to suit themselves. But with the
advent of carpetbagger rule times began to change. Certain
elements in Dewitt County, led by William Sutton, aligned
themselves with the Davis regime in Austin. Slowly, over a
period of years, the Sutton faction had gained influence. At
first their efforts to undermine the Taylors had been insidious, chipping away at the edges, just as a river at floodtide
erodes and weakens the shoreline. Within the last year,
though, their efforts had become bolder. And somewhat murderous, in a pragmatic, backwoods sort of way.

Still, those who knew William Sutton found nothing
strange in that. For he was a pragmatic man, a firm believer
in the old adage that the end justified the means. At stake
was the land itself, the very foundation of power and wealth.
Dewitt County, situated some seventy miles southeast of San
Antonio, was split down the middle by the Guadalupe River.
The Taylor clan's domain lay south of the river, and as the
power struggle intensified, the Sutton forces came to control
the lands north of the Guadalupe. Yet whoever had a hammerlock on county politics might well end up with control
of both the river and the land. It was the classic battle of the
haves against the have-nots. Cattle was king, but the corner-
stones of that kingdom were water and graze. The stakes

were monumental, and unlike man's lesser games, there were no rules.

Just last year, with an organized and well-financed campaign, the Sutton faction had gained control of several county offices. Perhaps their most critical victory was the election of Jack Helms to the post of sheriff. For Helms was a practical man, with all the moral conscience of a scorpion. He devoted himself not to causes but to the highest bidder. In this instance that happened to be the Sutton forces. And with the law behind him, William Sutton set in motion the oldest and most expedient of all power plays. He began murdering his opponents.

Several lesser members of the Taylor clan were killed first. Charged with rustling, they were taken captive by Helms' Vigilance Committee, and according to reports, gunned down while attempting to escape. Retribution was swift and decisive. Several Sutton men were bushwhacked with brutal efficiency. Obviously, stronger measures were needed, something closer to home. The Kelly brothers, married to Pitkin Taylor's eldest daughters, were run to earth and shot. The coroner's verdict was but another verse of an old song— killed while attempting to escape.

Yet the desired effect was not forthcoming. Instead of quaking submission, the Taylor clan bowed its neck and prepared to fight. Apparently still stronger medicine was needed, an object lesson that would destroy all will to resist. The patriarch himself, Pitkin Taylor, was lured from his house on a dark, moonless night and blown to kingdom come by several quarts of buckshot.

Again, the Sutton forces had misjudged their adversary. Bill Taylor, the old man's son, hadn't been shorted on grit. He marched into a billiard parlor the next night and accused William Sutton of murder. When the smoke cleared Sutton was badly wounded and Billy Taylor assumed leadership of the clan. But even as Taylor walked from the pool hall the name of the game changed.

The fight had become a feud.

As a spectator to the gathering storm, Wes Hardin felt a queer sense of being sucked along by forces beyond his control. Yet, for the first time in his life, he allowed himself to be drawn into somebody else's troubles. The Taylors had given him sanctuary—made a place for him and his family on their lands—and it wasn't an obligation to be shunted aside lightly. While it gave him an occasional fitless night, this idea of fighting another man's fight, he threw his support behind the Taylors all the same. And in Texas the support of John Wesley Hardin was a matter of no small consequence. His name was a household word, and unlike most outlaws, it was common knowledge that he had never resorted to murder or backshooting. This, coupled with the fact that he had killed more than twenty men, made him a formidable enemy.

The Sutton forces treated him with kid gloves, and since the day he rode into Dewitt County, they had never once attempted to brace him. Quite the contrary, Sheriff Helms had made several overtures of peace, suggesting that he remain neutral in the days ahead. Wes turned him down out of hand, and calmly went on about his business. He rode where he pleased, when he pleased, and it was plain he feared neither Sutton nor the Vigilance Committee.

Shortly after joining the Taylors, Wes had entered the cattle business. He had a family to support, and with the cow market at its peak, he saw a chance for quick gain. But he quickly discarded the idea of buying land and making another stab at ranching. The year on the Brazos had taught him much about the vagaries of life; he meant to wait and watch for a while before sinking roots. Instead of a rancher, he became a cattle buyer. After hiring a crew, he traveled around the county contracting ahead of season with various outfits. He offered the ranchers a fair price, thereby assuming the risk that the market would hold and he could later turn a profit. The cattlemen took to the idea readily, for it gave them a fair price on part of their herd and acted as a hedge against fluctuations in the summer market.

With spring, Wes and his crew began trailing small

bunches to holding pens at Cuero, the nearest railhead. From
there the cows were freighted to Indianola, the closest port
on the Gulf Coast, and then shipped to a contractor in New
Orleans. As he'd suspected from the start, the venture turned
a neat profit. The cattle market held strong throughout early
April and it appeared he had drummed together a thriving
little business. Though he was a speculator of sorts, the hazards entailed never bothered him. Life itself was a gamble,
with shorter odds than poker or faro or chuck-a-luck, and
cattle speculation seemed tame by comparison.

Some ten days after Bill Taylor shot William Sutton, Wes
and his crew drove a small herd into Cuero. This was the
last batch needed to round out a trainload; by late afternoon
the holding pens were empty and the cattle cars packed with
bawling cows. It was hot, dusty work—longhorns were contrary beasts and had an inborn fear of being hazed up loading
chutes—the men were soaked with sweat and grime when
the last door clanged shut. Wes felt parched, and he could
almost taste the foam on a cool beer, but he still had affairs
to conduct at the bank. After debating pleasure before business for a moment, he sent the crew on to a saloon and
headed uptown toward the square.

Cuero was the county seat, and as with most country
towns, the courthouse had been built in the center of the
square. Wes cut across the courthouse lawn to the bank, and
withdrew enough money to pay his crew and meet current
expenses. Stuffing the money in his pocket, he retraced his
steps and entered a saloon on the southwest corner of the
square. While he gave it little thought at the moment, he was
aware that Sheriff Jack Helms had watched him the entire
time from a downstairs window in the courthouse. He considered Helms a four-flusher, all brag and no show, and
promptly put the incident from his mind.

He found the crew bellied up to the bar and spent a few
minutes settling accounts. Then he ordered a large schooner
of beer and downed half of it in a long, thirsty gulp. He was
still wiping foam off his mustache when the door swung
open and Jed Morgan, a deputy sheriff, stepped inside. Nor-

mally he wouldn't have given the man a second glance. But
coming on the heels of the Sutton shooting and the sheriff's
undisguised interest in his movements, he was the least bit
leery. Something about the man's bearing alerted him as
well, a furtive look, as if a quick appraisal had just been
made. He straightened and shifted the schooner to his left
hand, watching Morgan from the corner of his eye.

The lawman walked to the bar, ordered a drink, and
knocked it back in a single motion. Then he stood there a
few moments, as if deliberating something, and beads of
sweat popped out on his forehead. Finally he drew a deep
breath and glanced over at the bartender.

"Guess you heard we're gonna clean them Taylors out."

Everybody in the saloon stopped talking at once. The barkeep went rigid, slewing a sideways look at Wes, but the
young outlaw merely studied his beer with wooden detach-
ment. Swallowing hard, as though he had something lodged
in his throat, the deputy tried again.

"Them Taylors are a bunch of backshootin' sneaks anyway. We're just gonna give 'em what they deserve."

Wes smiled and carefully set his glass on the bar. "Morgan, you're so full of crap your breath stinks."

Silence in the room deepened to a turgid stillness, and the
lawman flushed cherry red. Then he flicked a glance toward
the back of the saloon and his backbone seemed to stiffen.
He stepped away from the bar, hand on his gun, and turned.

"Hardin, you're under arrest."

Wes waited for the deputy's gun hand to move, then threw
himself away from the bar, drawing and firing as he dropped
to the floor. The slug caught Morgan just over the shirt
pocket, above his badge, and he cartwheeled backward in a
nerveless dance. Wes had hesitated only long enough to snap
off the shot and then rolled sideways across the floor. Now
he reversed himself, rolling backward a full turn, and came
up on one elbow facing the rear of the saloon. A rifle barrel
was suddenly withdrawn from outside and the back door
slammed shut. He drilled two shots through the door, knowing it was wasted lead. The bushwhacker was off and running

by now, but he wouldn't forget the splintering whine behind him an instant after he turned away. Next time he would be even shakier when he tried to backshoot somebody.

Uncoiling, Wes climbed to his feet and holstered the Navy. He slapped dust from his shirt and let his gaze drift around the room. Everybody but his own men suddenly got busy with their drinks, apparently unwilling to meet his stare. After a while his pale eyes settled on the bartender and he smiled.

"I got an idea the sheriff won't show up till I'm gone, so give him a message. Tell him I said it didn't work." The barkeep bobbed his head and Wes turned away. But as he neared the door, he stopped and looked back. "One more thing. Tell him if he comes lookin' for the Taylors I'll personally send him home in a box."

The young outlaw jerked his chin at the crew and strode from the saloon. The men trooped along behind him and outside they found a crowd gathered in the street, drawn by the sound of gunshots. Wes ignored them and walked toward the hitchrail. Their morbid curiosity irked him somehow, but as he stepped aboard the grullo, it came to him that they would soon have plenty to talk about.

Plainly the Vigilance Committee was set to raid the Taylors. Otherwise Morgan wouldn't have spouted off so strongly. But Helms had made a big mistake. In trying to weed out one fast gun, he hadn't just tipped his hand. He had pushed an outsider off the fence and made himself another enemy. For there was no longer any lingering doubt. Not so much as an iota.

All of a sudden it had become a very personal fight.

2

"Boys, I reckon it's time we faced facts."

Billy Taylor was tall and lean, with a ruddy face, eyes deeply socketed between high cheekbones and a big hawk-like nose. As he spoke a fiery glint appeared in his eyes, and his head swung from side to side, studying faces around the room. Upon hearing of Deputy Morgan's death he had acted at once, calling the clan to a council of war in his parlor shortly after supper. Men were jammed up back to the door, filling every chair and lining the walls in a crush of hard, sweaty bodies.

Down front were Taylor's three younger brothers, Jim, John, and Scrap. Seated next to them was Wes, and beside him, Jeff Hardin, a distant cousin who had drifted into Dewitt County some months back. Off to one side were the Dixon brothers, Bud and Tom, and with them, Bill Cunningham. Standing behind the settee were the Andersons, James and Ham, and their brother-in-law, Jim Milligan. All told some twenty men had squeezed into the crackerbox room, and while a few were missing, they comprised the Taylor clan. Whether by blood or marriage, they were related in some way, and south of the Guadalupe their word was law. Or had been, at least, in years past.

Now, crowded together in a stifling parlor, their numbers seemed pitifully inadequate for the task that lay ahead. Already they had lost nearly ten men, and not one among them doubted that the toll would mount higher before the fight was done. Yet, they came and they would fight, knowing in advance that some were marked for death. They had no choice, really. It had come down to sink or swim. And whichever way it fell, they would go together. Old Pitkin Taylor had drilled that into their heads relentlessly over the years, and they had come to accept it as gospel truth. Divided, they were nothing. But if they stood together, strong in their solidarity, the family could have anything it wanted. Dewitt County, most especially.

At last, Billy Taylor finished his inspection. Since assuming the reins, this was the first time he had called them to council, and they waited patiently to hear him speak. He was the patriarch's eldest, the rightful leader of the Taylor clan, but they would follow him only so long as he won. Though unspoken, every man in the room knew it, and perhaps no one sensed it so strongly as Billy Taylor himself. He drew a deep breath and let it out between his teeth. Then, choosing his words carefully, he began to talk.

"Seems to me Wes Hardin is right. The fat's in the fire. Now, I don't know whether Sutton is pullin' the strings from his sickbed or whether Jack Helms just decided to go whole hog. But one thing is plumb certain. They mean to burn us down and run us out of the county. And they're not gonna be long in makin' their play."

Ham Anderson screwed up his face in a tight frown. "Billy, I'm not throwin' rocks, but it seems like somebody ought to say it before this goes too far. If Wes hadn't killed Jed Morgan we might've just sat tight and weathered this out. Fact is, there's some of us here that still thinks that way. If you was to go have a talk with Helms and—"

The young outlaw started out of his chair but Taylor motioned him down. This was the first challenge to his leadership, and if it was to be the last, Taylor had to handle it in his own way. "Ham, I'll slap the puddin' out of the next man that says anything against Wes. This fight's been buildin' for a long time, and him killin' Morgan don't mean a hill of beans. Helms was already set to raid us and the only choice we got is how we're gonna put a knot in his tail."

"Well, I'll tell you one thing," Jim Milligan snorted, "you shore sound like your daddy. If ol' Pitkin had been willin' to bend a little a few years back we wouldn't be in this fix now. The Sutton bunch is rared up and ready to fight 'cause that's the only way they can get us to budge a notch."

"Now, Jim, you and the Andersons listen to me real close." Taylor barked the words out, squinting hard at the three men. "My daddy fought to get this county and he kept it for better'n twenty years 'cause he was willin' to bust heads anytime somebody looked at him cross-eyed. And that's the only way we're gonna keep what we got left. Fight for it. Talkin' to the likes of Sutton and Helms won't get you nothin' but a quick buryin'. That's the way I see it and that's the way I'm gonna run things. Only one man can call the shots, and unless you fellas vote me out, I'm him. Savvy?"

Milligan and the Anderson brothers shifted uncomfortably, darting sheepish glances at one another. The other men remained silent for the most part, but a few nodded their heads in agreement, and everybody seemed satisfied with the way Taylor had handled the situation. After allowing several moments to pass, just to drive the point home, Taylor took up where he'd left off.

"Like I said, it's not a matter of whether we fight. The only question is how we go about it. I got some ideas of my own but I'd like to hear what you boys've got to say. Floor's open to anybody that wants to talk."

Ham Anderson stood up. Taylor stared at him a moment then nodded. Anderson glanced around at the group and it was clear from their expressions that they expected more talk of peace.

"If we've got to fight, then I say let's go about it the right way. I served under some good officers in the war, and they all stuck pretty close to the same rule of thumb. Protect what you got before you go after more. Where we're concerned, that means we got women and kids and horses and cattle to think about. Some way or other, we got to come up with a plan to protect that before we get itchy and go lookin' for a fight."

Bud Dixon grunted. "What the sam hill you talkin' about, Ham? Fortin' up or some such thing?"

"Be sort of hard to fort up all them cows," Anderson replied quietly. "No, what I'm talkin' about is sentries, or scouts. Whatever you want to call 'em. Patrols of some kind to give us warnin' whenever Helms and his bunch head our way."

"Great Gawd Jesus!" Tom Dixon crowed. "You got any idea what that'd mean? Hell, there's better'n thirty miles of river where they can cross anywhere it suits their fancy."

"Hold off a minute." Taylor threw up his hands as several men began talking at once. "Seems to me Ham's got a point. I grant you they could come through lots of places, but there's only three or four good fords. And that's where they'll most likely come through. If we had scouts watchin'

those spots, we'd get warnin' enough to spring a little surprise on Helms.''

The men wrestled with that for a while and it was finally
decided to place Ham Anderson in charge of the scouts. If
and when the alert was sounded everybody was to gather at
the Taylor house. Some talk developed as the best way to
meet such an attack and everyone in the room suddenly
turned into a general. At last, Wes Hardin climbed to his feet
and stood watching them until an uneasy quiet settled over
the room. Then he turned and looked straight at Taylor.

''I've never fought in a war but I have come clear of a
few scrapes. Just listenin' to you fellows talk, it seems to me
we're barkin' up the wrong tree. Near as I recollect, fights
are generally won by the man that gets in the first lick and
keeps stompin' till it's all done with.''

''By golly, he's right!'' Jim Taylor jumped to his feet with
a shout. The four brothers were almost indistinguishable,
alike as peas in a pod, but Jim was the youngest, and by far
the loudest. ''Don't wait for 'em. Go get 'em!''

''My sentiments persactly,'' Bud Dixon chimed in from
over against the wall. ''I'd a heap sooner carry a fight to a
man than have him bring it to me.''

''Hogwash,'' Jim Milligan growled. ''At best we got
maybe thirty men. We'll be facin' twice that many, easy.''

''All the more reason to hit 'em first,'' Wes observed.
''Fast and hard. Clobber 'em good and get the hell out. Couple of shots like that and they'll call it quits.''

James Anderson cut the others off short. ''Wes, I gotta
say I think you're wrong. I served in the war, too, and believe
me, it was just plain suicide to try attackin' when you was
outnumbered two to one. Take my word for it, we'd get
chopped up in little pieces.''

''Yeah, but we're not fightin' a war,'' Wes countered.
''We've got our backs to the wall, and like as not, there'll
only be one battle. If we wait and let 'em come after us,
they'll gobble us up a piece at a time.''

Taylor broke in. ''Boys, you could hash that around all
night. Trouble is, you're overlookin' the big problem.

There's no way we can just haul off and attack the law. Not without stirrin' up a hornet's nest in Austin. We've got to let them start it and then figure out some way to finish it.'' He paused and looked around the room. ''Suppose we leave it at this. Until somethin' changes, we'll just sit tight and let them make the first move. After that it'll be dog eat dog and nobody'll be able to say we took the law in our own hands.''

Not everyone in the parlor was satisfied, but they were forced to admit that he had a point. None of them wanted the county overrun with State Police, and it could happen if they struck the first blow. A short while later the meeting was adjourned. Taylor had assigned men to Ham Anderson's scouts, and ticked off others to sound the alarm in case of attack. From there on out, he concluded, they would just have to play it by ear. Wes wasn't overly impressed with the tactics; he remained convinced that they were borrowing trouble by sitting back and waiting. But as he filed out the door it suddenly came to him that he should have kept his lip buttoned.

It was their fight. And they had a right to lose it any way that suited them.

3

Pitkin Taylor had built the main house to last. It was a rambling affair of log and stone, constructed to withstand the ravages of time and the elements. For a site he had selected a majestic grove of live oaks on a slight knoll, commanding a view of the shimmering prairie in all directions. The house had weathered well, surviving Indian raids, blue howlers hurtling down out of the wintry north, and coastal squalls that sometimes swept far inland. As the years passed, and his sons married, the old man built other houses nearby. Wedding presents, he called the smaller houses, though everyone was painfully aware that he wanted only to keep his sons close at hand. Or under thumb, according to men like the Andersons and Jim Milligan, who sometimes thought for themselves.

Still, if Pitkin Taylor had been a tyrant of sorts, there was never any question of his generosity. Three sons married—Billy, John, and Scrap—and three houses complete with furnishings. Only Jim, spoiled and unruly, remained in the big house. But the grove of stately oaks was not merely for living. It was also a place of work. As outbuildings sprouted around the base of the knoll, it became a complex of rough-hewn structures resembling a small town. There were corrals and barns, several bunkhouses, and a scattering of pens and sheds thrown up as the need arose. From a distance it looked like a handful of dice sprinkled haphazardly across the earth, but up close there was something foreboding about it, as if it had need of nothing save itself, and those who rode in unasked did so at their own risk. And in truth, except for Indians, the Taylor compound had never been threatened by an outside force. Until that night the bushwhackers left Pitkin Taylor riddled with buckshot.

Now, the Taylor ranch was inviolate no longer. Men of greed and ambition were even then mounting an attack. What Pitkin Taylor had built over a lifetime, a legacy to his sons and their sons after them, was in danger of being destroyed in a single night. There was a somber air to the compound. Lamps had been turned low and the laughter of children was curiously missing. Men stuck close to home, near their families, and the bunkhouses were unusually quiet. Oddly, not a single dog had barked since sundown, as if in some brutish way they had been spooked by fears beyond their ken. For fear was thick, like a noxious mist, and those men who slept at all slept lightly, with their guns never far out of reach.

Like the others, Wes felt the growing tension and he was in a skittish mood. Waiting curried him the wrong way, and given a choice, he would have ridden on the Sutton forces that very night. Still, the decision had been made and he was willing to follow Taylor's lead. For the moment anyway. If a hitch developed then he'd shuffle and see about dealing new cards all around.

Seated on a porch step, gazing out over the compound, it occurred to him that he owed Taylor the chance to make his own mistakes. The house he and Jane were living in had been Taylor's, and they had it to themselves because of his openhanded nature. After the old man's murder Taylor had moved into the big house, and despite grumbling from certain quarters, he had given the Hardins his own home. Which suited Wes just fine. There was too much commotion in the big house, people coming and going at all hours, and he much preferred to be off by himself. Besides, what with Jane expecting again, it had worked out better all the wayaround. She got a little snippy when she was in a family way, and had never felt at ease with the gang of women constantly swarming through the big house.

Overhead a shooting star flashed through the sky and he watched it fizzle out in a silvery streamer. Out of nowhere came the thought that people played out their lives in much the same manner. A brief spurt, snatching at the goodies and hollering to beat the band, and then it was all over. They hadn't accomplished much—except to whelp a bunch of kids and make fools of themselves—and when it was done with there wasn't much left to show. Just a few teary-eyed mourners and a headstone with some nitwit inscription a man wouldn't rightly have picked out for himself. The hell of it was, most folks didn't know any better. They went out thinking they'd really left their mark on things. In spades.

Suddenly it struck him that he was being mighty goddamn pompous. Anybody with a half brain would see that he hadn't made any great shakes of his own life. He had a wife and a family, which took care of the whelping department. Then he had a good horse and a few thousand dollars in gold. Other than that, he didn't have much more than the clothes on his back. Not a square foot of land or a house or the first stick of furniture. Matter of fact, the roof over his head had been built by someone else and he was sleeping in another man's bed. Which sort of put him to rowing the same boat as the nincompoops he'd just been sneering at.

He grunted sardonically and a mocking chuckle rumbled

up out of his gut. Yessir. He had a lot of room to talk.

"Must be awfully funny."

Wes craned around and saw Jane standing in the doorway. The lamp inside silhouetted her figure, outlining the barest hint of what he hoped would be a son. She was some months away from being ungainly, but the thought of what was to come had put her out of sorts lately. Not unlike most attractive women, she disliked losing her looks, and absolutely despised waddling around like a clumsy she-bear. Still, she'd wanted lots of babies, and she damn sure couldn't blame him for being accommodating. Besides which, he kind of liked it when her belly was big and round and her face filled out. Gave her a nice rosy glow, all flushed and apple-ripe, that she didn't have other times.

"Lady, don't you know it's not polite to eavesdrop?"

"Not on your husband, it's not." She came out of the house and sat beside him on the step. "I even listen when you talk in your sleep."

"Judas Priest! Just ain't no privacy anywhere, is there?"

"Well, how else is a woman to learn? You big hairy men walk around like you had lockjaw all the time. Besides, I find out some very interesting things that way."

"Yeah. Like what for instance?"

She smiled and flashed a mischievous look. "I'll never tell. But you don't have as many secrets as you thought you did. That's for sure."

Her light mood both surprised and pleased him. The last couple of weeks she had been cross and mighty hard to live with. He put an arm around her shoulders and drew her closer. "Woman, why don't you quit walkin' around in a man's mind? Like I said, it's not polite."

"You still haven't told me."

"Told you what?"

"What tickled your funny bone a minute ago."

"That? Wasn't nothin' at all. Just ruminatin'."

"Wes Hardin, don't you dare pull that lockjaw stunt again. Ruminating about what?"

His tailbone suddenly felt as though it was spiked to the

porch, and he found himself faltering for words. "Awww, hell, honey, it wasn't nothin'. Honest. I was just thinkin' about people and how most of 'em sort of piddle around trying to make something of their lives."

"And?"

"What do you mean *and?*" he demanded. "That's what I was thinkin'."

"There you go again. Shutting me out." She arched her head back like a schoolmarm and gave him a quizzical little frown. "There was more to it than that. Now, be truthful. Wasn't there?"

Sometimes he thought he never would understand women. Especially when they were in a family way. Seemed as if their brains took curiosity, then multiplied it by nosiness, and somehow came up with a wife's right to know. It left a man damn little privacy, and even less peace of mind.

"Well, if it's that al'fired important, I was thinkin' that most folks go to their graves never havin' done half of what they set out to do. Then I chewed that over a little more, and much as I hate to admit it, I guess I couldn't say much better of myself."

"What a horrible thing to say!" She was positively indignant. "You've done lots of worthwhile things."

"Yeah? Name me a couple."

"Why, you've built a ranch—"

"And lost it."

"—and made a pile of money."

"And spent it."

"Oh, Wes, stop mocking me. Good Lord, you're barely twenty. You've already accomplished more than some men twice your age."

"Sure have. Livin' off my kin. Can't even give my family a house of their own. Just a regular ball of fire."

Jane caught her breath, then snuggled closer and buried her head against his chest. "Sugar, it scares me when you talk like that. It's not like you. And I'm scared enough already without having a stranger in my bed."

His hand came up, stroking her hair, and he gave her a

gentle squeeze. "What kind of foolishness is that? There's nothin' for you to be scared about."

"It isn't either foolishness. And you know it very well."

"You're talkin' riddles. What d'you mean?"

"I mean the man you killed today. And all those other men. There's just no end to it."

"Janey, lemme tell you somethin'." His words were soft, almost inaudible, so quiet she had to strain to hear. "I never in my life killed a man that wasn't tryin' to kill me. Don't you know that?"

She sniffed and poked him in the ribs. "Wes Hardin, you're thick as a rock sometimes. That's what I'm talking about. All these men trying to kill you. The State Police and now you've taken sides in the Taylors' fight. Where does it stop?"

"Gawd A'mighty!" He'd finally caught the clue. "You're not worryin' yourself silly thinkin' somebody's gonna put me under?"

"Of course I am, you big ninny!" She jerked away from him. "I have a baby in my arms and another one on the way and half the men in Texas want to kill my husband. And you have the gall to sit there and tell me I shouldn't worry. You're—oh, damn! I don't know what you are."

"Quit sputterin' and listen a minute." He pulled her back into his arms and hugged her tight. "There's nothin' gonna happen to me. That's a natural-born fact, and you can bank on it."

She turned her head up, entreating him with her eyes. "Promise?"

"Take my word on it." His voice went husky and something odd happened to his face. "The man ain't been born that can punch my ticket."

"God, I pray not, Wes. Every night I pray that."

"Then you can quit worryin'. Looks like somebody's listenin'."

High overhead a star fell from the heavens and rocketed earthward. Then the sky settled once more into velvety darkness and the winking stars were like a zillion eyes staring

down at them. Drawing her close, Wes closed his mind to
all but the inky sky and the woman and the little cameo doll
that slept inside.

It was enough. Let tomorrow worry about itself.

4

A scout rode in on a lathered horse early the next evening.
The Sutton forces, some fifty men strong and led by Sheriff
Helms, were headed toward the Guadalupe. Under stiff questioning by Taylor, it came out that Ham Anderson had sent
men snooping around Cuero. Toward sundown the vigilantes
began gathering in front of the courthouse and there was little
doubt as to their purpose. The scouts raced back to the river,
informing Anderson, and he in turn sent riders fanning out
across the southern half of the county to sound the alarm.
However much he resented Anderson's casual disregard of
orders, Billy Taylor could hardly fault the man. It was a
shrewd move, and because of it, the Taylor faction had
gained a couple of precious hours.

Shortly after nightfall the clan began pouring into the compound, and by full dark close to thirty men were formed in
a loose knot before the steps of the big house. They were
armed to the teeth, many of them carrying the new repeating
Winchesters, and spoiling for a fight. Young Hardin still favored the shotgun for hunting men, but he was packing a .45
Colt Peacemaker. Just on a whim he'd bought the pistol earlier in the year in Indianola. It was the latest model, firing
cartridges instead of cap and ball. Yet, for all its advantages,
he had never used it. The battered old Navy rested squarely
on his right hip, and the Peacemaker was stuck in the waistband of his trousers. He'd brought it along as something in
reserve, and from all reports, he had picked the right night.
It promised to be a fight where a backup gun would come
in mighty handy indeed.

The men were talking in low tones, speculating on what
they faced, when Billy Taylor walked out of the house. He

stopped at the edge of the porch, grim-faced and watchful, waiting for the murmured conversation to slack off. After the men fell silent, he waited a moment longer, then cleared his throat.

"Boys, I guess you've all heard what's headed our way. Last time we met I told you I had some ideas of my own about how to handle this. I've give it lots of thought since then and I'm still convinced it'll work."

He paused and gestured out over the compound. "It stands to reason they'll hit this place first. If they burn us out here then the waltz is pretty well done with. But there's one thing they didn't count on. This whole hill is ringed with buildings of one sort or another. That makes it real easy to defend. I figure if we put men in ever' building, and give 'em a hot welcome, they'll play holy hell bustin' through. After a couple of blasts right up their nose, I got an idea they'll take off like scalded dogs."

There was a moment of silence while the men digested that. The porch lantern cast a dim glow out over their ranks, and it was apparent that many of them were having a hard time swallowing Taylor's plan. Considerable grumbling broke out, and several men muttered outright disagreement. Finally, James Anderson stepped forward.

"Bill, I hate to be the one to say it, but I don't think your idea'll work. First off, we got too few men as it is. You stick 'em off in them buildin's and we're gonna be spread mighty thin. If Helms was to keep his bunch all together, and charge one spot, they'd bust through this defense of yours like a hot knife cuttin' through butter. Then they would be behind us and we'd find ourselves in some fix."

A hoarse murmur swept back over the men, but Anderson motioned for quiet. "Now, lemme finish, then anybody that wants can have his say. There's another thing Helms could do and that worries me even more. Bill, just suppose we greet 'em with lead like you was talkin' about and they back off. You think they're gonna call it quits and ride on back to town? Not by a damn sight they won't. They'll just ride off and put the torch to ever' house south of here. And we'll be

sittin' on our butts back here watchin' 'em do it. Now I grant
you, that'd save this place. But it'd sure play hob with the
rest of us. We'd get home and not find nothin' but a pile of
ashes.''

Before anyone could get his jaws unlocked, Wes Hardin
stepped out of the crowd. He walked to the bottom step and
looked up at Taylor. ''I owe you a lot, Billy, and I don't like
causin' you grief. But I agree with Anderson. Only for a
different reason. It just don't make sense to fight that bunch
where we got women and kids to worry about. If they ever
busted through and got up here our families wouldn't stand
a chance. I'm still of the notion that we ought to ride out
and meet 'em somewhere. Ambush 'em maybe. Like I said
before, take the fight to them and hurt 'em bad.''

A moment elapsed while the two men stared at one another, and then the young outlaw's gaze went hard as flint.
''You know I'm not a quitter, and I'm willin' to oblige any
man here that thinks different. But I won't take a chance on
my wife and baby gettin' caught slambang in the middle of
a shoot-out. If you can't see your way clear to fightin' Helms
somewhere else, then I don't have no choice but to pull out.
I'd sooner back your play and have this thing done with, but
that's up to you.''

Bud Dixon and Jim Taylor stepped forward flanking Wes.
Dixon pulled himself up straight and squared his shoulders.
''Billy, none of us wants to go against you, but it 'pears to
me Wes is talkin' sense.''

Young Taylor bobbed his chin. ''And Jim Anderson, too.
You're my brother, and I wouldn't cross you for the world,
but it ain't fair to ask these fellas to protect our place while
their own gets burned to the ground.''

Billy Taylor's ruddy face paled and little knots bunched
tight at the back of his jaws. He stood there for a long time,
staring at the four men who had stepped forward, and the
still night seemed charged with tension. At last, he let go a
deep breath and looked out across the waiting crowd.

''What do the rest of you boys say? You of the same
mind?''

Aside from the other Taylor brothers, none of the men could meet his gaze. They ducked their heads, hawked and spat, and looked everywhere except at the tall man on the porch. Quite plainly, they had swung over to Anderson and Hardin. But they couldn't bring themselves to tell Pitkin Taylor's eldest son that he'd already been outvoted.

After a while Taylor shrugged and made a chopping motion with his hand. "That's answer enough, I guess. Put it to a vote and pick yourselves a new ramrod. But don't fiddle around. We stand here runnin' our gums much longer and Helms will be lookin' down our throats."

The men all started yammering at once, but Wes suddenly jumped up on the steps and faced them. "Hold your horses! Just slow down a minute and listen." Taken by surprise, they fell silent and stared back at him in mild puzzlement. "Now I'm sort of a Johnny-come-lately around here. And I reckon most of you figure it's not up to me to commence preachin', but I'm gonna speak my piece just the same, and I'll make it sweet and short. Any man that can admit he's wrong has got lots of sand. Leastways he does in my book. Seems to me Billy is the best man to lead this outfit, and to my way of thinkin', he deserves the chance. Hell's bells, how's a man gonna get to be a general if he don't get his feet wet? And besides, now that I take a closer look, I don't see no Stonewall Jacksons among you, anyhow."

The lantern sputtered and the men stood there gawking at him for a couple of seconds, baffled that he had switched horses in midstream. Wes was a little confused himself, but his feeling was genuine. He somehow sensed that Taylor had the stuff to make a good leader if given the chance to prove himself. All of a sudden someone at the back of the crowd let go with a snorty chuckle.

"Looks to me like there ain't no Robert E. Lees here, neither."

Everyone broke up laughing and the tension drained away, restoring their spirit of solidarity. Soon they got down to the real problem—where to jump the vigilantes—and began batting various schemes back and forth. All of them knew the countryside in the way of men born to the land, and a lively discussion evolved as the best place for an ambush. Then, quite unexpectedly, Ham Anderson rode in and stepped down from a jaded horse. His message needed no elaboration. Helms and the vigilantes were headed south along the Yorkstown Road.

And that put an end to the debate. Every man in the group was thinking of the same spot. The perfect place to throw a surprise party.

Tomlinson Creek.

Less than an hour later Billy Taylor had his men spread out along the south bank of the creek. The night was dark, with ghostly patches where starlight filtered down through the trees. Taylor had chosen well, selecting a site that afforded both cover and a clear field of fire. The men were hidden behind massive cottonwoods, far back in the shadows; he had positioned them on angles, two men to a tree, so that on signal their fire could be directed to the exact center of the creek. Across the stream there was a small clearing in the woods, where the road sloped down to the ford. Both the stream and the clearing shimmered faintly in a soft haze of starglow. Any movement toward the crossing, could be seen. And a man on horseback—or a whole gaggle of horsemen— would stick out like a parade of elephants.

Wes had been assigned a choice spot. Beside the road, not ten yards from the ford, where his shotgun would do the most damage. He stood with his back to a tree, loose and easy, with just the slightest tingle dancing over his nerve ends. It was a feeling he knew well, an old companion. A sign that he was alert and ready and keyed to just the right pitch. On the other side of the tree, Jim Taylor was squatted down on one knee, rifle butt resting against his hip. Directly across the road, screened by a cottonwood, Billy Taylor had his eyes glued on the dimly lighted clearing.

Nothing moved and the sounds of the night went undisturbed.

Their wait was prolonged only a short while. Hoofbeats
drifted in on a faint breeze and then the earth quivered under
the thudding rhythmic pace of animals moving at a steady
gait. One moment the clearing stood empty, a silvery blur,
and in the next a solid wedge of horsemen materialized out
of the night. They came on at a fast walk, unsuspecting and
careless, bunching up where the road sloped off to meet the
creek. When they hit the center of the ford, water splashing
up around their stirrups, Billy Taylor edged out from behind
the tree.

"Surrender or get your heads blowed off!"

The lead rider reached for his gun and Wes blasted him
out of the saddle. Others screamed and clutched at wounds
as the double load of buckshot whistled through their ranks
like snarling hornets. Their horses went berserk, wheeling
and bucking, as the night came alive with the orangy splat
of rifle fire. Wes flung the shotgun aside and jerked his Navy,
amazed that some of the vigilantes were actually firing back.
He thumbed off three shots in a blinding roar, and then froze
as the Navy snapped on a dead cap. Just for a moment he
couldn't believe it—the Navy had misfired—but his stupor
lasted only an instant. He dropped the gun, cursing savagely,
and pulled the Peacemaker from his waistband. As he earred
the hammer back, he saw another rider topple over and
splash headlong into the creek. Then, maddened with fear,
the vigilantes somehow got themselves unscrambled and
spurred back the way they had come.

Stepping clear of the tree, Wes emptied the Peacemaker
in a spitting, staccato bark. Around him, the drum of rifle
fire increased at a steady beat, but so far as he could tell
none of the riders were hit. Suddenly, like specters on
horseback, the vigilantes simply vanished into the woods and
were gone. An eerie silence settled over the clearing, and
along the tree line a dense cloud of gunsmoke hung still for
a moment, then scudded away on the breeze. Men appeared
all up and down the creek bank, staring quietly across the
stream. It had happened so fast—the rout was so complete—

that they could scarcely believe it. Words seemed inadequate, somehow wanting, and so they said nothing. They just stared, dazed and vastly relieved.

But Wes Hardin shared none of their wonder. Nor did he feel any sense of relief. In fact, he was angry, and just the least bit unnerved. An old friend had betrayed him. And under less favorable circumstances might easily have gotten him killed. Still cursing, he gave the Navy a sharp kick and watched as it hit the creek and sank to the bottom.

Then he hefted the Peacemaker, smiling, and calmly reloaded it.

5

The fight at Tomlinson Creek was hardly decisive. Helms's vigilantes left behind two dead, and according to word from town, several had been wounded. Curiously enough, most of the casualties were suffering from buckshot wounds, but the *Cuero Eagle* reported that none of them were expected to die. Yet, in some small way, it was a victory for the Taylor clan. They had driven the Sutton forces from their land, and not one of their own had received so much as a scratch.

There was considerable rejoicing among the womenfolk, and some talk that the victory might at last put an end to the feud. However much they wished it were true, wiser heads knew different. William Sutton, though still confined to bed, was not a man so easily dissuaded. Ham Anderson observed that the vigilantes were like a rattler. It remained dangerous until somebody cut off its head. And the feud would end when Sutton was dead. Not before.

But if their victory had a hollow ring, the Taylors at least had themselves a ring-tailed bravo to admire. Wes Hardin not only had real grit, he also had something between his ears besides mush. From the beginning, he alone had counseled the wisdom of an ambush, and while it hadn't been a spectacular success, it had damn well put the vigilantes to rout. Over and above that, tales began circulating about his deadliness in a fight. Even in the heat of battle men had seen him step from behind the tree, opening the fight with a double load of buckshot and then coolly emptying his revolvers into the massed riders. And all the time slugs whistling about his head and thunking into the tree at his shoulder. There were no longer any skeptics among them. Everything they had heard about young Hardin—the twenty-odd men he'd killed and his ice-cold nerves—was the straight goods. He was a slick article, sharp as a tack and deadly to boot, and they took immense pride in knowing he was on their side.

For his part, West hardly seemed to notice the change in attitude, the way everybody had commenced buttering up to him. Though he accepted their version of the fight, he had no recollection whatever of slugs chunking around him. He remembered firing and cursing the Navy and the heavy rattle of rifle fire. And in looking back, he remembered that those rifles, some thirty strong, had killed only one man. It was a chilling thought, and one he wouldn't soon forget. If a man wanted to go on breathing, particularly in a shoot-out at night, he was well advised to keep a shotgun close to hand.

All in all, it came as no surprise when Wes announced two days after the fight that he was going into town. Nor was anyone overly shocked that he meant to go alone. It merely confirmed what they had seen on the banks of Tomlinson Creek. The youngster had more guts than a three-legged bulldog.

Billy Taylor tried to argue him out of it and Jane pitched a fit that could be heard clear across the compound. But his mind was set and he wouldn't budge. He had business to conduct and the likes of Jack Helms was no reason to avoid Cuero. Matter of fact, he observed dryly, it was all the more reason to ride into town bold as brass. If backshooters ever thought they'd run a sandy on a man, there'd be no end to it. Better to let them know right from the start. Anybody who tried any monkey business was fair game. And deserved whatever he got.

Down the road a piece, Wes heard hoofbeats coming on

fast and reined up. Jim Taylor appeared a couple of moments later, fogging it at a dead gallop, and slid his horse to a halt. He had a big, toothy grin plastered across his face and looked as though he had just swallowed a canary.

"Thought I'd ride along with you." His eyes glittered with excitement. "Few things I need from town."

"Yeah?" Wes gave him a slow up-and-down scrutiny. "What's that?"

The question flustered him, but Taylor dismissed it with an idle gesture. "Oh, y'know. Tobacco and rollin' papers and stuff like that. Just little things."

"Stuff that just wouldn't wait, huh?" Wes studied him a moment longer, then smiled. "Billy know you tagged along after me?"

"Aw, hell's fire, Wes, I'm full-growed. Billy don't have to wipe my nose."

Which was true, after a fashion. Though three years younger than his cousin, Jim Taylor pulled his own weight and did a man's work. Thinking back to earlier days, Wes had to admit that the boy had a point. Every man was entitled to get his nose bloodied whichever way it suited him. And if he needed permission, then he wasn't big enough to try.

Wes reined the grullo north, toward town. "Glad to have the company."

Taylor brightened and pulled alongside. "Think there'll be any trouble in town?"

"Not unless somebody else starts it. Why, you lookin' for trouble?"

"Not me! Just askin', that's all." The boy's reply was overdrawn, a little too guileless. They rode in silence for a while, though it was obvious Taylor had something on his mind. Finally, clearing his throat, he worked up the nerve to spit it out. "Y'know, I got a confession to make. The fight at the creek the other night? That was the first time in my whole life I fired a gun at another man."

Wes gave him a sidewise glance, holding back hard on a smile. "That a fact? Well, you could've fooled me. I thought you did real good."

"You did—honest?" Taylor perked up and his chest swelled a couple of notches. "Cripes, I didn't even know you was watchin'. Tell you the truth, I was so scared I don't hardly recollect much of anything."

"Nothin' wrong with that. Plumb natural."

"Aw, c'mon. You wasn't scared. Not the way you was slingin' lead."

Wes smiled cryptically. "You think Ham Anderson's right? That this thing won't end till Sutton's been planted?"

Taylor was young but he was no fool. He took the hint, and set aside the string of questions he wanted to ask about gunfighting. "Can't see how it'd end any other way. Leastways, according' to Billy, Helms don't hardly take a leak less he checks with Sutton first."

"Yeah, that was sort of the impression I got. Too bad Billy didn't finish him off when he had the chance."

"Cripes, Wes, Sutton was down and bleedin' like a stuck pig. Billy couldn't hardly shoot him again. I mean—well, hell—it'd almost be like murder."

"Hadn't Sutton tried to shoot him?"

"Sure he did. Billy cussed him out so bad he had to draw."

Wes stared straight ahead, revealing nothing. "All the more reason Billy should have finished him. If there's cause to shoot a man, then there's cause to kill him. However it's gotta be done. Leave him alive and you wind up lookin' over your shoulder the rest of your life."

Jim Taylor started to say something but it clogged down in his wind pipe. What he'd just heard sent a chill rippling up his spine. But it made a hell of a lot of sense. So much so that only a lame brain would argue otherwise.

It was the real article. Straight from the horse's mouth.

They rode into Cuero shortly after the noon hour. The grullo needed to be shod, which was one reason for the trip to town, and their first stop was at the blacksmith's shop. Taylor wanted some odds and ends from the mercantile, so they separated at the northeast corner of the square. Crossing the street, with one eye glued on the courthouse, Wes strolled off toward the bank. Unlike the last time he was here, the sheriff wasn't gawking at him from the office window. But he had the feeling of being watched all the same. Some enterprising citizen would spot him and scurry off to inform the sheriff. Of that, he had no doubt whatever. Still, it didn't trouble him one way or the other. He had legitimate business here, and them that didn't like it could damn well lump it. Or try something stupid, if they were feeling lucky and right with God.

Whistling a cheery refrain from "The Old Rugged Cross," he entered the bank feeling cocky and light on his feet. Twenty minutes later, with the institution's flabbergasted president trailing him to the door, he walked out about thirty pounds heavier. In the money belt around his waist was five hundred dollars in gold and three letters of credit totaling nearly four thousand.

Headed back the way he'd come, his conviction remained strong that it was a wise move. And none too soon, either. The feud with Sutton had only just begun, and as any fool knew, it was always darkest before the storm. The way things were shaping up it was going to get a hell of a lot worse. And there looked to be a long dry spell before it got better. Which seemed ample reason to have his money out of the People's Bank of Cuero. Chances were better than even that he wouldn't have another opportunity anytime soon. If ever.

Feeling pretty smug, and just the least bit foxy, he set a brisk pace along the block east of the square. But as he came around the corner his cockiness went numb as an icicle and he slammed to a halt. The blacksmith shop was on the other side of the street, in the middle of the block, and in front of it stood Jack Helms. There was a gun in his hand and he had it pointed at something inside the smithy. Wes had a moment of gut-wrenching fear, a dead certainty that the lawman was only an instant away from killing Jim Taylor.

"Helms!"

The sheriff's head jerked around at the sharp cry, and he blanched, staring wide-eyed with terror at the young outlaw.

Then he spun, clumsily setting himself in a crouch, and brought the gun to bear. But his hand shook so violently that he couldn't align the sights, and he quickly brought his other hand up to steady the pistol.

Under different circumstances Wes would have laughed. It was a bumbling performance. All the same, Helms's intent was real enough, and in that he found nothing amusing. The Peacemaker was already out and cocked, and as he squeezed the trigger a gusher of red blossomed just above the sheriff's belt buckle. Aiming higher, he stitched a row of bright little dots straight up Helms's shirtfront. The big slugs jolted the lawman back a step at a time, like a puppet with his strings gone haywire. The last one caught him in the brisket, splattering bone and gore with the impact of a thunderbolt, and he went down in a jarring, head-over-heels somersault.

Jim Taylor ran from the smithy, his face wild and crazed. He halted, towering over Helms, and the body suddenly twitched in a final spasm of death. Unnerved, past caring that the man was dead, Taylor's reaction was one of sheer reflex. The gun in his hand came up and he methodically emptied it into Jack Helms's head.

Hurrying forward, Wes tried to call out, but the words wouldn't come. The act was so fundamental that its savagery spoke eloquently enough. When a man goes down make sure he stays there for keeps. And green as he was, the kid had taken the message to heart.

Jack Helms would rise no more.

CHAPTER 8

1

Peace of sorts had come to Dewitt County. Though the Sutton-Taylor feud flared sporadically the balance of '73, neither party seemed anxious for another full-scale battle. Instead they went back to bushwhacking one another, engaging in a prolonged if indecisive campaign of attrition.

With Jack Helms dead and William Sutton once again on his feet, the feud settled into a slow and deadly chess game, one in which the players painstakingly stalked each other, patiently awaiting the day that time and circumstance might sandbag the odds. Both sides hoped to whittle the other down, seemingly satisfied to destroy their enemies piecemeal rather than in a body. While there were long stretches of calm, there were also isolated spurts of violence, and those who sacrificed their lives rarely had any warning. They were simply murdered. Quickly, efficiently, and in ways that could never be traced.

A Taylor man was shot to death outside the Yorkstown general store. Another was picked off while hunting strays in a remote section of brush. One of Sutton's men was gunned down on a dark night as he made a final trip to the privy. And Sutton himself was ambushed twice. Both times his horse was shot from beneath him, and by whatever quirks that guide men's lives, he escaped injury. Curiously, there were no witnesses to the shootings. Like the three wise monkeys, the citizens of Dewitt County neither saw nor heard nor spoke. They merely watched and waited, content with the role of spectators. On the strength of this silence they bought the privilege to go on breathing. And if they kept quiet long enough, it seemed not unlikely that they would outlive the men who savaged one another in the struggle for power.

Shortly after New Year's, though, some of the more influential citizens came down off the fence. However misguided, they felt there was a genuine chance for peace. Secret meetings were arranged between William Sutton and Billy Taylor, and articles of truce were actually signed in the county courthouse. But the armistice was short-lived, if not stillborn. A spate of killings erupted and things went back to normal. Once again it became dog eat dog, and devil take the hindmost.

Throughout the winter Wes rode the countryside unmolested. Apparently the Sutton forces wanted no part of the brash young outlaw; he came and went as he pleased. Working both sides of the Guadalupe, he called on ranchers scattered across the county, again dickering ahead of time and allowing them to hedge against market fluctuations. Since spring roundup began early in southern Texas, he contracted for cattle to be delivered commencing in March and extending throughout the summer. But he rarely rode into Cuero except on urgent business, and even then, he never went alone.

Murder warrants were outstanding on Wes for killings of both Sheriff Jack Helms and Deputy Jed Morgan. Successors to the dead lawmen, appointed to fill their abruptly vacated terms, were deliberate rather than rash. They studiously avoided Wes, generally sticking close to the courthouse whenever he was in town. But as the months passed, and the old year gave way to the new, it became clear that local peace officers were the least of his worries. Nor were the State Police any longer a concern. The tides of change had swept over Austin, and in their wake was born a new and more formidable threat.

Edmund Davis, long the carpetbagger governor of Texas,

had at last been defeated at the polls. Elections were held
shortly before Christmas of '73 and Davis had been soundly
trounced by a former Confederate, Richard Coke. Upon taking office, one of Coke's first acts was to abolish the dread
State Police. But if Texans thought the slate had been wiped
clean they were sadly mistaken.

Governor Coke resurrected the famed Ranger Battalions,
disbanded in '65 by the Army of Occupation, and ordered
them to rid the state of outlaws. They were given a free hand,
what amounted to a license to kill, and told not to bother
themselves overly much with prisoners. The attorney general's office drew up a wanted list, one considerably longer
than that of the former State Police, and the Rangers were
turned loose.

Unequaled as man hunters, the Ranger Battalions went
through several counties like croton oil, flushing wanted men
with remorseless efficiency. Some outlaws were captured and
jailed, others fled west, but most were either shot dead or
hung to the nearest tree limb. Unlike the State Police, the
Rangers made little pretense of upholding the judiciary process. Their orders were to clean out Texas and they set about
it with the most expedient means at hand. Justice was arbi-
trary and swift, a kangaroo court where the Rangers sat as
judge, jury, and executioner.

One of the names heading the wanted list was that of John
Wesley Hardin, and the young outlaw watched with more
than passing interest as the Rangers worked their way toward
Dewitt County. While he had hoped for a general amnesty
with Coke's election, he was neither shocked nor disturbed
by the turn of events. It was simply another roll of the dice,
a matter over which he had no control whatever, and he took
it in stride. That his pursuers were Texans, rather than Yankee troops or carpetbagger police, seemed somehow strange
and just the least bit unfair. But he lost little sleep pondering
the inequities of life. After being hounded for five years,
killing peace officers had become something of a pastime, if
not habit. It hardly seemed important what badge they wore,
or under whose authority they rode. Stripped of political jar-

gon, it was simply him against them. Root hog or die. The man hunters sought to kill him and he in turn tried to stay alive.

That he was better at it than the lawmen was plainly their lookout. If they left him alone then he'd leave them alone. Otherwise they took their licks just like everybody else.

All the same, despite his jaundiced view, Wes had grown more cautious with time. It had nothing to do with fear, and only in a small way did his own safety bear in the issue. Instead, it had to do with his family. And an admission he had come to after much inner searching.

To live or die was no longer his choice alone.

In January Jane had given birth to a son. He was chubby and strong and the spitting image of his father. And they had named him John Junior, for it was the proudest moment of Wes's life. But with a new baby in her arms, Jane became oppressed with fear. She brooded constantly, afraid that Wes would ride off one day and be returned home in a box. Or worse, killed by the Suttons or lawmen and left for the carrion eaters on some remote stretch of prairie. Her fear was pervasive, touching their lives like an insidious growth, and she never let him forget.

Half the men in Texas want to kill my husband.

At first Wes joshed her for being a worrywart. But with the birth of their son his attitude underwent a curious change. Slowly, he came to grips with the fact that he was no longer a loner, answerable only to himself. Those days were past, and however reluctantly, he was forced to look at things in a new light. He had responsibilities that refused to be shunted aside—a wife and two children—and for them, if not for himself, he must somehow persevere. It was not enough that his daughter and son have as their legacy the hand-me-down tales of their daddy's fearlessness and daring. They must have a father, alive and kicking, to show them the way. On a chill wintry night, bundled close in their bed, it was a promise he had made to Jane. And he was as good as his word.

Unlike the old days, he had become an exceedingly cautious man.

But it was a curious brand of prudence, somewhat unorthodox and characteristic of the man himself. A stout right arm being the best defense, he sought to avoid his enemies not so much as he dwelled on ways to eliminate them.

Early in March, returning from the railhead at Cuero, he called a meeting with the Taylors. After supper he strolled across the compound and entered the main house. There he found the four brothers seated before the fireplace in the parlor. They had come to accept him as family, more brother than cousin, one of their own. The feeling stemmed in no small part from the fact that he had saved Jim Taylor's life. But aside from that, they admired him for his cool judgment and nervy quickness in a tight situation, qualities that had served the Taylor clan well, and repaid them manyfold for offering a kinsman shelter.

And now they waited expectantly to hear what he had to say. Plainly it was a matter of some consequence or he wouldn't have called them together. They had left him the place of honor, Pitkin Taylor's old rocker, and after seating himself, he wasted no time on formalities.

"Boys, I picked up an interesting piece of news in town today. Word's out that Sutton is gonna cut and run."

The brothers came up on their chairs, gaping at him in disbelief. Just for a moment they were shocked into speechlessness. Then Billy Taylor collected his wits and blurted out what they were all thinking.

"You mean he's quit the fight—give in?"

"Nope. Not just exactly, leastways. Seems like gettin' that last horse shot out from under him sort of soured his milk. He's gonna hole up in New Orleans awhile and let things blow over. Then, when he gets to feelin' lucky again, he'll come back and have another go. Course, that's all secondhand, y'understand, but it's the straight goods."

Scrap Taylor cocked one eye skeptically. "What makes you so sure?"

Wes gave them a wolfish grin. "He's got tickets on a boat out of Indianola a week from Saturday."

"Just him?" Jim Taylor demanded.

"Him and Gabe Slaughter." Wes paused and his grin widened. "And their wives."

"By Jesus Christ!" Billy Taylor slammed a meaty fist into his palm. "You're right. They're runnin'."

"And somebody really tricky," John Taylor crowed, "might catch 'em with their pants down."

"While they haven't got an army surrounding 'em!" Jim Taylor whooped. "Just the two of 'em by their lonesome."

Wes chuckled and set the rocker in motion. "I thought you boys might see it that way."

Billy Taylor shot him a quick look. "Was you figgerin' to deal yourself a hand in this?"

"Not unless I'm asked. Seemed to me it's a private game."

"I'm obliged, Wes. It's sorta personal. Just between us."

"Yeah. If somebody killed my daddy I guess I'd take it personal, too."

The four brothers nodded, glancing at one another and back at him. It was a gesture they wouldn't forget. And could never repay. After a moment he climbed to his feet, shook hands all around, and headed toward the door. As he hit the porch, they started talking at once, and he laughed softly.

Pitkin Taylor would have been proud of his sons.

2

Cuero was alive with rumors.

On every corner of the square men gathered in little knots to swap the latest gossip. Depending on which corner a man stood, and who was doing the talking, the speculation soared wildly. Local peace officers meant to brace Wes Hardin before the day was out. Lawmen from a neighboring county were in town, determined to collect the bounty on the young outlaw's head. The Texas Rangers were riding on Cuero, prepared at last to clean out the Taylors and their deadly kinsman. The rumors grew farfetched, even zany, as the day wore on, and the mood quickened as more and more people thronged to the square. Whatever took place, it promised to be spectacular. Nothing this exciting had happened since the circus came to town. And the townspeople meant to be on hand when the final curtain rang down.

It was the stuff of legend. A story to outlive them all. Or so they told one another as they stood gawking at the batwing doors of Wright's Saloon.

On the other side of those doors, Wes Hardin was bellied up to the bar, flanked by Jim Taylor and Bud Dixon. But the rumors, and the frenzied air of the town, seemed to concern him not at all. It was his birthday, and he had no time for fainthearts and their flimsy speculations. Today he was twenty-one years old, and celebrating it in a manner suitable to the occasion. Free, white, and twenty-one. A rare event in a man's life. All the more so since the law had done its damnedest to put him under before he reached voting age. And at the very least would have robbed him of his freedom. Tossed him in some stinking dungeon and thrown away the key.

He had earned a celebration. The hard way.

Not that he wasn't aware of an impending showdown. The state of things in Dewitt County had altered drastically, and again, he sensed a brewing storm. Only this time it wouldn't be so easily handled. Or so quickly ended.

Back in March, some two months past, the Taylor brothers had ridden down to Indianola. Docked at the wharf, they found the steamboat *Clinton*. And aboard the boat they found William Sutton. While John and Scrap guarded the dock, with four fresh horses hitched nearby, Billy and Jim mounted the gangplank. On the upper deck they cornered Sutton and his partner, Gabe Slaughter. The gunfight was fast and bloody, if somewhat one-sided. Sutton and Slaughter both went down, one dead and the other mortally wounded. But neither of the Taylor brothers received so much as a scratch.

It was a testament to their accuracy that every bullet fired
found the mark. The dead men's wives stood shrieking hys-
terically throughout the whole affair, but the only wounds
they suffered were those of anguish and sorrow. Clambering
back down the gangplank, Billy and Jim swung aboard their
waiting horses and the four Taylors made a beeline for Dewitt County.

With the death of William Sutton, a calm settled over the
Guadalupe. The faction he had organized and commanded
for so long fell to fighting among themselves. The King was
dead and a royal squabble broke out as to who would take
his place. Like their former leader, the men of the Vigilance
Committee still coveted the lands south of the Guadalupe.
And within their ranks were those who believed they could
succeed where William Sutton had failed.

This struggle for leadership gave the Taylor clan a momentary respite, and left them to fret over a new and more
resourceful adversary. The Texas Rangers.

Word seeped down from Austin that the killing of William
Sutton had been the last straw. The Rangers just then had
their hands full scourging Gonzales County, where the Clements family had ridden roughshod over their neighbors
since the end of the war. But once done in Gonzales, the
lawmen had explicit orders from Governor Coke. Their next
task was to clean out Dewitt County, and the natural place
to start, according to the big augurs in Austin, was with the
Taylor clan.

And a gold watch to the man who got John Wesley Hardin.

Hardly a bystander, Wes gave as much, if not more,
thought to the Rangers than did his kinfolk. In Dewitt County
alone he was wanted for the killing of two lawmen. Not to
mention a clutch of old warrants charging him with a dozen
or so murders. The fact that most of those he had killed were
either Yankees or carpetbaggers seemed to matter little. Not
to Austin or the Rangers. And certainly not to him, if he was
caught. They would stretch his neck from the nearest tree,
and the question of whom he had killed would soon be for-

gotten. Hung was hung, and it was just as final for drilling
a Yankee as it was for drilling a corrupt sheriff. Such hairline
distinctions clearly left the Rangers unimpressed, and for a
man facing the rope, they simply ceased to exist.

Still, even with time growing short, Wes hadn't broken
out in a nervous sweat. The Rangers had bitten off a mouthful in Gonzales. Unless they were something out of the ordinary—which he doubted, despite all reports—it would be
a while before they got around to tackling Dewitt County.
And when that time came he'd give them a dose of something they hadn't run across elsewhere. After all, they were
just lawmen, mortal men at that, and they weren't any more
bulletproof than the other toughnuts he'd laid to rest.

All in all, the situation left him unperturbed. He was
pleased with himself for arranging William Sutton's abrupt
demise, and thoroughly confident he could settle the Rangers' hash when it became necessary. Until then, he wasn't
about to give himself a case of blue swivets with needless
worry.

Instead, feeling his oats, he had come into town to celebrate his birthday. Accompanied by young Taylor and Dixon,
he started the festivities with an afternoon at the horse races.
This was a regular event, held every Saturday, and drew
people from all over the county. Betting was generally heavy,
and with an eye for good horseflesh, Wes won handily,
which was all the more reason to celebrate.

After the races, their spirits soaring, the threesome retired
to Wright's Saloon. There Wes bought several rounds for the
house and began promoting a poker game. Though it was
hardly sundown, he hoped to lure some of the town's sporting men into a little session of cutthroat stud. His luck was
running strong, the ponies had proved that, and he had a
hunch it was his night to howl.

Free, white, and twenty-one! Frisky and furry and full of
fleas! Never been curried above the knees! A ring-tailed la-
lapalooza from Bitter Creek!

Everybody laughed and drank heartily, since he was pay-
ing, but they couldn't be suckered into playing poker with

him. An hour later he was still trying to cajole someone into a game when the doors swung open and Cuero's new deputy sheriff walked through. He was a long drink of water named Dave Karnes, and until tonight he'd given the young outlaw plenty of elbow room. The saloon went still as a graveyard while he crossed the room and came to a halt in front of the threesome. Wes eyed him narrowly, not at all pleased to have a damper put on his celebration. The deputy darted a sheepish glance at the crowd and finally cleared his throat.

"Mr. Hardin, I wonder if we could have a few words?"

"Why sure, Deputy. What you got on your mind?"

"Well, it's sorta private." Karnes licked his lips nervously. "Reckon we could step outside?"

Wes gave him an inscrutable look, wondering if the sheriff had some notion of springing a trap right on the public square. If so, he'd gone about it in a mighty clumsy fashion. In fact, the idea was so absurd it was downright ridiculous. At last, the youngster shrugged and smiled at Karnes.

"Why not? Guess you wouldn't mind if my friends went along." It was more statement than request, and when the deputy bobbed his head, Wes gestured toward the door. "After you."

Karnes led off, with Wes trailing him. Taylor and Dixon brought up the rear, still a little confused by the swift turn of events. Outside they all came to a halt and Wes stiffened as he spotted the crowd. The square was jammed, and he was struck by the curious thought that it was him they had come to see. Suddenly alert, he turned a flinty gaze on Karnes.

"Deputy, I've got a hunch you know somethin' we don't."

"That's what I come to see you about, Mr. Hardin." Karnes broke out in a cold sweat and his words tumbled over one another. "The sheriff sent me over here to warn you. See, he's got an idea the Taylors could wind up runnin' the county and he wants 'em to remember that he did you a good turn."

"Warn me about what?"

"See that bunch up on the corner?"

Wes glanced up the street and saw a group of men standing off by themselves. They were strangers, and from the looks of them, a hardcase lot. Even as he watched, a man separated from the others and walked toward the saloon.

"Holy moses!" Karnes rasped. "The fat's in the fire now."

"Mister, you better do some fast talkin'." Wes scowled ominously. "Who's the jasper headed this way?"

"That's what I was tryin' to tell you, Mr. Hardin. Y'see, this fellar name of Charlie Webb, he's head deputy over in Brown County, and he got a posse together and they come over here—"

"To get me."

Karnes swallowed hard. "'Cause of the reward money."

Webb pulled up in front of them and Karnes's shoulders sagged like a wilted sunflower. The Brown County lawman and the outlaw stared at one another for a moment, saying nothing. Finally, Karnes got himself untracked, and in a froggy croak, made the introductions.

"Charlie Webb, this here's Wes Hardin."

"John Wesley Hardin." Webb beamed and stuck out his hand. "Been waitin' a long time to meet you."

Wes took the lawman's hand and nodded. "Pleased to make—"

Too late, he realized that Webb was packing a brace of Colts. Before he could move the lawman locked his hand tight, jerked the offside pistol, and shot him. Wes lurched backward, a dark blotch staining his shirtfront. But as he fell, he pulled the Peacemaker and thumbed off a single shot. The slug caught Webb in the face, tearing away his jawbone, and he slammed up against the wall. He hung there a moment, drilling another round into the boardwalk, then toppled forward. As he went down, Taylor and Dixon shot him four times in the back.

Suddenly Webb's posse opened fire from the corner and lead whistled all around them. Taylor and Dixon hammered off several shots, dropping one of the men, and the rest scurried around the corner. Working quickly, they grabbed Wes under the arms and got him aboard his horse. Then they mounted, leading the youngster's horse, and took off down the street at a dead lope. A moment later they turned the corner and disappeared from sight.

Dave Karnes suddenly doubled up and puked all over his boots.

3

The Texas Rangers rode into Cuero three days later. Though their bloody work was not yet done in Gonzales, one company had been detached from the Special Forces Battalion. Twenty men strong, their mission was to restore the law in Dewitt County. Other than that, they had blanket license to take whatever action deemed necessary. Austin was interested in results, not methods, and the Rangers' orders were both chilling and terse.

Convert the lawless. Make believers of them all.

This left the Ranger commander, Captain Sam Waller, considerable latitude in judgment. An avowed pragmatist, he chose not the best way, but the quickest. The big augurs in Austin had little patience with commanders who pussyfooted around, and Captain Waller was of the lean and hungry school. While not overly bright, he was exceedingly ambitious, and he knew that nothing impressed politicians quite so much as blood and thunder. A quick and violent campaign, with citations for bravery under fire, would be better for all concerned. Particularly Sam Waller.

With the problem reduced to fundamentals, Waller spent a day mapping his strategy. Basically, it was rather simple. There were two factions—the Taylors and the Vigilance Committee. And while the Taylors were acknowledged desperadoes, the Vigilantes at least had some tenuous alliance with the law. If he could eliminate the Taylors a semblance of order would be restored. Fast and efficiently. Then, if it was still necessary, he could turn and destroy the Vigilantes.

Yet he doubted that the second step would be required. A single campaign, conducted brutally and without quarter, was generally object lesson enough.

The strategy was neither remarkable nor inventive. It was merely the shifty reasoning of a pragmatic man, employing the expedients of ruthlessness and fear. And for Sam Waller, zealot without mercy, it was nothing less than a holy quest.

He would convert the Taylors with a baptismal of fire.

The Rangers' sudden appearance in Cuero was unexpected, but hardly a secret. Word travels fast in a small town, and by noon the grapevine was working overtime. Before nightfall the news had spread throughout the county, and the most avid listeners were known partisans of the Taylor cause. None more so than John Wesley Hardin.

Though he was not a deliberate man, tending to react as the situation demanded, Wes had already sorted through his alternatives. The three days' grace, laid up in bed with Jane playing nurse, had given him time to think. His wound was superficial, if painful, a neat hole drilled front and back through the side. So there was nothing to stop him from simply riding out and making himself scarce. Except loyalty to the Taylors.

Yet that bothered him only briefly. The clan itself was divided on the wisest course of action. Some intended to run. Others meant to hold their ground. What it came down to was how much trust a man placed in the law. That the Rangers were partial to bloodbaths, having demonstrated it in several counties, was apparent to many Taylor supporters. But most were determined to stand pat and take their chances. They felt they were in the right, that once the facts were known the law would declare them the aggrieved party. With some slight reservations, they welcomed the Rangers to Dewitt County. Now their families could rest easy, and a man might go about his work without fear of being bushwhacked.

Wes found it difficult to share that conviction. Years of dealing with lawmen had left him with an unshakable cynicism for the breed. They weren't to be trusted, however much they spouted slogans of equal justice for all the people.

Somehow it generally worked out that certain people were more equal than others. And based on past experience, not to mention the governor's wanted list, he figured his name had already been entered on the wrong side of the ledger.

The swing vote, though, was cast by the Taylor brothers themselves. They were split down the middle, and this fracture dispelled any lingering sense of loyalty the young outlaw might have had. John Taylor took off like a turpentined bear for parts unknown. Billy and Scrap forted up in the big house and declared themselves ready to fight till the last. Young Jim simply crossed the compound and threw in his lot with Wes. Guileless to the end, he made no bones about his decision. The chances of coming out alive were vastly improved by sticking with someone who had managed to survive similar predicaments. It was just that elemental.

Wes couldn't have agreed more. Only a fool fought the law on its own terms. The way to beat the Rangers was to play cat and mouse. Hit and run. Keep them guessing. Never give them a chance to get set. It had worked with the Yankees and the State Police, and it would work with the Rangers. After a couple of weeks of being led in circles, they'd call it quits and head on back to Austin. Lawdogs were a sorry bunch, as everyone knew, and had never been known for their gumption.

That night, after a teary farewell with Jane, Wes and young Taylor went on the dodge. They traveled light, carrying bedrolls and grub, and by dawn they were some miles south on the Guadalupe. There, they holed up for the day in a grove of pecan trees along the riverbank. Wes planned to shift their hideout each day, traveling only at night. While he entertained little hope of eluding the Rangers altogether, he knew the odds improved if they kept moving.

Downstream from camp, they hobbled the horses and turned them loose to graze on a grassy patch of bottomland. Afterward, they washed down cold biscuits and beef with river water. That part of being on the run was what Wes resented most. He missed his coffee. Thick and black and heavily larded with sugar. Being chased was an inconven-

ience. And people taking potshots at him was a bother of
sorts. But to be denied his coffee seemed the ultimate sacrifice. Damn near intolerable. Still, a fire was a luxury they
could hardly afford. Smoke on a clear day was a dead giveaway. Better to hire a brass band and parade into Cuero in
style.

The thought made him smile inwardly. A sardonic smile,
mocking himself. He was getting too old for this nonsense.
Like some crotchety vinegarroon, he sat there bemoaning his
coffee when he was lucky as hell somebody hadn't already
planted daisies over him. It just went to prove that God
should've given a man an extra bunghole and shorted him
on brains. Thinking could get a fellow in real trouble.

Watching him, Jim Taylor swallowed a mouthful of dusty
biscuit and arched one eyebrow. "You look like somebody
just gigged your funny bone."

Wes grinned and shook his head. "Not lately. Fact is, I
was thinkin' this outlaw business is gettin' to be a pain in
the rump."

"Sounds sorta queer comin' from you. I mean, hell, you
been on the dodge so long. I always figgered it was the kind
o' life you just naturally cottoned to."

"You mean like I picked it out special? The way some
people set their cap to be a doctor or a lawyer?"

"Well, no, not just exactly." Taylor frowned, searching
for the right words. "I know you sorta backed into it. But I
always thought"—his voice trailed off lamely—"well, you
know."

"That I got a charge out of killin' people?"

"Now, Wes, I didn't say that neither. It's just that"—
flustered, his face turned red as cherry pits—"I just s'posed
you liked the excitement. The way some folks get weaned
into likker. Guess I was wrong."

Wes grunted, fixing him with a rueful stare. "Lemme tell
you somethin', Jim. This stuff of being a badman ain't all
it's cracked up to be. It's a mighty lonesome occupation."

"Lonesome? Cripes, you got more friends'n any man I
know."

"And more enemies. Ever think of it like that?"

"Sure, I reckon that's part of it. But your name stands for somethin'. Hell, people all over Texas look up to you. You ain't some saddle tramp with a boil on his ass. You're special."

"Think so, huh? Well, you try cuddlin' up to that some night when all you got between your butt and the ground is a sweaty blanket. I guaran-dam-tee you there's nothin' *special* about it. After a while you get to wishin' you'd signed on as a ribbon clerk, so you could go home to a hot meal and a little nuzzlin'. 'Cause, Jimbo, when you get right down to the nubbin, that's what special really is."

"You ain't talkin' about a wife and kids and all that stuff?"

"That's exactly what I'm talkin' about. I had it for a year one time out on the Brazos. And there hasn't been a day since that I wouldn't 've traded my left nut to still be there. It was a good life. Lots better'n a man knows till he loses it."

"Christ A'mighty, Wes, that don't hardly make sense. Not the way you was livin' it up in town the other night. And the look on your face when you get in a fight. Hell, I've been there. I seen it for myself. You got a natural-born taste for them things. Sticks out like a sore thumb."

"Yeah, I guess it does. What I'm tryin' to tell you, though, is that there's things I like better. Y'know, sometimes a fellow has to play the cards he's been dealt and just do the best he can. But you stick with it long enough and that sportin' life, and all the time windin' up in a gunfight, gets old real quick. Take my word for it."

Taylor fell silent for a long while, staring distractedly at his biscuit. At last, he sighed and looked up with a bemused frown. "Well, that's shore a revelation. I don't mind tellin' you, it purely is. All this time I had it figgered that you was hard as nails and sudden death 'cause that's the way you liked it. Now you up an tell me you'd sooner been a ribbon clerk. Damned if that don't take the cake."

Wes knuckled his mustache back and drew a deep breath.

"Jim, lemme give you some free advice. When we come clear of this thing with the Rangers, you forget about the fast life and settle down. The only thing special about being a big, tough hombre is that you generally wind up lookin' like a sieve. And sooner or later somebody's gonna put a leak in you that a sawbones won't be able to get corked up. It's not a hell of a lot to look forward to."

The young outlaw's words proved prophetic. Shortly after dusk the next evening they stopped at Bill Cunningham's place to grain their horses. Cunningham met them at the door with a shotgun, his house darkened, and the tale he related left them dumb with shock.

While the Rangers were busy chasing Wes Hardin, the Vigilantes swept across Dewitt County exacting deadly retribution. In a single night they had lynched Jeff Hardin and the Dixon brothers, Bud and Tom. Then, their bloodlust aroused, they attacked the Anderson place. Ham and James had finally surrendered, fearing the women and children would be harmed, and the Vigilantes riddled them with buckshot right in their own front yard. Oddly enough, the Rangers didn't bat an eye. It was as if the law had joined forces with a pack of mad-dog killers. All in the name of justice. And however murky the alliance, their purpose was clear. The Taylor clan was to be hunted down and exterminated.

Wiped clean from the face of Dewitt County.

4

The hunt was well organized and relentless as death itself. Working separately, the Rangers and the Vigilantes methodically scoured the backcountry south of the Guadalupe. After their mindless night of savagery, which had cost the lives of five men, the Vigilantes' thirst for revenge appeared slaked somewhat. Their bloodlust had been curbed in no small part by Joe Tomlin, the man who now led them. Tomlin was crafty and unburdened by scruples, but he was an astute judge of character. All of which had helped him outwit his

rivals in the struggle for leadership of the Vigilance Committee. Upon taking command, he focused that same shrewd-
ness on the problem at hand, and quickly put an end to
needless violence.

With Ham Anderson and Bud Dixon dead, the Taylor
clan's lieutenants had been effectively eliminated. Those who
remained were either unwilling or incapable of leading the
ranchers below the Guadalupe. That left only the Taylor
brothers themselves. And their upstart kinsman, Wes Hardin.
Once they were dealt with, Dewitt County would become a
fat, juicy plum, ripe for the picking.

Word had leaked out that two of the Taylor brothers, John
and Jim, had taken to their heels. It was also known that the
other brothers, Bill and Scrap, had barricaded themselves in
the main house. Tomlin had seen that house, remembered
old Pitkin Taylor bragging that it had been built along the
lines of a fort, and he wanted no part of it. Wisely, he left
it to the Rangers to flush Billy and Scrap. At the head of the
Vigilantes, he rode off in search of John and young Jim. That
seemed the more prudent course, chasing the pair who had
taken flight, and if nothing else, Joe Tomlin was a prudent
man. He meant to live a long time, and enjoy his newly won
position as the he-wolf of Dewitt County.

But the best-laid plans, even those of prudent men, all too
often run afoul of the unknown. Tomlin had made a single
miscalculation—he assumed Jim Taylor had tagged along
with John, the second-eldest brother. It was a serious error
in judgment, one that became evident only when it was too
late.

Toward sundown on the second day of their hunt, the Vigilantes found a spot on Salt Creek where two men had made
a cold camp. Horse droppings and other signs indicated that
the men had spent the day hidden in a small stand of trees.
And most revealing was the fact that they hadn't built a fire.
Translated, it meant the men had reason not to be seen.

The tracks were still fresh, less than an hour old, headed
due southwest out of the woods. Like coonhounds on warm
scent, the Vigilantes set off at a fast pace in the failing light.

They trailed the two horsemen straight as a string to the farm
of Everett Nix, scarcely three miles from the cold camp on
Salt Creek. A known Taylor supporter, Nix was a hardscrabble sodbuster who had little stomach for gunplay. The
hunters had every confidence that the Taylor boys would
surrender rather than endanger Nix and his family. Boldly,
just as dusk settled over the land, they rode into the front
yard, fanned out in a rough crescent. This was Tomlin's idea.
He wanted the Taylors to see them, to understand that there
was no escape. It was his second mistake, but not his last.
That came when he stood tall in his stirrups and shouted
toward the house.

*"You Taylors got ten seconds to give up! Then we open
fire."*

Tomlin's jaw popped open as Wes Hardin appeared at the
parlor window and laid a double-barreled greener over the
sill. For an instant in time, frozen in space and motion, the
Vigilantes stared bug-eyed at the young outlaw. Then the
scattergun exploded in their faces. The first charge snatched
Tomlin from the saddle and sent him tumbling over the back
of his horse. A moment later another quart of buckshot sizzled through the air, wounding several men and stampeding
their horses. From the kitchen window a Winchester opened
fire, and the ugly snout of a Peacemaker replaced the shotgun
in the parlor window. Caught flat-footed, the Vigilantes pan-
icked and took off in a wild melee of squealing horses and
cursing men. The Winchester and the Colt peppered their
backsides, wounding two more men, and within seconds they
disappeared into the dusky night.

Joe Tomlin stayed behind. Dead as a doornail.

The Vigilantes were hardly out of sight when the back
door flew open. Wes and Jim Taylor rushed out and ran
toward the barn. Several moments later, saddles hastily
cinched and spurs whirling, they quit Everett Nix's farm in
a thundering gallop. Circling west for a mile or so, they
turned and doubled back, then struck off toward the Guadalupe. Neither of them said a word the whole time. And in
truth, there was no need. They were both thinking the same

thing. Their escape had nothing to do with foresight or brains. Nor was it a favorable commentary on their cunning.

It was a fluke. Sheer outhouse luck. One in a zillion.

Late the next night, the young fugitives warily rode into Slim Joiner's place. They had spent the day hidden in a marsh bordering Slough Creek; their clothes were crusted with swamp mud, they were hungry and frazzled, and their horses shuffled along like crippled elephants. They needed hot food, grain for their mounts, and a good scrubbing with lye soap. Taylor had suggested Joiner's place since it was off the beaten track and less likely to attract the law. Just at the moment, however tempting a soapy tub and a decent meal, that was their main lookout. Avoiding the law.

Slim Joiner could offer them little cheer, though. Aside from corn bread and a pot of warmed-over stew, his news was all bad. The worst yet.

Upon returning to town the night before, the Vigilantes discovered that a small battle of sorts had been waged at the Taylor compound. Early that morning the Rangers had attacked, surrounding the main house. But after a long, and mostly wasted, exchange of gunfire, it became apparent that they would never dislodge the Taylors from their fort. Captain Sam Waller ordered hay wagons set afire and sent them barreling into the house from front and rear. Within an hour the house was shrouded in flames and roiling clouds of smoke. Shortly afterward, with a choice of being roasted alive or surrendering, the survivors called it quits. Three of the defenders had been killed in the gunfight, but the Rangers took into custody Scrap Taylor, Joe Tuggle, and Dan White. Incredibly, Billy Taylor somehow managed to escape in the smoke and confusion.

The captured men were manacled and whisked off to jail in Cuero. That night, smarting over the death of Joe Tomlin and fueled with Dutch courage, the Vigilantes stormed the jail. They demanded the prisoners, threatening to take them by force if necessary. Captain Sam Waller, ever the pragmatist, formed his Rangers and beat a hasty retreat to the hotel. Still in chains, Scrap Taylor and the two unfortunates with him were promptly marched to the courthouse steps. There, without any great ceremony, the Vigilantes hung them from an overhead railing. The entire town turned out to watch and it was generally agreed that justice had been served.

Then, next morning, irony had the last laugh. Billy Taylor was captured attempting to board a boat in Indianola. It was the *Clinton*, the same boat on which he had killed William Sutton. Word came over the telegraph that he was being held without bail, awaiting arrival of the Rangers. Beaming, Sam Waller sent a squad to collect the prisoner, and then strutted around town as though he'd rolled in catnip. And as any fool could see, he had reason to be proud. The Sutton-Taylor feud was history. However questionable their tactics, the Rangers had ended a decade of bloodshed in a single week, and their captain had every confidence that he was about to become Austin's fair-haired boy.

When Slim Joiner finished his grisly tale, young Taylor was woozy with shock and Wes had his jaws clenched in a tight knot. But the outlaw's thoughts dwelled only momentarily on the dead. His mind turned instead to the living. Joiner had related all there was to tell, but in deference to his guests, he had left out one salient detail. There were two fugitives still to be caught. And come morning both the Vigilantes and the Rangers would be combing the countryside. For however much the lawmen gloated and swaggered about town, there were a couple of loose ends yet to be trimmed. One named Taylor and the other named Hardin.

And not until then would the matter be officially closed.

Joiner thoughtfully passed around a jug of his own white lightning, and the jolt of hard liquor seemed to snap Taylor out of his funk. Afterward, Wes took him outside and gave him some hard talk. It was straight from the shoulder, and the youngster winced a couple of times, but it had to be said.

Grim as it was, he had to face the fact that one of his brothers was dead, another would face the hangman very shortly, and the third was probably halfway to China by now. That meant he was the last of the clan. The last of Pitkin Taylor's sons still in Texas. If he had any hope of living— of returning someday to claim the family birthright—then he must run fast and run far. Otherwise there would be another Taylor sent to the boneyard before the week was out. Better to run, and find a hole, and live to fight another day.

Jim Taylor bowed his neck at first, but Wes persisted, and the boy finally caved in. They talked, weighing various hiding places, and Wes eventually remembered Barnett Hardin. Polk County was better than a hundred miles north and the Hardin farm was back off in the sticks. A perfect hideout. The kind of spot where a fellow could change his name, walk the straight and narrow, and get himself fixed for a comeback in Dewitt County.

An hour later, they shook hands and the youngster stepped aboard his horse. When he rode out of Slim Joiner's yard there were tears in his eyes. Green as he was, he knew it was a pipe dream. He would never come this way again. But he also understood why Wes had saved his life, and somehow he felt as though he'd lost the only friend he ever had.

Shortly before sundown next day Wes ambushed the Rangers. He figured they had earned some licks and he'd gone looking for them early that morning. They weren't hard to find. Just as he expected, they were out looking for him, and he cut their trail in late afternoon. After tagging along for a while it became clear that they were headed for the Thomaston Crossing on the Guadalupe. Thinking it over, he decided it was as good a spot as any for a surprise party. It was a deep ford, heavily screened by brush on both sides, and damned hard to back out of once a horse was in the water. Satisfied, he'd circled north ahead of the lawmen and took a position on the far side of the stream.

Not unlike times past, when he'd ambushed Yankee soldiers and State Police, he felt no remorse whatever. They were worse than the men they hunted, using the law as a license to kill, and they deserved everything the got. His only regret was that he had but one shotgun. A dozen would have been better. And a cannon better still.

Nerveless, holding off till the last second, he waited until they were in the deepest part of the ford. Then he blasted Captain Sam Waller straight into kingdom come. The second load he emptied into the men behind, chuckling to himself as their horses reared and another man splashed dead in the water. As they sawed at the reins, hauling their horses around, he jerked the Colt and thumbed off five shots in a blinding roar. A third man pitched from his saddle on the far bank and an instant later the Rangers were gone, pounding back the way they had come.

Without moving, Wes calmly reloaded, satisfied that in his own way he had helped even the score. Hefting the shotgun, he walked back to where the grullo was tied. Then he mounted and rode toward the Taylor compound.

5

The night was still and black under an overcast sky. There was a smell of rain in the air; the katydids were silent; nothing moved in the compound. Light blazed in the smaller buildings, but what had once been the big house lay ominously dark and quiet, a pile of charred rubble. A soft breeze carried the scent of burnt timbers, and unless a man put it from his mind, there was even a faint trace of scorched flesh.

Try as he might, it was a smell Wes couldn't set aside. It clung in his nostrils, thick and cloyed, sickly sweet yet putrid in the way of something tainted and gone to rot. He knew his mind was playing tricks, a ghoulish joke of some sort, for by now the dead men had been removed from the ashes and buried deep. But the odor stuck with him all the same.

He was hunkered down behind a tree, at the base of the knoll, and for the past hour he had been watching the compound. It was unlikely that either Vigilantes or the Rangers would return to this place on this night. Yet the risk was

always there, and this late in the game it was better to hedge
his bet. Another hour, waiting and watching, would cost him
nothing. Yet it might easily spell the difference between a
new life and a hangman's knot. For John Wesley Hardin had
decided to take his own advice.

He was leaving Texas.

After convincing Jim Taylor to quit the fight, Wes had
given it considerable thought. The advice was sound, wholly
realistic, yet coming from him it was laughably absurd.
Worse than that, it made him the world's greatest hypocrite.
For in all truth, Jim Taylor was small potatoes, a piker where
the law was concerned. If ever a man had reason to run fast
and run far, it was Preacher Hardin's wayward son. The stiff
lecture he'd given the boy went double for himself. But only
after mouthing the words to someone else, listening to his
own pearly wisdom, did it jar his brain loose, force him to
separate illusion from reality, and to take a long, hard look
at the folly of muleheaded pride. From the Rio Grande to
the Red, there had never been a man with more reason to
call it quits in Texas.

Nor was there any reason to stay. The opposite side of the
coin made that painfully clear. Bitter as it was to swallow,
loathsome even, an era had ended. He was no longer a knight
in shining armor, the people's champion against tyranny and
injustice. He was merely a common outlaw.

The people themselves, across the breadth of Texas, had
proved that. There had been no outcry of public indignation
over the Rangers' murderous campaign against lawbreakers.
The Clementses and the Taylors and the Hardins, once a
breed apart, had outlived their time. Union troops no longer
ruled Texas. The carpetbaggers had moved on to new swin-
dles. And the dread State Police were now a nightmare of
the past. Texas was once again governed by Texans, and its
citizens no longer sanctioned the wanton slaughter of lawmen. The people wanted peace and an end to the terrors of
Reconstruction. In short, the Rangers were Texans, not Yankees, and that made the difference. However savage their
bloodletting, the people backed them solidly.

And at the jaded age of twenty-one Wes Hardin found himself an anachronism. A legend who had outlived his era and suddenly had no place in the new scheme of things.

This realization was all the more painful because Wes had come to it so late. Almost too late. Years ago his father had advised him to run, to leave Texas. Mustanging on the Brazos had been a compromise of sorts, but stubborn pride wouldn't allow him to run farther. Had he done so things might have been different. And not just for him alone.

That was a thought much on his mind as he watched the Taylor compound. Had Billy Taylor been right after all? Would the politicians in Austin have supported the Taylor cause if that first ambush had never taken place? The ambush Wes had argued so strongly to bring about. And what of the lawmen he himself had killed in Cuero—Jed Morgan, Jack Helms, and Charlie Webb? Would the Rangers have ridden against the Vigilantes instead of the Taylors if an outlaw named Hardin hadn't stripped Dewitt County of peace officers? These questions vexed him, and yet they were moot, unanswerable. Whatever he'd contributed to the Taylors' downfall had been done with their blessing, and while he felt sadness, he felt no guilt. The dead were dead and flailing himself wouldn't bring them back.

But what of the living?

His eyes wandered to the compound, settled on the house where even at that moment Jane sat in mourning with the Taylor widows, doubtless waiting for word of his own death. What of her and Molly and the baby? That was a question which could be answered. A question, in fact, that had already been resolved. They deserved happiness and protection and freedom from fear. And above all else, it was for them that he had set aside his pride. Taken his own advice. Yielded to common sense and determined to put Texas behind him for good.

Yet there were things he mustn't tell her. Not until later. Like this latest stunt. One man ambushing an entire company of Rangers. There had been enough death and bloodshed to last her a lifetime, and to tell her now would merely add to the burden. It could wait until they were clear of Texas, the killing behind them.

Still, mulling it over, he wasn't sorry about the ambush. It had worked out well. All things considered, a pretty tricky maneuver. A little risky, perhaps, something he'd done in the heat of anger. But it had bought him a couple of days' grace, and at a moment when he desperately needed time. With Waller dead it would take the Rangers a few days to get organized. After the licking they'd taken, it wasn't likely they would go looking for a fight until Austin sent in a new commander. As for the Vigilantes, they already had what they wanted. The Taylors were dead or scattered to the winds. Which meant there was little chance of anyone organizing a fresh manhunt. Not anytime soon.

The thought sounded good, just logical as hell, but it made him laugh. However much it justified the risk, time wasn't the reason he'd ambushed the Rangers. He'd done it for the Taylors and the Dixons and the Andersons. And for himself. It was a damned fine way to leave Texas.

When the compound finally went dark, with the last lamp snuffed out for the night, Wes figured it was safe to move. Shotgun in hand, he left the grullo tied in the trees and cautiously worked his way up the knoll. Skirting open spots, he stuck to the shadows and within ten minutes he was standing alongside the house. He waited a while longer, letting his eyes roam from building to building, until he'd satisfied himself there was nothing out of kilter. Then he edged around the front of the house and eased quietly through the door.

Silently, he moved to the bedroom and found Jane snuggled up with both children. It was about what he'd expected. With the big house in ashes it made sense that Billy Taylor's wife and the old woman would take over the spare bedroom. He leaned the shotgun against a wall and very gently placed his hand over Jane's mouth. She came awake with a start, eyes wide with fear, a muffled scream choked back in her throat.

"Sshhh," he whispered, "it's me."

She whimpered, then big tears puddled up in her eyes and

she threw her arms around his neck. They clung to one another, rocking back and forth, and she smeared his face with salty kisses. Suddenly she began to shake, heaving great sobs, and she buried her face against his shoulder to hide the sound. He stroked her hair, gentle and soothing, and after a while she seemed to get hold of herself. With one eye on the children, he eased her back onto the pillow. Then, tapping his lips with one forefinger, he cautioned her to whisper.

"Stay quiet. I don't wanna draw a crowd."

"Oh, God, Wes." Tears brimmed over and spilled down her cheeks. But she sniffed softly and kept her voice low. "I thought you were dead. We heard about the fight at Nix's place and then somebody brought word that the Rangers were after you. I prayed and prayed, but I just knew they would find you. And then—"

He stilled her with a soft touch on her lips. "Take it easy. I'm fit as a fiddle. Matter of fact, you can quit worryin' altogether. I'm finished."

"Finished? I don't understand. What's finished?"

"The fightin' and killin' and everything else." He drew her close and breathed the words in her ear. "We're leaving Texas."

She gave a little yip of joy and threw herself into his arms. "Do you mean it? Sugar, do you really mean it? Oh, thank God. Thank the Lord and all the stars. It's a miracle. I can't believe it. Are you sure? We're actually leaving?"

"I mean it. Cross my heart. Now quit raisin' such a ruckus. I'd just as soon not wake the Taylor women."

"You couldn't. They have cried themselves sick with grief. But I don't understand, Wes. Why can't we let them know? They'd never tell. Never."

"Never's a long time. And people have a way of gabbin' when they shouldn't. This here's our little secret. Just between us Hardins. Now get your clothes on and let's see if we can get the kids dressed without any big commotion."

She sat bolt upright. "You mean we're leaving now? Tonight!"

"I mean we're pullin' out quicker'n scat. Now quit talkin'

and get busy packin'. I'll tell you all about it when we're down the road a ways.''

Jane Hardin wasted little time. While Wes hitched a team to a buckboard, she packed their meager belongings, and when he returned she was ready to go. The children were bundled warmly in blankets, still fast asleep, and Wes carried them out in his arms. Jane trailed along with a carpetbag in one hand and a tow sack stuffed full with food in the other. Within the hour they were off the knoll, the grullo tied behind the buckboard, and headed eastward into a gloaming dawn. By dead reckoning, Wes calculated it was two hundred miles to the Louisiana border.

And beyond that a new life in a new land. A land of fruit and honey, where people didn't know John Wesley Hardin from Adam's off ox.

What the good book called the Promised Land.

BOOK THREE
1875–1877

CHAPTER 9

1

The train rattled northward like a scorched centipede trying to escape the fireball lodged high in a cloudless sky. Smoke belched from the engine in thick black spurts, wheels meshing with steel rails in what seemed a slow and tortuous race with time. The noonday heat was oppressive, a brutal mace hammering down against the coach roofs, and inside, the passengers sweltered as if trapped in a crackerbox rocketing through the fires of hell.

Seated beside a window, Wes Hardin stared wearily at the monotonous landscape rushing past. His eyeballs were gritty and raw, smarting with flecks of engine soot, and his clothes were covered with a fine layer of powdered grime. The damp tropical heat left him sitting in a puddle of sweat, and his mind felt numbed, somehow sated, with the sight of palmettos and Spanish moss. Swaying with the motion of the coach, caught up in the mesmerizing *clickety-clack* of the wheels and the stifling heat, he fought against the drowsy lassitude that threatened to suck him under.

While he sat at the rear of the coach, his back against the compartment wall, he still felt jumpy and on edge. And that bothered him. There were no Pinkertons aboard this train, on that score he was certain, and the knowledge should have relaxed him, allowed him to settle back and catnap through the noonday inferno. But it hadn't and probably wouldn't until he was across the state line. Although what difference it made, skipping from Florida into Georgia, he wasn't all that sure. State borders meant nothing to the Pinks, as he'd learned the hard way, and even now they were probably sniffing out his trail.

Which was what he wanted. To lure them away from Jane and the kids. And perhaps that's what had him nettled. Some inner foreboding that the dodge hadn't worked. The Pinkertons were a dogged bunch, and nobody's dumbbells. Slippery as his maneuver had been, they might well have tumbled to the game.

Thinking about it, as the train chuffed northward toward Georgia, he had to admit it was a little childish. If anything, he had spooked himself. His unease was founded on nothing more than superstitious nonsense. The mind playing tricks on itself. A damnfool notion that Florida was a hex. That the Pinks had gotten the Indian sign on him, and that he wouldn't be rid of it until he was safely out of the land of sand and sun.

The hell of it was, everything had started out so well. And he had been so careful. Playing it cagey right from the outset. Looking back, though, hindsight was an illuminating if somewhat mortifying eye-opener. Clearly, he hadn't been cagey enough. Or else the Pinkertons had just been slicker. Or luckier. Or maybe both. But however the chips had fallen, he could see now that his first mistake was that paddle-wheeler.

A mistake he had compounded every step of the way.

Upon reaching New Orleans last summer, Wes had felt safe for the first time in years. The buckboard ride from Texas hadn't been any picnic, but Jane and the kids had held up well. All the same, they had needed a breather, rest and soft beds and some decent food. He'd picked a new name for himself—Harry Swain—and taken rooms in a swanky hotel. They spent the next week roaming the French Quarter, stuffing themselves with fancy meals, and generally lazing around. Then, with everyone back on their mettle, Wes decided it was time to lose himself for good. And the farther from Texas the better.

While Florida wasn't exactly the end of the earth, the young outlaw figured it was far enough. He booked passage on a steamboat to Cedar Key, a small port on the Gulf. Although he stayed seasick most of the voyage, the family enjoyed it immensely, and from Cedar Key they took a train to Gainesville. Wes had chosen the town because it was off the beaten path, about halfway across the state, and yet still large enough for a newcomer to pass relatively unnoticed. A couple of days spent looking the place over seemed to confirm his judgment.

It was sleepy and slow-paced, like most southern towns, and other than church socials, rarely had any excitement. All in all, it appeared perfect. A most unlikely place to stumble across the Texas Rangers.

Harry Swain rented a house, got his family settled, and then began scouting the business opportunities. Within a week he bought a saloon and quietly set about fading into obscurity. Over the next several months he refrained from gambling and operated an orderly, well-run drinking establishment. The townspeople came to know him as a friendly, if somewhat laconic, saloonkeeper, and the Swains were slowly accepted into the community. At Jane's insistence, the family joined the Methodist church, and everyone was pleasantly surprised by Saloonkeeper Swain's rather remarkable grasp of the good book. Quite shortly he was invited to join the fraternal order of the Masons, and being a devout Christian as well as a devoted family man, he readily accepted. With some reluctance on his part, Harry Swain had become the talk of Gainesville, and the townspeople counted themselves fortunate to have a real up-and-comer in their midst.

Not long after the New Year, however, Harry Swain's house of cards began to fall apart. The sheriff, who coincidentally happened to be a Mason, came to him with a disturbing story. There was a stranger in town asking questions, and despite a clever smoke screen, he quite obviously was a Pinkerton agent. More to the point, the questions he asked had to do with a man whose description bore an uncanny

resemblance to the young saloonkeeper. Like most Southerners, the sheriff had little use for the Pinkertons, who had
served the Union cause throughout the late war. While he
had told the detective nothing, and refrained from asking
questions of his own, the sheriff advised Swain to watch his
step. It wouldn't do for a good Christian and a brother Mason
to wind up in the pokey.

Harry Swain couldn't have agreed more. That afternoon
he gave his lawyer power of attorney to sell the saloon and
closed out his rather sizable account at the local bank.
Shortly after sundown, the Swain family appeared at the depot and caught the evening train for Jacksonville. Somewhat
stunned, the people of Gainesville awakened next morning
to find that the personable young saloonkeeper had departed
town bag and baggage. Without so much as a fare-thee-well.

But certain men not only knew of Swain's whereabouts,
they gave him a brotherly boost as well. In Jacksonville he
was put in touch with George Haddock, owner of a slaughterhouse and by no mere coincidence, a fellow Mason. They
exchanged the secret handshake and Swain became a contract
cattle buyer for Haddock & Company.

Once again the Swain family rented a house, joined the
church, and became active in community affairs. Jacksonville
was a sprawling city, bustling with growth, and Swain felt
confident he could lose himself for good this time. As the
months passed, his business grew and prospered, and his
family settled down at long last to a peaceful, untroubled
life. Yet, blissful as things seemed, he had reckoned without
the bulldog determination of the Pinkertons.

Toward the end of June he returned from a cattle-buying
trip and was informed by George Haddock that a stranger
had appeared just that morning asking questions. Haddock
told the man that Swain had moved to Tallahassee and let
the matter drop there. But from his description of the
stranger, Swain had little doubt that it was the same Pinkerton who had traced him to Gainesville. Why the Pinkertons
were after him was a question that had perplexed Swain for

the past six months. And despite many sleepless nights, he still hadn't resolved who might have sicced the detectives on him. Yet there was one part to the puzzle about which he no longer had even a smidgen of doubt. The Pinks were somehow tracing him through the transportation he used. First the steamboat from New Orleans. Then the train out of Cedar Key. And now the train from Gainesville to Jacksonville. It was the only answer that made sense.

With any luck at all, though, it might be made to work against the Pinkertons. Sucker them into a real Texas-type wild-goose chase.

Rushing home, he broke the bad news to Jane. She became despondent for a time, shattered that they were again forced to flee their home. All her apprehensions of the past boiled over and she burst into tears, fearful that they would be hounded the rest of their lives. But as he outlined his plan she slowly got hold of herself. And by the time he finished she was positively glowing.

Jane and the children were to hire a buckboard and drive to Baldwin, farther west along the railroad. From there they were to catch a train and make their way to Alabama, where Jane had relatives in a small farm town. Wes, meantime, would be acting as a decoy to lure the Pinkertons in the opposite direction. If they could pull it off, they might just lose the law forever.

And it had worked perfectly. Leaving everything behind, as if they were merely off for an afternoon in the country, Jane and the children headed west in a rented buggy. Wes appeared at the depot shortly afterward and bought a ticket on the noon train to Savannah. Quite innocently, he sparked a conversation with the ticket agent and managed to let slip that he was Harry Swain with Haddock & Company. When he boarded the train he was feeling pretty smug with himself. The hook had been baited and he had every confidence the Pinkertons would swallow it whole. They would follow him to Savannah and then on to Atlanta, and there the trail would vanish. For once in Atlanta Wes was finished with trains.

Aboard a horse, he would simply melt into the countryside, invisible among the crowds of horsemen entering and leaving Atlanta every day of the week.

Late that night, when the train arrived in Savannah, Wes found a nearby cafe and ate supper. Then he returned to the depot. This, too, was part of the plan. He purchased a ticket for Atlanta, spent a few minutes chatting with the agent, and finally stretched out on a bench to catch a nap. The train for Atlanta departed early in the morning, and when it left he meant for the ticket agent to remember him quite clearly. Naturally, being crackerjack detectives, the Pinkertons would have no trouble at all in following his trail.

The thought amused him, but he suppressed a mild chuckle. Hitching himself around on the hard bench, he was asleep an instant after closing his eyes.

Some hours later he came awake with a start. It took a moment for it to register, then it dawned on him that a train was slowly screeching to a halt outside. And it had come in from the south.

He bolted to his feet as the ticket agent came around the counter. "What train is that?"

Rubbing sleep from his eyes, the agent gave him a puzzled look. "Beats me, mister. Nothin' due in here from Jacksonville till tomorrow. Somebody must've run a special."

Wes had a sinking feeling who that somebody was. Striding past the agent, he slammed out the door just as the train groaned to a halt. Hardly to his surprise, the train consisted of an engine and a single coach. Apparently the Pinks had made up in speed what they had lost in time. Out of the corner of his eye he saw three men step off the coach and he began walking faster. Suddenly a voice behind him racketed over the hiss of steam.

"You, there! Stop right where you are."

Wes leaped from the platform and took off running across the train yard. Back at the depot, he heard shouts and the thud of heavy brogans pounding along the platform. Then something hot and angry fried the air beside his head, followed an instant later by the report of a gun. Disgusted, cursing inwardly, he skidded to a halt.

The bastards could never let well enough alone. Chasing him was one thing. Like gnats, it was an irritant he could overlook. But when they started shooting, that was just too damn much. Whirling about, he jerked the Colt and dropped to one knee. The Pinkertons were standing at the edge of the platform, blasting away as if they were lined up in a shooting gallery. Lead whistled all around Wes, kicking up cinders and zinging off rails, but he closed his mind to everything except the men on the platform. They were standing almost shoulder to shoulder, silhouetted perfectly against the depot lantern, and the muzzle flash from their guns winked orangy-gold in the night. He raised the Peacemaker, supporting his gun hand in the palm of his left hand, and aimed deliberately.

Suddenly the tables were reversed, and quite literally, the Pinkertons became sitting ducks. The first slug sent the man on the left reeling backward in a windmill of arms and legs. Shifting aim slightly, Wes thumbed off another shot and saw the next man buckle at the knees, then pitch headlong off the platform. The third man caught on that it was his turn next and he abruptly quit the fight. Spinning away, he ducked low and ran toward the station house. Turning back saved his life, but he hardly escaped unscathed. Wes snapped off a hurried shot that was just wide of the mark. It drilled into the doorframe beside the detective's head and a jagged splinter laid his cheek open to the bone. An instant later, leaving his feet in a headlong dive, he disappeared through the door into the depot.

Wes came to his feet and moved off through the train yard. As he walked, he reloaded, still cursing the Pinkertons. Rather neatly, they had upset his little red wagon, and the plan would have to be changed. Damned fast. Then he grunted, smiling to himself. Somewhere in Savannah there was a man who was about to sell him a horse.

Even if the transaction took place at the point of a gun.

2

Ed Duncan was a not a man easily intimidated. He had served with honor during the late war, sending a small legion of Johnny Rebs to their reward. And more recently he had exchanged lead with the James Boys and the Youngers, receiving both a raise and a citation from the agency for his coolness under fire. Few men sported such impressive credentials, and among his professional colleagues, it was said that the pale-eyed Scotsman had the brass of a billy goat. In short, he was tough, resourceful, and hard as nails.

But as Duncan walked along the hotel corridor he felt just the least bit shaky, and there was a brackish taste in his mouth. Waiting in a room down the hall was the Old Man himself, Allan Pinkerton. And for all his daring under fire, Duncan's qualms about this meeting were not without reason. Agents who muffed an assignment go the pucker reamed out of their puckerhole, and the Old Man seldom minced words in the process. He was hell on wheels, with the sting of a yellowjacket and all the warmth of an aroused cobra.

On the long train ride to Atlanta Duncan had thought of little besides the upcoming confrontation. What he might say in his own defense still eluded him. Or more precisely, it posed yet a more vexing question. What was there to say in defense of an agent who not only had queered a manhunt but at the same time managed to get two of his fellow agents killed? So far as he could see, the answer was plain and simple—not much. Certainly nothing that would get him off the hook.

In retrospect, Duncan found himself wishing he had never heard of John Wesley Hardin. Jesse James and his gang of cutthroats were cream puffs by comparison. The young Texan seemed to have more lives than a cat, and the luck of the Irish as well. Which in itself was a dirty word to the square-jawed Scotsman.

Yet, from the very outset, he had felt a grudging respect

for Hardin. Admittedly, the youngster was cold-blooded as a shark, and as a man-killer he had few equals. But he wasn't the garden-variety desperado. Nor was he an outlaw in the accepted sense of the word. Despite their best efforts, the Texas Rangers had failed to produce one shred of evidence linking Hardin to cattle rustling or bank robbery, or any other form of skulduggery for profit. It seemed that the most infamous gunman in Texas killed for only one reason—a desire to remain free. Duncan found nothing unnatural about that, and given the circumstances, he couldn't wholly condemn it. Particularly when it was common knowledge that Hardin supported himself and his family through honest labor, and rarely went out of his way to provoke trouble. The problem in a nutshell was that he had a disturbing way of ending arguments. And fully a baker's dozen of those he had killed were peace officers.

Scarcely a year ago, in the capitol building at Austin, Duncan had listened to vitriolic tirades from the governor and the attorney general on this very subject. The Scotsman had thought then that Hardin was perhaps one of a kind—an honest outlaw. But this distinction, however singular, was lost on the governor. Wes Hardin had made the Rangers look like bumbling asses, killing three of them in what could only be described as a turkey shoot. Then he simply vanished, leaving not only the Rangers but the governor himself the laughing stock of Texas. It appeared certain that Hardin had departed Texas and the governor wanted him run to earth. With one proviso. The Pinkertons were to take him alive and return him to Texas for trial. Only then would the good name and reputation of the Coke administration be restored.

Though unimaginative, Duncan was a student of logic, and he spent several months investigating the most obvious escape routes from Texas. Doggedly persistent, he questioned ticket agents at train depots and ship lines all along the Gulf Coast, slowly working his way into Louisiana. Finally, in a steamboat office in New Orleans, he struck pay dirt. From there the trail led to Cedar Key and then on to Gainesville. After talking with the sheriff, who was a poor liar, Duncan knew he was very close. The tradesmen he questioned around town—who were by turn reserved and startled and hostile—merely confirmed his judgment. Still, more than a week elapsed before he discovered that Hardin, posing as Harry Swain, had once again slipped through the net.

Simple deduction, and a small bribe to the depot agent, led him next to Jacksonville. There he called for support, and Allan Pinkerton assigned two agents to work under his supervision. They combed the city, slowly eliminating all possibility that Hardin had bought a saloon or returned to gambling. Then, Duncan had a brainstorm. He recalled Hardin's dealings in cattle and began investigating the city's slaughterhouses. Again he struck pay dirt in the form of a poor liar—George Haddock. And again Hardin slipped through his grasp. Only this time it was by a mere whisker. Duncan and his men traced Hardin to the depot less than two hours after the train had departed for Savannah.

The Scotsman wired Pinkerton in Chicago and within the hour he had a special train at his disposal. Later that night they roared into Savannah and through sheer happenstance almost stumbled over Hardin. Except that Duncan's orders were to take the outlaw alive, and he in turn shouted orders for his men to aim low. Try for a crippling shot.

It had been a harsh and costly introduction to John Wesley Hardin. Duncan's agents had been killed where they stood, and the Scotsman would carry a livid scar to his grave. He still remembered the leaden thunk as a slug slammed into the doorjamb beside his head, and at times he could even feel the splinter knifing through to his cheekbone. But what he recalled most was that the youngster had fired only three shots, which was not so much a testimonial to Sam Colt's equalizer as to Wes Hardin's accuracy. And it had stimulated a healthy respect in Ed Duncan for this one-of-a-kind outlaw.

He now knew what it was to have a shark turn and fight.

But while all of this mitigated his failure, none of it stacked up well as a defense. The unvarnished facts, galling as they were, told the tale. He'd had three chances to trap his man, and at every juncture Hardin had made a monkey of both him and the Pinkertons. It was the cardinal sin, besmirching the reputation of the agency, and on that score he must answer to the Old Man himself. Pinkerton rarely stirred from his headquarters in Chicago, and his presence in Atlanta could mean only one thing. Heads were about to roll.

Duncan halted before the door, removing his hat, and knocked. A gruff voice ordered him to enter, and as he stepped inside the room, any lingering hope went by the boards. The agency chief was standing in front of the fireplace, scowling one of his famous scowls. Quite pointedly, he declined to shake hands. Instead, he motioned to a chair and cut straight to the heart of the matter.

"I would like to know the present whereabouts of John Wesley Hardin."

"So would I, Mr. Pinkerton." Duncan lowered himself into the chair and squirmed about uncomfortably. "However, I'm forced to report that we've come up empty. He simply vanished into thin air."

Defeat in any form was unacceptable to Allan Pinkerton. Short in stature, pushing sixty, with a graying beard and muddy brown eyes, he seemed an unlikely hunter of men. Yet his looks were deceptive, cloaking an iron will and a fierce determination to win. In 1860 he had saved Abraham Lincoln from assassination, and afterward established the Secret Service. During the war he commanded all espionage and intelligence-gathering activities for the Union, and came away with a record unblemished by failure. He was shrewd, chillingly perceptive, and at heart, tougher than any outlaw he'd ever chased. Now, something flickered in his eyes, and he nailed Ed Duncan with a corrosive stare.

"Suppose you tell me how a man vanishes?"

Sweat beaded Duncan's forehead, but he returned the look squarely. "I don't know, Mr. Pinkerton. He's a will-o'-the-wisp. Like smoke. You reach out to grab him and all of a sudden he's not there."

"Am I to understand that after three weeks you still have

no clues whatever? That with two of our agents shot dead and the reputation of this firm at stake, you've turned up nothing?''

Duncan bristled at the tone and his pale eyes went stony cold. "That's correct, sir. Nothing. I've turned Savannah upside down and have yet to find a trace of Hardin. But I'm still looking, and unless you take me off the case, I'll find him. And that isn't an idle promise, Mr. Pinkerton. It's a statement of fact.''

Pinkerton glared back at him for several moments, then the muddy gaze abruptly softened and he smiled. "Ed, that's what I came all this way to hear. You are as good an operative as we have in the agency, and I never for a moment doubted that you would fail me. But I wanted you to hear yourself say it. Most of the time, it's what a man believes of himself that makes the difference.''

The Scotsman's mouth quirked in a dour smile. "I'll get him. It's just a question of when and where and''—he paused, no longer smiling—''whether or not you still want him alive.''

There was a long silence, and at last the older man nodded. "Take him alive. We'll make an example of young Mr. Hardin.''

Allan Pinkerton took a chair and thoughtfully steepled his fingers. After a moment's contemplation a foxy look settled over his face, and he peered across at Duncan with an intensity that fairly crackled.

"Now let's discuss tactics. I have a few ideas I believe might interest you.''

3

Polland in many ways reminded Wes of Mount Calm. It was a quiet little town, somewhat backwoodsy, and people tended to follow the rule of live and let live. Not unlike most small communities in Alabama, it was neither prosperous nor destitute. There were a couple of wealthy men who pretty well controlled things, notably the local banker and a former plantation owner who had managed to fend off the carpetbaggers and scalawags. But for the most part people made do with what the Good Lord provided and counted it a blessing after the horrors of Reconstruction.

Not that ambition in Polland was dormant. Nor was it suffering some acute form of stagnation. There were several small businesses, owned by men whose moderate means adequately satisfied their moderate needs. Yet everybody else, when they worked, generally found themselves in the employ of the banker and his major depositor, or if things got desperate, they trudged five miles to the sawmill at Wawbeek and hired out for the day. Things seldom got that desperate, though. For the people of Polland were content with chicken on Sunday, grits the rest of the week, and old-time religion around the clock.

Except that their pace was a little slower and their drawl a little heavier, Wes found them not all that different from the people back in Mount Calm. In many ways, it was as if he had come home again. Particularly when he discovered himself living among a regular beehive of Bowens.

Somewhat like the Taylors and the Clementses back in Texas, the Bowens were a loving, close-knit clan. An offshoot of Jane's family, blood kin to her father, they were easygoing and rarely bothered themselves with things outside their own small world. They knew, of course, that Jane's husband was a wanted man, and it rather tickled their fancy to have a famous outlaw as part of the family. The scars of Reconstruction were hardly healed, even in tiny Polland, and a man who had killed so many Yankees was a prize catch indeed. The Bowens welcomed him into the clan with open arms, but his identity remained their own-guarded secret, a private joke of sorts on the community, and so far as anyone knew, he was simply Harry Swain, young, obviously well-to-do, and come to Polland to settle among his wife's family.

All of which suited Harry Swain very much indeed. He was tired of running, wearied even with the killing, and he wanted to sink roots. The time had come to commence build-

ing something for his family, to give their lives a measure
of peace and stability. While that could never become a reality in Texas—he had discarded all hope of ever returning
west—it might well come to pass in Alabama. Polland was
isolated to a great extent, the nearest city some fifty miles
across the Florida line, and if he kept his nose clean it was
doubtful the world would ever again hear of John Wesley
Hardin.

Yet his rosy outlook for the future was mixed with just a
tinge of watchfulness. Never again would he underestimate
the Pinkertons. After his near disaster in the Savannah depot
they had won his grudging admiration, if not for their marks-
manship then at least for their genius as bloodhounds. Perhaps more precisely, he had developed a keen appreciation
for the skills of a stumpy little Scotsman with pale frosty
eyes and a square jaw.

Newspapers across the South had ballyhooed the Savannah
shoot-out in front-page headlines. Liberal quotes were also
included from one Edward S. Duncan, Special Agent in
charge of the manhunt for John Wesley Hardin. Duncan
freely admitted that he had lost the trail in Savannah, but
went on to observe that this presented nothing more than a
temporary setback. He had tracked Hardin from Texas to
Louisiana to Florida to Georgia, and he planned to go right
on tracking. Furthermore, he had every confidence that the
wanted man would be taken into custody within a very short
while. The newspapers ate it up. Having a woolly-booger
western desperado loose in the southland made hot copy.
Editorials teetered between outraged indignation and droll
amusement, and the public couldn't get enough. For weeks
every new development was trumpeted in Gothic bold, and
reporters employed prose so livid it all but glowed in the
dark. Then, quite abruptly, there was nothing. No news stories. No editorials. And no quotes from Edward S. Duncan.
The detective had dropped out of sight, and with him, all
speculation about the manhunt.

But if the public quickly forgot, the wanted man himself
grew all the more reflective. Having devoured the news sto-

ries as avidly as everyone else, he now knew something of his pursuer. The man had a name, and a souvenir from their gunfight in Savannah, which tended to make it more personal. He was obviously resourceful, double-wolf on guts, and not in the least discouraged by what he termed a temporary setback. And the fact that he had dropped from sight was not a matter to be taken lightly. Detectives seemed to be most dangerous, judging from past experience, when they suddenly turned unobtrusive and silent. And so it evolved, in the little town of Polland, that while Edward S. Duncan was out of sight he was hardly out of mind.

Harry Swain had much going for him in Polland. After escaping Savannah on a hastily purchased horse, he made his way across Georgia and Alabama, sticking to backcountry roads, and had come at last to the home of Brown Bowen. As the eldest in the family, Bowen had made him welcome, offering both friendship and refuge. Jane and the children had arrived some three weeks previously, and since then, the clan had been waiting expectantly for the daring young outlaw to make an appearance. They threw a celebration in his honor, with hickory-smoked hog and hoedown dancing and a hair-curling blend of white lightning. And when it was over, his eyeballs afloat and his step none too steady, the guest of honor found himself adopted. The Bowens, it seemed wouldn't take no for an answer. He and Jane and the children were to remain in Polland, settle down, and consider themselves full-fledged members of the family.

The lazy summer days slowly drifted into fall, and as the nights became cooler, Harry Swain made his decision. While he'd never refused the Bowens' offer, he felt it best to await events before sinking roots in yet another town. But with the coming of October, and still no sign of the Pinkertons, he concluded it was safe to try his hand at some form of business. After all, his family had to eat, and since money didn't grow on trees, it was high time he set about making some.

But as things worked out, it appeared that money did, in fact, grow on trees. Scouting around town for likely investments, Swain quickly learned that prospects were far from bright. Polland already had a saloon, which served its needs nicely; gambling was looked upon as a sin only slightly less heinous than adultery; and the cattle business, as such, was virtually nonexistent. By process of elimination the trades in which he had a working knowledge seemed to have been chalked off rather neatly.

Then, quite by accident, opportunity came knocking. Having exhausted the more attractive possibilities, Swain marched into the local bank, unstrapped his money belt, and made a sizable deposit. This fact was duly noted by Lionel Culpepper, the bank president, and Swain was shortly ushered into his office for a private chat. Culpepper had his finger on the pulse of things and there was little in Polland that escaped his scrutiny. While he had long since dismissed the Bowens as a vital force in the community, he sensed something altogether different about their young kinsman. Like most bankers, Culpepper believed that money talked loudest, and Swain's deposit slip was a highly persuasive introduction.

Which was no great revelation to Harry Swain. It was what he had expected, and the reason he'd played the money belt as if it were the case ace in high-stakes showdown.

After a bit of small talk, Swain let it drop that he was looking for an investment. Nothing speculative but something solid and reliable. Something a family man could get his teeth into and build with an eye toward the future. Having determined to settle in Polland, he wanted to contribute to the growth of the community and at the same time further his own fortunes in some small way.

This was the kind of talk to warm a banker's heart, and Culpepper took a fancy to the young man right off. It so happened that he did know of an investment. One of the bank's oldest customers, owner of a small logging company, was currently in a financial bind. While the company was basically sound, the owner, Joe Dan Adair, was a good logger but a poor manager of money. Forced to take the conservative view, the bank had recently declined his request for a loan. But a man with a head on his shoulders, who was

willing to pitch in and work hard, might well make his fortune in partnership with Adair.

A meeting was arranged between Adair and Swain, and
the two men struck it off immediately. Adair was on the
sundown side of forty, clearly a hard drinker with an Irishman's mercurial temper. But he needed money and he was
bright enough to recognize that a partner with brains could
prove a real asset. It took only a brief discussion, especially
the part dealing with money, to see that Swain qualified on
both counts.

Playing it cozy, the young investor spent a full week inspecting Adair's operation. The logging itself was done along
the upper tributaries of the Escambia River, some ten miles
west of Polland. After being felled and stripped, the logs
were snaked through the woods by mule teams and eventually brought to the river. There they were floated downstream
and sold outright to the sawmill at Wawbeek.

And it was at the sawmill that Adair was slowly losing
his shirt. The owner of the sawmill had a hammerlock on
the loggers, since his was the only mill along the stretch of
river that flowed through Alabama. He could set his own
price, take it or leave it, and thumb his nose at anybody who
yelled about the rules. There were plenty of loggers, but as
he was quick to point out, there was only one sawmill.

Swain disappeared from Polland for a few days, giving
Adair a mild case of heart flutters, and returned looking as
as though he'd just swallowed a canary. They sat down for
another talk, and while Swain was oddly cryptic about his
trip, he proved that he had brains enough for both of them.
The dickering went on far into the night, at times verging on
a bare-knuckle donnybrook, but the younger man couldn't
be swayed from a telling argument. He had the money and
without it Adair would sink like a rock. When they finally
shook hands, Swain was a full partner with authority to run
the business end of the operation any way he saw fit. All Joe
Dan Adair had to do was get the logs to river. From there,
Polland's newest entrepreneur would handle the rest.

Harry Swain came away from the meeting walking on air.

He had big plans for the future, and with a gambler's instinct for a winner, he knew he'd backed a sure thing. But he also knew there was risk involved, that he might well be constructing another house of cards. And though he allowed himself a pat on the back, he wasn't quite ready to stop looking over his shoulder.

Not until he knew the whereabouts of one Edward S. Duncan.

4

Polland was agog with wonder.

Joe Dan Adair's young partner had just turned the logging industry topsy-turvy. People around town could talk of nothing else, and wherever they gathered the topic of conversation seldom strayed from Harry Swain's nifty sleight of hand. The Bowens were beside themselves with glee, flushed and jubilant that the family had at last produced a live-wire eager beaver with the magic touch. Lionel Culpepper, though equally impressed, merely sat in his office at the bank and brooded. Somehow he couldn't shake the feeling that this Johnny-come-lately had stolen the march on him. And worse yet, hoodwinked him into helping.

It was a day that shook the order of things.

That afternoon Joe Dan Adair and his crew hit town howling like banshees. They tromped into Polland's one saloon and promptly ordered drinks for the house. Then, though the youngster himself had declined to join them, they proceeded to tell everyone within shouting distance of the tricky, underhanded, positively dazzling cunning of Mr. Harry Swain.

Adair & Company had felled their usual quota of logs that week. But when it came time to make the run downstream, Harry Swain had a little surprise for them. And it revolved around his mysterious trip a few weeks past, those two days he'd disappeared from town.

Horseback, Swain had ridden the shoreline of the Escambia River all the way to Pensacola. There, as any fool could have told him, he found a sawmill at the mouth of Escambia Bay. Being neither a fool nor a logging man, which many people considered one and the same, he sat down to talk turkey with the mill owner. When he departed, he had a firm offer for all the logs Adair & Company could deliver—at twice the price being paid in Wawbeek.

Ignorance is bliss, according to know-it-alls, and if so, then Swain was riding on a cloud. But it was a thin and delusive cloud, the stuff of pipe dreams. For no one had thought to tell him that logs couldn't be floated down seventy miles of winding, treacherous river. At least it hadn't occurred to anyone to mention it until he announced the scheme that day along the upper Escambia.

Then Joe Dan Adair told him. Loudly, in no uncertain terms, and with the profane artistry of a drunken mule skinner. After the sour-tempered Irishman sputtered to a halt, Swain fixed him with that stony look and asked a single question.

"How do you know it can't be done?"

"Because, goddamnit," Adair thundered, rolling his eyes at the innocence of fools, "nobody's ever done it before."

Swain just smiled. "Then it's time someone tried."

There was plenty more cursing after that, and at one point the two men almost came to blows. But at last Swain gave his partner the double whammy. First off, he had ridden every foot of the river, and logger or not, he was of the opinion it could be done. More to the point, their contract gave him the authority to call the shots, and like it or not, he was exercising that power.

Joe Dan Adair fumed and cussed and kicked at rocks. But he was snookered and he knew it. They set the logs afloat.

Later, recalling it for his goggle-eyed audience in the saloon, Adair admitted that the high point of his life was when they drifted past the sawmill at Wawbeek. The owner, Pud Moore, stood on the landing like a hayseed gawking at his first tent-show freak. That dumbfounded look, Adair cackled, a mixture of raw disbelief and faunching rage, was worth the price of admission. Even if they'd lost every log in the run, he would have felt amply rewarded.

But as it came about, they lost very few logs. The only hitch they encountered was below Century City, at a sharp bend in the river. There, everything came to a halt in a massive logjam, a bottleneck of sorts that had Adair stumped and the rest of the men scratching their heads. Swain, who hadn't yet got the hang of walking logs, was trailing them along the shoreline. He stepped down off his horse, pulled a stick of dynamite from his saddlebags, and calmly lit the fuse. As the loggers scattered like peppered ducks, he tossed the dynamite into the bottleneck.

Afterward, laughing about it, the men labeled it a stroke of genius. The explosion made kindling of the logjam, sending a plume of debris rocketing skyward, and in the blink of an eye the pileup simply ceased to exist. They again started the logs downriver and from there on out it was smoother than a ride on a brand-new hobbyhorse.

They roared into Escambia Bay cocky as a bunch of bulldog pups. What nobody had ever tried before, they had just done. And if they could do it once, they could do it again. Any damn time they pleased. Yet the frosting on the cake was still to come. They got that when everybody ganged around and watched the mill owner pay Harry Swain double the price their logs would have brought upriver.

The partners called a stockholders' meeting of Adair & Company right on the spot, and voted a week's bonus for every man in the crew. Then they swaggered into Pensacola and got blind, stinking drunk. Somewhere along the line— Adair seemed to recall it was after they'd wrecked the third saloon—Swain pulled another disappearing act. Him being a family man and all, they figured he'd headed on home. Which was the Christian thing to do, and dampened the spirit of their celebration not at all. With a full load under their belts, they invaded Ma Smalley's riding academy, the fanciest sporting house in town. And as the police informed them later, they put the girls out of commission, pretty near demolished the house, and gave Ma herself a case of the nervous twitters.

All in all, it had been a mortally satisfying experience.

Their story finished, Adair and his men announced that they were holding a little contest. And they needed the counsel of the sage minds gathered there at the bar. Somehow it didn't seem proper that young Swain be stuck with such a commonplace given name. After all, with what he'd done *Harry* just didn't fit the ticket anymore. The opening of the Escambia to loggers demanded something more elegant, a moniker with class.

The trouble was, Adair and crew had come up with a couple of dandy names but they couldn't decide between them. Trailblazer Swain had a good ring to it. But the other one, Pathfinder Swain, wasn't anything to sneeze at either. So they were going to leave it up to the town. Whatever folks started calling the youngster, that's how he'd be known.

Personally, Joe Dan Adair observed, he didn't give two hoots and a holler. Whether it was Trailblazer or Pathfinder, it all worked down to the same thing. That Swain kid was a goddamn wizard. Still squiffed to the eyeballs, Adair was soon overcome by the blubbery look common to all melancholy Irishmen with short fuses and tender hearts. So he saved the moment with that honored and most ancient of all Gaelic traditions.

Hammering the bar, he ordered another round for the house.

Jane Bowen Hardin Swain was proud as punch and mad as a wet hen, which was a little hard to manage all at one time. She gave the cake batter a vicious lick and grumped something very unladylike to herself. The more she thought about it the madder she got, and just then, she was thinking about it plenty.

Her husband had again proved himself. Shown that he was something more than a common outlaw and killer of men. He had a keen head for business, not to mention shrewd judgment, and the gift of swaying others with nothing more

than reason and soft words. That was apparent in the way
he'd made this logging venture pay so handsomely. While
stodgy old-timers sat mired in worn-out methods and hide-
bound customs, he looked deeper, sought new insights, and
came up with a better way. Like visualizing the Escambia as
one long water chute. Daring something no one else had ever
tried. And doubling the profits!

It was grand and glorious. To her, almost godlike.

But how did that fool Irishman repay him? Not to mention
the townspeople and her own family. With a childlike contest
and a name pirated straight out of Fenimore Cooper's books.
It was outrageous. Humiliating. More than that, it was crude
as spit.

She heard footsteps and got busy whipping the batter. A
moment later her husband came through the kitchen door,
whistling softly, and gave her a swat on the rump.

"What's for supper, woman? I'm hungry as a bear."

Sniffing, she gave the batter a savage whack. "You seem
awfully chipper."

"Well, I oughta be. Just got Adair and his boys sobered
up and packed off to camp. Which, in case you don't know
it, is one mighty full day's work." She thumped the batter
harder, saying nothing, and studied her a bit closer.
"Somethin' the matter? You look like you just swallowed a
mouthful of hornets."

"Very funny. I must say, you're certainly taking it
calmly."

"Taking what calmly?" Puzzled, he shot a glance back
toward the front of the house. "Is there somethin' wrong
with the kids?"

"No, there is nothing wrong with the children. They're
having a nap. And you know perfectly well what I mean."

"Well, if I do it's news to me. What the sam hill are you
gettin' at, anyway?"

"What I'm getting at is the latest town joke." She
slammed the batter in a cake pan, then spat out the words,
her lips pinched tight. "Trailblazer Swain."

"Great God A'mighty. Is that what's got your goat? They

was just havin' some fun. Nothin' but a bunch of drunks jabberin' whiskey talk.''

"That's exactly what I mean!" Her eyes blazed and she waved the mixing spoon overhead like a broadsword. "Drunks sit around giving you nicknames and the good people of this town laugh themselves hoarse. It degrades everything you've accomplished in the last month."

"Now is that a fact?" He grinned and cocked one eyebrow. "What would you say if I told you that Mr. Lionel Culpepper—the big-dog banker himself—asked me in for a little chat today?"

"He did?" She blinked and lowered the spoon.

"Yes ma'am, he did. Thought I might be interested in a deal he's been hatchin' up. And I was."

"You were?"

"Yep. Seems like he's got his hooks on some timberland down below Wawbeek and he thought we might figure some way to divvy up the profit. Turned out to be simple as pie. He wanted half and I let him twist my arm into givin' him a quarter."

"But why did he—I mean, he owns the timber."

"Yeah, but I know how to get it to Pensacola. See, that's what had him stumped all these years. There ain't no way to float logs upstream."

Her cheeks went red as beet juice. "I was silly to worry, wasn't I?"

"Sure you were. Them swells, the good people you was talkin' about, they don't care what handle a man goes by. Not so long as he can make 'em some money. You just wait and see, before long they'll be invitin' us to come have supper at their big fine houses."

"You really think so?"

"Know so. Fact is, I'm givin' odds."

Jane grabbed up the cake pan and whirled across the kitchen in lazy circles. "Oh, Wes, I'm happy as a pig in mud."

"The name's Trailblazer, ma'am. And I'm right proud to see you smilin' again. 'Course, you oughta be, squatted down amongst all these Bowens. It's like havin' a whole tribe for your very own family.''

She shushed him. ''You know that's not it. It's being clear of the law and you so successful and having men like Mr. Culpepper seek out your advice. Don't you see, we might really make it this time. Have—well, you know—all those things we talked about and didn't really believe.''

''Speakin' of which.'' A funny little gleam flickered in his eyes. ''How long you reckon we've got before the kids wake up?''

She slid the cake pan in the oven and spun like a dizzy butterfly to the door. Then she turned, tossed her apron in the air, and gave him a lewd wink. ''Mr. Trailblazer, I figger we got an hour 'fore that cake is done. Now, if you need any help findin' the path, jest stick with me.''

She danced away and he followed her through the door.

5

The preacher lifted his hands to heaven.

''Now, if y'all will stand and please turn to page one-nine-three in your hymnals.''

The congregation rose, an obedient flock, and there was a rustling flutter as they thumbed through their hymnbooks. From the front of the church, hidden by a screened partition, came a muffled *thump-thump-thump* as one of the Butler kids jackhammered air through the pump. Then the organ wheezed to life, and Maybelle Floskins, grinning like a horse eating briars, assaulted the keyboard with her stubby fingers. The faithful drew a collective breath, watching Preacher Cleve Blalock's lead, and raised their voices on high as the organ thundered out of the prelude.

On a hill far away
Stood an old rugged cross
The emblem of suffering and shame

Singing loudly, if slightly off key, Harry Swain stood in the second pew from the front, on the left side of the aisle.

Beside him were his wife and children, and together they comprised a living model of what every Methodist family aspired to be. Little Molly, going on four, was starched and fluffed, a flaxen-haired cameo of her mother. The youngest Swain, two-year-old Johnny, was decked out in a little man's suit and already displayed the roughly chiseled features of his sire. Jane, whose clear alto compensated somewhat for her husband's jarring baritone, was never more radiant.

And never more proud. Deacon Ura Suggs, not ten minutes past, had ushered them down the aisle and seated them only one pew from the front on the left-hand side, directly behind banker Lionel Culpepper and his family. In the Polland scheme of things, it was an engraved announcement to one and all. The Swains had arrived.

After the hymn, Reverend Blalock led his flock through the Lord's Prayer and motioned for them to resume their seats. Then he drew himself up to his full height, eyes glittering with fire and brimstone, and launched into a fist-pounding sermon on the insidious horrors of demon rum. His topic for the morning was prompted in no small part by a courtesy call from the Ladies Temperance League earlier in the week. The good reverend, not only supported their cause with fervor and straitlaced rectitude, he also knew who wore the pants in most Polland families. His sepulchral wrath set the church rafters to vibrating, and predictably enough, John Barleycorn took a real thrashing from Christ as the sermon built to a crescendo.

Harry Swain listened with only half an ear. Demon rum posed no threat to him personally. He could take it or leave it, and mostly he left it. Moreover, several Sundays each year throughout his boyhood, he had heard John Barleycorn raked over the coals in a manner that made Preacher Blalock's sermon a pale imitation of the real article.

The thought made him smile inwardly. Reverend James Hardin had few equals when it came to Fundamentalist, Bible-thumping old-time religion. The mellifluous, honey-tongued voice—interspersed at key moments with a crisp, barking jolt—kept his congregation wide awake and in fear of their mortal souls. Looking back, it seemed that his delivery was inspired, evangelical more than rehearsed, the stuff that made believers of fornicators and idolaters alike. After one of James Hardin's sermons the people of Mount Calm knew better than to monkey with God.

Here lately the young businessman's thoughts had returned frequently to those days. The time of his boyhood. Warm, golden years filled with discovery and never-ceasing marvels. He felt a void, an aching lonesomeness, something unfulfilled. And however much he resisted the idea, he knew it stemmed from his folks.

The plain and simple truth was that he missed them. Perhaps living among the Bowen tribe, seeing the love and tenderness they lavished on one another, had triggered some wistful memory of his own family. Not that it was enervating, or caused him to brood himself into the dumps. His folks had been strict and unbending, never the kind to display affection. So it wasn't that. They loved him, and had proved it in their own way, and he'd never felt the need for syrupy talk and hugs and kisses. It just boiled down to something he sensed in his gut, something he couldn't put a name to or label or spell out even in his own head. He missed them.

Sitting there in the pew, only dimly aware of Preacher Blalock's fire and fury, it came to him that the Hardins hadn't derived much joy from their youngest son. How long ago was it that they'd set their sights on him becoming a schoolteacher? Only seven years. Yet it somehow seemed like more. Another lifetime. And instead he'd brought a different sort of fame to the Hardin name. Scarcely anything to make his folks burst with pride or beat the drum about their secondborn.

Of course, the last couple of years had been better. While there was no way of returning home, or bringing them to visit Polland, he did write them fairly often. The letters were long, filled with news of the kids, and the logging venture, and the fine life he and Jane had made for themselves. But it disturbed him, even after all this time, that his folks couldn't reply. The only word he had of them was through

Jane's family, for she could write her parents using the Bowens as a cover. His letters were mailed on business trips to
Pensacola, just in case the Rangers were still nosy about who
was writing the Hardins.

Yet, as he considered it now, the whole thing struck him
as a little overcautious. It was close to two years since he'd
skipped Texas, and just shy of a year since his shoot-out
with the Pinks in Savannah. In all likelihood the law had
chalked him off as a lost cause and gone on to fresher game.
Perhaps things weren't so risky anymore, and handled just
right, he might work out a way for his folks to write back.
If he got a post-office box in Pensacola, under still another
alias—who would be the wiser? It was something to think
about anyway. And it would damn sure beat getting the news
secondhand. Which was what it amounted to with the tidbits
passed along by Jane's mother.

Just for a moment his mind drifted back to the sermon and
he was reminded that it was Cleve Blalock who had baptized
his children. That must have hurt the old man mightily. To
know that some footwasher in Alabama had done the hocus-
pocus on his own grandchildren. Doubtless his folks were
proud to see him back in the fold, and to know that he had
arranged salvation for the kids, but it must have chafed all
the same. James Hardin was made of stern stuff, but he
wasn't as hard as he put on. Dunking his own grandkids
would have been a mortal delight. All the more so since he'd
never seen them. But, as every preacher knew, life was no
bowl of cherries. Otherwise there would be no need for religion. Or preachers.

Somehow, although he couldn't quite make the connection
between preachers and bankers, his mind suddenly jumped
to Lionel Culpepper. The banker was seated directly in front
of him, and it passed through his mind that for all of Culpepper's righteous ways, there was no forgiveness in the
man. Over the last several months they had become thick as
thieves, working out a number of deals that had proved mu-
tually profitable. Along the way, though, he had learned
much about the man who cracked the whip in Polland. Harry

Swain was accumulating a tidy little nest egg not because
Culpepper liked him, but because the banker occasionally
needed a front man who was quick with his head. Culpepper
called him astute and gifted, buttering him up with four-bit
words, but beneath that oily smile beat the heart of a real
man-eater. One miscue, like that fiasco last month in Mobile,
and Culpepper would toss him to the wolves. Which meant
he would have to watch himself closer in the future. A damn
sight closer.

   He still couldn't figure how things like that happened. It
wasn't just that he was a backslider and couldn't resist temptation. There was more to it than that. Had to be. Like maybe
some voodoo cloud trailed him around—his own special
hex—read to dump on his head whenever he strayed off the
straight and narrow. And the hell of it was, he hadn't strayed
all that far.

   After delivering on a big timber contract, he and Adair
had taken the boys to Mobile for a well-earned spree. While
the others had swilled booze and sampled half the brothels
in town, he'd played it close to the vest. Kept his nose clean,
and more than anything else, hung around to bail them out
when they finally landed in jail. But after a couple of nights
of such nonsense, he'd gotten bored and let himself get
sucked into a poker game. And like any damn fool should
have expected, there sat a tinhorn who fancied himself
greased lightning with both the cards and a gun. The upshot
of it was, he called the man for dealing seconds and had to
put a leak in his ticker. Outside the saloon, with Adair and
the boys in tow, it went from bad to worse. A trigger-happy
constable came running up, already primed for bear by the
gunshots, and somehow they ended up swapping lead. That
part was still a little hazy, but he finally winged the lawman
enough to put him down and they made dust going away.
Adair awakened a liveryman, paid top price for a team and
wagon, and the whole bunch of them quit Mobile that very
night.

   It was the kind of tomfoolery he could no longer afford.
Not just because of the Pinkertons, either. Had anyone tied

him to the shootings it would have reflected badly on Culpepper. Everybody knew the banker had taken him under wing, and a scrape like that would have seriously compromised Culpepper's position in the community. And if it was dangerous to monkey with God, it was sheer lunacy to jeopardize the social standing of Lionel Culpepper. A miscue in that direction, just one little slip, would put Harry Swain and family back on the road again. Without a pot and nowhere to squat.

Which was something to ponder. Long and carefully.

Reverend Cleve Blalock was coming down to the wire, flailing John Barleycorn with some choice Scripture. As the sermon mounted to a pitch, and the preacher worked himself into a proper frenzy, the head of the Swain family silently swore the oath. No more booze. Or cards. Or honky-tonk saloons. From here on out it was nose to the grindstone, right around the clock.

Straight as an arrow and stiff as starch.

CHAPTER 10

1

The muggy coastal heat hung over Pensacola like a sweaty blanket. Not unlike most Gulf ports, the city in August was hot and fetid and thoroughly unpleasant. That it was a major railhead, gateway to Alabama and the Florida Panhandle, simply made matters all the worse. Tracks fanned out from the city in a latticework of steel, narrow-gauge arteries linking it with hundreds of inland towns and countless whistle-stops. Throughout the day, trains chuffed in and out of Pensacola, a snarl of fire-breathing monsters drawn to the switchyards as dragons to a den. But along with the human cargo disgorged, and tons of freight embarking overland from the wharfs, the trains left an unmistakable spoor. Thick smoke and grimy soot drifted across the city; combined with the soppy heat, it left Pensacola sweltering in a filthy steam bath.

Coat slung over his shoulder, Ed Duncan stood on the depot platform, eyes riveted on the bands of steel running west from the city. Beads of sweat streamed down his face, and in the humid noonday heat, his shirt stuck to him like a mustard plaster. He felt soaked, limp as a dishrag, a human puddle caught in a vapid blast furnace. Lips pinched tight, his mouth a small cavern of salt, he silently cursed the heat and inept railroads and the South. Mostly the South. At times such as this his thoughts returned to the Orkney Islands, off the coast of Scotland, where he had grown to manhood. It was a land of cool ocean breezes and emerald fields and untainted air, and he found himself wishing he'd never left it.

A wish he'd dwelled on much this past year.

Never a believer in luck, except that which a man made for himself, Duncan had come to a brooding uncertainty about the caprice of time and circumstance. Seemingly, the gods had conspired with fortune, and so far as he, personally, was concerned, the outcome had been nothing short of catastrophic. He had crisscrossed this miserable, steamy land since late last summer, and in all that time he had turned up not one lead as to the whereabouts of John Wesley Hardin. The only thing he'd accomplished was to prove to his own satisfaction that southern hospitality was a fable. Outsiders, which included both Yankees and bandy-legged Scotsmen, were as welcome as a plague of locusts.

After the Savannah shoot-out, Allan Pinkerton had ordered him to resume the manhunt. The young fugitive was to be brought in, according to Pinkerton's directive, regardless of how long it took. Neither the agency chief nor the governor of Texas thought it would be a snap. The man they sought was a most uncommon outlaw, as he had demonstrated to the embarrassment of everyone involved. But none of them, Duncan most especially, had believed that the hunt would consume another year.

The search was resumed in Savannah, where Hardin had disappeared, and it quickly became apparent that Duncan was looking for the proverbial needle in a haystack. Pinkerton had made the case his sole responsibility. There was only one outlaw, the Old Man declared, and it should require only one detective to find him. Duncan struck off alone, checking steamboat lines, outlying railroad depots, and fully a hundred livery stables in surrounding counties. Finally, having exhausted the more likely prospects, Duncan was forced to admit that Hardin had outfoxed the hounds. However he had escaped, it broke the pattern he'd followed since departing New Orleans in the summer of '75.

Duncan returned to Savannah, and began a house-to-house

canvass of farms along roads leading from the city. Late in November, what was now the winter of '76, the drudgery at last paid off. He stumbled across a farmer on the Claxton Road who had sold a horse the summer before to a man answering the description of Wes Hardin. The date fitted, and as the stranger had appeared afoot early one morning, the timing dovetailed neatly with the Savannah shoot-out. After four months of dogged legwork, Duncan finally knew how his man had eluded capture. And more than that, he knew Hardin had headed west into Georgia.

But what seemed good fortune quickly proved nothing more than a fluke. The trail simply evaporated, as if Hardin went up in a puff of smoke after buying the horse. Duncan's line of search, which roughly paralleled Sherman's March to the Sea, became a study in futility. The natives were aloof, hostile, and at times downright insulting. They gave him little conversation, and even less information. If any of them had seen a rider fitting the fugitive's description, they betrayed it by not so much as a flicker of an eyelash. Whatever else they were, Duncan wrote in his reports, these Georgia crackers were good haters and damned accomplished liars.

Before long he came to feel like a blind man groping from one cul-de-sac to another, and by the New Year, he reluctantly called it quits. Hardin had once more slipped through his grasp.

Then, as if fate meant to toy with him a while longer, a shot in the dark bore fruit. At their meeting in Atlanta last summer, Allan Pinkerton had ordered him to have a surveillance placed on Reverend James Hardin's mail. Duncan wrote Austin, suggesting some sort of arrangement be worked out with the postmaster in Mount Calm, and the attorney general set the wheels in motion. Afterward, the detective forgot about it, never once dreaming that Hardin would be so foolhardy. But in early January, with his spirits at a low ebb, he received an astounding communiqué from the Pinkerton office in Chicago. According to Austin, the elder Hardin had gotten two letters, a month apart, both postmarked Pensacola. Implicit in this new wrinkle was the curious fact that the letters bore no return address. While scarcely hard evidence, it was enough to galvanize the Scotsman. At an impasse in Georgia, with the letters his only fresh clue in months, he immediately boarded a train for Florida.

Pensacola proved to be—if anything—more of a dud than Savannah. Duncan at first spent his days haunting the post office and his nights sifting through outgoing mail. When that drew a blank, another month down the drain, he began combing the city. Hardin's favorite hangouts—saloons and gambling dens, cattle auctions and slaughterhouses—were investigated with painstaking care. But all to no avail. By late spring the detective was forced to a distasteful conclusion. John Wesley Hardin had changed his method of operating, doubtless disguising himself behind an occupation completely unrelated to his past. That, or he was living elsewhere and merely using Pensacola as a mail drop. Or he might have played it very cagey and done both.

Which brought things full circle. Another cul-de-sac.

Duncan went through the motions, but his heart wasn't in it. As in Savannah, he widened the search to outlying towns, expecting little and finding less. His actions were those of a skilled man hunter reduced again to the drudge of procedure and legwork. The red-necks of Florida were even less co-operative than the crackers of Georgia, and as the summer wore on his mood slowly soured in the juices of its own frustration.

All the more so since communiqués from Allan Pinkerton informed him that letters continued to arrive in Mount Calm. And with the exception of a stray bird from Mobile, the postmark never varied—Pensacola. Clearly, the man he had tracked so far and so long had come to earth within close proximity of the port city. But where, and in what guise, were questions that defied answer. The detective simmered and stewed, more from his sagging spirits than the heat, and doggedly plodded about the countryside in a game of blindman's buff.

Then, in late July, he received a cryptic telegraph message from Allan Pinkerton. He was to meet Lieutenant John

Armstrong of the Texas Rangers in Pensacola. Armstrong's
train would arrive on the first day of August, and at that time
he would explain the purpose of the meeting. There the message ended, and Pinkerton left him to grapple as best he
could with his own impatience. Not to mention a seething
indignation at a move which had all the earmarks of impending demotion. Otherwise, he could think of no logical
explanation for calling up the Rangers.

And now, dripping sweat and boiling mad, he waited on
the depot platform as the train slowly screeched to a halt.
Several passengers stepped off the coaches, but he had little
trouble identifying the Ranger. John Armstrong was tall and
rawboned, weathered lean with time. His mouth was straight
as a razor slit, covered somewhat by a bristly mustache, and
his jutting chin had a cleft so wide it might have been split
with an ax. The high-crowned hat, spurs, and six-gun were
merely window dressing, like ornaments on a Christmas tree.
Plainly, he was a Texan, and from the way he carried himself
and kept his eyes squinted in a hawklike scowl, he was
damned proud of it.

The two men spotted one another and came together on
the platform. They made an odd contrast—the tall, lantern-
jawed Texan and the diminutive, pale-eyed Scotsman—and
a moment passed as they stared at each other with mutual
distaste. Armstrong didn't like Yankees, even the imported
variety, and Duncan had an aversion to swaggering gunmen
who passed themselves off as peace officers. Which sort of
got them off to an even start. The Pinkerton stuck out his
hand and the Ranger gave it a perfunctory shake. Then Armstrong shifted his cud and squirted tobacco juice off the edge
of the platform.

"Take it you must be Duncan."

"Which rather obviously makes you Armstrong."

The Texan grunted. "Anybody tell you why I was
comin'?"

"I was informed by our Chicago office that you would
tender an explanation upon arrival."

"Meanin' I was to give you the lowdown."

Duncan drew a long breath and sighed. "Yes, I believe we can say that was the gist of the message."

Armstrong's hawklike gaze flicked around the depot and he lowered his voice to a near whisper. "Hardin finally slipped up. Week ago Saturday, his daddy mailed him a letter to a post-office box here in Pensacola." He jerked his chin back toward the train. "It's in the express car. Oughta be put in his box sometime tonight."

"I presume we're to maintain a watch on the post office and take him into custody when he appears."

"That's the gen'ral idea. Leastways, if he don't make a fight of it."

"And if he does?"

"Let's hope he don't. The governor wants him alive, and I'm the kinda fella that likes to follow orders."

"Apparently the governor didn't feel the Pinkertons could handle the situation without help."

The lawman smiled and squirted the cinders again. "Well, s'pose we just say he thought the Rangers oughta be in on the showdown. However it works out."

Duncan gave him a short look. "Translated, that means after I've chased him for two years Texas wants to claim some of the glory for itself."

"Yeah, but you just chased him. You ain't never caught him. Makes a whole heap of difference."

The little Scotsman conceded grudgingly. "Your logic underwhelms me."

Armstrong liked four-bit words even if he didn't always understand them. "Shorty, you and me is gonna get along just fine. Now what d'ya say we find ourselves a waterin' hole and lemme sluice some of the dust out of my innards. Goddamn, I'd sooner take a whippin' than ride a train."

Duncan turned without a word and headed uptown. The Ranger tagged along, lugging a war bag, thoroughly pleased with the way things had gone thus far. Back in Austin they'd told him to watch himself, warning him that the Pinks would

attempt to grab the headlines. But plain to see, he didn't have
nothing whatsoever to worry about.

This little fella was the runt of the litter.

2

Adair and the loggers looked like a bunch of overfed
schoolboys out on a lark. Laughing and yelling and playfully
swapping punches, they walked forward to where Harry
Swain awaited them outside the sawmill. Under Adair's supervision, the crew had just brought a run down driver and
they were in a mood to celebrate. Over the past year this had
become something of a tradition with Adair & Company.
Several weeks' backbusting work in the woods, then skating
the logs down the Escambia, and afterward, a volcanic spree
that left Pensacola's red-light district in a shambles.

The laughter faded to smiles and some of the exuberance
melted away as they halted in front of Swain. A remarkable
change had come over the young businessman in the last six
months. He was decked out in a conservative suit and looked
spiffy as an undertaker. These days he seldom worked with
the crew, and since the blowout in Mobile had never taken
part in their celebrations. That part they could understand—
killing a gambler and wounding a policeman was reason
enough to lay back for a while. But they knew him as a
carouser and a man who loved a good scrap, and they
couldn't quite fathom his sudden taste for the straight and
narrow. His time was now spent flitting about the countryside, wheeling and dealing on assorted ventures, and rumor
had it that he was becoming wealthy as sin. The men still
liked him, and admired his style, but the closeness, that old
sense of easy familiarity, was gone. Somehow, in a way none
of them could articulate, he was no longer a part of the crew.
He was the boss, both to them and his partner, which was
clear in the way Joe Dan Adair deferred to his judgment. It
sort of put a damper on things at times such as this, and for

that reason alone, they lost some of their raucous good humor in his presence.

Smiling, Swain waited till they ganged around, then gave his partner a steady look. "Joe Dan, I hate to spoil your fun, but Timmons is waitin' for us in his office."

"Aw hell, Harry, there ain't no sense in me bein' there." The Irishman's face wrinkled in a hangdog expression. "All that horse tradin' and contracts and such is your bailiwick."

"Just the same, I think you ought to sit in. We're gonna be talkin' tall cotton, and I want him to know we're both of a mind."

Adair grumped something to himself and fell silent. After a moment Swain glanced around at the crew. "Boys, I'm afraid your wingding is liable to be a little short this time. If we pull this deal off I wanna catch the three-ten back to Polland and get things movin'." He pulled a fancy pocket watch from his vest and checked the time. "That gives you about four hours to tie one on. And don't get yourselves tossed in the jug, neither. I wanna see everybody at the depot bright-eyed and bushy-tailed."

The men sulled up, groaning their displeasure. But he cut them short by hauling out a roll of greenbacks and peeling off several bills. He stuffed the bills in the shirt pocket of Monk Birkhead, the foreman.

"That ought to cover drinks and a quick trip to Ma Smalley's for everybody. Just be sure you get 'em to the train station on time." He started away, then turned back and fished a small key from his vest pocket. "Monk, I'd be obliged if you'll do a little errand for me. This here's the key to my mailbox. Pick up any letters I've got and bring 'em on to the depot."

Swain grinned, waved the crew on their way, and walked off toward the sawmill office. Adair ambled along beside him, hands thrust deep in his pockets, plainly out of sorts. They skirted the scrap heap, picking their way over slabs of bark and refuse, and finally the Irishman couldn't hold it any longer.

"Harry, I don't like to be throwin' rocks, but you're makin' it awful hard for me to live with them boys. I mean, hell's fire, they bust their butts for us and they got a right to blow off a little steam."

"Horseapples! We've got 'em spoiled rotten and you know it." Swain stopped and fixed him with a tight scowl. "Joe Dan, lemme tell you somethin'. We're about to talk turkey on the biggest contract we ever negotiated. Now, I haven't got time to wipe noses and listen to people bellyache. If this deal goes through we'll all be sittin' on easy street. But we're gonna have to quit playin' kid games and buckle down to work."

He paused, scrutinizing the older man closely. "I'd like to know you're with me on this."

Adair nodded and ducked his chin. "Hell, I'm here, ain't I? But that easy street ain't as easy as it sounds. What makes you think Timmons won't beat you down on price?"

Swain flashed a cocky grin. "Because I'm holdin' a club over his head. Pud Moore is just itchin' to sell me his sawmill, and that sort of puts Timmons between a rock and a hard place. I suspect he'd roll over and do tricks to keep me out of the millin' business."

Laughing, he threw an arm over Adair's shoulders. "C'mon, you old goat. Let's go get ourselves a contract. And stop actin' like you're gonna swell up and cry. God A'mighty, I never saw a man fight so hard to keep from gettin' rich."

Adair chuckled despite himself and playfully rapped his young partner in the stomach. Then, of a mind, they marched through the sawmill door. It promised to be a lively session, and in a way, the Irishman was glad he'd been strong-armed into coming along. All of a sudden he had an idea that being rich wouldn't be half bad. Not at all.

Things generally slacked off at the post office after noon-time, and the rest of the day became a grinding bore. Back in the mail room, Duncan and Armstrong tried to stay awake swapping stories, but by now they had pretty well exhausted their supply of tall tales and anecdotes. Three weeks had passed, and every minute of every day their eyes remained glued on a certain box and the single letter it contained. They arrived at the post office when it opened each morning and left when the doors were locked each night. And the waiting had slowly become a test of their endurance.

That they had endured one another was no small feat in itself. The only thing they had in common was the man they pursued. Their views on politics, religion, the law, and most particular, methods of apprehending the lawless were poles apart. Their storytelling began as a means to pass the time, but gradually evolved into a device to rankle the one listening. They bickered constantly, sparking some heated arguments, and three weeks sequestered in the post office had hardly brought them closer together. Yet they were both under orders, and despite their antipathy, forced to make the best of a bad bargain. Until Hardin showed it was like it or lump it, and for Ranger and Pinkerton alike, it was strictly a matter of lump it.

The two men had suffered one another's company so long that they had finally come round to rehashing stale arguments. Just now Armstrong had his mouth stuffed with Climax and was glaring fiercely at the little detective.

"The hell you say! There ain't one iota of proof. You're like a possum hound barkin' up an empty tree."

Duncan's mouth quirked in a patronizing smile. "And your problem, Lieutenant, is that you seem blinded by facts. First, the postmarked date on a letter mailed from Mobile to Hardin's father. Next, on the day after that date, a gambler is killed—remember now, Hardin likes his poker—and a policeman wounded. Last, and perhaps most significant, was the fancy pistol shooting. There aren't many men that handy with a gun. Not even in Texas."

That stung and Armstrong recoiled. "Fat lot you know. I could name you a dozen men that could've done better'n that. And them's just the Rangers. Why, hell, there must be a hunnert fellers that good with a gun. Mebbe more."

"In Mobile?" Duncan countered dryly.

"Judas Priest! Arguin' with you is like talkin' with an

anvil.'' Armstrong squirted a spittoon and knuckled tobacco juice off his mustache. ''What I'm tryin' to get through your head is that—''

The detective stiffened, staring wide-eyed at the mailbox. Armstrong looked up in time to see a hand extract the letter and slam the door. Both men leaped from their chairs, guns drawn, and ran to a door at the far corner of the mail room. But once through the door they skidded to a halt. The man walking away from the box was wrong in every respect. Too short. Several years too old. And ugly enough to stop an eight-day clock.

''Sonovabitch, that peckerhead ain't Hardin.'' Armstrong seemed genuinely perplexed. ''What the hell do we do now?''

Duncan's stumpy legs were moving even as the man disappeared through the street door. ''We follow that letter. Wherever it goes!''

Then he was gone and the Ranger hurried after him. They hit the street, spotted their man turning downtown, and tagged along a half block behind. For the first time in three weeks, their common denominator brought them together in a union of purpose and mutual need.

Harry Swain was seated on the aisle and next to him Joe Dan Adair sat gazing out the coach window. Last-minute pasengers were hurrying to board the train, but Adair seemed oblivious to the commotion, humming softly to himself. Though his drinking time had been cut drastically short, he was pretty well squiffed and feeling no pain. An hour ago they had signed the largest contract in the history of Adair & Company, and he was fairly bubbling over with good cheer. Just as his partner had predicted, he was on the verge of joining the well-to-do. And for that he thanked neither God nor his lucky stars, but Harry Swain, the slickest horse trader to come down the pike since Heck was a pup.

Their crew was spread out through the coach, ossified on cheap liquor and a bit sapped from their brief but hectic tussle with Ma Smalley's girls. While they were accustomed to somewhat longer benders, a couple of days at least, they really couldn't complain. The boss had footed the bill, plus forking over their regular bonus, which showed that his heart was in the right spot after all. They settled back in the stiff, uncomfortable seats, their hunger slaked for the moment, and began daydreaming about the next time.

The young businessman was preoccupied himself, but with matters of a loftier nature. Monk Birkhead had brought a letter from his mailbox—the first letter in two years from his folks—and he was rapidly devouring the hometown news. Although his head swirled with contracts and figures and potential profits, he set such things aside as he skimmed through the letter. Everybody in the family was well and overjoyed that he had again found the Lord, and, of course, they were delighted with his business success. Not to mention the children and the steadying influence of his good wife. Mount Calm was peaceful and thriving, and church membership was on the rise. Old friends often inquired about him, and the family offered prayers each night that he find a horn of plenty in the land where he had built a new life.

Reading that, he chuckled to himself. It seemed that nothing had changed in Mount Calm. Or in the Hardin household either. Maybe that was the way of it, though. How it was meant to be. Some places and some people never changed. Smiling, he again focused on the letter.

"Hands up! Anybody moves gets shot."

The letter fluttered to the floor. Just for a moment he sat there in a witless stupor, hardly able to credit his eyes. A man stood at the front of the coach with a pistol leveled on his chest. And from the garb, and the weathered rawhide look, he scarcely needed to be told who the man was. The Texas Rangers, incredible as it seemed, had found him at last.

Uncoiling, he sprang to his feet, clawing at the Colt in the waistband of his trousers. But the gun refused to budge, its hammer snagged on the bottom of his vest, and he tugged frantically to jerk it clear. Beside him, Joe Dan Adair encountered no problem whatever. Through an alcoholic haze,

the old man pegged it as a holdup and fumbled a bulldog
pistol from his hip pocket. As he brought it to bear, a little
man in a rumpled suit at the back of the coach shot him
between the shoulder blades. The impact of the slug drove
him forward, angling sideways through the open window,
and he fell headlong to the tracks outside.

The young outlaw was still struggling with his own gun,
distracted for a moment by Adair's death and the unsettling
fact that somebody had him covered from the rear. Then, in
the next instant, the Ranger somehow materialized in the
aisle, directly in front of him, and clubbed him over the head
with a long-barreled Peacemaker. His eyes rolled back in his
head like glazed stones and he staggered crazily against the
seats. Suddenly he went limp, a huge doll with its stuffing
torn loose, then he rebounded off the cushion and slumped
unconscious to the floor.

Ed Duncan walked forward, waving his pistol at the rest
of the crew. "You men just keep your seats and nobody will
get hurt."

He stopped beside Armstrong, who was staring down at
the young outlaw. They stood there for a while, hardly able
to believe that it had gone so smoothly. That they had captured John Wesley Hardin at last. When the detective finally
spoke there was something new in his voice. A note of respect.

"That was a nervy thing you did, John. The lad might
well have killed you."

"Naw, hell, there's the nervy one." Armstrong jerked his
chin at the crumpled form on the floor. "Had the drop on
him and the bastard kept right on tryin' to get that gun un-
tangled."

"You could have shot him, though. I suspect most men
would."

"Mebbe. But all I could think of was the governor sayin'
he wanted Hardin alive. Been sort of embarrassin' if I'd
brought him back in a box."

They fell silent for a moment, then Armstrong glanced
down at the detective. "Ed, I'm obliged to you for takin'

care of that other feller. What with me bird-doggin' Hardin the way I was, I got an idea you saved my bacon.''

Duncan smiled. ''Professional courtesy, John. You would have done the same for me.''

The Ranger's mouth creased in a small grin. ''Yep, reckon I would at that. But I owe you, all the same.''

Armstrong extended his hand and the little Scotsman gave it a hearty shake. Then, while Duncan kept the logging crew covered, the lanky Texan grabbed Hardin by the heels and dragged him off the train. As he backed through the coach door, Ed Duncan was whistling softly under his breath. A sprightly tune, Scottish in origin, and better played on the bagpipes. But it seemed fitting nonetheless, for he was a happy man, at peace once again with himself.

Two years and twenty-one days. And done with at last.

3

The cell was nothing to write home about. It was small, with a bunk and washstand on one side, and a table with a couple of chairs on the opposite wall. Under the bunk was a slop jar, but as the guards emptied it only once a day, the whole place reeked of an outhouse. The view wasn't bad, though. Not if a man liked to look at the capitol building. The jail fronted San Jacinto Street, right in the heart of Austin, and they had given him a cell on the top floor. Standing at the window, he could gaze out over the bustling city, and ironically enough, had a beeline view of the governor's office.

Which was where he spent the most part of every day. There, staring out the window, or else pacing back and forth like a caged animal. The jailers kept a wary eye on him, for he was restless and seldom off his feet. Not until late at night, when he was worn out from pacing, did he flop on the bunk and try to sleep. But even then, it was difficult to rest. He felt trapped, a great lobo caged in steel, the freedom he prized above all else gone forever. Better had they shot him, put him in the ground, for a wolf deprived of his freedom was no wolf at all. He was simply a beast, mindlessly pacing his stinking lair in numbed rage.

He paused at the window, staring out across at the capitol. Again he was struck by the question that ate on him, nibbling at his bowels with sharp little teeth. What good is the law in a land where there is no justice? Like Texas. Where the men in power twist the law to suit their own ends.

The governor wanted him caught and caged. So the man hunters had tracked him down. Taken him captive in a state where their badges meant nothing. Killed an innocent man in the process. All without warrant or legal right of seizure. Then, compounding the illegality of their act, they had spirited him back to Texas. And again, on order from the governor. Simply shunted aside the judiciary process. Ignored the accused's right of habeas corpus and the fundamental privilege of extradition proceedings. Slapped him in irons and shoved him aboard a train. Hustled him across half a continent in defiance of all laws ever written to protect the rights of an accused man. The trial had been held in absentia—a kangaroo court invoked by the law-makers themselves—and the verdict rendered. Innocent until proved guilty ceased to exist. The law and the governor and the state of Texas had decreed that justice was better served if certain men were shortchanged on their rights, brought to bay and caged in the most expeditious manner possible.

Which made them worse than the man they jailed. Their lawlessness was larded with deceit. The act of hypocrites. A mockery of the very system they were sworn to uphold. Beside them, an outlaw was an honest man. He risked all in open defiance. They risked nothing, for it was within their power to pervert the law according to the needs of the moment. To make justice a sham and evil a virtue. All in the name of honor and decency and the state's inviolate right to an eye for an eye.

Standing there, his gaze fixed on the windows of the governor's office, Wes Hardin was an embittered man. Not from hate or a thirst for revenge. Nor as an outgrowth of his long vendetta with those who enforced the law. They were merely hired help, mercenaries earning their daily bread. Instead, his rancor was for the kingfish. The high and mighty. The men who called the shots. He felt like a gambler who had played the game squarely, calling every bet and never questioning the stakes, only to find in the end that the cards had been marked all along.

A game rigged by the anointed. The lawmakers themselves.

Footsteps in the corridor broke his train of thought, and he became aware that someone had stopped outside his cell. He turned from the window, and seeing them there, such an unlikely pair, made him smile. Standing outside the door was his nemesis, Ed Duncan, and the detective's lanky sidekick, John Armstrong. Curiously, he felt no bitterness toward these men. They had taken him alive, when they might as easily have killed him, and on the long journey back to Texas they had treated him fairly and with respect. Against orders, they had even allowed him to pen a hasty letter to Jane, informing her of his capture. Perhaps they were lawdogs, but they weren't bastards. In a queer sort of way, he'd grown to like them. What his educated lawyer called friendly adversaries.

He crossed the cell and stuck his hand through the bars. "Mornin', gents. How's tricks?"

Both men shook his hand and Duncan returned the smile. "Can't complain. How about yourself?"

"Why, I'm livin' in the lap of luxury, Ed." He motioned back toward the cell. "Soft bed, three squares a day, and somebody to empty my johnny-pot. All the comforts of home."

Armstrong, who rarely smiled anyway, wasn't fooled by the light tone. He shifted his quid to the off-cheek and gave the cell a sour look. "Not much, is it? Seems like they could've done better for a fella of your caliber."

"John, I don't suppose it matters much. However it was fixed up, it'd still be a cage." Wes flashed them a sudden grin, dismissing it with an idle gesture. "Listen here now, that's enough of my troubles. What brings you gents callin' so bright and early?"

"Couple of things," Duncan replied.

"Mebbe three," Armstrong amended, slewing a sidewise glance at the detective. "You recollect that leetle debate, don't you?"

"Yes, to be sure. Our bone of contention. But the good news first." Duncan beamed, thumbs hooked in his vest pockets. "Wes, by rights your lawyer should be telling you this, but since we're feeling particularly fond of you today, we wanted to be the bearers of good tidings. The court has approved the motion for change of venue. Your trial will be held right here in Austin."

Wes was genuinely surprised. "Well, I'll be dipped. Never figured that had the chance of a snowball in hell."

Armstrong clucked, bobbing his head like an old tom turkey. "You're mighty lucky, Wes. Mighty lucky. If that bunch down in Dewitt County had ever got their meat hooks on you, that'd been all she wrote."

"You'll get no argument there. Folks on the Guadalupe wouldn't exactly remember me with what you'd call Christian charity."

He hesitated a moment, studying the lawmen with a quizzical frown. "Speakin' of which. How come you fellows are feelin' especially fond of me today? Old man Pinkerton give you a citation or somethin'?"

"Better'n that." Armstrong managed what passed for a smile.

"Much better." Duncan rocked up on his toes, eyes bright. "Wes, the state has authorized payment of the reward for your capture. John and I will share in it equally. Which is only fair, of course."

"Five thousand simoleons." Armstrong spoke the words with a poor man's reverence.

"Well, kiss my dusty butt!" Wes lit up with a big smile and he pumped their arms in a warm handshake. "By God,

NOBLE OUTLAW   291

I'm proud as punch. You boys earned it. Ever' nickel of it. If I was out of here I'd stand you to a round of drinks.''

The irony of his statement struck them at the same time and they all burst out laughing. Then, after their laughter slacked off, Duncan gave him a sober look.

"Wes, we're pleased you took it this way. John said you would, and I tended to agree, but we're gratified nonetheless.''

"Hell's bells, I don't hold you fellows no grudge. You was just earnin' your keep, and that's all there is to it. Besides, I come out smellin' like a rose. Listen here, I damn near keeled over when I found out they was only gonna prosecute me on one count. And for shootin' Charlie Webb, too! Christ, that's the biggest joke I ever heard.''

"Don't let it tickle you too much," Armstrong commented glumly. "They got witnesses on that one, and the word's out—they're figgerin' on stretchin' your neck.''

Wes waved it off. "Hide and watch. We got a few tricks up our sleeves. Might turn out a whole lot different than most folks think.''

The lawmen exchanged a look more eloquent than words. Clearly, they didn't share his optimism. A moment passed in silence, and then Duncan snapped his fingers.

"Say, that reminds me. What John said about our debate. Now, if you would rather not talk about it, we'll understand. And naturally, anything you say is off the record. But we've had this argument going, and if you could clear up a few loose ends, we would certainly be in your debt.''

Wes nodded, mildly puzzled. "Argument about what?''

"The fact of the matter is"—Duncan faltered, groping for words—"Wes, there isn't any easy way to ask this. You see, our debate has to do with your gunfights.''

"Aw, quit pussyfootin' around, Ed." Armstrong shifted his quid and glanced back at the outlaw. "What he's trying to ask you is how many men you've killed.''

The Ranger gave him a sly wink and Wes just nodded, solemn as a judge. Then, pursing his lips, he looked over at the little detective. "Well, Ed, lemme ask you—was you talkin' about white men, or did your argument include Injuns and greasers?"

Duncan's eyes went round as saucers. "Why—uh—I don't know, really. I suppose men are men, regardless of their color." He paused, still uncertain, and shrugged. "In all fairness to John, I think it's the overall number we would have to consider."

Wes rubbed his jaw and spent several moments in deep calculation. Finally he grunted. "Course, you understand, I never notched my guns or any such foolishness. So I might be off a couple either way. But near as I can figure, I'd say forty would come pretty damn close."

Duncan blinked, plainly startled, but Armstrong cackled softly and slapped him across the shoulders. "See there, you little runt. Told you, didn't I? Next time you won't be so quick to put your money where your mouth is."

The Scotsman swallowed, and then, quite softly, "Forty?"

"Give or take a few. Gets a little fuzzy that far back."

"Lad, I've done you a grave injustice. A man should never underestimate his adversary. Particularly in our line of work."

Duncan was still shaking his head when they left, not at all himself. But for once Armstrong actually appeared jovial, as if he had pulled off some rare coup that only a Texan could fully comprehend.

A little later Wes heard footsteps and thought they had returned with more questions. Pleased with the joke, and himself, he crossed the cell ready to lay it on thick. Then he froze, everything suddenly gone blurred and somehow distorted, like looking through a windowpane smeared with the splatter of raindrops.

Standing at the cell door, were James and Sarah Hardin. They had never been a family to show affection, but his arms went through the bars now and embraced them in a tight hug. There were tears streaming down his mother's face, and as far back as memory served, it was the first time he remembered his father turning loose. They held him close

through the bars, content just to touch, and for a long while
nobody spoke. At last, the old man cleared his throat, swallowing hard, and looked up.

"Son, if it's not too late, we've come to help."

4

The trial was an event. A Texas-style Roman circus. The
biggest thing to happen in Austin since the carpetbaggers
departed back in '74. The newspaper ballyhooed it with
reams of purple prose. John Wesley Hardin, Texas' most
notorious desperado, was to be tried for murder. By early
September the sensationalism had built to a fever pitch, and
people converged on Austin from all directions to see the
spectacle. Their mood was carnival, laughing and high-
spirited, and a holiday atmosphere settled over the city. They
had come to gawk at the most deadly gunfighter of them all,
the swaggering young bravo who reputedly had killed a man
for every year of his life.

But if the trial was a drawing card, the main attraction
would come afterward. At the scaffold, where condemned
men spent their last moments dancing on air. Feeling ran
strong on that score, though. Some people remembered the
days of Yankee oppression, and their sentiments were with
the youngster. Yet others had shorter memories, and were
perhaps more honest. For those who flocked to Austin on
that warm September day—whatever their jangled emotions;
whatever their heated disclaimers—were there of one mind
and one purpose and but a single expectation.

They came to watch Wes Hardin be hung.

An overflow crowd filled the courtroom, with spectators
jammed shoulder to shoulder along the walls. Down front, a
company of Rangers, armed to the teeth and primed for trouble, stood ready should the onlookers become unruly. Seated
at the defense table was the accused and his attorney, Horace
Adams of Waco. Directly behind them, on the other side of
the rail in the front row, was Jane Hardin and the defendant's

294

Matt Braun

parents. The prosecution table was across the room, nearer the jury box, and on the bench sat Judge Marcus White. Earlier that morning the jury had been impaneled, but only after Horace Adams exhausted all his peremptory challenges. A noted criminal lawyer, with a flair for drama and a mellifluous voice, Adams had left the impression that his client was unlikely to receive a fair trial anywhere in the state of Texas, much less in the capital city itself.

Afterward, Judge White gave everybody a stiff lecture about their conduct in his courtroom and the trial began. Tate Belford, special prosecutor appointed by the governor, made a lengthy opening address in which John Wesley Hardin came off as a cross between a depraved scoundrel and a mad-dog killer. He vowed to prove beyond a shadow of a doubt that the accused had gunned down Deputy Sheriff Charles Webb in cold blood. Defense counsel held his opening remarks to a minimum, gently ridiculing the state's inflammatory assertions. He drew laughs from the crowd, which Judge White quickly silenced, and tentative smiles from the jurors. Having harpooned Belford where it hurt, he quit while he was ahead.

The prosecutor was an old hand, and while rankled by the gibes, he was never in any danger of losing his composure. With the stage set, and the spectators hanging on his every word, he began to unravel the state's case. Throughout the morning a half-dozen witnesses, freshly imported from De-witt County, were paraded to the stand. Without exception, they were former members of the Sutton Vigilance Committee, and with only minor variations, they all told the same story. The accused and his kinsmen had killed Deputy Webb without provocation or reason. Foul murder, three against one, with the peace officer riddled full of holes. Belford even managed to sneak in some testimony about a conspiracy, hinting that the death of Charles Webb was, in fact, premeditated murder. Adams strenuously objected and Judge White ruled the testimony inadmissible. But the jury had heard, nonetheless. After several gory recountings of the killing itself, and heavy stress on three gunmen against a lone peace officer, the notion of a conspiracy was easily swallowed.

Adams' cross-examination was brutally incisive, leaving the witnesses rattled and bathed in sweat, but he failed to dislodge them from their story. The prosecution had drawn first blood, and the jurors began eyeing Hardin as if he were a molester of little girls.

Then, pausing for effect, Tate Belford offered up the *coup de grâce*. He called to the witness stand Clarence Spivey, sheriff of Dewitt County. They worked well together, and made a hard act to follow. Tate knew the questions and Spivey had all the answers. In ten chilling minutes, Spivey related how he had stood on the courthouse steps and watched Wes Hardin, assisted by Jim Taylor and Bud Dixon, murder Deputy Charles Webb. There was no doubt as to the identity of the killers, and having witnessed it with his own eyes, he could verify that the dead man never had a chance to defend himself. It was outright murder, with all the mercy of three men slaughtering a hog.

Belford resumed his seat, looking immensely pleased with himself, and Adams rose for cross-examination. He approached the witness stand scratching his head, almost hesitant, apparently puzzled by something he'd heard.

"Sheriff, I confess I'm at a bit of a loss. You stated you were on the courthouse steps when the shooting occurred. Is that correct?"

Spivey was a paunchy, whey-faced man with a nose the color of rotten plums. On guard now, he squinted back at the lawyer through rheumy eyes. "It is."

Adams still looked perplexed. "You weren't in your office?"

"No."

"Afraid to show your face?"

"No."

"And isn't it a fact, Sheriff"—Adams turned to face the jury and his voice cracked like a bullwhip—"that on the day in question you were *dead drunk*?"

Belford leaped to his feet. "Objection! Counsel is badgering the witness, your honor."

"Sustained," Judge White intoned. "Watch your step, Mr. Adams."

Adams nodded and turned back to the witness. "If you weren't drunk, Sheriff, perhaps you could tell us where your deputy was during the shooting. I believe his name is Dave Karnes."

Spivey batted his eyes a couple of times. "Why, I seem to recollect he was back in the office."

"Wasn't that rather odd? That he wasn't with you while a shooting was in progress?"

"Not especially. We had no way of knowin' there was gonna be a fight."

"You didn't know that Charles Webb was in town for the express purpose of confronting John Wesley Hardin?"

"I did not."

"And I suppose you'll tell us next that you did not send Deputy Karnes to warn Wes Hardin of Webb's avowed intention to shoot him dead?"

Spivey bridled with indignation. "That's what I'm gonna tell you awright, 'cause it never happened."

"By the way, Sheriff, where is Dave Karnes now?"

"I wouldn't know. Turned out he didn't have the stomach for law work and I had to fire him."

"Oh, when was that?"

Spivey's nose purpled and his store-bought teeth clacked together. "Couple o' weeks back."

"Now, isn't that strange? You mean to say that after three years as your deputy you decided he wasn't fit to be a peace officer?"

"That's right."

"Wasn't that a little—sudden?"

"Nope. He had a family and I just hated to do it, that's all."

"Very commendable. A lawman with a soft heart." Adams stalked back to the defense table, then whirled, leveling his finger at the witness. "Sheriff Spivey, I offer you one last chance. Will you here and now recant the lies you have just told this court?"

Belford bounced out of his chair, sputtering with rage. Judge White waved him silent and looked across at the jurors. "The jury will disregard defense counsel's last question." Then he turned back to Adams. "Counselor, you are bordering on contempt of court. Let this be my last warning."

"I understand perfectly, your honor." Adams took his seat. "Defense has no further questions of this witness."

Presently, after the spectators were quieted and order restored, it became apparent that Spivey was the state's final witness. Belford rested his case for the prosecution and Judge White called noon recess. Adams conferred briefly with his client, expressing guarded optimism. They had lost ground, he admitted, but the day was still young. Wes was allowed a few minutes with Jane and his folks, and he could see from their quivery looks that they were worried. As he was himself. The morning hadn't been a spectacular success. Then, all too suddenly, the jailer tapped him on the shoulder and he was returned to his cell for lunch.

Shortly before two that afternoon court was reconvened. Everyone was in place as Judge White took the bench. He rapped his gavel several times, hammering the crowd into silence, then peered over his glasses at Adams.

"Does defense counsel wish to make an opening statement?"

Adams rose. "No, your honor. Our remarks will be reserved for the summation."

"Very well. You may proceed with your case."

"If it please the court, defense will call but two witnesses. The first is former deputy sheriff of Dewitt County, David R. Karnes."

The crowd erupted in a buzz of speculation and Judge White again hammered them into silence. Dave Karnes, who had been secreted into town only that morning, came forward and took the witness stand. After the oath had been administered Horace Adams crossed the room and stood where he could watch the jurors' faces.

"Mr. Karnes, I believe you served as deputy sheriff of Dewitt County for three years. Is that correct?"

Karnes had put on weight, but he was still fidgety and somewhat unsure of himself. "Yessir, that's correct."

"And you were dismissed from that position two weeks past. On August 27, I believe."

"Yessir, I was."

"Correct me if I'm wrong, Mr. Karnes, but wasn't that just four days after the defendant was captured in Pensacola, Florida?"

"Yessir."

"I see. Now if you will, please tell the court the circumstances prompting your dismissal."

Prosecutor Belford jackknifed to his feet. "Objection! Irrelevant and immaterial, your honor. This has no bearing on the murder of Charles Webb."

"On the contrary," Adams countered. "With the court's indulgence I will show the connection."

Judge White steepled his fingers, considering a moment, then peered down from the bench. "Overruled. Make your point quickly, Mr. Adams. You're skating on thin ice."

Adams smiled and focused once more on the witness. "You may answer the question, Mr. Karnes."

Dave Karnes gulped, took a long breath, and let it all out in a rush of words. "Well, at first, when we heard that Hardin had been captured, nothin' much happened. Ever'body took it real calm. Then a few days later—the twenty-seventh, it was—we got word he was gonna be tried for killin' Webb and quick as scat some of the old Sutton bunch showed up at the sheriff's office."

"You're referring to the followers of William Sutton, who opposed Hardin and his relatives in the Sutton-Taylor feud?"

"Yessir, them's the ones."

"Proceed."

"Well, they shooed me out of the office and there was a lot of yellin' and cussin', and then finally they left. Afterward, the sheriff called me in and told me I was fired. I asks why and he says there's certain people that don't want me around to tell what I know about Webb gettin' hisself killed. When I commenced makin' a fuss the sheriff gave it to me straight. Told me he couldn't protect me. Said if I didn't get out of town, and keep my mouth shut, them same people would turn me into worm meat.''

"So you ran. To protect yourself and your family."

"Yessir, I shore did. That very day."

"And why have you come forward now, Mr. Karnes?"

"Why, 'cause you subpoenaed me and had me shanghaied up here. I ain't no damn fool."

The crowd burst out laughing, and Adams noticed several jurors smothering their smiles. Judge White banged his gavel, and when things settled down, Adams picked up the thread of Karnes's testimony.

"You made a statement that interests me, Mr. Karnes. You said, and I quote—certain people didn't want you around to tell what you knew about Webb getting hisself killed. What did you mean by that phrase—Webb getting hisself killed?"

"Just what I said. Webb come over from Brown County with a bunch of hardcases, all likkered up he was, and commenced braggin' around town how he was gonna kill John Wesley Hardin. Said it'd be easy as shootin' fish in a barrel. Well, a little before sundown, right after the races, the sheriff sent me over to the saloon to warn Hardin. Webb didn't mean nothin' to us, him bein' from another county and all, and the sheriff said he figgered he'd keep hisself in good with the Taylors just in case they won the feud.''

Karnes paused for breath, acutely aware of the jurors watching him and the hushed stillness that had fallen over the courtroom. After a moment, he resumed. "Well, anyhow, I called Hardin outside and about that time Webb walks over. I introduced 'em and Hardin offered to shake hands and that's when Webb shot him.''

"Excuse me, Mr. Karnes. You're absolutely sure of that? Webb shot first? While Hardin was offering to shake hands?"

" 'Course I'm sure. Webb shot him and then Hardin shot him back. Hardin only got off one shot, 'cause he was fallin', y'see. And then Taylor and Dixon opened up and pumped Webb full of holes. Never saw nothin' like it. And don't want to again.''

''Now, let me see if I have it straight. Hardin shot only once and his companions fired a number of times. Is that correct?''

''That's exactly correct.''

''Very well, Mr. Karnes. Now think carefully. You were standing there, the only true eyewitness to the shooting. Is it possible that Charles Webb could have survived the *one shot* fired by Hardin?''

Karnes shrugged. ''Yeah, I suppose so. Leastways Hardin lived through the one Webb give him.''

''Quite true. Now consider carefully again, Mr. Karnes. Is it possible that Charles Webb could have survived the multiple wounds inflicted on him by Taylor and Dixon?''

''No way on earth! They riddled him like a sieve.''

''Then isn't it extremely likely that Charles Webb was killed not by John Wesley Hardin but rather by Jim Taylor and Bud Dixon?''

Belford slammed out of his chair. ''Objection! Calls for a conclusion on the part of the witness.''

''I withdraw the question, your honor.'' Adams moved away from the jury box, then stopped and looked back. ''One final question, Mr. Karnes. Is it your belief that Hardin fired in self-defense?''

''Why shore. Webb shot first. 'Sides, Webb didn't have no business in Dewitt County, anyways. He always was pushin' in where he didn't belong.''

''Thank you, Mr. Karnes.'' Adams strolled to the defense table, then turned and gave Tate Belford a genial smile. ''Your witness, counselor.''

The prosecutor tried, but with each question his cross-examination seemed to spill more worms from the can. He badgered, bullied, and browbeat, and the witness squirmed like jelly throughout the ordeal. But for all his fidgets and gulping of air, Dave Karnes couldn't be swayed from his story. He told what had happened, what he had seen, and nothing could change that. Not even an enraged special prosecutor. When he finally left the stand, bathed in a cold sweat, the former lawman's testimony was still intact.

A nervous murmur swept back over the spectators as Karnes walked from the courtroom. They knew what was coming next, the opening refrain in a dance of death. The very thing that had brought them to Austin. And Horace Adams didn't disappoint them. He stepped away from the defense table, nodded to Judge White, and in a deceptively quiet voice spoke the words they waited to hear.

"The defense calls John Wesley Hardin."

Staring straight ahead, wooden-faced, Wes marched to the stand and repeated the oath. Then he lowered himself into the witness chair and waited. Counsel for the defense again positioned himself at the far end of the jury box. He wanted nothing to distract the jurors from his client, or what they were about to hear, and his first question claimed their attention like a clap of thunder.

"Wes, did you or did you not shoot Charles Webb on the afternoon of May 26, 1874?"

"Yessir, I did."

"Had you ever seen Webb before that day?"

"No sir. I hadn't. Fact is, I'd never even heard of him."

"To set the record straight, then, will you please tell this court why you shot him?"

The defendant shifted slightly, and his gaze came to rest squarely on the jurors. "Webb walked up to me friendly and smilin' like, and when he was introduced, I offered to shake. He latched onto my hand and jerked a gun with his left hand, and then he shot me. He was yellow clean through to pull a trick like that, and as long as he'd started it, I figured I was within my rights to shoot him back."

"And you fired solely in self-defense, is that correct?"

"Yessir, it is."

"Were you aware at the time that Charles Webb was then a deputy sheriff of Brown County?"

"I was. Dave Karnes had just got through tellin' me. But Webb had no jurisdiction in Dewitt County, and even if he

had, he never said a word about arrestin' me. He just said
somethin' like, 'Pleased to meet you,' and then he shot me.''

''Other than the shooting itself, do you have any particular
reason to remember the occasion?''

''Yessir, I do. It was my birthday.''

''How old were you that day?''

''Twenty-one.''

''And you were out celebrating with friends?''

''Well, I was. Webb sort of busted up the celebration.''

Adams paused, watching the jurors smile and nod, and
waited for a twitter of laughter to subside among the spectators. ''Now, Wes, I have but one final question. I want you
to take your time and answer it in your own words. It is
rumored that you have killed a man for every year of your
life. There is no reason for you to confirm or deny that rumor. Still, it is common knowledge that you have killed a
number of men over the years. And for that reason I ask you
now—before this jury and this court—have you ever in your
life killed a man except in self-defense?''

The courtroom went deathly still. Wes looked from the
lawyer to Jane and his parents, then out over the crowd, and
at last brought his gaze back to the jury box. ''When I was
fifteen I killed a man who was tryin' to kill me. Happened
he was black and Yankee soldiers came after me, so I had
to kill some of them. After that the law never let me be.
Someone was always tryin' to kill me—soldiers, carpetbagger police, different kinds of lawmen. But none of 'em ever
gave me a chance to surrender peaceable, to tell my side of
the story. They just came after me and they tried to kill me.
I can't say I regret killin' them, because they brought it on
themselves, and I reckon most of 'em got what they deserved. But as God is my judge, I never killed a man who
didn't try to kill me first. I never robbed nobody or broke
the law in other ways, and I never took pay to kill a man. I
just killed to stay free, and I guess if there's anything worth
killin' for, it's a man's right to freedom.''

He stopped, still looking at the jury, then his eyes moved

to Jane and his mouth ticced in an imperceptible smile. She nodded, blinking away tears, and her lips curved in response. The courtroom remained still, absolutely silent, for perhaps a dozen heartbeats. Then Adams wheeled away from the jury box and strode past the prosecution table.

"Your witness, counselor."

Tate Belford knew better than to monkey with a loaded gun. Never in a month of Sundays could he rattle Hardin. The man appeared made of flint and ice. And just then, it seemed highly improbable that he could even discredit the outlaw for killing a score of men. Somehow, the way Hardin told it, the killings sounded curiously noble, almost patriotic. He would let well enough alone.

"The prosecution has no questions of this witness."

The defendant stepped down from the stand, shoulders squared and head erect, and crossed the courtroom. There was a slight stir in the crowd as he took his seat, then the room froze in utter silence. Horace Adams rose, eyes fastened on the bench, and nodded to Judge White.

"Your honor, the defense rests."

5

Texas was electrified by the news.

John Wesley Hardin would not hang. A jury of his peers had convicted him of second-degree murder. Later polled, the jurors admitted that had it been anyone besides the notorious gunman they would have set him free as a bird. Circumstances surrounding the case, however, made it impossible to render an acquittal verdict. Yet, in all conscience, neither could they send him to the gallows. The outlaw's impassioned, almost eloquent plea from the witness stand had swayed their vote. That, along with the evidence, the jurors readily agreed, had saved him from the rope. Nonetheless, from that same witness chair, he had acknowledged killing a small legion of men. Twenty, perhaps more.

And displayed no sign of either remorse or contrition. Nor did he attempt to excuse the killings, which was to his credit. A proud man to the end, he had not begged.

But if the jurors could not hang him, neither could they turn him loose, perhaps to kill again. However noble a man's intentions—and defending his freedom was perhaps the noblest cause of all—the law demanded payment. Justice must be served. The jury found him guilty of murder in the second degree.

And Judge White sentenced him to twenty-five years.

Newspapers across Texas bannered the story. The youthful outlaw, now only twenty-four, had been spared by the grace of God. And the compassion of twelve very mortal men. Yet, as most editorials agreed, twenty-five years at hard labor in Huntsville Prison was hardly a slap on the wrists. Another jury and another judge might have hung him. But in the end, perhaps mercy was the better choice after all. It was right that Texas bind up its wounds. Set aside its grim memories of Yankee injustice and carpetbagger rule. Turn its eyes onward, to a new day and a fresh beginning.

The time for vengeance had passed.

Oddly enough, everyone seemed satisfied with the verdict except the convicted man himself. Wes Hardin had not compromised himself on the witness stand. Nor had he pandered to the jury, hoping to touch their soft spot and exact some form of clemency. He staunchly believed in man's God-given right to defend the most precious of all possessions—his freedom. The testimony he gave was not meant as an appeal. Nor did he seek to mitigate the act of killing itself, or the fact that in seven brief years he himself had killed some twenty-odd men. Instead, he had played for all the marbles, staking everything on his belief that a man who relinquished the right to defend himself was no man at all.

And in that, he had lost.

But any gambler worth his salt knows when to check the bet. However much he believed himself innocent of wrong-doing—especially in the killing of Charlie Webb—the jury had met him only halfway. That they had not voted acquittal,

he found it difficult to accept, or comprehend. That they had
shown him mercy, instead, both astounded him and unnerved
his deep-rooted conviction that man was the least tolerant of
all God's creatures. Yet, the fact remained, he had gambled
and lost.

Which was a damn good time to fold his cards and call it
a day. There were other murder warrants outstanding, more
than he cared to recall. And to appear ungrateful—or even
worse, angry—might well goad the state into having another
try. They had a grab bag of warrants to choose from, and
next time they might dust off one that would give him a
short, if somewhat unpleasant, acquaintance with the hangman's noose.

Better to hold his peace. Keep his thoughts to himself. Let
them send him to prison. Give the governor his bone. And
the public its sugar tit—a substitute of sorts—for not seeing
him hang. Then, after biding his time for a while, anything
might happen. It was a mortal wonder what a man could do
when he set his mind to it. And Huntsville was scarcely
impregnable. Either from without or from within.

Freedom was illusive but it wasn't yet lost.

Now wasn't the time, though. Nor was the place just exactly right. He was in the visitors' room of the Austin jail,
manacled hand and foot, and outside the door stood a company of Rangers waiting to escort him to the penitentiary.
The Ranger captain had allowed time for final farewells, and
only moments before his folks had left the room. Their parting had gone well, all things considered. His mother wept,
which was to be expected, and his brother Joe, who had
finally put in an appearance, smiled a lot and told him to
keep his dauber up. But the old man had surprised him.
James Hardin talked not of God or those who live by the
sword, and made no mention whatever of his youngest son's
misspent life. Instead, he spoke of the future, and the dawn-
ing of a new era in Texas. And how, in time, Wes would
come back to them and take his place in a more orderly
world. It was farfetched, little more than a fairy tale, but Wes
had indulged the old man's fantasy. If it gave his folks hope

and some measure of comfort, then it was the least he could do. A token gesture, perhaps, but one which would let them sleep easier in the years they had remaining.

All the same he hadn't mentioned his true feelings, or his own plans for the future. Nor would he reveal these things to Jane. What people didn't know couldn't hurt them—or worry them—and what he had in mind was not a thing to be shared. It was best kept in the dark, out of sight and out of mind, until the time was right. Then, if his luck held, and the cards fell right, they might yet find the land of milk and honey, where all roamed free.

The door swung open and Jane stepped into the room. He found it incredible, a small miracle of sorts, that she hadn't changed a bit since those long-ago days on the Brazos. Her smile was still smoky and warm, soft as an autumn sunset. And her eyes, like violets glistening damp with morning dew, were a sight he would carry to his grave. She was one of a kind, this woman of his. Full of fire and mettle, tenderness and love. The stuff that made a man more than he might have been. A restorative not just for his soul, but an elixir that gave reason and purpose to life itself.

She came into his outstretched arms, sliding underneath the manacles, and for a long while they said nothing. The warmth and softness he had known so well seemed all the more precious in these last moments, and he was content just to hold her close. At last, their time fleeting swiftly, she eased back, tilting her head upward, and gave him a searching look.

"You'll never be out of my heart or my mind. Not for a moment. And the day you come home I'll be right there waiting."

There were no tears in her eyes, and never had he been prouder of her than at that moment. He forced himself to smile. "The kids still at your folks'?"

She nodded. "I thought we would stay with them awhile and then visit your folks. They're both close enough to Huntsville, so I'll be able to see you every month on visiting day."

"How you fixed for money?"

"You may be a scamp, Wes Hardin, but you're a very good provider." She cocked her head in that funny little smile. "We'll get along very nicely on the investments you made. So just put that out of your mind."

There was a heavy rap on the door and they both stiffened. Suddenly her eyes went misty and she struggled to hold herself in check.

"I love you, sugar. I always have and I always will."

"Maybe I never told you, but I should've. You're the only woman I ever loved, Janey. Even before we were married, there wasn't nobody but you."

She came into his arms and gave him a kiss that was meant to last. They clung to one another, unable to speak, and then, very slowly, he lifted his manacled hands over her head and stepped back. She sensed he wanted it this way and she didn't move, standing proud and tall as he shuffled to the door. He looked so fine, just the way she would always remember him, strong and vital, like a young hawk floating free on a high, soft wind. Somehow, at that moment, there were no manacles or leg-irons. There was just the boy she had married and the wild, free spirit she had grown to love.

At the door he turned back, flashing that old grin. "Remember that sayin', be careful what you wish for 'cause it might come true?"

Her bottom lip trembled, but she gave him a bright nod.

"Wish real hard, and when the moon's down some dark night, keep a sharp lookout. Maybe your wish'll come true."

She understood. "I'll be waiting. Every night of my life."

The door opened and closed and he was gone. Several moments passed while she listened to the rattle of his leg-irons as he hobbled down the hall. There were voices, muted noises for a bit, then all went silent.

And the waiting began.

EPILOGUE

Never had a man tried so hard to keep a promise.

When the gates of Huntsville Penitentiary clanged shut behind John Wesley Hardin it signaled a battle of wills between prison authorities and the determined young outlaw. It was a battle in which an irresistible force quite literally hurled himself against an immovable object—in this case a stone wall. And with only brief interludes, it was to last for five agonizing years.

Less than a month after entering prison Wes Hardin engineered an escape attempt unlike anything Huntsville had ever seen. In scope, it was actually more of an armed insurrection than a prison break. Assigned to the wheelwright's shop, he allowed himself a week to inspect the layout. What interested him most was the armory, located some seventy-five yards across the prison compound. There the weapons of off-duty guards, both rifles and pistols, were stored in a small building that looked as impregnable as a fortress. But he had no intention of storming the armory. Instead, after considerable reflection, he decided to tunnel underneath the prison yard and enter from below.

With his plans perfected, Wes enlisted into the conspiracy some thirty lifers and long-term convicts. His reputation had preceded him inside the walls and he had no trouble whatever in organizing the revolt. The men selected readily acknowledged his leadership, and digging began on the first day of November.

Their goal was to tunnel into the armory, seize the guns, and arm upward of a hundred convicts. Then they would demand surrender of the prison, taking it by force if necessary, and liberate the inmate population of Huntsville. Afterward, in the confusion and uproar, with better than five hundred convicts scurrying across Texas, Wes had every confidence he could pull a vanishing act.

The tunnel progressed smoothly, burrowing on a direct line beneath the carpenter's shop and the superintendent's office. Working from the wheelwright's shop, one man dug at all times while the others covered for him and kept watch. Dirt from the tunnel was secreted outside and scattered in the prison yard during exercise period. Wes had the men organized into shifts, with no one man off the floor for more than a half hour, and the wheelwright guard never once tumbled to their scheme. Three weeks after the digging began, late on the afternoon of November 20, the tunnel was completed. All that remained was to wait for guards supervising work parties outside the walls to return their weapons to the armory. Then the conspirators would break through the floor of the arsenal, distribute guns to everyone in the wheelwright's shop, and seize the prison.

But Wes had failed to reckon with life inside the walls. Huntsville crawled with men willing, if not eager, to play the part of Judas. In exchange for information, they curried the favor of prison officials, which brought them privileges denied other inmates. The young outlaw's single miscalculation proved a fatal flaw.

Shortly before the break was to occur, armed guards swarmed over the wheelwright's shop. The plot had been betrayed at the last minute, and twelve men were hustled off to the warden's office for questioning. Several talked, more concerned with their own skin than honor among thieves, and Wes was quickly tagged as the ringleader. Before nightfall he was thrown in a dank dungeonlike cell, with a ball and chain attached to his leg. There he spent the next fifteen days, isolated in total darkness, subsisting on nothing except bread and water.

Upon being released he was assigned to the shoe factory, more determined than ever to escape. His time in solitary had been spent in analyzing the first attempt, and he saw now that it was doomed from the start. Besides being much too elaborate, it depended on far too many men, which made it susceptible to the prison grapevine, and ultimately exposure to the authorities. Having sampled the folly of trusting others, he reverted to a role more in keeping with his character. He became a loner, and began planning his next break.

On the day after Christmas he was again betrayed, this time by his own cellmate. In his possession the guards found a pistol, which had been smuggled into prison, and a homemade master key which unlocked every door and gate between the cellblock and the front wall. Clearly, Huntsville's most illustrious inmate was not a man to be dissuaded by bread and water alone. Harsher measures, it seemed, were necessary to speed his adjustment to life inside the walls.

That night Wes was stripped naked, spread-eagled on a stone floor, and tied face down. Then the underkeeper, a bullet-headed bruiser who gloried in his trade, stepped forward with the Huntsville nutcracker. This was a whip consisting of four straps, each twenty inches long and constructed from thick harness leather. It was designed to crack toughnuts and hardcases who had proved unresponsive to gentler discipline. Under the supervision of the warden, Wes was administered thirty-nine lashes, all the law allowed. Afterward, his back and buttocks reduced to bloody quivering jelly, he was dragged to solitary row and held in isolation for thirty days.

Yet the lash had somewhat the opposite effect intended. Although half crippled by the flogging, and unable to perform hard labor for some months afterward, Wes was hardly broken in spirit. He set about hatching new plots for escape.

Over the next three years he attempted seven breaks. When he wasn't betrayed by fellow convicts, he was discovered by guards, and again hauled off to solitary. With each attempt he was flogged the limit; his back became a latticework of heavy, discolored welts. And his keepers added a new wrinkle—they tried to starve him into submission.

Nothing worked, though. He was incorrigible, bullheaded, and from the punishment he had absorbed, seemingly indestructible. Within Huntsville he became something of a legend—the man who wouldn't break—and the inmates spoke of him in awed tones. Prison officials grew increasingly bewildered, completely stymied by a man who evidenced only contempt for their brutal methods. At last, convinced that the lash and starvation were a waste of time, they simply chained a ball to his leg and assigned guards to watch him around the clock.

Then, early in 1885, a curious thing happened. After seven years' imprisonment, Wes Hardin got religion.

Some of those in Huntsville, most especially the warden, declared it was nothing short of a miracle. Others, perhaps more skeptical, allowed that all else having failed, Hardin had merely made peace with his God and accepted the inevitable. Those who knew him well, a scant handful within the prison walls, traced his conversion to another source. Soon after the New Year his mother and father had passed on within weeks of one another. Hardin had accepted the news stoically, displaying no emotion whatever, but he was never again the same man.

However the transformation came about—and this remained a bone of contention for years afterward—there was no dispute as to subsequent events. Wes Hardin embraced the Lord God Jehovah with the same fervor and vitality that had made him the most feared gun in Texas. Under the prison minister's guidance, he became an avid student of theology, exploring the Bible and the rudiments of Holy Writ with the zeal of a reformed drunk. Before long he was assisting in church services, and within a few months had been appointed superintendent of the weekly Sunday School class.

On a sweltering Sunday night early that summer, he penned a letter to Jane which read in part:

I can tell you that I spent this day in almost perfect
happiness, as I generally spend the Sabbaths here,
something I once could not enjoy because I did not
know the causes or results of that day. I had no idea
before how it benefits a man in my condition. Although
we are all prisoners here we are on the road to progress.

That, even from a man who detested braggarts, was something of an understatement. Once on the road to salvation,
Wes Hardin pulled out all stops. He ransacked the prison
library, in short order mastering Stoddard's *Arithmetic* and
Davies' *Algebra*. With that under his belt, he next undertook
an intense study of history, broadening his perspective of
man's place in the scheme of things. And along the way he
discovered what was to become his grand obsession—the
law.

The years passed swiftly after that, months rippled off the
calendar like golden leaves in an autumn wind. Caught up
in his hunger for knowledge, Wes devoured Blackstone,
Bishop's *Criminal Law*, Walker's *Introduction to American
Law*, and fully a hundred additional volumes ranging across
the wide spectrum of jurisprudence. He began corresponding
with judges and noted attorneys around the state, seeking
interpretations and shadings of what he had read. By 1892
his comprehension of the law *per se* was awesome, and in
terms of statutes and legal technicalities, he was acknowledged to be better versed than most practicing attorneys.

Later that year, however, he received a severe blow. Jane
Bowen Hardin suddenly sickened of ague and died. She had
remained faithful to him throughout his long imprisonment—
proud to the end—urging him to continue his studies and
hope for a brighter day. Now she was gone, his staunchest
supporter through good times and bad, and life without her
seemed hardly worth the effort. For a time his mood darkened, and he fell into a fit of depression, unable to shake the
thought that she had wasted her best years waiting for him
to return. Slowly, though, he came to see that wallowing in

self-pity demeaned her memory, belittled the love and happiness she had brought him. While Jane was gone, their children still waited, and what he had never given her, he might yet give to them. He returned to his studies with a vengeance.

Then, early in 1894, judged to be fully rehabilitated, the former outlaw was granted an unconditional pardon by Governor J. S. Hogg. After sixteen years behind the walls at Huntsville, John Wesley Hardin walked through the gates a free man. There to greet him were his children, Molly and John.

While saddened that his wife hadn't lived to see him freed and his citizenship restored, Wes bore no grudge against society. He had matured greatly while in prison—graying a bit at the temples as he approached his fortieth birthday—and he had no wish to dwell on the past. Time laid scars on a man, and whatever else he'd learned in Huntsville, he knew now that wisdom came when a man could accept the bitter with the sweet. There were good years remaining, and instead of looking back, he looked forward, to the future.

And as Jane had believed all along, it was a brighter day.

Before spring Molly, who was married to a storekeeper, made him a grandfather, and a month later he served as best man at John Junior's wedding. Then, in May of that year, shortly before his birthday, the fruition of his love affair with Blackstone came to pass. He was admitted to the bar as an attorney-at-law. It was a warm day, cloudless and not unlike most spring days, but a day that many men, John Wesley Hardin among them, would not soon forget.

Texas' deadliest outlaw had hung up his guns at last.

BEFORE THE LEGEND, THERE WAS THE MAN...

AND A POWERFUL DESTINY TO FULFILL.

On October 26, 1881, three outlaws lay dead in a dusty vacant lot in Tombstone, Arizona. Standing over them—Colts smoking—were Wyatt Earp, his two brothers Morgan and Virgil, and a gun-slinging gambler named Doc Holliday. The shootout at the O.K. Corral was over—but for Earp, the fight had just begun...

WYATT EARP

MATT BRAUN